Cell Tower

Frank Lazorishak

Cell Tower is a work of fiction. Names, characters, places, and incidents are either the product of the author's imagination or are used fictitiously. Any resemblance to actual persons, living or dead, events, or locales in entirely coincidental.

ISBN: 978-0-557-96804-6

CHAPTER 1
Tuesday, Early March
(Peter)

I really don't like my job anymore. Actually, that's not true. I do like my job. I just don't like my working environment anymore. I guess that would take some explaining. If anyone was listening to me talk to myself.

It's 7:26 on a beautiful Tuesday morning, and I'm driving east on Ohio Route 2 near the beginning of a forty-five minute commute. I left a great view of Lake Erie and Herring Gulls and Great Blue Herons in lovely suburban Lorain, and I'm on my way to a terrible view of cloth-covered partitions and cement blocks in my four by six cubicle in ugly urban Cleveland.

Howard, the latest addition to our management team, will be watching to see what time I show up at the office. Our management team. The team I fondly refer to as the Three Stooges.

* * *

As I drive down Route 2, I'm sort of on automatic pilot. It's a four-lane, limited access highway, and there's not a lot to see. Traffic is building nicely. It'll be a mess by the time I get to Interstate 480. I'm driving into the rising sun, and visibility is bad.

To keep from having to look into the sun, I've got the visor down, and I'm sort of scrunched down to look under it. My eyes are wandering off to the sides of the road; there's not a lot to look at, but it's better than looking into the sun constantly.

I pass under a high voltage transmission line crossing the road, probably coming from the Avon power plant and heading south toward Akron or Columbus. There are lots of generating facilities along Lake Erie, and their lines seem to go every which way. My wife, Kate, says nobody notices these things. But I do. I'm an engineer -- I can't help it.

There's a cell phone tower coming up on the south side of the road. They are almost as ubiquitous as the transmission lines. There are more of them popping up every week, it seems.

Did the tower wobble? Nah. Must be the sun glare playing tricks. The towers they plant around here are massive. They don't wobble. This one looks typical: a tapered steel cylinder a little over a 100 feet tall and about four feet in diameter at the base. No, they don't wobble.

Oh, shit. It did wobble! I'm sure of it. It can't be the wind. There's very little this morning, certainly not enough to make the tower move. I touch the brake to disengage the cruise control, and my Mustang starts to slow down. I check the rear view mirror. There's nobody close behind me. I let the car coast. The tower definitely moved. It's moving east and west. Not far, but it *is* moving. I'm almost abreast of it. I decide to pull over. I signal and touch the brakes again.

I watch in disbelief as the tower crashes to the ground. It just falls over! Sort of like a tree being chopped down…

How can that be? There's no explosion. No fuss. No muss. No nothing. It just fell over. It's gone.

I pull off to the side of the road and stop. I'm just past the tower. It's about fifty feet from the road. As far as I can see, there's nobody around. No workers. No spectators. Nobody.

The site looks recently constructed, and it's typical of what they're building these days. There's a small fenced in area with a prefab equipment building next to the tower. There's a gravel access road to the tower running parallel to Route 2. Or I should say, ex-tower, because it's now lying in the scrub brush.

The tower fell parallel to the road. The antennas are a jumble of scrap. There's a little smoke coming from the building, but no obvious fire.

A whole bunch of cell phones had to just quit working. I check my Sprint Blackberry. I still have lots of bars. I wonder whose tower this was.

I'd love to go investigate, but I'll be ten minutes late for work as it is. I'm paranoid about giving Howard any opportunity to question my performance. Investigating the tower will have to wait 'til I'm on my way home.

I've never seen -- I've never heard of -- anything like what I just saw. This borders on unbelievable. Do cell phone towers fall over? I don't think so. But this one just did.

CHAPTER 2

(Gregory)

I am pumped! I did it. And, my first cell tower wasn't really *that* hard. Well, yes, it was *really* frickin' hard, but I did it!

What a pain, though. I had to make three trips before I actually accomplished my mission, and I risked getting caught every time. That in itself was scary.

It took me most of the night to actually take the tower down. I intended to drop it before dawn, but undoing the nuts took longer than I planned, and it never went over until seven-thirty. I intended to drop it toward the highway, but the wind didn't cooperate and it dropped parallel to the highway.

But I did it. I destroyed it. I made my first attack on Vista Tel. And there will be more. Many more.

* * *

The tower I picked was along Ohio Route 2, a four-lane, limited access road with a wire mesh fence along the perimeter. Why do they build those silly-ass fences anyway?

Anyway, the tower was about fifty feet south of the wire mesh fence, and sat inside its own twenty-foot square chain link security fence. There was an equipment building to the west of the tower and an ice bridge connecting the tower and the building. "Ice bridge" is a term I learned doing research on the Internet. It's the steel guard above the cables going from the tower to the equipment building. It's crazy, the amount of information available on the Internet.

There was a gravel road about a quarter mile long leading to the site. It had a cable across it at its entrance, but that was okay. I wasn't going to drive back anyway. There was a small used car lot nearby. I would stash my beat up Honda there among the other beat up cars, and walk in. Nobody would even notice.

* * *

I hate to sound like a Mafioso, but company number one on my hit list is Vista Tel, one of the smaller cell phone companies around here. They're spending a lot of money building towers, advertising, and trying to expand. I want them to go away, merge, or sell out -- not expand.

I couldn't believe how easy the Internet made it to do my research. There are actually websites that show you who owns which towers. That made it easy for me to find the perfect tower. I found my first victim near Amherst. The location was very visible to passersby -- I wanted people to see what I'd done. But, the approach was very secluded -- I wanted to be able to get in and work on it without being seen.

Amherst was a very good location for several reasons. One, it's pretty far from home. I live in the eastern suburbs of Cleveland, in a small city called Euclid, but Amherst is west of Cleveland. It's far enough away that I'm not a local. Two, I know the area well. I was raised near Akron, and my father keeps a boat on Lake Erie. We made a gazillion trips through the Amherst area when I was growing up.

My parents have moved to the Vermilion Lagoons near Amherst now that they've retired, and I still go there to see them on occasion. As I've driven from Euclid to Vermilion, I've watched the horrible proliferation of cell phone towers throughout this area. There are dozens just along Route 2.

I hate frickin' cell phones. They are radiation hazards. I hate frickin' cell phone towers. They are ugly. I hate frickin' cell phone companies. They are greedy.

But starting with the Amherst tower, I'm going to fix the problem. I *will* stop them!

CHAPTER 3

Tuesday afternoon

(Peter)

I really don't like my job anymore. Hmm. I don't think I've said that to myself since this morning!

I just came back from taking my lunch break at Home Depot. I usually don't eat lunch. I got out of the habit a long time ago. I survive just fine on two meals a day. But our management team, Larry, Moe and Curly, insist that everybody take a one-hour lunch break. Something about a mid-day break making people more productive. I think it's bull. All it does for me is make an almost ten-hour workday into an almost eleven-hour workday.

At lunchtime, I go somewhere -- anywhere -- just to get away. I once told my wife that I leave the office so I don't accidently work on my lunch hour!

Today, I sat in the Home Depot parking lot and listened to the noon news on WTAM. There was nothing about the cell phone tower on the radio. I find that very odd. "Amazing" is a better word. You'd think a cell phone tower falling over would be a big deal. Maybe it's too soon for it to have I hit the news. I'll bet some cell phone company is getting a ton of phone calls though.

I wandered around the store for a while and thought about what I saw this morning. I haven't told anyone about it. I don't know why. I saw what I saw. But I didn't think things like that happened in the real world. In movies, maybe. In Cleveland, no.

* * *

I'm a professional. In any job I've ever had before, I would just scan the local TV station websites. But the management team frowns on people surfing the Internet during business hours.

I'm salaried. In most jobs I've had in the past, I would just leave the office and go investigate the cell tower site myself. But not now. Not here.

I'll have to wait until tonight. I'll investigate on my way home.

* * *

I'm sixty-two years old. I retired early from a good job in the automotive industry in Warren, Ohio, to take an even better job with an engineering consulting firm in Cleveland, Ohio. For the first two years, I worked out of a home office and flexed my hours as I wished. The work always got done. The customers were happy. The company was happy. I was happy. Quite frankly, I didn't work too hard. All was well with the world. And perhaps most importantly, my job supported our life-long, but rather expensive hobby.

My wife, Kate, and I love to sail. For many years, we lived near Warren, Ohio, and kept our sailboat at the Vermilion Yacht Club on Lake Erie.

Kate works out of a home office too, but for a different company. Our respective companies didn't really care where we were physically, as long as we had good VPN computer connections, good landline and cell phone service, and could travel to our real offices when necessary. Kate's company headquarters was in Chicago, and was a ninety-minute drive from Warren to Cleveland Hopkins Airport, and a short flight to Chicago. Mine was in Cleveland, and was a ninety-minute drive, too. She made the drive once or twice a month. I made the drive once or twice a week. Most importantly, it was a two-hour drive from Warren to our boat, and we made that drive every weekend, at least when it wasn't snowing. We were spending too much of our life driving, and we spent years dreaming about and looking for the ideal place on the lake.

Then we found it! It was an absolutely beautiful condo right on Lake Erie. Actually, it's more like a home than a condo, with 3 floors and over 5000 square feet. It was located right on the beach! We studied and planned and agonized and prayed. And in November -- dumb time to buy a new home -- we did it. We owned a lake front condo.

We have five adult kids between us, two from my first marriage, and three from Kate's. All five of them agreed that we were nuts, that we should be thinking of a little retirement home, not a monster condo on Lake Erie. But it was ours. Literally, a dream come true.

Kate's commute to the airport dropped to thirty minutes, mine to the office to forty minutes. The trip to our boat was only ten minutes. It was going to be marvelous.

We both spent the last six months firmly ensconced in our new home and home offices watching fall turn into winter and winter turn into spring. We absolutely loved it. Somebody has recently made a ton of money selling caps and shirts and stuff that say, "Life is Good." It truly was.

* * *

Then Howard came into my life. Howard is not a bad person; he is just a control freak. Howard was hired to become a new layer of management between my old boss, Damien, and me. Somebody like Howard was probably a necessary addition. Damien had too much work to do. So Howard appeared one day.

My first real contact with Howard was two weeks after he was hired. He invited me into the conference room. He told me that I was the highest paid employee in his department, that he didn't have enough work to keep me busy full time, and that he needed me to become a contract part time worker. I told him that was unacceptable and immediately went to Stan, the owner of the company. To make a very stressful two-week-long story short, the outcome was that I would continue to be employed full time, but since Howard needed to have me available at all times, I would have to commute to the office every day. I'm not sure if he really felt that way, if he didn't trust me to actually work at home, or if it was his way to encourage me to quit. In any case, I was now a very reluctant Cleveland commuter.

And that's why, "I really don't like my job anymore."

CHAPTER 4

(Gregory)

My father is fond of telling people that I'm in the sixth year of a four-year degree. Does he *know* how that makes me feel? I don't tell people that he took twenty-five frickin' years to get *his* degree. In his case, it was college, to getting my mother pregnant with me, to the Air Force, to a fifteen-year bout with alcoholism, to college again. So I don't think six years in my case is so bad. Besides, I have a very good reason, at least a better reason than getting some girl pregnant.

I started out in electrical engineering. I think studying electricity is fascinating. When I was a Cub Scout, I made a crystal radio. It amazed me that I could make something that would actually receive a radio station. It only received one station, and not very loudly, but it actually worked. I was frickin' hooked. The radio led to a hobby in electronics, to an amateur radio license, and then to college and electrical engineering. I was proud to be one of the geeks. But in college, my goals started to change.

CSU exposed me to a whole bunch of new ideas. I discovered how badly big business is screwing up our planet. Yeah, I know that sounds like a cliché. I know I sound like some

Greenpeace environmentalist, but they really are screwing up our world. Badly.

In time, I came to the horrible realization that the world really doesn't care how badly big business is screwing things up. People care about driving their fifteen-mile-per-gallon SUVs down a six-lane highway at seventy miles an hour, spewing out pollution where the deer used to feed. They care about taking their 400 horsepower convertibles out for a spin on Saturday, burning more gas in an hour than a hybrid does in a week. They care about shopping at a nice hundred-acre mall where Winnie the Pooh used to have Adventures in the hundred-acre woods. They care about driving their hundred-gallons per hour speedboats faster than anyone else, leaving the fish to cope with the oil slicks they leave behind them. They say they are concerned about global warming. Then they decide to let their children -- and grandchildren -- deal with it. They really think we can wait that long!

And then there are cell phones. I hate frickin' cell phones, and cell phone towers. Passionately! Cell phones are an electromagnetic radiation hazard -- people should be afraid of them. And the towers are ugly -- they're a blight on our landscape. And the companies just don't give a shit -- they only care about their frickin' profits.

The bigger problem is that there are several dozen cell phone companies all erecting their own towers, and making the blight worse. Find a nice high spot in the countryside, and you will see three or four towers. You can't drive more than a couple of miles without seeing a frickin' tower. Even cell phone companies realize that their towers are a blight on the surface of our planet. They are actually hiring companies to try to disguise their towers as trees! Fat chance.

This is a prime example of why we need more government control of industry. Companies should be forced to share towers and antennas, or even better yet, there should be only one band of frequencies shared by all companies. There is simply no reason why we should have to tolerate the huge number of towers that exist. At last count, there were over 250,000 of them!

Anyway, I decided to tell the world what I had discovered, and I switched majors to journalism. I was going to share my newfound awareness of how badly big business was screwing up the world *with* the world. I spent a couple of years learning to be a writer. I was a promising one, my favorite professor told me. Of course he was a fellow environmentalist. I think the creep was also gay. He hit on me a couple of times, and when I didn't encourage him, he lost interest in my budding career as an environmental activist writer.

But after a while, I realized that just writing about what we were doing to our world was futile. If I didn't commit to actually doing something about the problem, I was just as frickin' bad as the "they" I was complaining about. Maybe I was worse, because I saw what was happening when they didn't. I decided that perhaps science and technology could help solve some of the problems that were being caused by science and technology, and I switched my major back to electrical engineering. I should finish in another year.

In the meantime, there is something I can do *now*. I can "encourage" cell phone companies to combine. If I can destroy enough of one company's towers, I can destroy their business model. I can force them to combine with another company -- to either merge or sell out. Either way, there will be fewer companies, and fewer towers.

I can find others who see the problem, and we can force companies all over the country to combine, one company at a time. Eventually there will be just one company -- or maybe even one government agency -- with towers. One set of towers will be a whole lot better than dozens of sets of towers, and everyone will get better coverage, too!

Then, we can concentrate on finding ways to eliminate towers entirely. There is already research being done on using antennas buried in road surfaces to provide communications. Other means have to exist. If cell phone companies find that their towers come down as fast as they put them up, they will look to other means of providing communication.

But for now, I can do my part to start them moving in the right direction...

CHAPTER 5

Tuesday evening

(Peter)

Shit! I meant to go home via Route 2 so that I could check on the downed cell phone tower. Instead, I took my usual way home via the Turnpike. Don't ask me why, but I always go to work via Route 2 and come home via the Turnpike.

Kate's expecting me for dinner, so I don't want to backtrack. I'll tell her about what I saw and check it out on the news after supper. Maybe we'll take a drive up later and have a look-see.

* * *

There is nothing on the local six o'clock news. Nothing at all about the cell tower. There is nothing on the Web. This is weird.

Kate has some work to do tonight, so I'm going to drive up by the downed cell tower and see what I can see. I might stop to pick up a local paper, too. No, wait. It's a morning paper in Lorain, so the tower won't be in today's paper. I'll pick one up in the morning. Maybe then.

I change from my work uniform to my standard non-winter, non-work uniform. When I go to Cleveland, I wear what has become the standard at the office: clean pressed jeans and a golf shirt with an embroidered company logo. I suspect that Stan Johns, the owner of my consulting firm, encourages the look because he thinks it's workman-like or something. I think for an engineer it looks just plain sloppy. Stan is a graduate mechanical engineer and a licensed Professional Engineer to boot, but he looks, talks, and dresses like a millwright. I hate to sound prejudiced, but Johns is anglicized from Janoski, and he fits the stereotype. I'm amazed that he's done as well as he has.

Anyway, it's out of those clothes and into faded tan Tommy Bahama shorts, a well worn dark blue tee shirt from Port Dover, and a pair of somewhat beat up Sperry Top-Siders. I don't know whether it's an affectation, a fashion statement, or just because I find the attire comfortable. I *am* a sailor, and I dress the part from the time the weather breaks in the spring 'til it turns cold in the fall.

I'm what an old-timer friend of mine calls a river rat. He says two kinds of people live along the water: river rats and tourists. River rats feel the pull of the water and have to live near it. Tourists like to impress their friends and themselves by pretending to feel the pull. I really am a river rat. When I travel on business, after my work is finished for the day, if it is nearby, I head for the waterfront. I never get tired of the water -- it's always the same -- and always different.

I drive south to Route 2 and then east toward the site of the downed tower. As I approach the site, I can see a mobile crane and two flatbed eighteen-wheelers on the access road to the tower. One of the flat beds has several sections of tower loaded on it. There are about a dozen workers milling about near the downed tower. It's pretty obvious that they are removing the tower. I can also see several official-looking vehicles blocking the entrance to the access road. And no bystanders. I would have expected a situation like this to attract quite a crowd.

I slow down as I'm moving along Route 2 so that I can take a better look. In the breakdown lane, even with the downed tower, there are four cars pulled over: two State Highway Patrol sedans and two SUVs. The patrol cars do not have their red and blue lights going. It almost looks like the troopers have two cars pulled over for some traffic violation, but the no flashing lights is odd. As I slow down and go by, I notice that there are four men standing together by one of the patrol cars: two troopers in uniform, and two men in dark suits, white shirts and ties. They are not talking. They are watching the cars going by.

I go beyond the cars, slow down, signal and pull into the breakdown lane about fifty feet in front of them. One of the uniformed troopers immediately starts moving quickly toward me. They obviously don't want me here. Odd. Oh well, I'll get off at the next exit and double back to the county road going past the site. Maybe I can find out what's going on down there.

* * *

Did that State Trooper just take a picture of my car? I swear he pulled out a camera. But it was so quick, I'm not sure.

CHAPTER 6

(Gregory)

I absolutely could not believe that there was no frickin' mention of my handiwork on the news. The lack of anything on the morning news didn't surprise me. It was too soon. I had listened to Cleveland's biggest news-talk station all morning for a breaking news bulletin -- nothing. I flip-flopped between all the noon TV news shows -- nothing.

Since I was up all Monday night, I spent all day Tuesday napping on and off, and checking the radio, TV and radio station websites for news about my handiwork. That, and reliving the demolition of my first cell tower.

* * *

I arrived there past midnight, parked in the lot of a used car dealer just south of the tower access road. One more car in the lot would be completely un-noticeable. I waited 'til there were no cars in sight and then quickly walked to the access road, and out of sight of the county road.

My entry was straight out of a hundred spy movies I've seen: sneak up with a pair of bolt cutters, cut a door in the chain link fence, bend back a flap of fence, and I'm in. I discovered on the Internet that many towers are protected with surveillance cameras. A casual hike by the tower during the day had revealed no cameras. Apparently, Vista Tel's not that big or sophisticated, yet.

The tower base was a steel plate about four feet square. It had sixteen inch and a half diameter anchor bolts going down into the concrete pad. Each bolt had two nuts: one load bearing, and one lock nut. They were big suckers; I'd need a three-inch socket, and a long breaker bar. My first visit over, I made sure I didn't leave any obvious signs of entry. I carefully folded the chain link fence back where it was. Someone would have to look very hard to see my door.

* * *

Next came a trip to a truck stop outside of Akron. I used to live near there, and I knew that they had a tool store that catered to truckers. The joint was full of redneck truckers, and I felt completely out of place, but they had what I needed, and they wouldn't remember me.

Now I was ready. I needed a windless night with not much moonlight. My plan was to arrive at the cell tower about midnight, remove the bolts, and run like hell when the tower started to go over. I figured I could be long gone by the time Vista Tel realized what had happened and alerted the police. My Internet research had revealed that entering the protected area of a tower site is a federal crime, so I had no romantic illusions of what I was doing. I knew the FBI would be looking for me. I needed to be out of there fast. I intended to watch it on the news like thousands of others.

* * *

On the big night, I parked in the car dealer's lot again, waited to make sure no cars were around, and then quickly carried my tools to the access road.

I walked back to the tower, pushed my stuff through my door in the chain link fence, and set up a small LED work light. I needed enough light to see what I was doing, but not enough to be seen from Route 2. My idea was to remove all the locknuts, and then work around the base removing one load-bearing nut at a time -- kind of like removing a wheel from a car -- until I was down to one nut on each side. Then I'd remove the last nuts and drop the tower. With no wind, I would also be able to drop the tower the way I wanted, directly toward Route 2. It should come down with the antennas in the grass between the fence and the pavement. It would be quite a frickin' sight for the morning commuters.

The installers had tumbled the threads on the bolts to prevent the lock nuts from working loose. At first I panicked, but with a good tug on the breaker bar, I was able to break loose the lock nuts. Once I was beyond the damaged threads, they came off easily. I think I would have tack welded the two nuts together to prevent vandalism. Apparently Vista Tel didn't think of that, or perhaps they don't think vandalism is an issue. They're about to learn differently!

Suddenly, I had a problem. An unexpected problem. A big problem. The first load-bearing nut wouldn't budge. I am not a small guy. I stand six feet tall and weigh just at 200 pounds. I'm not a jock, but I'm in pretty good shape. Even so, I strained until I literally got shaky. The nut would not come off. I rested and then tried another nut. Same results, except it took me less time to realize this wasn't going to work. My one-inch breaker bar was over two feet long, but it didn't give me enough leverage to break the nuts loose. I once saw some road workers removing nuts from the base of a streetlight with a breaker bar and a sledgehammer. Now I knew why. I couldn't risk the noise caused by beating on the breaker bar with a sledgehammer. I'd have to come back with something that gave me more leverage. That really pissed me off!

So I left, again. I made sure I left no obvious sign of entry. I put the lock nuts back on the anchor bolts. I carefully smoothed out the scuffed spots in the ground cover around the tower base. I had really dug my heels in trying to break the nuts loose. I went back out through my door in the chain link fence. Like last time, no one would be able to tell that I'd been there -- until the next time.

I decided to leave the breaker bar and socket stashed in the brush near the access road. I'd have less to carry next time, and I would be less suspicious-looking if somebody saw me.

The following week, I went to an industrial supply house in Toledo. I told them my uncle was doing some work on a ship and needed a ten-foot-long piece of two-inch schedule eighty pipe. I paid cash. They were fine with that, and I had my leverage. Schedule eighty pipe is strong and heavy. I'd cut it into two pieces, one four feet long, and one six feet long. I'd try the four-footer first. If that didn't work, I'd try the six-footer. If that didn't work, I'd have to come up with a different scheme.

* * *

Third trip. Another windless night. Another midnight. Back to the used car dealer's parking lot. Back to the tower. Two lengths of two-inch pipe are pretty heavy, so I was moving slowly. Halfway to the access road, I saw lights coming over the crest in the road ahead of me. I dropped the pipe in the ditch and tried to look like someone walking home from the local bar down the road. I even stumbled a little. The car never slowed down. I was safe. I went back, picked up the pipes and hurried to the access road.

I carried the pipes back to the tower fence and retrieved the socket and breaker bar. Then I moved back through my door in the fence, and back to the tower base. The lock nuts came off easily again, and I was ready to try my four-foot lever on the handle of the breaker bar. The first load-bearing nut broke loose amazingly easy, but removing it was still slow going. I worked my way around the tower and removed three of the four load-bearing nuts on each side base. Sixteen lock nuts and twelve load-bearing nuts took a lot longer than I had planned. It was starting to get light in the east, but I only had four to go.

The tower was south of Route 2. If I removed the nut from the south side last, the tower should drop to the north, just like dropping a tree. I learned how to fell a tree the way I want in the Boy Scouts. Scouting has lots of benefits, but I suspect they won't list cell tower felling as a useful skill to be learned.

An early morning breeze had started to build. The temperature felt like it was dropping. I hadn't checked the weather for the night. I should have. A cold front and the accompanying wind could screw things up a lot.

The pre-dawn wind was blowing out of the west now hard enough to rustle the leaves on nearby trees. Wind out of the west meant I'd never get the tower to go north. I'd have to settle for east, and I wasn't at all sure I'd be able to remove the nut on the west side with the wind pressure on the tower. I took off the north and south nuts. Two nuts left. I started to loosen the load-bearing nut on the west side and felt the tower base move enough to put pressure on it. It stopped. I couldn't move it. *Now* frickin' what?

Then I realized that I could feel the tower moving east and west slightly. It was, after all, like a giant frickin' fishing pole. It flexed. The wind was making it move back and forth slightly. If I timed it right, I might be able to loosen the nut on the west side when the tower was moving west. I put a little pressure on the breaker bar and one hand on the tower. When I felt the tower go west, I yanked. The bolt moved. It was going to work. About ten more yanks at the right time, and the nut was loose enough that I could see the tower base starting to move with the wind. The base started to groan. I timed my efforts and loosened the east bolt a little. It was past dawn now, and I could see the top of the tower moving against the morning clouds.

It was getting late. I didn't want to be here now that it was morning. I could see cars going by as morning traffic started to build. Now, the tower was getting scary. I had a horrible feeling that the last nuts were going to strip, or the anchor bolts were going to snap. If that happened, the breaker bar could go anywhere, the tower base could become a giant baseball bat, the antenna cables would become dangerous whips. I didn't want to be nearby when that happened. I stopped to consider my options and leaned up against the fence to figure out what to do next.

Suddenly there was a gust of wind -- and a sharp crack. It sounded like a .22 caliber rifle shot. The anchor bolt had snapped! All hell broke loose. The breaker bar went flying past my ear so close that I felt the wind from it as it whizzed by. It bounced off the fence above my head and as I watched it fly across the enclosure toward the other side of the fence, I saw the tower starting to go over. I dove through my door in the fence and rolled away. I didn't stop to look as I heard the crackle of electrical circuits frying. I rolled for about fifteen feet, and got up to run down the access road. The tower was going east and I was going west. When I got to the cover of the trees along the road, I stopped to look. Squatting among the trees I was pretty well hidden from Route 2. I watched as the tower toppled. It went slowly -- and tore the ice bridge and cables from the electronics building. Smoke started to come out of the vents in the equipment building. It was less noisy than I expected. There was no loud crash as the tower hit the ground. Just a "whomp" that I felt as much as heard. There was no explosion of electronics. A few more crackles and then even the smoke went away. It was kind of disappointing actually. Not much to show for a hard night's work.

But I was high on adrenaline! This was the first tower! I had done it! There would be more. I'd learn to do it better. They *would* listen -- or they would pay.

CHAPTER 7
(Peter)

I get off Route 2 at the exit past the downed cell tower, and work my way back to the county road near the tower site. I pick it up just north of Route 2, and head south.

I go through the underpass, and see the same thing I saw up above: two Ohio State Patrol cars and two SUVs. There is a similar group of characters: two in uniform and two in suits.

I tend to avoid cops. In an earlier life, I often had good reason to, but that's another story. This evening I decide to be really brave. As I approach the first State Trooper, I come to a stop. There is a beat-up Honda following me, but he doesn't seem to mind. He pulls to a stop behind me. The trooper waves me on. I sit still. I have the top down, but it's getting chilly, so I have my windows up. I roll down my window and wait for the State Trooper to approach. He walks up to my door and starts to say something. I smile and say, "What's going on, officer?" He pauses for a few seconds, almost as if he is planning his response. Then he says, "They're removing an unused cell tower. Trucks are entering the road here. You'll have to move on, sir."

This whole thing gets, "Curiouser and curiouser!" It just doesn't feel right somehow.

* * *

I decide not to push my luck. I still think that State Trooper up on Route 2 might have taken my picture.

I move on past the access road and continue south. I notice a used car lot not far beyond the underpass. It's a small lot with about a dozen cars and trucks. The sign says "SHAWN'S DEALS ON WHEELS." I signal and pull in. The Honda goes on by. I shut off my car. I need to think about this whole deal with the cell tower. After I stop, I realize that stopping here might be a little obvious. Maybe I'm getting paranoid. Oh well, too late now. I'm already committed.

The lot is open, and a guy who is apparently the owner/salesman/mechanic/handyman comes out of the little trailer that serves as an office. As he walks up, I get out of my car. He introduces himself as Shawn and says, "Thanks for stopping." Shawn either owns a bunch of car lots like this, has another source of income, or has delusions of grandeur. He looks like he just stepped out of an ad in GQ: red Polo baseball cap, red and blue Polo dress shirt, tan khaki Dockers, well-polished tasseled Bass loafers. Is he for real? Or is he a plant? Or is this more paranoia on my part?

I hold out my hand. "Hi, Shawn. I'm Peter. I was going by and noticed that you have a couple of work trucks. I'm really just browsing at this point. If it's okay, I'd really like to just look around a bit by myself."

"No problem. I've got some paperwork that I have to finish before I close. Holler if you have any questions, or if you want to take anything for a drive."

"That's great. Will do."

As Shawn turns to leave, I say, "Question." He turns back, and I ask about the cops up the road. I try to act curious and casual.

"I really don't know much. They were there when I opened about noon. I walked up a while ago and got shooed away. They told me the cell tower was being removed and that I'd have to stay out of the area for safety reasons."

"Humph."

"Yeah. And it struck me as odd that they were removing the tower, because it's been up less than a year."

"Oh, really?"

"Yeah. I know that for a fact because my cousin leases them the land. But I didn't ask any questions because I have an agreement with cops: I leave them alone and they leave me alone."

"I understand. Me, too..." I kind of doubt that he would volunteer information like that if he was a plant. Or would he?

Shawn goes into his trailer and I try to look like I'm checking out the trucks. I'm really trying to check out the tower site. I hear the crunch of tires on gravel, and look up to see the tired looking Honda pulling in to Shawn's Deals On Wheels! He went on by just a minute ago. He must have turned around and come back. He parks next to my Mustang and gets out.

The driver looks to be mid-twenties. Kind of hippie looking with shoulder length brown hair, a scruffy beard, and one of those dumb knit hats. Why do they wear those hats? It's March. It's sixty degrees, for God's sake. Actually, he looks too well fed to be your typical unemployed druggie-hippie. He's about six feet tall, weighs about 200 pounds, and looks pretty fit.

As the Honda driver gets out of his car, Shawn comes out of his office trailer. They exchange about six words. Shawn turns, and with a slightly irritated look, heads back in to his trailer. Joe Honda smiles, waves, and heads straight for me!

CHAPTER 8

(Gregory)

By early afternoon, I couldn't keep my eyes open any longer. I'd been up all frickin' night. I decided to take a nap, but I set my alarm for five-thirty, 'cause I didn't want to miss the big story on the six o'clock news.

* * *

There was nothing on the six o'clock news! *Still* nothing! Why? Hadn't they discovered the tower? Didn't they know what I did? Where they keeping it quiet?

I couldn't stand waiting. I decided that I needed to take a drive, and go get a firsthand look at what was going on. It was a forty-mile drive from Euclid to Amherst, so by the time I got there, it was pushing seven o'clock. I decided to drive past the site on Route 2 and see what I could see. I planned to go by heading westbound. That way, I'd have the four lanes and a median strip to buffer me from any activity.

It was a good thing I did. As I approached the site, I saw four cars parked on the south side of Route 2. There were two state cop cars and two SUVs. The staties were just sitting, with no flashing lights. The two SUVs looked like stereotypical CIA SUVs. Black vehicles -- I think they might have even been actual Chevy Suburbans -- with blacked out windows, and no markings. There are four men standing by one of the cars: two state cops in uniform and two civilians wearing dark suits. FBI? Homeland Security? CIA? I didn't know, but I didn't want to find out.

I couldn't see much at the cell tower site. I thought I saw a crane, but I really couldn't be sure. I needed to get off Route 2, and get down on the county road to really see what was going on. The next exit west was about five miles down the road, so it took me a while to double back. It was after seven as I drove along the county road and approached the Route 2 underpass.

I was following a guy in a Mustang with the top down. The dude was going about thirty-five, and looking around as he drove. He had a beard and looked to be in his late fifties. A Sunday driver out cruising on a Tuesday evening. Actually, I didn't mind in the least. Him going slow gave me an excuse to go slow and look around too.

Before we even got to the underpass, I saw that there were state cops and black SUVs here at the access road, too. Just like on Route 2, there were two of each, and just like on Route 2, there were four men standing along the road. The Mustang driver came to a stop beside the men. One state cop stepped toward him and waved him on. He just sat there. I pulled up behind him and waited. The other cop and the two civilians looked in my direction. I fiddled with the radio to avoid making eye contact. Cop number one walked up to the Mustang. The driver said something to him, the cop answered, the driver said something else, the cop responded and waved the driver on. While I waited, I sneaked a look at the nearest SUV. It had federal government plates. The Mustang guy drove slowly away. I nodded to the state cop as I passed him, and followed the Mustang past the access road to the tower site. I could see a flat bed trailer with several sections of tower loaded on it. The driver was up on the trailer checking the load. He was getting ready to pull out.

* * *

The Mustang guy pulled into the same used car lot I used during my midnight visits to the cell tower site. Could this be yet another coincidence? Am I getting paranoid? I drove on by and checked out the driver. He was pretty much what I expected: beard, late fifties, but he didn't look like "a Sunday driver on a Tuesday evening." He looked curious, puzzled, like he knew something was wrong. He looked like he was thinking hard.

As I drove by the car lot, I decided to take a chance and go talk to the dude. I drove down the road about a hundred yards, found a driveway, and turned around. I went back to the used car lot, pulled in, and parked next to the Mustang. I don't think the state cops and their friends noticed me. At least I hoped not.

As I got out of the car, some guy came out of the office trailer and said, "Hello, I'm Shawn. Thanks for stopping." What's up with this dude? He's really well dressed for the owner of a rural twelve-car car lot. He had on fancy clothes that looked like they just came from the cleaners. Was he really the owner, or was he a plain-clothes cop? I should have checked out Shawn's Deals On Wheels before I started using it as a midnight parking lot. Then I'd have known if this was the real Shawn. I filed this little goof away for future use.

"Hi. I saw my uncle's Mustang sitting here, and I just stopped to see what he's up to."

Shawn looked momentarily irritated, then he smiled, said okay, and started back inside. I waved to "Uncle Joe," smiled, and started walking toward him.

CHAPTER 9

(Peter)

So Joe Honda keeps smiling and comes walking toward me. Like I'm his long lost uncle.

When he gets close, he says, "Hi. My name's Gregory. I told the guy who works here that you were my uncle." My mouth falls open, and I just blink at him.

"Huh?"

"I saw you talking to the state cops back there, and I was curious about what they had to say, but I didn't want to explain that to this guy. Hope you don't mind."

"Oh... I'm Peter," I say, holding out my hand. "You turned around and came back to find out what they had to say?" More "Curiouser and curiouser!"

"Yeah. It's not every day that they dismantle a cell tower. There are way too many of them anyway. I wouldn't mind if they dismantled *all* of them. They are so frickin' ugly. Besides, judging from the damage I saw, it looks like it might have fallen over rather than been dismantled."

Why did he say "fallen over"? I couldn't see any sign of damage when I drove by. What had Gregory seen that I hadn't?

What does he know that I don't know? I decide that I really don't want to share what I saw this morning with Joe Honda, aka Gregory.

"Odd that you should say 'fallen over.' The State Trooper said they were dismantling an old unused cell tower, and shooed me away because of the trucks entering the highway."

"It takes two state cop cars and two government SUVs to frickin' direct traffic?"

"Government SUVs?"

"Yeah, I noticed the plates while I was stopped behind you. That really made me wonder. So, what do you think *is* going on?"

"I don't know. Actually, the whole thing strikes me as a little odd." Gregory seems motivated by more than just curiosity. He's looking for information. I decide to feel Gregory out just a little. But to do it cautiously.

"Shawn said they were working on the tower when he got here about noon. He got the same story I did from the cops. He also told me that he thought it was weird that they were dismantling the tower. He said that his cousin leases them the land, and that it's been up less than a year."

"They don't spend the money to build a tower, and then just tear it down. Something is just not right, here. There are more state cops and more SUVs up on Route 2. Are they there to direct traffic, too?"

I *know* Gregory could not have seen the cars up on Route 2 as he came through the underpass. He must have been up there, too. Am I being followed? Time to end this conversation.

"Don't know. Well, Gregory, they really don't have any trucks here that I like. I'm sort of looking for a work truck. Gotta get home for supper. Nice talking to you. See you."

As I walk off, he catches up to me. We walk silently back to our cars.

Can you do a Google search on a license plate and find out the owner's identity? As we approach our cars, I start silently repeating his license number. My short-term memory isn't what it used to be. I'll jot his license down as soon as I get in the car.

He has a bumper sticker for Cleveland State University parking, and it's for this semester. He certainly looks the part. He's in the standard attire of a liberal arts major, and he sounds like one, too: God, but I hate words like frickin.' Either use the real word -- or don't -- but don't use cutesy substitutes!

We're about thirty miles from Cleveland State. Maybe he lives around here. I don't want to restart the conversation, so I say bye and get in my car. He does the same. He just sits, so I decide to leave. I pull out of the car lot and head home, still saying his license number to myself.

CHAPTER 10

(Gregory)

Meeting Peter at the used car lot was just sheer dumb luck. When I saw him talk to the state cop guarding the tower access road, and then pull in to the used car lot almost next door, I didn't know what to think. I'm glad I decided to turn around and go back.

After I told Shawn that the driver of the Mustang was my uncle, I walked toward him as though I'd known him all my life.

He was looking at a beat up old truck. No, that's not right. He was looking over the hood of the truck, and toward the tower site. I walked up to him and said, "Hi. My name's Gregory. I told the guy who owns the joint that you were my uncle."

He just kind of stared blankly at me and said, "Huh?" I obviously caught him off guard.

I quickly explained why I came back. I started to babble about there being way too many cell towers in the world. He looked at me suspiciously, and I realized I was talking too much. I needed to draw him out. I paused. I asked him what *he* thought was going on.

He told me he thought the whole thing was a little weird.

When I told Peter about the state cops and SUVs up on Route 2, I immediately knew I goofed. He looked very surprised. He knew that I couldn't have seen them from here, but he also knew that they were there. This guy was more than just a casual passerby. He must have been up there, too.

I needed to find out who this guy was. I decided to copy down his license plate number when I leave. I thought I could do a Google search and find out who he was.

Peter looked really uncomfortable. Time to beat feet.

He ended the conversation for me. He said he had to get home for supper, and he walked off. I caught up to him. He was supposed to be my uncle, after all. We walked silently back to our cars.

As we approached our cars, I looked at his license number: CAPTAIN. His license plate holder said Vermilion Yacht Club. That made him easier to find. He's a boater. Maybe he knows my father. Now was not the time to ask. He was spooked enough.

I thought he was looking at my license plate, too. But all he said was, "Bye," as he got in his car. I did the same, and fiddled with the radio waiting for him to leave first. So his license was CAPTAIN, and he was a boater from the Vermilion Yacht Club. I could work with that info.

CHAPTER 11
(Peter)

There is something just not quite right about the kid who I met this evening at Shawn's Deals On Wheels. Gregory, if that's really his name, was trying very hard to be naturally inquisitive -- nosy, if you will. But I could sense a much deeper interest in what was going on. He knew more than he let on. He was dying to ask me more questions, but he didn't want me to know that he had more than a passing interest. He had to have been up on Route 2. He couldn't have seen the State Troopers and Feds up there from down here. I need to see what I can find out about him.

For that matter, there is something not quite right about Shawn himself. His dress doesn't fit his position. Rural used car dealers don't wear Ralph Lauren. They wear jeans and maybe a golf type shirt. Besides, his clothes looked like they just came out of the Macy's bag. I need to see what I can find out about him, too.

I wrote down Gregory's license plate: C4226D. Whenever I wonder out loud about something, Kate says somewhat facetiously, "So look it up on the Internet." I should be able to do just that. I'll try when I get home.

Finding out about Shawn might be a little more difficult.

* * *

A Google search for Ohio license plates yields a ton of hits. There are a gazillion sites that offer personal information based on a license plate number. Unfortunately they all cost money. Anywhere from ten dollars to seventy-five dollars. And I don't know which ones to trust to provide the information I need. More importantly, I'm not sure I want to trust these sites to give me a name and address without recording information about me. Many sites profess that inquiries are confidential, but are they? Why would I trust a site that is giving out personal information not to give out mine? However, if I knew Gregory's last name and address, I think I could find out a lot more about him. I also suspect that he is or was a CSU student. How to find out more?

Okay, let's see what we can find out about Shawn. A Google search for Shawn's Deals On Wheels yields lots of hits, but nothing looks like the one I want. I try using quotes and get nothing. I try quotes and caps. Still nothing. How about "DEALS ON WHEELS" plus "Amherst"? Nothing. How about "DEALS ON WHEELS" plus "Lorain"? Still nothing. Shawn must not have a website. I'm not surprised. Maybe the Better Business Bureau knows something. Nothing on the BBB Amherst site or Lorain sites. I'll try driving by Shawn's on my way home from work tomorrow night. Maybe I can get some more useful information. An address, or Shawn's last name.

It's getting late. Kate gets weird if I spend too much time on my computer. I think I'll go fill her in on my evening's detective work.

CHAPTER 12
(Gregory)

I knew that there was something just not quite right about the guy who I met at Shawn's Deals On Wheels. Pete was trying very hard to be just curious, but I suspected that he knew more than he let on. He really wanted to ask me more questions, but he didn't want me to know that he was more than "just curious." He had been up on Route 2. He picked up on the fact that I knew about the cops and Feds up there. I needed to see what I could find out about him.

Actually, when I thought about it, I suspected that there was something not quite right about Shawn either. Rural used car dealers don't wear fancy clothes like he had on, they get their clothes at K-Mart. I needed to see what I could find out about him, too.

Memorizing Pete's license plate had been easy: CAPTAIN. I decided that when I got home, I'd see what I could find about license plate lookups on the Internet.

Then I'd see what I could find out about Shawn.

* * *

A Google search for Ohio license plates yielded a ton of hits, but all the sites cost money: ten dollars and up. Besides, I wasn't sure I wanted to trust any of them enough to give them my credit card information to pay for a search. What if he was a cop too and they alerted him that I was checking up on him? Still, if I knew Pete's last name and address, I could find out a lot more about him.

I'll figure it out later. For now, I decided to see what I could find out about Shawn. I Googled Shawn's Deals On Wheels every way I could think of and got nothing. I just couldn't get a good hit. He must not have a website. Mr. Shawn must not be into the computer age yet. A frickin' hick in fancy clothes out in the middle of frickin' nowhere!

I decided to drive by Shawn's tomorrow night. I thought maybe I could find out some more info that'd help in my search.

CHAPTER 13

Wednesday

(Peter)

I saw the tower go down yesterday morning. There still has not been anything on TV or the radio about it. I picked up a Lorain morning paper on my way to work today. There is nothing in the paper about the tower either.

I hate to sound like Mel Gibson in *Conspiracy Theory*, but this really is beginning to look like some sort of cover up. I really want to doubt that I am witnessing a cover-up. But it's very odd that there has not been anything anywhere about the tower going down. Then again, Mel Gibson turned out to be right.

Kate and I were talking about the tower incident, as we've come to call it, again over coffee this morning. She has come up with a great idea on how to find out more about Gregory, and maybe even Shawn.

Mike.

My oldest son, Mike, is a U.S. Marshall. He is currently working with the Air Marshalls flying out of Denver. I'm sure it's not completely kosher, and possibly even illegal, but I suspect that he can check into both Gregory and Shawn for me.

Mike is a product of my failed first marriage. He was raised by his mother, and we have never really been close, but we do communicate regularly. Maybe "irregularly" is a better word, but we do communicate. I'll call him today at lunchtime.

CHAPTER 14
(Gregory)

I took down the first tower on Tuesday morning. As of Wednesday morning, there still was no news about it anywhere. I checked the Cleveland Plain Dealer. Nothing.

Why were they not talking about it? Could there be some sort of agreement between the government and the industry to cover up these things? Was the media in on this, or were they clueless, too? Were they fed the same story that Pete was fed about the tower being dismantled?

I read a statement on the cell phone tower manufacturer's association website that they did not release information on tower failures or tower vandalism. It didn't say why, but my guess was that they didn't want to give people ideas. Could their keeping this quiet be part of the same plan? It's *not* going to work.

I ran into a girl I knew at school on Wednesday, and I asked her if she had heard anything about a cell phone tower collapse. Rachel said no, and she added that she wouldn't mind if they all collapsed. An ally?

* * *

I've got an idea. Rachel may be my answer to finding out about Pete and Shawn. She is: one, pretty radical; two, anti-government; three, a genuine computer nerd; and four, cute. I think I need to ask her out for beer and pizza, tell her I need her help doing some personal research, and see what she says.

CHAPTER 15

Thursday

(Peter)

I usually leave the office at lunchtime. I go to Home Depot or the marine store or the hobby shop, or if it's nice, I go to the park. I just go. And, it's also a good time to make personal phone calls.

Today is another beautiful spring day. I'll head for Big Creek Park, put the top down, and enjoy the sun.

Time to call Mike. When I dial his number, I get his voice mail. I'm not surprised. These days, he's traveling almost constantly.

"Mike, it's your dear old Dad. I need a favor. It's kind of complex, and I'll need some time to explain, but I need to do some background searches on a couple of people. I'm hoping you can help. Or at least point me in the right direction. Give me a call on my cell phone when you can. Say hello to Eric. Bye." Eric is my grandson. I wish I could see him more.

* * *

My cell phone is one of my few remaining fringe benefits. It's a company phone, but I use it as my own. It rings. It's 2:45. I'm back in the office. "Hello. This is Peter."

It's Mike. He still talks like an Army First Sergeant, gruff and loud. "Hi, Mike, let me go outside where the signal is better." And where nobody can overhear.

I go out to my car. "Hi, Mike, how you doin'?"

"Same old, same old, Dad. Either riding around in planes, or struggling to not punch out some idiot supervisor. How have you been?"

"Pretty good. Spring is springing and I'm looking forward to lots of sailing this summer. I know what you mean about idiot supervisors. I'm dealing with my share, too. I've taken to calling our president and his two fair-haired boys Larry, Curley, and Moe."

"So which one is which?"

"I had to do a little research, but I found out that Moe was the ringleader. That has got to be our president. The other two have yet to be identified."

"And I thought you worked for this high powered consulting firm."

"Maybe high powered, but also high stupidity. But that's another long story. I can't talk too long, but I need your help. I've gotten involved in some strange goings on outside of work. I need to look into the backgrounds of a couple of people I have met. I need to do it without attracting any attention to myself -- or to them. It's kind of a long story. Can you give me a call at home tonight? I'll explain it all to you."

"Sounds like the beginning of a good spy novel. I'm off on a flight in a few minutes, but I'll be back tomorrow. How about I call you tomorrow night about ten your time?"

"Funny you should say that. This is a really weird situation, and I've had similar thoughts. But it can wait 'til tomorrow night. Talk to you then."

"See you, Dad."

"Bye."

Spies? Probably not. But I've got this strange feeling that I'm getting into something weird. I may need Mike more than either of us knows.

CHAPTER 16

(Gregory)

I made it a point to run into Rachel Thursday. We were walking in different directions between buildings. I was going to a controls class that I absolutely hated. It was not something I'd ever use, it was a lot of work, and the professor was boring and arrogant, but it was required for the degree. Rachel was heading to the Computer Center, either to a class, or to work.

I know she works the help desk several hours a week. I asked her why once. She said it gives her some additional income that she sorely needs, and it gives her time to study between calls. It also gives her access to the considerable power of the university computers.

"Hi, Rachel."

"*Ciao*, Gregory."

Using cutesy words like "*ciao*" is one of Rachel's less endearing traits, but I can live with it. I'm not so sure about her tendency to throw quotes from movies into her conversations. She is very good at it, but it can be frickin' annoying. However, her general good looks make the less endearing traits easy to overlook. She is just plain attractive. Jewish, I think, but not with the stereotypical Jewish features. She is much softer looking. She sort of reminds me of Michelle who was on the TV show *24* from some years ago. Sometimes her clothes and makeup are a little too Goth for my liking, but not so much that it is a major turn-off.

"Got a minute?"

"I'm on my way to work, 'What's new pussycat?'"

Groan. "I need the expert services of a genuine computer nerd, and the word on the street is that you're the best on campus. Can we get together tonight over pizza and beer to talk about it?"

"If you're buying. I'm just a poor working girl."

"No problem. I'm one of those trust fund students who is just amusing himself with school until he comes into his inheritance. 'Mummy' and 'Poppy' do give me a substantial allowance, though. Not enough to keep my Porsche in gas for many trips out to Cape Cod, but enough for pizza. How about the Inner Circle about ten? Or is that past your bedtime?"

"I get off work at 9:30. That works great. See you later, alligator."

"After while, crocodile." Double groan. Is that a movie quote, or just a really bad cliché?

I don't know Rachel well. I've seen her around campus, and I've talked to her a few times. We travel in different social circles, so I haven't really had the chance to get to know her. Actually, I shouldn't say we travel in "different social circles." She travels -- I don't. She hangs out with the computer crowd. I often see them all sitting around a big table at Arby's just off campus. I don't really hang out with anyone, either from school, or otherwise. I'm not really a social kind of person. I have lots of casual acquaintances. Well, I have some casual acquaintances. I have no really good friends.

I did not date at all in high school. I came to college a virgin. I had a brief fling my first year here and lost my virginity, but I've never really had a girlfriend. Nor have I felt the need. But Rachel's different. Rachel fascinates me.

CHAPTER 17

(Peter)

"Hi, Mike. Thanks for calling back. How goes it with you and Eric?"

"Great. I had a couple of days off last week, so we took the trailer up to the mountains to do some fishing. We had a ball. I really don't understand his mother. She says I'm trying to turn him into an outdoorsy type when he doesn't want to be. Everything I see says he loves the outdoors. Maybe those kinds of differences are why we're divorced. That and the fact that she has turned into a real nut case."

"I hate to say it, but those kinds of things were why I think your mother and I were doomed from the start."

"I kind of figured that. By the way, Eric says thanks for sending him Grandpa's .22 rifle. He loves it. His mother wanted to make him wait until he was eighteen before giving it to him! So, what is this about me doing some background checks under the radar?"

"Glad he likes the rifle."

"He remembers his great-grandpa. Just barely, but he does, so the rifle is special."

"I'm glad. Anyway, on to the background checks thing. It's a classic long story. And I don't want you to do anything that might get you in trouble."

"Let me decide that, Dad. What's the long story?"

"I was driving to work Tuesday morning, and I saw a cell phone tower fall over. No big wind, no earthquake, no explosion, no workers around, no cops around, it just toppled over. It sat about fifty yards from the highway, and it fell over parallel to the highway as I was driving by at about seventy miles an hour."

"Okay?"

"I went back to the site Tuesday night. The site was guarded by Ohio State Patrol Troopers and Feds in plain clothes who were driving honest-to-God black Suburbans with government license plates. They wouldn't let me near the site, but I saw workers demo-ing the wreckage. One of the State Troopers told me that they were removing an unused cell tower. I don't buy that. I saw the tower fall over Tuesday morning. I saw construction workers cleaning up a wrecked tower Tuesday night. They were not dismantling an unused tower."

"That does smell suspicious. There's more?"

"It gets worse. After my encounter with the State Trooper, I drove to a nearby used car lot to park unobtrusively and see what I could see at the cell tower site. The owner of the car lot is person one who I have suspicions about. He introduced himself as Shawn, and the lot is called Shawn's Deals On Wheels -- it's a dinky lot out in the middle of nowhere with about twelve cars. He did not dress like Shawn of Shawn's Deals On Wheels. He dressed like somebody who went out and bought some civilian clothes real quickly so that he could pose as Shawn to field any questions about what was going on at the cell site. I never thought to ask him about his cars. That might have revealed whether he was really the owner of the lot. Anyway, I'd like to know if Shawn is really Shawn. By the way, Shawn said he was curious about the tower, too. He told me his cousin owned the land on which the tower sat. He said that the tower was less than a year old, and that he thought it was unlikely that it was unused. So maybe Shawn just dresses funny. But I'd like to see a photo ID. I don't know Shawn's last name or the address of the lot. I can mark it on a MapQuest map and email it to you if you like."

"My guess is that Shawn is just weird. In my opinion, all used car salesmen are a little weird. Send me that map. I'll find out who Shawn is and email you a copy of his DMV record. It'll have a copy of his driver's license photo. That one's easy. But yesterday you said there were two people?"

"Yeah. While I was at the used car lot a college-aged kid drove up, parked next to me, and I think tried to pump me for what I knew about the cell tower site. He said he saw me talking to the State Trooper and was curious about what was going on. But I got the very distinct impression that he knew more about what was going on that I did. The details aren't real important, but I believe that he knew more than he was telling me. He was more than just a drive-by curiosity seeker."

"What'd he look like?"

"Long-haired, hippie type. The kind I see every day at LCCC."

"LCCC?"

"Oh. I think I forgot to tell you I'm teaching again. At Lorain County Community College. I'm teaching an evening class in electronics -- actually microprocessors. Anyway, this kid looked like one of my typical students. The kind who is playing at being a hippie now, but will clean himself up when he has to go out into the real world and get a job. He identified himself as Gregory, and was quite well spoken, except he says 'frickin" a lot. He had a Cleveland State University parking sticker on his car. My guess is he's a student there, probably in science or engineering. Gregory looked old enough to be bordering on professional student status, maybe as old as mid twenties. He is person of interest number two. I love that phrase: 'Person of interest.' I wonder who invented it?"

"Actually John Ashcroft first used it when he was Attorney General. I think in 2001, when he was talking about a scientist named Hatfill who was being investigated in the anthrax cases. But tell me more about Gregory."

"It figures that you'd know that. Before I tell you about Gregory, I need to tell you something else. I am very proud of you.

You went from being one screwed up teenager to someone I love to brag about. I loved to tell people about your Ranger days, and now that you're a U. S. Marshall, I really brag about you. Well done, son."

"Aw, 'Gee willikers,' Pop."

"Just know that I'm proud of you. Anyway, maybe it's just a conspiracy theory, but I think that tower coming down was *not* planned by Vista Tel, and *not* an accident. And I think Gregory knows something about what really happened. I got his license plate number, and I'd like to know more about him: background, prior arrests, groups he's involved with, that kind of thing. I don't know what I'm looking for. I guess I'm just looking. And maybe I'm all wet -- maybe he was like me -- just passing by, and curious."

"Dad, I respect your insight enough to believe that he *is* worth looking into. What's his license plate number? And what kind of car was it?"

"Beat up Honda. I don't know the model or year. The plate is C4226D. Ohio."

"Okay, Dad. I obviously don't know what's going on, either. Yet. I don't know that anything is going on. But you're right. It just doesn't feel quite right. Let me do a little checking into Shawn and Gregory. I'll get back to you in a couple of days. Okay?"

"Yeah. That'd be great. Maybe I read too many books, but this really *does* feel like some kind of conspiracy thing. Call me on my cell phone anytime. I always carry it. Take care, Mike. And tell Eric he is welcome for the rifle. My dad would be pleased that Eric had it now. I think my dad bought that gun when he was an apprentice before he and my mom got married, so it's older than I am. And that's old! See you."

CHAPTER 18

(Gregory)

"Hi Rachel. Been waiting long?"

"I just got here. I'm hungry enough to eat the proverbial horse. Let's order."

"What do you like on your pizza?"

"Anything but anchovies or Soylent Green!"

"Anything but what?"

"Never mind. It's from an old Charlton Heston movie. You'd have to see it to understand. I like Italian sausage, pepperoni, and mushrooms. Is that okay?"

"That's great. I'm a carnivore, too. And I love mushrooms. Pitcher of beer okay?"

"'Go ahead. Make my day'"

"Be back in a few."

* * *

"They said twenty minutes for the pizza. But we can start on the beer and I can explain why I need a computer nerd."

"You're talking to the best."

"Here's the deal. I would like to know more about two people I met the other day. I tried searching on line, but either found nothing, or I found sites that are going to cost more than I want to spend. Also, I'm skittish about leaving tracks on the Internet."

"'Tell me more. Tell me more.'"

"One guy is a fifty or sixty-some year old who lives over in Lorain or Vermilion. His first name is Peter. He's a sailor, and he drives a Mustang with a vanity license plate that says CAPTAIN."

"Why do you want to know about him?"

"It's kind of a long story. It involves the cell phone tower that was knocked down the other day. Besides, it's just possible that knowing too many details could get you in trouble down the road. Are you sure you want to know the details?"

"Like I said, 'Tell me more. Tell me more.'"

"Okay. You know -- I think you know -- that I absolutely hate the proliferation of cell phone towers. Well, I actually saw one demolished on Tuesday. I think it was a willful act of sabotage. There has been nothing on the news about it."

"Go on."

"While I was trying to find out more about the tower, I met two guys who might know more than they were willing to admit. They might have just been curious like me, I suppose, but I don't think so. I just want to find out a little more about them. I might want to talk to them more. Well, one of them, at least, but I don't know how to get in touch with him. The other one might be an undercover cop or something, and if he is, I don't want to talk to him. Do you think you can help me find out more about them?"

"I didn't hear anything about cell phone tower terrorism. Where was this?"

"Like I said, there has been nothing on the news about it, and I didn't say 'terrorism,' I said sabotage."

"There's a difference?"

"I think so. Anyway, it was west of Cleveland, over by Amherst."

"What were you doing over there on a Tuesday?"

"Why all the questions? I was going to visit my parents. Okay?"

"Don't get paranoid. The questions are because you said, 'It could get me in trouble,' and I want to know what I'm getting into. Besides, it strikes me as odd that you were going all the way to Amherst to visit your parents on a Tuesday night."

"Actually they live in Vermilion, and it was Tuesday morning. I decided to take a frickin' mental health day and spend it at the lake. Maybe go screw with the boat."

"You have a boat?"

"No, my dad does. He has a thirty-six foot sailboat. I can use it if they're not using it. Do you like sailing?"

"I've never been sailing. I've never been on a boat, but I'd love to try it."

"Maybe we can go some time."

"I'd like that."

"So, do you think you can try to find out about these guys for me?"

"'Do, or not do. There is no try.'"

"I know that one. It's Yoda!"

"Huh?"

"Do you know that you use a lot of movie quotes in your conversations?"

"'Well, nobody's perfect.'"

"Is that another one?"

"'Elementary, my dear Watson.'"

"I'm going to have to keep a list or something. Anyway, will you help? With the checks, I mean."

"Don't bother. You'll never get them all. Yes."

"I'll go get the pizza."

* * *

"Boy does that look good. 'The stuff that dreams are made of.' I should be able to get in to the DMV records and find out Peter's last name. From there it's easy: address, SSN, DOB, phone number, whatever you want to know. Arrest record, credit report, 'et cetera, et cetera, et cetera.'"

"That would be frickin' great."

"I haven't had Inner Circle Pizza in a while. This is outstanding! Who's the other guy you want me to check out?"

"Right near where the cell tower went down is a little used car lot called Shawn's Deals On Wheels. I met a guy there who said he was Shawn, but I'm not sure he really was."

"What makes you say that?"

"Well, the cell tower site was guarded by state cops and guys in plain clothes. Shawn's was right next door. The Shawn I met wasn't dressed right to be the owner of a dinky little country used car lot. He had on brand-new-looking fancy clothes. I would have expected Shawn to be in jeans and a polo shirt. He just looked too well dressed. How can I find out if he's really Shawn of Shawn's Deals On Wheels?"

"Well, his DMV record would have a picture."

"Yeah, I guess. Of course, if they faked Shawn, they could fake his picture."

"I've got to go potty. Be right back."

* * *

"Greg, level with me. What's going on here? You're a lot more involved in this than you're telling me, and it's starting to creep me out. If you want me to help, you need to be straight up with me."

"Can I trust you?"

"With what, for God's sake?"

"This has to go no farther."

"*What* has to go no farther?"

"Okay. I told you I saw a demolished cell tower. Well... Well, I did it."

"Did what?"

"Demolished it. I took it down. I'm responsible. And they're frickin' covering it up."

"You took it down? Oh, shit! 'Toto, I've got a feeling we're not in Kansas anymore.'"

CHAPTER 19

Friday

(Peter)

I'm off to visit the Three Stooges again. I slowed down a little as I went by the cell tower site. There appeared to be no activity at all, no sign of the tower, no wreckage, no nothing. Even the equipment building is gone. It's like it never existed. And there is still nothing on the news.

Kate and I always chat in the morning over coffee. No TV. We sit in our living room overlooking Lake Erie, watch the boats and the birds go by, and discuss the day to come. I told her about my talk with Mike last night. She said that I've been watching entirely too many Mel Gibson movies, but I could tell she was intrigued.

Sometimes Kate tries to play the "I'm just a dumb housewife" role, but it doesn't work. She is well educated with an AAS in electronics technology, a BS in mechanical engineering and an MS in organizational development. She's employed by a Fortune One Hundred industrial supplier as a project manager for multi-million dollar accounts. Kate works with high-level sales people and managers all day long, and more than holds her own. She is interesting, and interested in the whole world. A "dumb housewife," she is not. But then, that's why I married her. Well, that and the fact that she is cute: 5'6", 120 pounds, blond hair, green eyes, and freckles. Plus, she loves the water in general, and sailing in particular. But then, I'm prejudiced.

She will insist that I tell her all about what Mike has to say. If I know Kate, she'll be as involved in this thing as I am.

My cell phone rings just as I'm pulling into the parking lot.

"Good morning, this is Peter."

"Hi Dad, I've got some information for you."

"Boy, that was quick! Unfortunately I'm just going into work, and I don't want to discuss this where other people might hear. Can you call me back between noon and one? Or I can call you?"

"I was intrigued with your story. I stayed up last night and did some research. Some very interesting things surfaced. But it'll wait 'til noon. Call me when you can talk. I'll be home until tomorrow morning. See ya."

"I'll call you at lunch. 'Bye, Mike. Thanks."

* * *

The morning really dragged. "Very interesting things," huh? At noon, I leave the office and drive a mile or so to Big Creek Park. It's one of my favorite spots to spend my lunch hour. It's just a long skinny park that follows the creek for a few miles in the city, but it's quiet, shady, and away from the office.

"Hi, Mike, is this an okay time to talk?"

"Hi, Dad. It's a good time. Here's what I found out.

"Person of interest number one: Shawn Rainbow. Yeah, that's really his last name. He looks legit to me. Assuming the Shawn you met matches the photo I emailed to your home email address. Does fortyish, about 5'7", somewhat pudgy, fair complexion, glasses and very little hair sound right?"

"Sounds like him. You think he's okay?"

"He looks okay to me. He has an ex-wife and a couple of teenage daughters wandering around somewhere. He's originally from Georgia, a real redneck, and he's trying hard to live that down. He's known to dress well, and talk more sophisticated than he really is.

"He's worked in the auto business in and around Cleveland for most of his life, and finally managed to scrape together enough cash to go out on his own. Why in almost rural Amherst, I have no idea. He owns a modest condo in Amherst. His tax records indicate that he is making it work, though. Well enough to support himself, his ex, his kids, and a live-in girlfriend, at least. He's been in Amherst for a couple of years. My guess is that he is what he seems: a typical small business man."

"Okay. I'll check the photo tonight. Could they have changed the photo to match a plant?"

"I doubt it. I know the federal government well enough to doubt that they could work that fast. You could always go back in a few days and see if the same Shawn is still there."

"That's a thought. I just might do that. What about Gregory?"

"Ah, yes, person of interest number two: Gregory Zaremba. He's the interesting one. Semi-professional student at Cleveland State University -- six years so far -- switched majors from electrical engineering to journalism and then back to electrical engineering. He lives alone in Euclid, and supports himself with occasional inconsequential jobs, supplemented by money from his parents. He is currently not working."

"Your description fits what I saw perfectly, Mike."

"Not only is he a person of interest to you, he is a person of interest to Homeland Security! When I started digging into him and his past, red flags started going up. I backed out of the databases I was in as unobtrusively as possible, but I suspect that I may hear from HS concerning my inquiry."

"Red flags?"

"Yeah, but I did find out a few things before I backed out. He has a history of student activism. He's always marching and protesting for or against something, but usually against. He is anti-government and anti-business, pretty much believes in anarchy. His apparent credo reminds me of a druggie I knew some years back who thought, 'I should be able to do whatever I want as long as it doesn't interfere with the right of others to do the same.' That, of course, is what all of English Common Law, and our own law, is all about."

"Interesting."

"Gregory may be anti-government, but he is not apolitical. He has actively campaigned for the Green Party candidate of the month, whoever it happens to be. Apparently, he thinks they will disassemble the government."

"I run into his brethren all the time at LCCC."

"More importantly, he has a YouTube posting that is a rant about cell phone towers! He complains about how many there are, and how ugly they are. They are, in his words, 'a frickin' blight on the landscape!' He compares them to chain link fences. Don't ask me what he has against chain link fences. He thinks cell phone towers should be banned, consolidated, replaced with some green technology, etc., etc., etc. He even suggests that all cell phone towers should be destroyed!"

"You're kidding!"

"No, I am not. I suspect that the cell phone tower thing is what got Homeland Security interested. Cell phone tower vandalism is as much a concern to HS as the vandalism of any utility. Utility vandalism is considered a national security threat and is treated as such by HS and the FBI. It's a very serious issue. One you don't want to get involved in."

"Really?"

"Dad, you need to be careful. I don't know why Gregory was there. I don't know how he found out about it so quickly. I suspect that this dude is more than just a curious passerby. It's not a coincidence that he was there. He was attracted to this tower falling over for a reason. In my experience, coincidences are usually not."

"Wow. Now what?"

"That, dear old Dad, is up to you, but I'd be real tempted to let it drop. Of course, having said that, you should know that I won't let it drop. And I suspect this is a 'like father, like son' scenario. I have a few sources that I can check to see what I can find out about the cell tower itself. You have certainly piqued my curiosity."

"Okay, Mike. I've got to get back to work. Keep me posted."

"Will do. See you, Dad."

And so it's back to work. I know Howard is monitoring emails. I wouldn't put it past him to be monitoring Internet traffic as well. It'll kill me to not spend the afternoon digging around on the Internet. But it'll have to wait 'til tonight. Again!

CHAPTER 20

(Gregory)

It's the night after I broke the news to Rachel, and we're back at Inner Circle sharing a pitcher of Bud and waiting for our pizza.

Rachel looks sharp tonight, a little less Goth than usual. I definitely approve. Dressy black denim pants and a gray light weight sweater that compliments her short black hair and startlingly blue eyes. She's about 5' 5", and thin, but definitely not skinny. I think "sleek" is a good word. She has a nice figure, and looks like she might work out, but she's not muscular. Just sleek.

"'Fasten your seatbelts. It's going to be a bumpy night.'"

"I take it that means: one, you decided to help me; and two, you found something out about Shawn and Pete."

"'Yeah, Baby,' on both counts."

"Well, where do we start?"

""Splain, Lucy.' We start by you explaining just why you did what you did. If I like your explanation, I'll help. I'll fill you in on what I found out. If I don't like your explanation, I walk, and this ends here and now."

"That's fair. It's pretty simple, really. I hate cell phone towers. They are frickin' ugly. They are, in large part, unnecessary. I consider them a blight on the countryside. They --"

"Wait. Why do you say that they are, in large part, unnecessary?"

"Think about what you see scattered around the countryside. It's not at all unusual to see two or three towers very near to each other with several sets of antennas on each tower."

"And?"

"The reason you see so frickin' many is because there are dozens of cell phone companies putting up towers and antennas to compete with each other for our cell phone dollars."

"And?"

"We could eliminate many of these frickin' towers by forcing providers to share technology. Or better yet, we could have a quasi-governmental monopoly like the regular telephone and gas and electric companies used to be before big business convinced Congress to deregulate them. Deregulation was supposed to promote competition by eliminating the monopolies, but it backfired. We have a big mess with all of the utilities now. But that's another story."

"Go on with this one."

"One government regulated cell phone company would mean one set of towers with one set of antennas. We could probably eliminate two-thirds of the existing towers. As an added bonus, that one company could add new towers in dead spots to improve overall coverage. Our coverage is terrible compared to Europe."

"And?"

"If a bunch of companies weren't spending a substantial portion of their bloated profits putting up towers, they could invest in research to find alternatives to towers. There has been some promising research in that area, but nobody wants to spend money on it. It's frickin' easier to just throw up more towers!"

"And?"

"And what?"

"I get everything you're saying, but I don't see how destroying one tower in northern Ohio will have much effect on this blight."

"I won't stop with one frickin' tower. I started with a new small company just moving in to this area. Here's the plan: I'll inform them that I'll destroy their towers as fast as they put them up. My demand is simple: Vista Tel is to sell out to a bigger existing company, and get rich in the process. Alternatively, they can share bandwidth with another company, or they can lease space on existing towers. Or I drive them into bankruptcy!"

"And so that's one small company in one small area..."

"It doesn't stop there. When Vista Tel caves, we move on to the next company. Eventually we enlist other like-minded people in other areas of the country to do the same thing. And just maybe we can make a difference. Just maybe we can drive the industry to that one quasi-governmental monopoly. Like the landline-based telephone company used to be."

"Just maybe."

"And just maybe, we can convince the government to go back to the way it used to be for the other utilities. One gas company, one electric company, even one cable company."

"That makes a lot of sense."

"We have to be very careful involving others. The cell phone companies will fight this, and they'll enlist the help of the police to stop us. I've done my homework -- utility vandalism is considered a federal issue, so the FBI and maybe even Homeland Security will get involved. That's why I want you to be sure you want to do this. It'll be dangerous, but I truly believe that we *can* make a difference."

"Like I said, or actually like Bette Davis said, 'Fasten your seatbelts. It's going to be a bumpy night.' I think our Pizza's up. Will you go get it, please?"

* * *

"Okay, Greg, 'It's Showtime!' You convinced me. At least, for now. Here's what I found out.

"Shawn of Shawn's Deals On Wheels is Shawn Rainbow, an unremarkable person. The description I have is forty-three years old, 5'7", 190 pounds, fair complexion, glasses and very little hair. Sound right?"

"Perfect description. 'Unremarkable,' you say?"

"Shawn is your stereotypical used car salesman. He's a redneck from Georgia. He made enough money working at several big dealerships to start his own used car lot. He's divorced and supporting a couple of teenage daughters that live with his ex-wife. Shawn's trying to convince his girlfriend and everyone else that he's a cool dude. He just bought a motorcycle, for God's sake."

"You really nailed him from what I saw. Where do you get your information?"

"'You don't want to know.' But here's a picture."

"Well, there is no doubt that the Shawn I met is this Shawn. Like somebody once said, 'What you see is what you get.'"

"Geraldine."

"Geraldine?"

"Yes, Geraldine. Flip Wilson's character Geraldine always said, 'What you see is what you get' on *Rowan and Martin's Laugh In*."

"Oh. You're good."

"I know. 'The stuff that dreams are made of.'"

"Oh, stop it. What about Pete?"

"Don't you mean 'What About Bob?'"

"I give up! I give up! Please."

"Okay. Okay. It's a game with me. A game I particularly enjoy with you. You're a good sport about it, at least so far."

"So far."

"Peter is much more interesting. The description I have is: sixty-two years old, 5'10", 215 pounds, sun-baked complexion, longish brown hair graying at the temples, brown eyes, and a well-trimmed full beard that he has worn for at least thirty years. Works part time for an engineering company and teaches part time at Lorain County Community College. He is a boater. He has a forty-three-foot Beneteau sailboat, and he's Vice Commodore of the Vermilion Yacht Club. Is this him?"

"'Bimbo!' Is that from a movie? Why do you say he's much more interesting?"

"I don't think so. Well, if Peter were Italian, we might say he is connected."

"Connected?"

"Yeah. How about this for connections? His sister is an Assistant Attorney General for the State of Ohio. His youngest son is a defense attorney in Fort Lauderdale. And here's the fun one: his oldest son is a U.S. Marshall!"

"You're frickin' shitting me."

"'Wait a minute, wait a minute. You ain't heard nothin' yet!' During the cold war, he spent several years overseas working for Raytheon, the big defense contractor. I can't crack where he was or what he was doing. It's a mystery."

"So, what do you think?"

"Zowee. 'Keep your friends close, but your enemies closer.' Let's eat."

CHAPTER 21

(Peter)

"Hi, Dad. Did I catch you at a good time?"

"Yeah, you did. I'm on my way home. I have the top down. Let me roll the windows up so I can hear you better. Okay, that's better. What's up?"

"Ever since we talked earlier, I have been thinking about this whole cell phone tower thing, Dad, and I'm concerned."

"How so?"

"I doubt seriously that this Gregory is just a lookie-loo. There are too many connections, and too many coincidences. It has been my experience that coincidences just don't happen that often. There is almost always something else going on."

"I agree. That's why I'm curious."

"You know the old cliché about curiosity and the cat. I don't want your epitaph to be 'Here lays Captain Curious Cat.' If Gregory is involved, he's unstable. And unstable people don't think like we do. You could get hurt. Bad. As in dead. I just heard on the news about a guy arrested for bombing a lab at USC to protest their using mice for drug testing. He sees nothing wrong with killing people to save mice. Gregory could be that warped. Okay?"

"I suspect that if he's involved, he is that warped. I told you he doesn't seem right. But consider this, my son. You were in the Rangers for twenty years and they taught you lots of really nasty ways to protect yourself. Remember that I spent some time working for the State Department and the Defense Intelligence Agency. They taught me similar things. I may be old, but I can still protect myself."

"Not against guns and bombs."

"No, not against guns and bombs. If it looks like that's where this is heading, I promise you that I'll bail out. I'm approaching the tollbooth. I've got to hang up to get money out. I'll keep in touch."

"Me, too, Dad. Be safe."

CHAPTER 22

(Gregory)

That was a really cool frickin' time with Rachel. It's amazing what she found out. My gut feeling is that both Shawn and Peter are pretty much what they seem. I think all the coincidental connections with Peter are just that -- coincidences -- but I still need to be careful with him.

God, am I glad it's Friday. This has been an incredible frickin' week. It's hard to believe I just took the tower down on Tuesday. This urban terrorism shit is stressful. I should have picked up a movie for tonight. I'm sure there's nothing on TV. Over a hundred channels courtesy of Time Warner, and nothing worth watching.

Who could that be at ten o'clock? "Hello?"

"*Ciao*, Gregory. Did I wake you?"

"No. I just turned on the TV to see if there was anything worth watching. There isn't. Did I give you my number?"

"You forget that we decided that I'm the best computer nerd you know. Let's see. Home phone is 216-555-1234. Cell phone is 216-555-5678. CSU user ID is gregoryz6623 -- that's predictable. You should not use part of your social security number. Do you

want me to tell the rest of it? Password is philmont -- that's odd --
why philmont? Should I go on?"

"Okay. So I've been hacked into. My life is an open book. I
have no secrets. You didn't call just to impress me. You did that at
the Inner Circle. What's on your mind?"

"I want in. I want to be a part of your cause, your quest,
your project, your dream, whatever you call it."

"You're serious?"

"Yes. I may not have the passion for your cause that you do,
but I agree with both your cause and your methods. Besides, it
sounds like a hoot. Urban terrorism. Zowee!"

"You understand that this could be dangerous?"

"That's what excites me."

"By 'dangerous,' I mean the 'Do not pass go. Do not collect
$200. Go directly to jail.' kind of dangerous. If we get caught, we
will be prosecuted -- and persecuted."

"'Louis, I think this is the start of a beautiful friendship.'"

CHAPTER 23

Saturday

(Peter)

It's a beautiful Saturday morning in March. Kate's heading to Youngstown for the day. She's going to a shower for her friend Susan's daughter. I should be going down to work on the boat. It's time to start getting her ready for launch. Actually, I've still got over a month, but I've got the bug.

Instead, though, I'm heading for Shawn's.

I think Mike's probably right. But...

* * *

I don't know how this guy makes a living. I've never seen a customer here. Oh well, I've often asked that about small business in general. How do they survive? I noticed that Shawn's got a Chevy S-10 in decent shape. That's going to be my excuse.

"Hi, Shawn. I was here the other day. I remembered that dark blue S-10. Might be the kind of thing I'm looking for. How much are you asking?"

"Hi, Captain. Want to take it for a ride?"

"Captain?"

"That's what your license plate says."

"Oh, yeah. Actually, it's Peter, but most people call me Cap'n."

"Cap'n as in the military or as in airline captain?"

"Neither. Captain as in Merchant Marine Captain. Though I've not really used it, I do have a Coast Guard License. Anyway, how much?"

"Why don't you look it over, take it for a drive, and then we'll talk? I'll go get the keys."

"Well, I'm not sure I'm that serious."

"I want to move it. I'll give you a great deal. Be right back with the keys. Pop the hood and check it out. It's got just a little over 100,000 miles and it's clean."

So, I play used car buyer. Shawn sure sounds like a used car dealer. Oh well, a quick trip around the country block and, "I'll think about it." I used to have an S-10 very much like this one. Mine was an '85. This looks a lot newer, but it's the same body style. The style I always liked. And Shawn's right, it is in good shape.

"What do you think? I told you it was clean."

"Yeah, it really is. I had an '85 almost identical to this. It was ten years old, pushing 200,000 miles and still going strong when I traded it for a Jeep Wrangler. What year is this?"

"It's a 1993, the last year for this body style. I like it better than the newer ones. It looks like a truck should look. Go ahead, take it for a drive. It's a stick. Is that a problem?"

"Not at all. So was mine. I won't be long."

Shawn heads back into his office trailer.

Oh well, I didn't really want to go work on the boat. This *is* in good shape. I turn right out of the lot, and go toward the Route 2 underpass. There's the access road to the cell tower. This is a good chance to check it out. I can always say I wanted to try the S-10 on a dirt road.

* * *

The entire site has been sanitized. The tower is gone. The little equipment building is gone. Even the power line from the road back to the site is gone. It's too clean. It's like they didn't want anyone to know there was ever a cell tower here. They? Now who's sounding paranoid?

CHAPTER 24

(Gregory)

So Rachel wants to be involved in my little project. That's good. On several levels. I need an assistant. I need a confidant. And I think I need a girlfriend. It's been a while. Maybe "girlfriend" is not the right word. How about a girl who can be a friend? How about just plain old sex? That, too. Rachel *is* smokin' hot.

Nice day for a drive to Vermilion, by way of Shawn's. Maybe I'll look for a new vehicle. Of course, that takes money. Oh well, I can look, can't I?

* * *

Shawn's the only one here, again. I'll tell him I'm thinking about trading my Honda in on a small truck. "That's my story, and I'm sticking to it." Uh, oh. I think Rachel's rubbing off on me. That sounds like a movie quote. I'll have to ask her.

"Hi. Boy, is this a coincidence. Your uncle was here this morning."

"My uncle?"

"Peter -- the Captain. He's thinking about buying that dark blue S-10 up front."

Uh, oh. "Actually it is a coincidence. I didn't know he was coming, but I saw the S-10 the other day, too. I'm thinking of trading my Honda in on a truck. And that might be the kind of thing I'm looking for. How much are you asking? Do you take trades?"

"Absolutely. The keys are still in it. Why don't you take it for a drive?"

"Not 'til I know what it'll cost me. I'm a student at CSU, and I'm pretty poor."

"You're a long way from CSU."

"I'm going to visit my parents in Vermilion, and I thought I'd stop."

"Who are your parents? I might know them."

Too many questions. "I doubt it. They just moved there. Anyway, how much?"

"Take it for a drive while I check out your Honda, and then we'll talk."

"I'm not sure I'm that serious. Let's talk first."

"I need to look at your Honda and do a little research. It'll take me ten minutes. Go ahead, take it for a drive. Don't tell your uncle I said this, but I'd rather sell it to you. He looks like he can afford something newer, and I'd like to help you out. I've been where you are. This would be a great little truck for you."

Okay, I'll play his game. Actually, this is a nice truck, and my Honda is getting tired -- very tired. I've got an idea.

"I don't want to blindside Uncle Pete if he's serious about this truck. I'd like to call him, but I don't have his number in my cell phone. Did he give it to you?"

"Yeah, I have it in the office. I'll give it to you when you get back."

Another idea. Let's check out the cell phone site. I am taking a truck for a test drive. I need to know how it handles dirt roads.

* * *

Wow! This is weird. Everything is gone. The cable across the access road is gone. The tower is gone. The equipment building is gone. The power line is gone. It's like they didn't want anyone to know there was ever a cell tower here. This is scary. Why aren't they talking about it? Why hasn't there been anything on the news? The silence is frickin' killing me.

CHAPTER 25

(Peter)

Mike's right. I can't leave this cell phone tower thing alone. Of course, he said he wouldn't be able to either. Must be in our genes. It's been on my mind ever since my visit to Shawn's this morning.

I did manage to spend some time this afternoon digging stuff out to start working on the boat. And that's exciting. Or at least, that's something to look forward to. Morning Star is our Beneteau 423. She doesn't need a lot of springtime care and feeding, but she does expect some attention. All the systems -- engine, water tanks, holding tanks, air conditioning -- need de-winterized. And that's my job. The hull needs waxed, but I pay the boatyard to do that. I think the bottom paint is okay for another year. But if it needs done, that's another job for the professionals. Kate will do a general cleaning below decks. She is not only a great first mate, she takes very good care of the cabin.

One of the few things that I don't like about the Beneteau is the teak toe rails. They look great, but they need attention before she goes in the water. I switched from many coats of spar varnish to one coat of Sikkens Cetol years ago, but it still needs done each spring. I keep her indoors for the winter, but the building is unheated. I think Sikkens says it has to be at least fifty degrees to apply Cetol, but I need to check on that.

Except for the teak, Morning Star looks great. Ready for another year. It'll be a month before she goes in the water. But she's getting restless. Boats are supposed to be in the water. They just don't look happy out of the water. Soon.

I'm restless, too. My mind keeps coming back to that sanitized cell tower site, and to what part Joe Honda, AKA Gregory Zaremba, has in all of this. Should I call him? Is it safe to call him? Can I call him? Mike didn't mention a phone number. As Kate would say, "Look it up on the Internet."

$$* * *$$

After dinner, I tell Kate that I'm going to try to find Gregory's number on the Internet. She grumbles. I go upstairs.

No phone number is listed for a Gregory Zaremba anywhere in the Cleveland area. I guess that shouldn't come as a big surprise. Lots of kids these days do not have landline telephones, and if you can get cell phone numbers on the Internet, I don't know how. Oh well, maybe next time I talk to Mike.

It is amazing how cell phone technology has changed the world. Debbie and Devin are two of my younger kids -- twenty-six and twenty-eight -- I don't think they have landline telephones either. They use their cell phones all the time. That and a cable connection for their computers is all they need. So, are telephone books, the good old white pages becoming obsolete, too?

My cell phone rings. It's almost nine p.m. Not a work emergency, I hope. "Hello?"

"Hi, this is Gregory Zaremba. Is this Pete?"

Wow! Talk about timing. "Peter. Yes…"

"Hi. I was back out at Shawn's Deals On Wheels late this morning, and Shawn said that my 'Uncle Pete' had been in earlier."

"Yeah, I was." Curiouser & Curiouser.

"Shawn said you were looking at a blue S-10 that he has. So am I. I don't think I can afford it, but I also don't want to screw you up if you're serious about buying it. I told Shawn I'd call you about it, but I didn't have your number in my cell phone. He gave me your number. He does think you're my uncle, after all. Hope you don't mind."

Should I go for it? Now is my opportunity. Okay. A little bait. "No, I don't mind. Actually, I'm not going to buy it. To be very honest, I was just using the truck as an excuse to see if the Shawn we met was still there, and to nose around a little."

"Wow! That's frickin' amazing. Me, too. I do like the truck, but no way can I afford it. You said you wanted to see if the Shawn we met was still there. What do you mean?"

Nibble, nibble. "Well, I thought the whole cell phone tower thing was just not quite right somehow. And when I met Shawn, I thought that he, too, was not quite right. I did a little checking, and he seems legit. But I wanted to talk to him again, just to reassure myself."

"What do you mean by 'not quite right'?"

Nibble, nibble. Wait. Don't set the hook yet. "I don't know exactly what I mean. The whole 'unused cell phone tower being dismantled' thing didn't sit well with me somehow. It was too pat to explain what I saw. When I met Shawn, he didn't sit well with me either. He was too pretty to be a country used car salesman. But I think he is what he says he is. I'm still not sure about the cell phone tower though."

"Wow! That's frickin' amazing. I keep saying that. Sorry. But this is amazing. I felt exactly the same way about the cell phone tower, and about Shawn. But you think Shawn is okay, now?"

Set the hook! "Yes. I have some ways of checking into these things that I'd rather not explain, but my contacts tell me that Shawn is legitimate. My contacts are also checking into the cell phone tower. They should be able to determine exactly what is going on there. It may be completely legitimate, but I'm not sure. I saw some things that don't fit the 'unused cell phone tower being dismantled' story. I may have more information soon."

"Wow! Again! I'm doing some digging, too. Can we compare notes in a few days? Your caller ID should show my cell phone number."

Caught him! "A few days won't work. I'm going out of town on business for a while, and it may be weeks before I know any more. How about I call you if I find out anything. If you don't hear from me, know that it was all nothing. As my wife says, 'Too many Mel Gibson movies.'"

"Well. Okay. But if you find out anything at all, please call me. Or email me at gzaremba@csuohio.edu. Or do you not use email?"

Time to end this before playing him too long allows the fish to get away. "Yes, I do. Hey, my other line is ringing and it's probably my wife. She's out of town so I've gotta take it. Real quick, spell gzaremba."

"g-z-a-r-e-m-b-a -- @csuohio.edu -- got it?"

"Got it. Gotta go. See you."

As Joe Honda would say, "Wow!" Now what?

CHAPTER 26

(Gregory)

I just don't understand why they are not talking about what I did. I did read something somewhere about them not publicizing cell phone tower vandalism, but I *destroyed* one! That's far beyond vandalism! That's newsworthy! I *want* it talked about.

I know. I can force the issue. I'll set up a bogus email account with Yahoo or somebody on a computer at the school library. I'll send an email to Vista Tel, and copy the news media.

It'll be a fine Saturday afternoon project.

* * *

Setting up a bogus email account was so easy it's scary. No wonder terrorists are using the Internet. I just logged onto Yahoo.com and it asked if I wanted free email! I clicked "Yes" and within three minutes, I established an account using bogus data. Then I emailed Vista Tel, and copied every radio and TV station in Cleveland, at least those I could find. Just for the frickin' hell of it, I copied the Cleveland Plain Dealer. This will attract some attention!

You have attempted to cover up the
fact that we destroyed your cell
phone tower along Route 2 in Lorain
County on Tuesday morning. Our
act is now public knowledge. We are
sending a copy of this email to the
Cleveland media.

You are hereby warned that we will
do everything in our power to put a
stop to the proliferation of these
ugly affronts to the beauty of God's
creation. Our demands are simple:
you are to sell out to a bigger
existing company, or you are to
share bandwidth and equipment with
another existing company, or you
may lease space on existing towers.
If you decide to stay in business,
figure out a way to do it without
erecting any more towers, or we will
drive you into bankruptcy!

Why Vista Tel? Because you are
here, and new, and erecting new
towers. We intend to stop the spread
of new towers. After Vista Tel has
met our demands, we will move on
to another company and do the
same thing to them. Our long-term
goal is one national array of cell
phone towers. The towers may
belong to a quasi-government
monopoly patterned after the U. S.
Postal Service, or they may belong to

a single government-regulated corporation like the Bell System used to be. There is no sane reason to have dozens of individual companies erecting their own towers. We will put a stop to it!

You have been warned!

* * *

Now we'll get some news coverage. It should be on the evening news. I've got to let Rachel know. I call her on my landline.

"Hello?"

Her voice sounds strange. "Rachel?"

"'Yeah, Baby.'"

"Hi. I didn't recognize your voice. It's Gregory."

"This is a really crappy phone. One of these days, I've got to replace it. What's up?"

"I've got a couple of extra phones. You can have one. Just come over and pick one out."

"Thanks. I'll take you up on that offer. But you didn't call to offer me a phone."

"Watch the news tonight. Listen to the radio. Buy a Plain Dealer in the morning. I sent an anonymous email to Vista Tel and to all the Cleveland media. They now know that I destroyed the cell tower, and they know why I did it. Actually, in the email I always used the term 'we' so they will think it was a group of people. I don't want to send you the email, but I have a hard copy if you want to read it."

"Zowee. That's exciting. I definitely will channel surf during the evening news. Better yet, I'll TiVo Channel 8 and listen to Channel 5. They have the best local news. I do want to see the email you sent. And I would like to replace this phone."

"I've got something to do this afternoon, and I'm going to be away tomorrow. Maybe we can get together Monday night?"

"I'd like that. Call me Monday during the day. I'll come over to your place to do some phone shopping, but I need to know where I'm going."

"Euclid. It's easy. I'll call you on your cell phone Monday."

"Great. Bye, Greg."

"Bye, Rachel."

* * *

The news is everything I hoped it would be. I don't know which is better, all the media talk about "urban environmental terrorists in our midst right here in Cleveland," Vista Tel trying to explain why they covered it up, or the government lamely denying any part in the cover up. As Rachel said, "Zowee!"

"Hello?"

"I don't know where it got started, but the word I've heard to describe what you've created is 'shitstorm.' You have caused one huge shitstorm. It's on local talk radio now. I'll bet it makes the 11:00 national news tonight and Rush Limbaugh on Monday. Congratulations. I want to go listen. I love it. You done good! 'May the force be with you.'"

"And 'May the force be with you,' too. I-- Hello? Hello?"

Boy, was she excited. As she said, I done good.

CHAPTER 27

Monday

(Peter)

"Hi, Dad. How goes it?"

"Marvelous. I just had a great dinner: salad with Asiago Peppercorn dressing, penne pasta with Italian hot sausage, fresh bakery bread. I'm stuffed and sitting here watching the seagulls go by. I love watching them soar into an onshore wind. They just look like they're having fun. I understand why the guy who wrote *Jonathon Livingston Seagull* was inspired to do so. How goes it with you?"

"Okay."

"'Okay' usually means less than okay. What's the matter?"

"It's not a real big deal. Eric is giving us fits. He doesn't like school."

"There's a saying about the acorn not falling far from the tree."

"But I grew out of it!"

"Yes, you did! A degree in Computer Science. A career as an Army Ranger. A second career as a U.S. Marshall. You grew out of it, and so will he. Just be a father, a better one than I was, and try to help him through it."

"You did okay, considering."

"I did try. When I was sober. But Eric isn't why you called. Even if it's been about the cell phone tower, we've talked more in the last few days than in the last few years, and I like it. So, what is up?"

"Well, I told you that I set off alarms when I started doing a background check on Gregory Zaremba. I had a call from Homeland Security today. HS wanted to know what my interest in Zaremba was. They connected his Cleveland location with yours. They surmised that I was doing a background check on him because you had contact with him. They wanted details. I told you, he is a person of interest to HS."

"They connected me and him? How?"

"Yep. Pretty easy, actually. You'd be amazed at what a Cray supercomputer can do with associations and interactions. You've heard of Venn diagrams. A Cray can do millions of Venn diagrams in microseconds, and make connections. It's kind of like that trivia game Six Degrees of Kevin Bacon. Everything is eventually connected, and you are the common connection between Zaremba in Cleveland and me in Denver."

"I don't think I like being the common connection."

"Dad, I can't tell anything less than the truth to HS. It's my job. I told them that you had met him near the site of a cell phone tower that had come down, that his demeanor caused you to wonder about him, and that you asked me to check into him. Of course, they know about your background, so they had reason to trust your instincts. They seemed satisfied for now, but there may be more inquires. Especially now that an unnamed urban terrorist organization is claiming credit for taking the tower down. You did hear about that, didn't you?"

"Oh, yeah. That's all that's been on the local news all weekend. It's really big news here. Mike, there is something I've got to tell you."

"Uh, oh…"

"'Uh, oh' is a good way to put it. As I understand it, Vista Tel and the media got the email from this group on Saturday afternoon. I don't watch the news much, and I didn't hear about it until Sunday. But Saturday night, I got a call from Gregory Zaremba."

"Uh, oh…"

"Yep. 'Uh, oh.' He was definitely feeling me out about my interest in the whole cell phone tower thing. Zaremba was agitated and excited. I led him along a little by telling him I suspected the 'unused tower demo' story, and that I also suspected that Shawn might not be legit."

"What did he say?"

"When I told him that I had been having someone investigate Shawn, he went ballistic with excitement. He told me he had the same suspicions, and that he, too, was investigating Shawn. I backed off a little at that point, but he pushed hard. He was really excited. I got the impression that he thought he had found a kindred spirit. He wanted to compare notes in a few days. I tried to cool his interest in me -- and my investigations -- by telling him I was going to be out of town on business for a while. And that's the truth, by the way. I'm going to LA to do some work at a customer's plant in Torrance. I'll be staying in Redondo Beach, so I'm looking forward to it. I should be gone for about a week."

"Dad, Zaremba's phone call to you is very troubling. Another coincidence. Did he say how he got your number?"

"Yeah. I went to Shawn's Deals On Wheels Saturday morning. I wanted to see if Shawn was still there and to snoop around a little. I know you told me not to get involved. What can I say? You're my son. You would have. You admitted it the other day. Anyway, I took a truck for a test drive and gave Shawn my phone number. Zaremba went there later Saturday. For the same reason that I did, he says. He took the same truck for a test drive. He told Shawn he wanted to call me about it, but didn't have my phone number with him. Shawn thinks he's my nephew and gave him my cell phone number. He says. And it sounds plausible."

"Okay."

"By the way, my test drive took me to the cell phone tower site. It is cleaned up like there was never a tower there. The word that came to mind was 'sanitized.'"

"'Sanitized' is exactly the right word. HS does not acknowledge that cell phone tower vandalism exists. They take the same approach with all utility vandalism. By not acknowledging it, by sanitizing the site, by making it a non-issue, they remove the incentive to do it for the sake of publicity or notoriety. The bad guys lose interest if they know it won't accomplish anything. Most vandalism is done to get attention. Why bother if you're not going to get any attention?"

"Well, they sure sanitized it here. Until that email hit the news, there was no mention whatsoever that it happened. I watched for it because I was curious about what I saw. I witnessed a cell phone tower fall over along a busy interstate highway. A newsworthy event. But there simply was no news. That's what piqued my interest."

"Dad, you're not going to like this, and I'm truly sorry. I'm going to have to pass this info on to Homeland Security. There are simply too many coincidences. I don't believe in coincidences. Homeland Security doesn't believe in coincidences."

"Now it's my turn to say it. 'Uh, oh.'"

CHAPTER 28

(Gregory)

"Hi, Rachel. I'm glad you came. Welcome to my humble abode. It's not much, but it's home."

"'There's no place like home.' Looks very nice, actually. It's bigger than mine."

Rachel looks really nice tonight, as usual. She has on brown skinny hip hugger jeans, and a beige lightweight, fuzzy sweater. She looks super hot.

"I much prefer an older home to a modern apartment. I think it has more character, and it has lots of room for all my junk. Speaking of junk, let's go phone shopping before I forget. The phone department is down in the basement. Not a pretty place, but it's great for storing stuff. It's dry, anyway, and the spiders are behaving this spring."

"I am not a spider person."

"I'll protect you." Or hug you.

"'My mother thanks you. My father thanks you. My sister thanks you. And I thank you.'"

God, but I wish she'd knock off the movie quotes. They're so frickin' annoying. "I was kidding about the spiders. They're not a problem down here. I've got a whole box of phones somewhere. Some good, some bad, some so-so. Do you have a color preference? Ahah, here it is."

"Zowee. Dial phones. Do they still work? Can I have one?"

Anything you want. "I think so. I bought them at a flea market for a dollar apiece. Take one and try it. If it works, keep it. I'll have to put a connector on the cord. Do you have RJ-11 phone jacks at home?"

"If that's the little plastic thingy about a half inch square that's similar to a computer Ethernet plug, yes."

"Yep, that's an RJ-11. Actually, the one computer networks use is called an RJ-45. I have no idea what 'RJ' stands for. Pick out a regular push button phone, too, just in case the dial phone doesn't work. If you like pink, this Princess phone works well."

"Princess phone?"

"That's what they called it. I think my sister might have had one during her Barbie phase."

"Princess. Barbie. And that fits Rachel, the computer nerd?"

"Yes. I think so." Definitely fits.

"I'm flattered. I think. I'll have to give it some thought."

"Let's take your phones upstairs."

* * *

"Let me find you a bag for your new collection of phones. And get a connector on that dial phone cord. I've got a crimping tool in the other room. Be right back. Better yet, come with me and I'll give you the proverbial fifty cent tour."

"'Lead on, MacDuff.'"

"Two bedrooms, this one for computers and stuff. Come on in while I find an RJ-11 and my crimping tool. So, what do you think of my shitstorm?"

"It is going exactly as I thought it would. You have gotten the attention of Fox News, CNN, even Rush Limbaugh today. I'm very impressed."

"I got more attention that I ever expected. Ok, I've got what I need. This is bedroom number two. I actually use it for sleeping. Nothing special here, just a bedroom."

"And the bed is actually made. Or did you do that just for company?"

"No. I hate getting into an unmade bed at night, so I always at least throw the covers back over."

"You're neat, too."

"Here's the bathroom. Part of the lease deal was the landlord would give me cheap rent if I did some remodeling. He pays for materials and I provide the labor. I just finished the bathroom."

"Very nice. You surprise me."

"Why?"

"'More than just a pretty face.' Seriously, I didn't expect you to be a home handyman as well as an urban terrorist."

"Actually I enjoy remodeling. Someday I'd like to tackle a really unique project. Near where I grew up, there is a barn, complete with silo, that a guy remodeled into a home. It took him fifteen years, but when he was done, it was stupendous. He was photographed and written up in House Beautiful, or something. I'd like to do something like that. Or build a really unique house, like the one in *The Lakehouse* with Sandra Bullock and Keanu Reeves. But for now I'm up to my eyeballs in urban terrorism."

"Kitchen."

"Kitchen. Next on my list to be remodeled. I might be looking for ideas. Do you know any 'Susie Homemaker' types that might be willing to help?"

"No, but I know a 'Princess Barbie' type who would."

"Great. Dining room. I don't know what you do with dining rooms now."

"Dine."

"And back to the living room."

"For living. And a comfortable one at that. And for sitting. It's been a long day."

"Yes, it has. This frickin' urban terrorism stuff is tiring. Want a drink? I have beer, Diet Pepsi and cheap red Italian wine. My Dad used to call it 'dago red.' I wonder where the word 'dago' comes from?"

"'Frankly, my dear, I don't give a damn.' Diet Pepsi will be great. I'm really not much of a beer drinker, except with pizza. And wine doesn't appeal to me. I'm just not a party girl, I guess. I don't do drugs either. Barbie complex?"

"If it's a Barbie complex, I approve. I don't drink much either. Or do drugs, I just remodel."

"I want to talk business for a couple of minutes. I think we should keep the shitstorm brewing."

"What do you have in mind?"

"I've been thinking about it a lot. Here's what I want to do. We make two phone calls from two different places to two different TV stations at exactly the same time. Each of us delivers exactly the same message. They'll both think they have an exclusive. They'll broadcast it as such. When their stories coincide, the shitstorm will rage on. Everyone will know that there is more than one person involved. And duplicate messages will verify the validity of the whole thing."

"I like the idea, but I don't like calling. They might be able to trace the numbers. They might record our voices and be able to use voice prints later to prove that it was us."

"We want them to record us, so they can play the messages over the air. I suspect that they record all incoming calls anyway. We call from pay phones so they can't trace us. I have software that modifies voice patterns to make them unidentifiable. We can record our messages and play them back into the pay phones. I have a cassette recorder. Do you?"

"I have a digital recorder. What do we say?"

"We keep it very simple: 'Deliver this message to Vista Tel. Be afraid. Be very afraid. You have been warned. Publicize your plans to meet our demands. Or we will destroy another tower.'"

"When do we do it?"

"Tomorrow, in time for the evening news. At four o'clock."

CHAPTER 29

Friday

(Peter)

It's been a quiet week for me. And quiet has been good. I talked to Mike on Monday night. I haven't heard a thing about the cell phone tower all week. Mike hasn't called. Gregory hasn't called. Quiet. Good.

It's not been quiet on the media outlets, though. There has been a constant babble from the expert analysts all week: Who did it? How many are there? Where are they? Will they do more? What's their real motive? Are they Americans? Are they foreigners? And on and on and on and on. They really don't know anything, but they'll never admit it. Even though I know that they don't know, Kate and I have been pretty much glued to the TV. We flip back and forth between FOX and CNN, except when the local Cleveland news is on. Then we flip back and forth between Channel 3, Channel 5, and Channel 8.

Now, things have changed dramatically. It's Friday afternoon, and I almost made it through the week. I just got off the phone with a character named Nick Patridis. He sounded like the stereotypical government agent. "Hello, I'm Nick Patridis from Homeland Security and we need to talk."

"But I'm at work. We're not supposed to get personal phone calls. Can this wait until after I get off work at five p.m.?"

Gruffly: "No, it can't wait. We need to talk. Now."

"Please make it quick."

Even gruffer: "How quick is up to you. You and I need to sit down and have a face to face. This weekend."

"But I really don't have anything I can tell you. I explained everything to Mike, and I'm sure he passed my story on to you. And I'm --"

He's a real hard ass: "Look, we are going to talk. We meet this weekend, or we meet at your office on Monday. Pick one."

"Okay. Okay." So, I try to placate him, to calm him down a little. I've worked with his kind before. I tell him that, as I'm sure he knows, I used to work as a contractor to the DIA.

"Look, Nick. It was Nick, wasn't it?"

"Nick Patridis. Homeland Security."

"I know the drill, I'm not trying to be difficult. I want to help. This kid, Gregory, scares me. However, you need to understand that I have a rather paranoid boss who hates personal phone calls."

"And how is this relevant?"

"I wouldn't put it past him to be recording our office calls, and I don't think either of us wants that."

He agrees and starts to act a little more civil. Crisis over. With Nick, at least.

I go on. "I'm leaving tomorrow morning for a week-long business trip to California. I can give you my flight numbers and where I'll be staying in Redondo Beach, if you want. How about I call you when I get to LA, and get settled in. I'll use my cell phone, so it'll be more secure than the motel phone. We can talk as long as you want. If we still need to have a face to face, we can do it when I get back."

"Okay. That sounds reasonable. However, call me on Sunday."

I don't ask why. That works better for me anyway.

CHAPTER 30

(Gregory)

It's Friday afternoon, and it's been quiet all week. I want to call Pete, but I don't think I should. I don't want to push him too hard and scare him off. He said he's going out of town. I'll give him another week and then call him. "How was the trip?" Etc., etc. And, "Anything new about the cell phone tower thing?" Etc. etc.

I want to call Rachel even more, but I don't want to seem too anxious. There is something starting between us that goes beyond the cell phone tower thing. And I don't want to scare her off either. But for a more personal reason, I think.

I've got to do something this weekend. Maybe I'll take a drive to Vermilion. I can offer to help my Dad get his boat ready to put in the water, and I can ask him if he knows a sailor named Peter Bradovich.

And Rachel calls. "*Ciao*, Gregory. Want to get together tonight for something to eat?"

I tell her I'd love to and I suggest that we meet at a little bistro I know in Lakewood. It's small, intimate, and inexpensive. It has very good, almost gourmet food. Rachel asks if that's not a long drive for me, and I say it's a drive, yes, but I don't mind. I tell her I was just trying to figure out what to do to get out of the house anyway. We agree to meet at seven.

* * *

Rachel is waiting for me at the hostess station, and she looks great as usual.

Bistro Diso is a little more crowded than I expected, but it is Friday night. However, we get a table almost immediately. As the hostess takes us to our table, I check out the other patrons. Rachel is the fox of the joint. Several guys check Rachel out as we walk through the small dining room. She has that effect on guys. She's attractive, but not super pretty. She's just one of those girls that you just have to check out when you spot her. It makes me feel good to be with her. When we get seated, we order iced tea for a start and study the menu.

Rachel likes the sound of the fish, something called Tautog that I've never heard of. The waiter says it's a mild Atlantic fish similar to Mahi Mahi, and it's done peppercorn crusted and grilled. It does sound good. Rachel says, "To quote Mikie, 'Try it. You'll like it.' I hope." I decide to try it, too.

I knew something besides dinner was on Rachel's mind. It takes her until the salad gets here to broach the subject. "I don't want to let the shitstorm die down."

"Me neither. I can't believe how quickly it has become back page news. What do you have in mind?"

"Vista Tel is ignoring us and hoping it was a one-time deal. They have made no statements to the media; they have not even acknowledged our demands. We have to do another tower to convince them!"

"I think we need to cool it, give them more time."

"No. They are ignoring us. They will only understand action. We need to hit them while they're down."

It's almost an argument. Well, "argument" isn't a good word. We're both just a little cautious of each other's opinions.

We're kind of feeling our way into a possible relationship. I don't want to alienate her, and I think she feels the same way. We just kind of toss ideas back and forth through the salad and the fish.

And the fish is absolutely frickin' delicious. I thank Rachel for suggesting it. "I often order a filet because it's safe, but I'm really glad I had the fish."

"It really is good, 'The stuff that dreams are made of.'"

By the time we have dessert -- tiramisu for her, carrot cake for me -- we are of one accord.

We're going to do two phone messages again. We'll each deliver the same message, her to Channel 5, and me to Channel 8 at the same time on Sunday. Our message will be, "Deliver this message to Vista Tel. 'You're not listening. You have seventy-two hours to publicize your plans to meet our demands. If you fail to do so, we will destroy another tower.'"

I like the idea, if not the timing. "That's it?"

"I can send an anonymous email with the same message to Vista Tel and to all the local media. And you, 'My little chickadee,' can find us target number two!"

CHAPTER 31

Sunday

(Peter)

I kind of lied to Nick when I told him I was leaving for California tomorrow. That was Friday and today is Sunday. Oh well, so I was off by a day. Now that I think about it, lying to him probably wasn't smart. I'm sure he can very easily check on my flight schedule.

So, we're off to the airport. Kate and I decided to go out to breakfast. An omelet at The International is always a good idea. I had their Liberty Omelet with a whole bunch of different meats, and Kate had the Western, I think. Kate loves their potato pancakes. I'm a crispy home fries person.

Kate is delivering me to the airport. It saves Stan some money on parking, and more importantly, saves me from dragging my suitcase and computer carry-on from the parking garage. Whenever we can manage it, we take each other to the airport and pick each other up. It's convenient for the traveler, and we like saying goodbye and hello at the airport. Kind of romantic, somehow. Twenty-five years, and we're still romantic.

I'm the one doing the traveling today, so I've got on my usual travel clothes: jeans, and a Ralph Lauren sweater with a zipper part way down the front and a turned-up collar. Comfort is key.

Kate is not going much of anywhere today -- just hanging out -- but as usual, she is dressed very nicely. Dark slacks over low boots with pointy toes and kind of square heels. A crew neck top with a little jacket sort of thing over it. The colors show off her blonde hair and green eyes. I suspect the outfit is from Chico's. Wherever it's from, it's nice. My dear old dad, God bless his soul, once told me I have good taste in women. He was right.

Since I'm getting out at the airport, she's driving: the lake to Route 2 to Interstate 90 to Cleveland-Hopkins. And I'm counting cell phone towers.

I think I counted eighteen towers in a twenty-minute drive. That's amazing. And many of them are shared by several different providers. I wonder how many exist nationwide. It's got to be a huge number.

What's really amazing is that many of them are in locations that would cause damage if they were knocked down. Some would hit buildings, stores, offices, gas stations, even homes. And some would hit power lines. What are they thinking?

CHAPTER 32

(Gregory)

I'm off on a Sunday morning drive to Vermilion. I decided to just show up at my parent's house. They're used to it. Mom will feed me; she always does. And she'll make her usual big fuss over me. My old man will act somewhat distant; he always does. But he'll be glad to see me. I'll volunteer to go down to the boat with him. He'll like that. Even if we don't actually do anything, we'll both enjoy it.

It's a long haul from Euclid to Vermilion. Sixty miles. The drive will take me just at an hour. But I told Rachel I'd look for tower number two, and there are a frickin' ton of them in that sixty miles. The trick will be to find one that is secluded enough to work on. There won't be anything until I get out of the urban area. There are lots of towers in the city, but none that we can safely do.

I can take Interstate 90 right through Cleveland and pick up Route 2 in Lorain. Traffic will be light on Sunday, so I'll make good time. Crap. Looks like an accident at dead man's curve. Only Cleveland would have a curve on an interstate called dead man's curve. And the name fits. A six-lane interstate in the middle of downtown Cleveland -- with a right angle turn and an underpass!

The accident wasn't as bad as I thought. It only added about ten minutes to my drive time, and I'm on Route 2 almost to the cutoff for Vermilion. Over the river -- the Vermilion River -- and through the woods.

I'm thinking about Rachel, and looking over towers as I go. Thinking about Rachel is fast becoming one of my favorite past times. It's been a long time since I have felt this way about a girl. I'm not sure I've ever felt this way, now that I think about it.

The only thing about Rachel that bugs me is her incessant frickin' movie quotes. They're a genuine pain.

There it is! Just north of the highway! The perfect tower!

It's the same type as the last one. It's gotta be Vista Tel. It's in the perfect location. It sits just off the highway. It's about three hundred yards back an access road behind what looks like an abandoned farmhouse on what, I think, is West River Road.

I'll check it out on the way home. If it is a Vista Tel tower, we have our next target!

CHAPTER 33
(Peter)

Ah, wonderful Los Angeles. As we approach the airport, I can actually see the copper colored cloud of smog hanging over the city. I've seen it every time I've come to LA. I've never noticed it anywhere but here. And I'm going to be breathing that stuff for the next week.

$* * *$

I've got my rental car, a new G6, and I'm on my way to Redondo Beach. The plant is actually in Torrance, but it's less than five miles from there to Redondo Beach. There is nothing in Torrance, and Redondo Beach is -- well, Redondo Beach. All I can say is, if you've never walked along the Esplanade or driven Palos Verdes Drive before you die, do it.

But as some commercial once said, "Getting there is half the fun!" It's less than ten miles from LAX to Redondo Beach -- straight down Sepulveda Boulevard -- but it's ten miles of typically insane LA traffic.

However, as I fight the traffic, I can't help but notice that every time I stop at a light, I see cell phone towers. Different from at home though. They're on buildings, on roofs, and on water towers. They're even on high voltage transmission line towers. I guess they don't really need to erect towers like we have at home. You can drive a hundred miles in the LA area and never leave the urban area. There is always some manmade structure that you can hang a cell phone antenna on, and they do.

* * *

I've gotten checked in at the motel, a Holiday Inn Express. It overlooks Seaside Lagoon, and it's right next to the marina. Perfect location. For me, at least. If John expects me to put up with the travel -- and he does -- he knows he has to treat me right. And this is right.

I change into my standard summer waterfront dressy clothes: white Tommy Bahama shorts, short sleeve pastel plaid Polo button down shirt, no socks, and Sperry Topsiders. The guys at work kid me about my "yachty" attire, but I'm comfortable. And I fit in.

I walk the short distance down Harbor Drive to the marina. I find a small restaurant; get a table for one by the window overlooking the docks. It's Sunday night, and just like our marinas at home, it's quiet. All the weekend people have gone home to get ready for work in the morning. Just the locals are left. It is my favorite time of the week on the waterfront. This one, or any one.

I order a hamburger with bacon and blue cheese, homemade potato chips, and a diet Pepsi. As I look out the window at the boats, my mind drifts back to cell phone towers here and at home. I'm still convinced that what I saw on my way to work two weeks ago was the deliberate destruction of a cell phone tower. I don't know if it was vandalism or terrorism, but it was deliberate.

Is there really a difference between vandalism and terrorism?

CHAPTER 34

(Gregory)

It was a nice day with my folks, but I was antsy to leave and check out the site I found. I stayed through supper, made an excuse about homework, and left. I left Vermilion via West River Road and found the site and the access road. The access road does join West River Road at an abandoned farmhouse. It looks perfect.

When I get home, I check the website. Yes! The tower is a Vista Tel tower. I still find it frickin' awesome that there are actually websites that show maps of virtually all the cell phone towers in the country, and identify who owns and operates them. Isn't the information age wonderful?

I've *got* to call her. "Rachel?"

"'Bond. James Bond.'"

"Miss Moneypenny, maybe, but not James Bond. Definitely the wrong sex."

"You noticed, huh? What's up?"

"I definitely noticed. I found our next tower."

"'I feel the need. The need for speed.' Where? When can we do it?"

"Easy. Easy. It's outside of Vermilion along Route 2. The access road is behind an abandoned farmhouse. It's a very secluded location. We can get in and out without being seen. I checked on the Web and the tower belongs to Vista Tel. I figure going west of the last one will make them less likely to look east for the perps -- us. I don't know when we can do it, though. I lost my frickin' tools at the last tower. It went down suddenly and it threw my pipe, big socket and breaker bar across the enclosure. I didn't take time to gather them up, I just boogied!"

"What do we have to do to make this happen? We warned Vista Tel that we'd do another tower if they didn't respond by this Wednesday. I think they're going to need convinced that we're serious. So, what do we have to do? 'Go ahead, make my day.'"

"We have to do a drive-by, check out the site, and make sure it's quiet enough to get in and get out. Then we go back and reconnoiter, figure out what tools we need to take it down. At the very least, we have to buy a new pipe, big socket and breaker bar. Last time it took me a couple of weeks to get the right tools without attracting attention. You can't just go into Home Depot and say, 'I want a set of cell phone tower demolition tools.' Then we figure out the logistics: where to park, how to get the tools back to the site, how to escape after the tower goes down, and so on. It's going to take us some time to get organized, make our plans, buy what we need, and then actually do it."

"It won't be nearly as complex this time. You know what to do. You already did it once. The second time will be easy!"

"But I don't know when we can even do the first drive-by, let alone all the rest of it."

"'Elementary, my dear Watson.' Tomorrow evening we take our bikes and do the drive by. The weather channel says it'll be a great evening for a bike ride! Zowee!"

CHAPTER 35

Monday

(Peter)

This is the fun part of my job, the part that I really like; working with the customer, and discovering what my company and I can do to help them have a safer and more efficient operation. Typically, I spend a few days at the customer's site, then go home and spend several weeks or even months designing an upgraded system.

This is the fun part, but getting here was not. It's only five miles, but five miles of surface streets in LA during rush hour is horrendous! Five missed turns, four Anglo drivers showing signs of severe road rage, three Hispanic drivers cursing at me in very non-standard English, two serious near misses, and a partridge in a pear tree. And people do this every day. I made it to the plant; only to be confronted with a virtually all Hispanic workforce, most of whom speak little English. The good news is that Victor, the electrician, does speak passable English. And we got a really good start on the job.

I spent a lot of time today taking pictures of the existing installation, and just asking questions. Because of the proprietary nature of their process, the pictures I took will have to be vetted by

Tom Angelo, the plant manager. Tom is very laid back. He looks, and acts, like an aging member of The Beach Boys.

Tom says he is busy tonight, but he suggests that we go out to dinner tomorrow night at a place he knows in Hermosa Beach. He says The Charthouse is one of the best restaurants around; he'll make the reservations.

The engineering staff quits at four. I've got several hours of daylight to explore the Pacific Coast Highway, but not until traffic thins out. I go back to the hotel, kick my work boots off, grab a Diet Pepsi, turn on the TV, stretch out on the bed, and just veg. My work boots are steel-toed clodhoppers with metatarsal guards. They're heavy, and wearing them all day is just plain tiring. The good news is that Tom told me today they are unnecessary at this facility. No boots, no hard hat, no fire-retardant jacket. Just safety glasses, and they're not too fussy about them.

Since I'm doing a big fancy dinner tomorrow, I'll eat light tonight. I'll pick up a sub and some chips from a convenience store while I'm out and about. And this evening, it's out and about south. No particular reason for south. It was a mental coin toss. Obviously it was south or north. I see no reason to go inland, not with the Pacific Ocean out my window.

Here in Redondo Beach, the Pacific Coast Highway, Route 1, doesn't go along the coast. So, I drive south on Catalina Avenue and then on Palos Verdes Drive to Long Beach. Terminal Island in Long Beach is amazing. It's got to be one of the largest container loading and unloading ports in the world. Almost five miles of ships and cranes and containers. Thousands of containers. I slow down crossing the Vincent Thomas Bridge to look and get beeped at a lot. So I'm a tourist.

Outside of Long Beach, I pick up the Pacific Coast Highway and just cruise. Seal Beach, Sunset Beach, Huntington Beach, Newport Beach, Laguna Beach. I'd love to keep going, but I'm about forty miles from the hotel, and it's getting dark. I'd better head back. I think it's about a hundred miles from LA to San Diego. Maybe I can finish up early enough one day this week to go all the way. I wish I had the Mustang.

CHAPTER 36

(Gregory)

Rachel has done Google maps of site number two and MapQuest directions. So, I let her drive while I navigate. Besides that, her car is nicer. She actually drives a Jeep Wrangler. It's dark green, fairly new and spotlessly clean; it's obviously well taken care of. Somehow, it fits Rachel. She even has a top-of-the-windshield decal that says, "Silly Boyz! Jeeps are for Girlz!"

It's still too cool to put the top down. We make good time on Interstate 90 through Cleveland to Route 2 and then onto side roads to the old farmhouse. We drive by slowly, and then decide to park somewhere else. We find a now closed dentist's office about a half mile north. I take our bikes off Rachel's bike rack, and check them over. Rachel says she is just a poor working girl, but she seems to be doing okay for herself. Not only is her car much nicer than mine, so is her bike. Hers is a relatively new mountain bike with a whole bunch of speeds and canvas bags and stuff. Mine is a rather beat up three speed that is just barely ride-able. I swallow my pride, and off we go. We ride south to the farmhouse, and then back the access road to the tower. To the casual observer, we're just a couple of college kids off on an evening bike ride, maybe looking for a place to rest and make out.

Tower number two looks just like tower number one. They are twins! The same tools will work. Of course, I'll have to replace the socket and breaker bar, and buy another length of pipe.

Oh, shit! I just thought of something frickin' awful! Not only did I lose my giant socket set, I left my LED work light there, too. I was very careful to always wear gloves when handling the tools. I wanted no fingerprints left to identify me, but I forgot the batteries in the work light. I know I handled them without gloves when I first bought the light. I wiped down the outside, but I forgot the frickin' batteries! They can tie me to the scene! How long do fingerprints last? Oh man, I'm screwed!

There is good news, though. I have never been fingerprinted, my prints are not on file anywhere. I almost got arrested a couple of times at some protest rallies, but I managed to skate. Good thing. So maybe I'm *not* screwed -- unless we get caught...

I don't dare tell Rachel about this. I can hear it now: "Batteries not included." But I do need to ask her about whether her fingerprints are on file anywhere. I have to make sure she always wears gloves, and doesn't touch anything now that might leave prints.

"Rachel, while we're back here, don't touch anything where you might leave a fingerprint. We don't want any evidence that we were ever here."

I'm trying to figure out how to ask her about whether she has ever been fingerprinted, whether she has any kind of record.

"'Round up the usual suspects.' I won't leave any prints, but even if I did, they wouldn't mean anything. I've never been arrested. I've never joined the military. I've never had my fingerprints taken. I'm not in anyone's database. How about you, 'My little chickadee'?"

"Me neither. I'm clean too." Except for the flashlight batteries.

The only problem I see with tower number two is parking. The abandoned farmhouse is too exposed. A car parked there at night will be a sure invite to some cop to come check it out.

Rachel has a solution. She will drive. She'll drop me off at the farmhouse with my tools and then go hang out somewhere until the tower goes down. Then she'll come back and get me so we can make our getaway.

"But how will you know when the tower comes down?"

"'You know how to whistle, don't you, Steve? You just put your lips together and blow.' Actually, I have a pair of walkie-talkies. I think they're called Family Service Radios. We can use those. You call me right before the tower comes down, and I'll be at the farmhouse to pick you up as soon as you come out."

"Sounds like a plan. Now all we have to do is restock our 'Cell Phone Tower Demolition Kit.'"

"Gregory. May I call you Greg? Greg, it's not a big deal. We need pipe, a socket and a breaker bar. You get the pipe and I'll get the socket and breaker bar. Tomorrow. What size do I want to buy?"

"Nobody has ever called me Greg. I don't know why, but I have always gone by Gregory. I like the way you say Greg. Yes, it's okay. What do you know about tools? Do you even know what a breaker bar is? And why tomorrow?"

"Probably because you introduce yourself as Gregory, not Greg. I think Gregory sounds rather stuffy. You are now Greg, 'My little chickadee.' And I know lots about tools. I'm something of a tomboy. I always helped my dad work on stuff around the house. My dad once said that I was the only Girl Scout he ever met who knew what a five-sixteenths inch open-end wrench looked like. Tomorrow, because today is Monday, and we are going to do this on Thursday. I promised Vista Tel!"

CHAPTER 37

Tuesday

(Peter)

A California style workday at Torrance. Nobody seems to work real hard -- definitely laid back -- yet the work gets done. Victor is a joy to work with. He is quite knowledgeable. Closer to engineer level than to electrician level. He was helpful, polite, and just plain a nice guy. If Victor is typical of the workers here, we could use a few like him in Ohio.

* * *

Tom stops by in the afternoon. "Are you going to be up for a great filet tonight?"

"Yes. I definitely will be."

"I've got a meeting now. How about I pick you up at your motel about seven-thirty?"

"Okay. What's the attire?"

"I call it California casual. You can wear anything from an Armani suit to cut off jeans. As long as you don't look like a tourist."

* * *

Tom shows up in a 2001 Mustang convertible. It's even blue. Almost exactly like mine except his is a stick shift V-8 and mine is an automatic V-6. I comment that I have a very similar car at home and that I was wishing I had it yesterday evening when I was driving the Pacific Coast Highway. He asks what I'm renting and I tell him a new G6. He says, "Let's swap for the week." I say, "Huh?" Tom says, "Why not? You can play tourist with this, and I can try out the G6. I've been thinking of buying one for my wife. After a week of driving it, both Sue and I will know if it's what we want."

"Well... If you're sure."

"Sure, I'm sure. It's a done deal. We swap tonight. Sue will be tickled."

* * *

The Charthouse looks exactly like it sounds. Nautical. Posh. Overlooking the marina. Expensive.

I could go on and on about the dinner, but I won't. The food fits the ambiance. Almost two hours. Almost $200. And I don't even drink. We talk very little shop. Families. Backgrounds. Hobbies. Just talk. If I lived here, we could be friends. And I think the feeling is mutual. Sometimes, you just connect. And we did.

I pick up the tab. Stan won't like it. My expense account actually has a maximum amount for each meal: $10 for breakfast, $10 for lunch, and $21 for dinner. Why $21? Beats me. But special customers call for a special meal, and Tom and his company are definitely special. I see several million dollars worth of work here over the next few years. So, Stan will bitch, but he'll pay.

Tomorrow will come early. But it was a great night. And I'm now driving a Mustang convertible. Fantastic!

CHAPTER 38

(Gregory)

"Well, hello, 'My little chickadee.' Glad you could come over."

"As somebody once said, 'You had me at hello.' Very nice place you have here."

"Tom Cruise as Jerry Maquire in the movie *Jerry Maquire*. 1996. Great quote. Terrible movie. Tom Cruise has come a long way since *Rainman*, a long way down. And thank you. I like Little Italy. It's a neat place to live. I'll show you around a little later."

"I should know better by now than to try to beat you at your own movie quote game."

"Don't stop trying, though. You'll get better. I've got years of practice on you. How about a beer, or a Diet Coke? We can order pizza or subs from Marco's, a really good place right down the street. Unless you'd rather have something else. There's a good Chinese takeout place down the street, too, and all the usual chain joints."

"Diet Coke, please. I like Chinese, as long as it's spicy, like Hunan or Sichuan. But a pizza sounds good."

"Let me go and find Marco's number. I'll order us a pizza."

*** *** ***

"Rachel, I really don't think we should rush the next tower. It's Tuesday night. We can't possibly be ready by Thursday night."

"Yes, we can be ready, 'My little Chickadee.' There is not that much to do."

I think I could learn to hate being called "My little Chickadee." I wish she'd knock it off. "But…"

"'But me no buts.' I have to buy a breaker bar and a socket. I know what I need. I know the size. I know where to get them. I can do it tomorrow. You have to buy a pipe to amplify the torque you apply with the breaker bar. You know what you need. You know where to get it. You can do it tomorrow."

"But…"

"No buts. What else do we need?"

"I lost my frickin' LED work light."

"Buy a new one tomorrow. And please quit saying 'frickin'. It's a very poor substitute for fucking, and I consider using profanity an indication of a poor command of the English language. You have a very good command of the English language; except for frickin'. Humor me, okay? What else do we need to do?"

I want to say, "Quit calling me 'My little Chickadee.' But I don't. Instead, I say, "Uh. Okay. What else? Uh."

"That's what I thought. Greg, it is no problem. We *are* ready. We *can* do this. Thursday night."

"But…"

"No buts! We are ready. We are going to do it. Thursday night."

"Well."

"'Well' is better than 'But,' Greg. One more thing. We should use your car. A Honda is less noticeable than a Jeep."

"Well, okay. Now what?"

"Now you go get the pizza. It's called Marco's, and it's on the right about three blocks west of here. I want to take a quick shower and change out of my work clothes."

"Okay. Be back in a few."

* * *

When I get back, Rachel is sitting on her couch and looking really good! Just plain sexy. A simple black top with string shoulder straps and lace around the neck. I think they call it a camisole. And very obviously nothing on under it. That and snug, but not tight, hip huggers with a silver belt. She is hot!

I busy myself with serving us pizza just so I can keep from staring at her.

* * *

I slide my chair back from the table. "That was really good pizza. Better than Inner Circle. I'm stuffed. I should go do some homework, but I'm too full to do much of anything."

Rachel moves to the couch. "So, stay for a while, 'My little chickadee.' Come here. Sit by me."

She pats the couch next to her. I move there -- a little hesitantly. "Greg, I'm not very good at this. I've not had a lot of experience. I've been too busy working and getting educated."

"Good at what?"

"Shh, 'My little chickadee,' just let me talk. I have a feeling you're kind of like me, not very good at... Oh, shit. Just kiss me."

"Huh?"

"I really like you. I think you really like me. I feel something I like when we're together. So, kiss me."

"Ahh."

"Quiet. Kiss."

* * *

"Zowee."

And that was my first night with Rachel…

CHAPTER 39

Thursday

(Peter)

I had a funny thing happen today. Funny-weird, not funny-ha-ha.

While I was working at the plant late this morning, I realized that I needed an RS-232 cable to connect my laptop to one of the processors. They didn't have one at the plant, so I got directions to the nearest big box electronics store, and off I went.

I'll not name the big box store for reasons that will become clear in a minute. But their initials are "BB," and that doesn't stand for Big Box. The chain normally sells what I need. Unfortunately, I found an empty hook on the display. I couldn't find any more cables in the vicinity. I also couldn't find a salesperson who was interested in helping me. I finally found a disinterested one, told him what I needed, and followed him to the empty hook on the display.

He studied the empty hook and the tag above it for at least thirty seconds. Then he profoundly announced, "We're out of them."

I said that I could see that there were none on the hook, but that I'd like to know if they had any in stock, perhaps in the back room. I suggested that perhaps he could check the computerized inventory system. He agreed that he could do that. And stood there. By now, I was getting more than a little impatient. His name tag said "Stephen." I said, "Stephen. Do it."

This got a somewhat surly "Okay" but he did move -- slowly -- to the POS computer and he punched in the SKU. He announced that they were out of stock.

I tossed an equally surly "Thanks" over my shoulder and headed toward the door.

The doorkeeper looked a little older and a little more sentient. I told him what I needed, about the empty hook and about Stephen's lack of helpfulness. I asked if he had any ideas. With somewhat less surliness than Stephen, he suggested a Radio Shack a block east. I said thank you, and off I went.

* * *

When I walked in to Radio Shack, a sales clerk actually greeted me. He said his name was George, and asked how he could help. I told him I was from out of town, and that I needed an RS-232 cable. I told him my big box story and said that is why I prefer Radio Shack.

He laughed, shook his head, took me to the cable display and pointed out several cables of different lengths and sexes. I asked him to let me think about what I needed, and he went off to help another customer. One who was looking at cell phones.

The cell phone customer was getting agitated. And he was getting frustrated. And just a little loud. Being basically curious, I pretended to be reading cable packages and watched and listened.

The cell phone customer appeared to be an Arab. Short, wavy black hair, deep-set dark brown, almost black eyes, slightly olive skin. He was about five foot ten, and obviously in good shape. My guess is he worked out regularly. He spoke English with absolutely no accent. His clothes were perfectly American, a Tommy Hilfiger polo shirt, and Dockers. And his clothes were too American somehow. My guess is he was an Arab national trying to pass as an American. I don't know why I thought that, but that's what I thought.

The Arab wanted to buy six prepaid TracFones. He said they were for his family members who were visiting. He wanted them so they could keep in touch.

George tried to convince him to buy an Alltel phone and sign up for their family plan. He said he could get multiple phones and lines. It would be more flexible and cheaper. And he could tailor the minutes on each phone to their needs.

The Arab said, "No. I just want TracFones with prepaid minutes. No family plans. No signing up. I just want to buy six prepaid cell phones. Please."

George knew he wasn't getting through to him. He genuinely wanted to help the guy get a good deal. He tried again: "But, sir, with Alltel's family plan, you…"

"No! No family plans! Please, you must sell me TracFones now! Or I will leave!"

"Okay, sir, if that's what you want," George said. And as he turned away from the Arab, I saw his lips moving. I'm not a lip reader, but my guess is he mumbled something like, "Well, screw you. I tried. Have it your way." About a hundred years ago, I managed a Radio Shack in western Pennsylvania, Oil City, to be exact. I mumbled things like that on a daily basis. And drank a lot.

George wrote up the sale for the six TracFones. The Arab took his phones and left.

After he left, I took the cable I needed to the cash counter. I said to George, "Boy was that guy a pain."

George said, "The boss says that the customer is always right. I was just trying to save him some money. It doesn't make sense to buy six prepaid phones when he could have gotten a family plan for a lot less. He could have even gotten push-to-talk. Oh well, at least he paid cash, so I'm not going to get screwed with a bad check or a stolen credit card."

"I take it you don't know him?"

"Never saw him before. Hope I never see him again. But there are a couple of nice shiny new Benjamins in the drawer. You found what you need, sir?"

"Yep. Ring this up, please, so I can get back to work."

* * *

I couldn't help mulling over the Arab cell phone buyer incident as I was going back to the plant. Like I said, funny-weird.

CHAPTER 40

(Gregory)

I really didn't want to do this so quickly, but Rachel is right. Vista Tel is ignoring us. Perhaps taking down a second tower as promised will get their frickin' attention.

It's after 2 am when Rachel drops me and my tools off at the farmhouse. It's warm for a March night, it's dead calm, and it's dead quiet. I hide by the farmhouse and watch for about ten minutes. Nothing. No cars. Nothing. "In the still of the night." The few locals around are all asleep. But not me. Me and my 'faithful sidekick' Rachel, waiting for my call. So, let's get on with it.

I stash the bolt cutters and breaker bar behind the farmhouse, and carry the pipes and LED work light back to the fence. It's about a five minute walk. Then back to the farmhouse. Another five minutes. And back to the fence with the rest of the tools. Another five minutes. It's pushing three a.m. -- the quietest part of the night -- at least out here in the middle of nowhere.

Time to get to work. Just like last time, cutting the fence is easy. This time, it's going to be a one-night job so I don't even have to worry about hiding my access hole. They will know I was here by morning. I bend the flap of chain link fence out of the way and start ferrying my tools in.

I hear a noise. It was soft, but it was there. An animal? It was soft, but it sounded big -- more like a deer than a rabbit. Maybe a person. Maybe I'm busted. No way could somebody know I'm here.

"Greg?"

"Rachel? What in God's name are you doing here?"

"I want to watch."

I can't believe she did this. "That wasn't the plan. Where's the car?"

"Screw the plan. I want to watch. If I'm going to be part of this, I'm going to be in all the way. The car is down behind the Dentist's Office. It's hidden. No one will see it."

What's *wrong* with her? "But, what if…"

"'But me no buts.' Remember? I'm part of this, a big part. I'm as guilty as you are. I want to see it happen. So, let's get on with it."

Crap. "How are we going to escape?"

"The car is ten minutes away. We'll be out of here long before anybody knows that anything has happened, Greg. I really do want to watch it go down. God, from this angle, it looks huge."

"It *is* huge. I really don't like changing the plan like this, Rachel."

"Greg, you got me into this. I'm in. Deal with it."

Well, maybe. "Okay. I still don't like it, but we're here so, yeah, let's get on with it. Help me carry the rest of the tools in. Grab the breaker bar and socket. And this time we leave no tools behind. When it goes down, you carry the breaker bar and socket and bolt cutters. I'll put the work light in my pocket and carry the pipes. Do you have gloves? We can't leave any finger prints."

"No gloves. But I won't touch anything except our tools. What do we do?"

I guess I'm kind of glad she's here. "There is no wind tonight, so we just remove the nuts around the base, and -- and -- and, I don't know. I think -- I hope -- it'll fall over. I hate to say this, but the last time the wind helped. This time there is no wind. I don't know what will happen when we remove the nuts. Maybe, if we remove everything but the nuts on the west side, it'll go east. Maybe."

"Let's just do it and see what happens. It can't just stand there without being fastened down. The slightest imbalance or puff of wind will make it fall over."

"I hope."

I brought something extra this time. I reach in the pocket of my cargo pants and pull out a small can of WD-40. I spray all the nuts, and put it back in my pocket. Can't hurt.

Like before, the lock nuts come off fairly easily once I get past where the threads are tumbled.

I try the breaker bar with the shorter length of pipe on one of the load-bearing nuts on the south side. It starts turning easily. WD-40 or lack of wind pressure? A little of both, I think. I work around the base plate taking off every other nut, just like removing a tire. When half are off, I remove the rest of the nuts on the north and south sides, and then all but one nut on the east side and one on the west side. Then the one on the east side. And finally the last nut on the west side. And nothing! It just sits there! It can't. It has no support, but it just sits there.

I sit back and look at Rachel. She stares back at me with such a dumbfounded look that I start to giggle. Then she starts to giggle, and pretty soon we're laying on the ground next to each other just kind of chortling. We hug, and kind of switch to snickering. Rachel gets up, while I prop myself up on one elbow to watch her. She looks at the tower. She points at the ice bridge, and says, "This is what's holding it!" She picks up the pipe, and whacks the tower with all her might. It makes a horrible clang. I look around and worry that somebody might hear. "Quiet."

"Oh, screw it. It's not going anywhere." And she flops down on top of me. "No point in wasting a perfectly good night." She kisses me. I kiss her back. Pretty soon we're taking each other's clothes off.

It looks like this will be my second night with Rachel.

Rachel and I are both panting. She unbuttons her jeans and I start to pull them off. Suddenly we hear a screech -- of metal tearing. I look up over my shoulder at the source of the sound. It's the ice bridge. The tower is slowly leaning over and pulling the ice bridge with it. It's going south toward Route 2. We quickly sit up and watch. We're mesmerized by what we see.

"Oh, shit."

"Zowee!"

It's awesome. It's like watching a slow motion movie. There are even special effects: sparks, smoke, crackles, and of course the sound of tearing metal. It's like we're spectators. It's leaning over at about thirty degrees from vertical.

"It's going toward the road."

"It won't actually hit the road, but it'll be close. If anyone is going by, they'll see it coming toward the road. Probably scare the shit out of them."

It's at about forty-five degrees, and starting to go faster. More sparks and crackles. The ice bridge tears free of the building. Cables start snapping inside the building and whipping out against the tower like broken rubber bands. It's awesome.

We hear the screech of tires on Route 2. Somebody sees it coming down.

It's at about sixty degrees, and moving fast!

More screeching tires. And headlights along the road.

And a huge whomp! And then, silence.

We just sit for a minute, almost hypnotized by what we saw. I recover from my trance "We've got to get out of here. Quick."

We gather up our tools, slither through the hole in the fence and start up the access road. We're walking fast and looking over our shoulders. We see lights, but hear nothing. We're at the farmhouse. No cars are in sight. Let's hope it stays that way. We start along the county road to where Rachel parked my Honda, worried about passing cars. We start to jog. Then we see lights in front of us. Between us and my car. We hit the bushes along the road and wait as the car goes by. He's going slowly, but seems not to be looking for anything. Just going slow, probably half asleep. He drives past us. We wait 'till he's out of sight, get back on the road and start to jog again. Rachel was right, it's less than ten minutes from the farmhouse to the car. We throw our tools in back, and get in. The road's empty. I pull out and head north toward Vermilion.

"Where are we going?"

"Away from the tower. As fast as I can go without attracting attention."

Another car approaches. This time it's a police car with his lights flashing and his siren going. He roars by us. In my rear view mirror, I see him hit his brakes as he gets near the farmhouse.

"Two minutes slower and we'd have been screwed! He's pulling into the farmhouse. That was too close."

"Speaking of screwed, I want to go to my place. We got interrupted. That was a turn-on."

"'Mrs. Robinson, you're trying to seduce me. Aren't you?'"

"You're learning. And, yes, I am!"

And it does look like this will be my second night with Rachel, after all.

CHAPTER 41

Friday

(Peter)

Ah, the infamous redeye. Leave LA a little before midnight, LA time. Spend four and a half hours in the air, and get into Cleveland a little before seven a.m., Cleveland time. And feel like shit. Oh well, at least I'll be home for the weekend.

The week in Los Angeles was great. I didn't get to San Diego, but Tom assured me that I'll be back soon. He promised to install me in his Mustang and kick me out of the plant soon enough to make the trip. Next time. There are times when I really don't like my job. There are other times when it is just great, and this week was one of them.

I've got the latest James Patterson paperback, the latest Scientific American, peanut butter crackers, and M&Ms. It'll be a long ride home. But I'll keep busy reading and munching. And maybe snoozing later. Or thinking about Nick.

We talked while I was in Los Angeles. We did it his way. I called him Sunday. I agreed to meet him. At my boat. This Sunday.

My boat is stored indoors for the winter. The building is pretty private. It will be a good place to meet Nick.

Something to think about on the flight home. When I'm not reading. Or munching. Or snoozing.

* * *

I get tired of reading after a while. As I lean back in my seat -- and that's not very much leaning these days -- I start to contemplate this Nick character. He and Mike know each other from some past life. When I consider Mike's past life, I realize that Nick is probably ex-military, too. Mike still sounds like a first sergeant, and Nick is just as gruff and business-like, but smoother, somehow. Ex-officer maybe? Perhaps Homeland Security training has mellowed him out. As I start to doze, I realize that he reminds me of me twenty or thirty years ago. Hmm.

* * *

They just gave us the requisite snack. Eight midget pretzels and a warm Diet Coke. At least they still provide ice.

Domestic airline travel isn't what it once was. I remember the days of full meals, not snacks; cute stewardesses, not middle aged (or worse) flight attendants. The days when airlines treated you like a valued customers to be pampered, not sheep to be fleeced. Oh well, as I think Bob Dylan once said, "The times, they are a changin'." Much as I hate to say it, it's our domestic flights that suck, not the internationals. I recently flew to Europe. KLM there and Lufthansa back. The aircraft were very roomy Airbuses. The flight attendants were young and cute. Even the guys. They acted like they enjoyed their jobs. They had fun and it was contagious. The food was good, and plentiful. It really was like TWA in the old days.

* * *

And I just came up with something else to think about. I keep mulling over the Arab cell phone buyer incident I witnessed in Los Angeles. That was funny. Funny-weird. It was one of those times where you want to know "the rest of the story," as Paul Harvey would say. Is he even still alive? Kate would know. Or she'd tell me to, "Look it up on the Internet." I've missed her. It'll be good to get home.

CHAPTER 42

(Gregory)

Last night was quite a night! The second tower went down easily. Even though it took a while to get started.

We've got to figure out a way to make them fall where we want them to. I learned in Boy Scouts how to do it with a tree. You notch the side towards which you want it to fall. But you can't notch a steel tower. I need to come up with an alternative. There has to be a way.

And yes, I did spend the night at Rachel's. We definitely finished what we started at the cell tower site. Rachel was practically undressing while I was parking at her place. She was ready!

I haven't had a lot of experience with women. I haven't been involved with a lot of girls. I think I can count the total number of girls I've screwed on one hand with fingers left over.

But I have to believe that sex with Rachel is something special. I'm not in love, but she could become addictive. I have to use words like "awesome" to describe what it's like with her. And "wow!" And -- I don't know -- just "wow!"

Afterwards we just lay in bed staring at the ceiling, sharing a cigarette, and talking. It was a genuine Marlboro moment. Rachel told me that taking down the tower was one of the most exciting things she had ever done. Ever. She said that she didn't understand why, but that she found it to be a tremendous turn on. She said, "I don't think I've ever been so horny! I just wanted screwed!"

And boy, did we. I keep saying "wow!" I may have to start saying "Zowee!" It was something I've never experienced before. Awesome. Addicting. Scary.

Rachel is showering. After she showers, we're going to go over to my place so I can do the same.

I watch her get dressed. I'm tempted to undress her. She stops and looks at me. "We have to do the phone thing again this morning. We have to tell the TV stations that we did the second tower because Vista Tel ignored us. We have to tell them when and where it went down; tell them to send their camera crews; tell them to tell Vista Tel to announce their plan to comply with our demands, or we will continue."

I say nothing. I just look at her. She continues. "We've got to find the next tower. We've got to be ready. If Vista Tel still ignores us, we will do tower number three and we will get the media involved somehow. The crime scene needs to become a media event. We need to get them there as close to real time as we can."

That worries me. I want to go slow. I want to plan our next tower carefully. I don't want to make any mistakes. Rachel wants to hurry. She's pushing too hard.

I start to say something, but she interrupts. "Another thing we need to do right now is send another email to Vista Tel. But I want to do it from your computer."

"Why mine?"

"Don't worry. My methods are safe, and completely anonymous."

So, why does she want to use my computer?

CHAPTER 43

Sunday

(Peter)

It's not time to put my boat in the water yet, but it is time to be working on her. A forty-three foot sailboat takes a substantial amount of work to get it ready to launch in the spring. And I enjoy just working on her almost as much as actually sailing her. Just being around boats and the water is relaxing. As Kenneth Grahame said in *Wind in the Willows*, "There is nothing -- absolutely nothing -- half so much worth doing as simply messing about in boats."

Morning Star, my Beneteau 423, is stored in an old lumberyard building in Vermilion. It's not heated, but it stays reasonably warm this time of year. And it's private. There are only about six boats in the building and I rarely see anybody there. The boatyard owner gave me my own key to the building. It's the ideal place to meet this Nick character.

I gave Nick directions on how to get here, and now I'm just "messing about." Nervously. But messing about. I'm stringing an extension cord from the shore power socket on the stern to an outlet about fifty feet away when I hear the door at the other end of the building open. I can't see the door from here.

"Peter?"

"Yeah, I'm back here. Who is it?"

"It's Nick."

"Meet you in the middle of the building near the bow of my boat. Right under the skylight."

"Okay."

As we walk toward each other, we each do a quick assessment of the other. He's a little shorter than I expected, maybe 5' 9". He's built like a fireplug, though. His clothes don't conceal the fact that he is all muscle. I probably outweigh him by forty pounds, but I have no doubt that he would easily win any confrontation.

Nick has straight black hair that he wears in sort of bangs. It comes about halfway down his forehead and he periodically pushes it off to one side. The quick motion somehow calls attention to his alert brown eyes. He's well tanned and has a few acne scars. He does not look Greek. My guess is that one of his parents was Asian.

"Anybody else here?"

"No. I'm Peter Bradovich." We shake hands. He is abrupt, but pleasant at the same time. "Nick Patridis, from Homeland Security."

"Can I see some ID?"

"Aye, aye, Captain." He pulls his wallet from his back pocket and flips it open. I see a badge and an official looking photo ID card.

My first impression is that he is something of a smart ass who enjoys his job immensely. "Actually I wouldn't know if that was real or not."

"It is. Want to see my gun?"

He seems to have a way of irritating me just a little, and of putting me at ease at the same time. "No, but that doesn't prove anything either. Bad guys carry guns, too."

"Point. What can I do to convince you that I am who I am and that I need your help?"

This will work. "I don't know. I guess we just need to talk it through."

"Nice boat. Big boat. Expensive boat. Have you been boating long?"

"Forever. I grew up around boats. My Dad had power boats as long as I can remember. Went on my first sailboat ride at fourteen, and immediately fell in love with sailing. Owned a small boat by the time I was sixteen. And I have had one most of the time since."

"I know that you have a Merchant Marine Officer's License. Ever use it?"

"No. It's just something I always wanted, so I studied for the test while I was recuperating from one of my ankle surgeries. Why am I not surprised that you knew about my Captain's License?"

"Ankle surgery? From your Air Force injury?"

"Yes. Why am I not surprised that you know about that, too."

"Your background in the military and with the Defense Intelligence Agency makes it pretty hard for us not to know a lot about you, Cap'n. I'm not trying to impress you with how much I know about you. Just trying to make small talk and put you at ease."

"Well, I'm not sure that it's working. I'm reminded of my last debriefing a whole bunch of years ago."

"How's that?"

"I was a young smartass. The debriefing officer was very full of himself, and trying hard to impress me with how serious he and the whole debriefing was. I finally got fed up and cracked, 'Well, if I move, should I notify you?'"

"I'll bet that went over well."

"He said, 'No. We'll know,' without cracking a smile. I decided that maybe he wasn't trying to impress me, and that maybe it was as serious as he was acting. I have discovered since then that guys like him -- and maybe you -- don't joke."

"Actually we do sometimes. But as you figured out then, yes, it is that serious. We have good reason to believe that Gregory

Zaremba is the perpetrator, probably with at least one accomplice. And they took down another cell phone tower Thursday night."

"You're kidding. No, you're not."

"No, I'm definitely not kidding. And they are threatening to take down another tower unless Vista Tel meets their demands."

"Their demands?"

"Yeah, they've got the bizarre idea that they can force Vista Tel to quit building their own towers, and to share existing towers belonging to other cell phone providers."

"'Bizarre' is a good word for that idea. Don't they know about capitalism and competition? So, why do you want to talk to me? I really have told you everything I know."

"You know Gregory. He knows you. He knows you have an interest. We want you to make contact with him, see what you can learn, and report back to us."

"You want me to spy on them?"

"In a word, yes."

"But, I don't know that I can do that. I don't know if I want to do that. If they're as wacky as they sound, it could be dangerous. I just don't know. And I do know that my wife will not want me to get involved."

"How much does your wife know about this?"

"Everything I know. Everything I told Mike. That's the kind of relationship Kate and I have. We don't keep secrets from each other. We talk."

Nick and I talked for a while about his theories on what was going on. What the motives of the terrorists might be. Whether or not Gregory was involved. Who else might be involved. He had little firm knowledge concerning the who's, but an amazing amount of insight into the why's.

"Cap'n, I don't know what you did for DIA -- that information is still *need to know*. But I do know the kind of work contractors for DIA do. Let me ask you a rhetorical question: Why did you do whatever you did? My guess is that you're a closet patriot. That you believed in what you were doing."

"I did it for the money! No, that's flippant. You're right. I did it because I believed I could make a difference. I'm not a closet patriot. I've been out of the closet for a long time. And I'm proud of it."

"Cap'n, you can make a difference here, too. You're right. Gregory and his group may be very dangerous people. They are doing serious damage. They may be affiliated with even more dangerous people. And they have to be stopped. You are our best hope. You can infiltrate their group, and find out who's involved. You may be able to find out who their connections are. That's all we're asking you to do -- gather information."

"I still don't know. I have to talk to Kate. I won't do this without her knowledge and approval."

"We can't involve your wife."

"She is involved. If you want me, you get her. Period."

"I'll have to talk with my supervisors."

"Period."

"Okay. I'll pass that ultimatum on."

"You do that."

"We'll be in touch, Cap'n."

CHAPTER 44

(Gregory)

I need some space. I need to figure this thing with Rachel out. It's like she's taking over. I can't let that happen. I can't even say frickin', and her movie quotes are driving me up the wall!

The whole cell phone tower elimination dream is *mine*. I came up with the plan. I came up with the target company. I came up with the methods. I don't think Rachel really believes in my campaign. I think she is in it just for the thrill of it.

I like having Rachel as my partner. I just flat enjoyed taking down the second tower with Rachel. Sharing. Or something like that. And then there's the sex.

But I can't lose control.

But I don't want to lose Rachel.

Sunday mornings are great times for drives. I do some of my best thinking while I'm driving. And I need to think this through.

I Rarely listen to the radio. I enjoy the quiet. Once in a while, I'll listen to a talk show. Rush or Shawn or Michael or some other right wing nut-case just to see what they're up to, but usually the radio is off and I just drive, enjoy the quiet, and think. I guess that's odd for a guy my age, but it is what it is.

And that's what I do this morning. I find myself heading west again. Why west? Familiarity? I think it's because if I go east, I'm in suburbia for a long time. Some of it nice, but most of it ugly. Going west takes me through the city, but then into some really nice suburbs: Lakewood, Rocky River, Bay Village. And then into the country. Spoiled by lots of frickin' cell towers. My targets.

As I drive the familiar route, I-90 to Route 2, I mull over the Rachel thing. I really enjoy her. I like being with her. I like doing things with her, whether it's destroying a cell phone tower, or sharing a pizza and a movie. But -- I've got to maintain control of my campaign, I've got to keep it on track. And I think I can do that. I need to sit Rachel down and have a heart to heart. Just tell her that I value her and her help, but I can't let her bulldoze me into making rash decisions. She'll understand, I think. I hope.

* * *

I'm approaching the Lorain exits. I think I'll head down to Lake Road. The lakeshore is interesting this time of year: boatyards coming out of hibernation as owners start getting ready for the season. It's still early in the year, but spring is springing. I do love being around the water. My mom and dad instilled that in me.

Holy shit! I just found our next target. How could I have not noticed it before? It's frickin' perfect!

It looks like a Vista Tel tower. It's new. It's the same style as the other ones I took down. The electronics building looks the same. I'll check on the Web when I get home, but I'd be willing to bet.

And it is perfectly located. Just off the exit. It's in a somewhat built up commercial area. There are a couple of one-story buildings on either side of the road, and a couple of homes that may or may not be occupied. One has a For Sale sign that says "Commercial." The area used to be rural until Route 2 went in, and now the area around the exit is going low-rent commercial: an insurance agent, a Chiropractor's office, a body shop, and a gas station. The spot is ideal. Lots of traffic during the day, lots of visibility, but it'll be dead at night.

I stop at the gas station, go inside, and buy a Diet Pepsi and a Butterfinger bar. I ask to use the restroom. The clerk gives me the key on a two-foot long piece of plastic. He says, "We only have one restroom. The entrance is outside and around to the right." Perfect. That puts the restroom on the side of the building toward the cell phone tower. I can look around a little without attracting attention.

* * *

Rachel will love this place! The media will go ballistic when we destroy this one.

We have to figure out how to alert them in real time without getting caught. The area is perfect for lots of rush hour news coverage. The tower location is perfect. It sits about fifty yards off of the road behind and between an insurance office and the house with the For Sale sign. The tower is adjacent to the insurance office rear parking lot and on the edge of a cornfield. It looks like the cornfield was never harvested. Most of the corn is still standing from last year. My guess is that the farmer lives in the house with the For Sale sign, and went broke. The house looks occupied and poor. I suspect that the ex-farmer is hoping to make some money by selling his property to a commercial developer. Good luck.

The tower is only about a hundred yards from Route 2, so once the news media hit here with their mobile units, the gawkers will tie up traffic on Route 2 as well as the local road.

And the really neat thing is that from the looks of it, if we can control the direction of fall this time, we can drop the tower right between the insurance office and the house! Talk about newsworthy!

CHAPTER 45

(Peter)

I screwed around at the boat for an hour or so after Nick left. I didn't get much accomplished. Basically I just stared off into space thinking about what he had to say. Thinking about whether I want to get more involved, thinking about what I might be getting myself into. I had the heater going in the cabin and I messed about in the relative warmth while I pondered the whole thing. No decisions. Well, that's not really true, I think I need to do what Nick wants. But, I have to run this by Kate. I meant what I told Nick. If Kate doesn't buy into this, I don't do it. I might as well lock up and head home.

* * *

"I've been wondering all morning what this Nick character had to say, Cap'n."

"Sorry to make you wait, honey. I wanted to wait 'til I got home to discuss it with you face to face."

"Well, we're face to face. And there is fresh coffee."

"Coffee sounds good. I'm chilly. Let's get some coffee, turn on the fireplace, and sit in the living room." The room we call the living room opens off the kitchen and overlooks Lake Erie. It's a great room. We furnished it for sitting, and talking, and reading. It has no TV, but it does have several big, comfortable upholstered chairs, Kate's leather recliner, a couple of love seats, a fireplace with gas logs, and huge two story high windows facing the lake.

"Well, what's up?"

"Nick Patridis is part of some kind of Homeland Security unit that specializes in home grown terrorists. People like Timothy McVeigh of Oklahoma City fame, and the Unabomber. He thinks that Gregory Zaremba has something to do with the cell phone tower destruction that's going on around here. We missed the news, but a second tower was destroyed Thursday night."

"You're kidding."

"No, I'm not kidding. The second tower was just off of Route 2 near Vermilion. Same cell phone company, same type of tower, same procedure, same messages to the media. And they are threatening to keep doing it unless their demands are met."

"Demands?"

"Some naive crap about forcing Vista Tel to quit erecting towers and share existing ones. And that sounds to me like something Gregory would come up with. He's weird."

"So, what does Nick want you to do?"

"He thinks that Gregory is at the very least, involved; and at most, that he may be the leader. He thinks it's a small group -- maybe just two or three -- operating independently. He wants me to contact Gregory, and see if I can get involved with their group. Basically, become an urban terrorist."

"And do what, for God's sake?"

"Report back to him. Find out who's in the group. Find out who's supporting them. Find out their plans for the future. And, I guess, eventually, Homeland Security will arrest them all. I assume that they have to gather enough evidence to make a court case."

"What did you tell Nick?"

"I told him that I won't do anything without your knowledge and approval. He didn't want me to involve you, but I told him that it was not negotiable. You had to know, and you had to give me the okay."

Kate gets up from her recliner, comes over to the loveseat, sits down next to me and hugs me. Hard. And long. "This is really scary."

"I know. But Nick says they do not fit the profile of people who would intentionally harm other people. They are idealists who look at this as a war against big business -- some faceless entity -- not against people. The problem is, if they are not stopped, people will get hurt."

"I don't want you to be one of them."

"Does that mean you don't want me to do it?"

"No. It means I want you to be very, very careful. I think that if you can help stop them, you have to do it. And I know you well enough to know that you have reached the same conclusion."

"You know me well, cutie. And I know you well. You're right of course. And I knew that you'd come to the same conclusion that I did."

"I'll be doing some heavy-duty praying."

CHAPTER 46

(Gregory)

"Hi, Rachel"

"*Ciao*, Greg. What's up?"

"I went for a Sunday morning drive today."

"And, 'Go ahead, make my day.'"

"And I found tower number three!"

"Zowee! 'I love the smell of napalm in the morning.'"

"Not napalm, but definitely an attention getter! It's near Route 2 and another major road, right between an insurance office and a house!"

"Within striking distance?"

"'You betcha.'"

"You *are* improving. Can I come over?"

"Now?"

"This evening. I have a couple of things to do first."

"Call me when you're on your way. I'll put coffee on. Or beer. Or something."

* * *

"So. Tell me, 'The stuff that dreams are made of.'"

"Come on in. Stay a while."

Rachel comes in, kisses me soundly, and plops down on the couch. "Well?"

"The tower I found is only about a hundred yards from Route 2, right next to one of the major roads into Lorain. Once the news media get there with their mobile units, the gawkers will tie up traffic on Route 2 as well as the local roads. All we have to do is figure out how to get them there quickly, and without getting caught."

"I have some ideas on how to do that. But tell me about the 'right between an insurance office and a house.' That sounds stupendous."

"Let me draw you a little map. Here's Route 2, and the exit to Broadway. Here's the insurance office, and the house. And here is the tower! If we can control the direction of fall this time, we can drop the tower right between the insurance office and the house! Talk about newsworthy!"

"Not 'between.' On."

"What?"

"*On* the house. They shouldn't have built it so close. That will really deliver our message."

"But I think the house is lived in!"

"Then on the insurance office. It might even be more effective. I can hear the media talking heads now: 'What if the terrorists had targeted the house instead of the unoccupied office building? A whole family was asleep in what they thought was the safety of their home. Children were innocently asleep in their beds, dreaming of puppies and cookies, not the carnage that was looming! The whole family could have been killed! This must be stopped! Vista Tel must take action!' It will be great!"

"Rachel, this is scary. I don't want to damage other property, just Vista Tel's."

"'What we've got here is a failure to communicate.' Greg, this is a war. A war against Vista Tel. A war against the horrible defacing of our God given earth. It is your war. And you've convinced me to make it my war, too. And in a war, there is collateral damage."

"But no people."

"No people. Greg, I'm glad you involved me in your war. I'm glad that I'm a part of it. I just want what you want. I want Vista Tel to listen. We'll do what we have to, but we'll make them listen. Come here. Sit. You're right, it is scary. Hold me for a minute."

* * *

"Can you stay tonight?"

"No. I've got to work in the morning. Maybe one night this week, Greg. I really want to."

"Me, too."

* * *

"Rats. Let me get the phone, and I'll walk you out to your car. I get almost no calls. It's probably some idiot salesman. Hang on."

CHAPTER 47

(Peter)

"I hope you've been doing some of that heavy-duty praying. I'm going to call Gregory and see if I can set up a meeting. Want to listen in?"

"Yes."

"Okay. Get the other phone. I'll dial his number. When I give you the high sign, hit the line one button and put your phone on mute."

"I know what to do. Are you ready now?"

"Yes. Okay, I'm dialing... It's ringing..."

"I'm on."

"Hello?"

Keep it light. "Is this Gregory?"

Yes?"

Be cool. "This is Peter Bradovich. Your 'uncle'? We met at the car lot near Amherst?"

"Oh. Hi. I was hoping you'd call. Hang on one. I just got out of the shower. I need to grab a towel."

* * *

"Okay, sorry about that. I'm back."

Honesty is the best policy. "I just got back into town. I was in Los Angeles on business."

"I've never been to California. Is it as cool as TV makes it out to be?"

Small talk. "Not really. The weather is great, but most of what I saw was a hundred miles of urban sprawl. Rather like around Cleveland. Just miles and miles of city."

"But nice? Like Westlake or Rocky River?"

I feel like a tour guide. "No. More like Euclid or Eastlake. Down along the Pacific coast is very nice, but I was working in a place called Torrance, and it has little to recommend it."

"I live in Euclid. You're right, it has little to recommend it. So, what's up? Did you find out any more about the cell phone tower?"

Here goes. "Yes. I got some answers from a friend who looked into it while I was gone. But the answers I got lead to more questions. I'd rather not discuss it over the phone. Any chance we can get together one night this week and to use your phrase, 'compare notes'?"

"Ahh. I don't know. What do you have in mind?"

Careful. "I work near Cleveland Hopkins Airport. I'm thinking we can meet for coffee after I'm done working. Like, maybe Tuesday?"

"You say you got some answers? I'd really like to know what you found out. But I don't know why we can't talk about it on the phone."

He has to watch TV. "As Jack Bauer would say, 'Trust me.'"

"Ahh... Yeah. I guess I can meet you. When and where?"

I should have thought of a place ahead of time. Think. "Do you know the area east of the Airport at all? Parma? Brookpark?"

"A little."

Got it. "Take Interstate 480 west out of Cleveland, get off at Ridge Road and go north. There's a plaza right there on the left. There's a Starbucks in the plaza. I get off work at five. Can you meet me about five-fifteen or five thirty?"

"Yeah, I can do that. Tuesday, right?"

Phew. "Yes. Tuesday evening. See you then."

"I'm looking forward to it. See you."

* * *

"Well, what do you think, honey?"

"I think you did good. But 'Jack Bauer'?"

"I felt like Jack Bauer. This is weird stuff. Did you hear what sounded like two people breathing on his end?"

"I wondered about that. I wasn't going to say anything, but I think you're right."

"Well, there were two of us. I wonder."

And I'll have to keep wondering for at least forty-eight hours.

CHAPTER 48

(Gregory)

I pick up the phone as Rachel stands by the door. "Hello?"

"Is this Gregory?"

"Yes?"

"This is Peter Bradovich. Your 'uncle'? We met at the car lot near Amherst?"

"Oh. Hi. I was hoping you'd call. Hang on one. I just got out of the shower. I need to grab a towel."

I cover the mouthpiece and stage whisper, "Rachel! Come here. Quick. It's that Pete from the used car lot. Come listen."

I tilt the phone so Rachel can hear. "Okay, sorry about that. I'm back."

Pete tells me he just got back from Los Angeles. I tell him I've never been to California, and ask him what it's like. I guess I'm trying to verify that he was really there. He says it's basically a big ugly urban area. He actually compares it to Euclid!

I finally can't stand the frickin' suspense any longer. I ask him if he found out anything about the cell phone tower.

He tells me he got some answers from a friend, but he doesn't want to discuss it on the phone. He wants to meet to "compare notes" -- my phrase.

So what's wrong with talking about it on the frickin' phone? I look at Rachel. She shakes her head up and down. She silently mouths, "Meet him!"

Pete says, "As Jack Bauer would say, 'Trust me."

So, who is Jack Bauer? Rachel is still shaking her head up and down. I agree to meet him early Tuesday evening.

He gives me directions to a Starbucks east of the Airport. I don't go to Starbucks; they're full of yuppies, but I agree to meet him there anyway.

Rachel is now doing the thumbs up bit with both hands. I say goodbye and hang up.

* * *

"Well, what do you think, Rachel?"

"'Keep your friends close, but your enemies closer.' I think you did good. We've got to meet him."

Oh, stop with the quotes!"We? And who is 'Jack Bauer'?"

"Yes,' we.' There is no way I'm not going with you. I keep telling you, I am involved. You're stuck with me, 'My little chickadee.' You don't know Jack Bauer? *24*? You've got to watch more TV."

"So, stay and watch some with me."

"I'm going home. But I'll be right back here Tuesday by four. Walk me out."

CHAPTER 49

Tuesday

(Peter)

Boy, is it hard to concentrate on work. All day, my mind has kept drifting off toward my meeting with Gregory. I did manage to get a few things done, but five more minutes and I'm out of here.

I will be a little early getting to Starbucks. I want to let him get there first. I'll stop for gas at the always-cheap BP station at Tiedeman Road.

* * *

Okay, this is it. I'm here. As I approach Starbucks, I see Gregory sitting by the window. With a girl! The breather from Sunday night?

* * *

Very tentatively. "Hello, Gregory. Let me go get a café mocha, and I'll be back."

"Hi, Pete. This is my friend Rachel. She knows everything I know about the cell phone tower crash. I hope you don't mind that I brought her."

I want to say, "Yes, I mind!" I don't. I say nothing. I just look him hard in the eye and go to the counter.

* * *

When I come back, Rachel is first to speak. "Peter. Should I call you Pete? I begged Greg to let me come along. This thing has really captured my curiosity. Greg and I have known each other for a while. He has told me everything he knows about the cell phone tower going down. He told me about meeting you at Shawn's Deals On Wheels the evening after it happened. I'm curious about your curiosity. And about you're promise to find out more about what happened."

Rachel is the strong personality here. "Call me Cap'n. Most everybody does."

"Are you -- were you -- an airline pilot? My dad has a friend who is a retired airline pilot, and everyone still calls him Captain Burrows."

I like her forthrightness. Her openness. She'll give me more information than Gregory. "No, I'm a sailor. I have a Merchant Marine Officer's License. That kind of Cap'n. It's a long story."

"I'd like to hear it someday. But right now, we're dying to know what you found out, and why you didn't want to talk about it on the phone."

Rachel takes Gregory's hand under the table for just a quick minute. But the gesture says tons. I ask, "Gregory, have you found out anything more?"

"Only what we've heard on TV. And that's not been very much. The media coverage has been suspiciously light. I'm sure they're not telling us everything they know. But they took down a second tower last week."

Rachel looks at Gregory. Her look says, "Shut up." "Rachel, I've been out of town. I did hear that they took down a second tower. But that's about all. Gregory has been aware of this from day one. You've come in later, I assume. What's your take on this from what you've heard on the news?"

"'What we've got here is a failure to communicate.' I thought you had information to share with us!"

"Rachel tends to talk in movie quotes."

Rachel is strong. Well, so am I. Movie quotes? Okay. "Paul Newman as Cool Hand Luke, right? Yes, I do have information to share with you, but I'm trying to catch up with what you've heard. I've been in California for a week and this hardly made the news out there. Humor me. Tell me what you've heard on the news. Then I'll tell you what I've found out."

Rachel and Gregory spend the next twenty minutes telling me what they've heard on radio and TV. They tell me a little too much.

Nick has provided me with synopses of what has been released to the media. There is always some information the media doesn't get. It's the police's way of sorting out legitimate confessions and tips from bogus ones. I can't put my finger on a specific unreleased fact that Rachel and Gregory knew, but the feeling that they know more than was released is there nonetheless.

Now it's my turn. "Okay. Your info tells me a lot that I didn't know. Here's what I did know before this meeting. I have some friends who have access to information you won't hear on TV. They tell me that the investigation has gone beyond the local police. Homeland Security, the FBI, the CIA, and an organization you've probably never heard of, the Defense Intelligence Agency, the DIA, have all gotten involved. Despite all this firepower, they do not have any idea who the perpetrators are. CIA and DIA are fairly certain that this is not the work of a foreign government or military. HS and the FBI feel that this is the work of a small local group. Probably amateurs. Their methods do not indicate a lot of sophistication in either their actions or their communications. The general feeling is that they are either idealistic college kids out to battle big business or fringe left-wingers out to save the environment. In either case, they will get caught."

"Who are your friends that are telling you all of this, Cap'n?"

Getting a little defensive are we, Gregory? "You're both smart enough to know that I won't answer that."

"Zowee! 'Louis, I think this is the beginning of a beautiful friendship.' I really want to keep digging into this. It's exciting. We can explore on the Web. You can keep quizzing your friends. We can go explore the sites. It's like CSI! Zowee!"

She is excited. "Bogart as Rick in *Casablanca*. Zowee is a good word, Rachel. Let's do our own things, but let's keep in touch. I never got into CSI, but I told my wife I felt like Jack Bauer working for CTU."

"I wondered who Jack Bauer was when you mentioned him the other night."

"Jack Bauer is the hero of a TV show called *24*. He works for a fictional government group called the Counterterrorist Unit."

"I don't watch much TV."

I have to ask. "There is one thing I've got to know. When I called you Sunday night, Gregory, was Rachel listening in?"

Gregory looks at Rachel. Neither says anything. "I thought I heard two people breathing. For what it's worth, my wife was listening in, too. She and I have no secrets. And I think she secretly agrees with what these guys are doing."

Rachel nods. "'All-righty then!' Yes, I was listening. That's why I insisted on being here tonight. I wanted to meet you. And if your wife agrees with what these guys are doing, I think I'd like to meet your wife."

Her incessant movie quotes could get very annoying very quickly. But that was an interesting comment about Kate. I let it pass for now. It's time to end this little meeting. "I think we've covered everything we can for now. I'm heading home for supper. Kate's cooking the last of the Perch we caught last fall."

CHAPTER 50

(Gregory)

Going to class today was a complete frickin' waste of time. So what else is new? Sometimes I think college in general is a complete waste of time. However, staying in school keeps my old man paying the rent for me. "Paying my dues" is the phrase he uses for school. All day, my mind has kept drifting off toward my meeting tonight.

Rachel should be here any minute. I'm not sure I want to take her -- I don't know how Pete will react. But how do I say no?

"Hi Rachel, right on time. Want me to drive?"

"Let's take the Jeep. I'll drive."

"Okay. I'm not sure if Pete is going to go for you being there. Maybe I should meet him alone first."

"'Nobody puts Baby in a corner.' It'll be our little surprise. I keep telling you -- I'm in!"

* * *

"You go get a table by the window. I'll get us a couple of coffees. What do you want, Greg?"

"I don't know. I'm not a Starbucks person. Do they have basic coffee?"

"Yeah, but you don't want it. I'll get you a Caramel Macchiato."

"A what?"

"'Trust me.'"

* * *

Good timing. Here comes Pete. I recognize the Mustang.

* * *

"He sees me. And you!"

I watch Pete. He looks troubled to see Rachel. He says Hi and starts to turn and head for the counter. I quickly introduce Rachel. I tell him I hope he doesn't mind that I brought her.

Pete says nothing. But his look says a bunch. He turns and heads for the counter.

* * *

When Pete comes back, Rachel is first to speak. She starts blabbing about us, and the tower and Shawn's, and about being curious about what he knows, and on, and on. And on!

Rachel! Quit talking, I think. Pete doesn't seem perturbed. He tells Rachel to call him Cap'n.

Should I interrupt? Rachel goes on and says we're dying to know what you found out.

At least Rachel said we. She takes my hand under the table for a minute, and squeezes. I think Pete sees it.

Pete looks at me for a minute, and then switches his attention back to Rachel. As we talk -- more correctly, as they talk and I listen -- I pick up on the beginnings of a bond forming between them. I'm not sure I like it. I'm not sure I can do anything about it.

As they continue, Rachel is almost bouncing off the wall. She is really excited. She throws out another movie quote, and Pete nails this one, too. I really hope I don't have two of them trading quotes now.

Rachel is making noises like we're all going to be one big happy family. She even admits she was listening in when I talked to Pete Sunday night.

Suddenly, the meeting is over. Pete abruptly slides his chair back. He gets up and says, "I think we've covered everything we can for now. I'm heading home for supper. Kate's cooking the last of the Perch we caught last fall."

He says goodbye and walks out the door!

CHAPTER 51

(Peter)

Well, *that* was interesting. Where did Rachel come from?

They are more than just curious. My gut tells me that they know more than they let on. If I had to bet money on it, I'd bet on Gregory and Rachel being involved. Involved? In what? In terrorism? Are they *terrorists*? Or just a couple of screwed up kids? But if they are a couple of screwed up kids who are destroying cell phone towers, does that make them terrorists?

I hope Mike is home. What time is it in Colorado? "Hello." He still sounds like a First Sergeant.

"Hi, Mike. Is this an okay time?"

"Yes. I'm cooking stuffed pork chops for Eric, Laurie and me, but I can talk and cook. What's up?"

"I just left a meeting with Gregory Zaremba. And he brought his girlfriend, a really cute, but mouthy girl named Rachel."

"Really? How did it go?"

"I think they might be members of the group that's taking down the cell phone towers. Hell, they might *be* the group."

"Did you call Nick?"

"Not yet. I wanted to talk it over with--"

"Dad. Do not pass 'Go.' Do not collect $200. Call Nick now."

"But--"

"Stop. This is serious shit. Call Nick right now. *Then*, call me back. Please do it, Dad."

"Okay. I have Nick's number in my cell phone. If you think it's that important, I'll call him now."

"It *is* that important, Dad."

Mike is not one to get excited without just cause. He spent twenty years in the Army Rangers, and did a lot of stuff he still won't talk about. I've never heard him be so insistent.

* * *

"Nick, this is Peter Bradovich. I'm on my way home from a meeting with Gregory Zaremba and his girlfriend, Rachel."

"I know who it is. Caller ID works very well. Do you know Rachel's last name?"

"No, I didn't think to ask."

"It's okay. We can find out easily enough. Start at the beginning, and as best you can, tell me exactly what happened at the meeting. Once upon a time, you were trained to observe and report accurately. Resurrect those skills now, Cap'n. We need to know what you know."

"Well, to start with, I think that they are possibly the ones responsible. I talked to Mike, and he said to call you immediately."

"Smart man, but then he has some background, too. And I think you may be right. We have some new Intel that may point to Gregory. Tell me exactly what happened tonight."

It's a good thing that it's a half hour drive home. It took me the whole drive to tell Nick the story of our meeting. Kate says that sometimes I get carried away and embellish my stories. But the old training kicked in, and I emulated a tape recorder, relaying the whole meeting to Nick, pretty much without editorial comment.

When I finished, Nick was silent. "Nick?"

"I'm here. Just digesting. And making notes. Anything else?"

"No, that's about it. What do you think? Are they the ones?"

"I can't answer that. But we need to proceed as though they are. Are you willing to continue this?"

"I think so. I don't think they're dangerous. Not to me, at least. What do you want me to do?"

"Give it a few days to percolate. I don't want to spook them. Then we'll have you make contact again, and try to get involved. We need to work toward making them think you sympathize with their cause, that you want to help. Let me give it some thought, and consult with some coworkers. I'll get back to you in a day or two."

"I'm going to tell Kate what went on at the meeting."

"I don't think that's smart."

"I didn't ask. I'm also going to tell her where you want me to go with this."

"That's even less smart."

"But that's the way it is. She's in or I'm out."

CHAPTER 52

(Gregory)

I'm really pissed at the way Rachel dominated the whole meeting with Pete. I'm silent as we drive back to my place.

"Well, 'My little chickadee,' what do you think?"

"Of what?"

"Of what went on at Starbucks. And why are you pouting?"

"I'm not pouting! However, I was a little irritated about the way you kept talking and wouldn't let me get a word in edgewise."

"'Gentlemen, you can't fight in here! This is the War Room!' So I got excited. I'm sorry, Greg. I really am. I know this is your show, but you got me involved with your cause and with you. I like being involved with both. I don't know what's going to happen with the cell phone towers. I don't know where our relationship is heading. They're both a little scary sometimes. But I want to see where they're heading. Both the tower thing -- and us. I do. Really."

"Well. But ..."

"'But me no buts,' 'My little chickadee.' We'll work it out. Besides, I've got plans for you when we get back to your place."

* * *

We walk into my apartment. I have my arm around Rachel's waist. I can feel the heat from her body, and it feels good. The phone is ringing. Shit. Nobody ever calls me. The caller ID says it's from area code 310. Where is that?

"Hello?"

"Hello, my name is Justin. You do not know me, but I have something important to say to you."

"If you're selling or begging, I'm not buying or giving. Bye."

And I hang up without waiting for a response. "Salesman. You said you have plans for-- Shit. Wait a minute."

Same area code. "I am on the Do Not Call List! There are federal laws against--"

"I know that you destroyed the cellular telephone towers."

"What? What are you talking about? Who are you?"

"Your anonymous emails are not nearly as anonymous as you think. If I can trace them back to you, so can the government. I sympathize with your cause. I can help. We must talk."

Oh, shit! I look at Rachel. "So talk."

"My name is Justin. I am calling from California. I am a sympathizer with your cause."

"What cause?"

"Just listen, please. Gregory, I have been able to back-trace the email that was sent to Vista Tel from your computer last Friday. I am referring to the email claiming responsibility for destroying their second tower. I have resources available to me to do such things. The government will be able to do so as well. If you continue, you will get caught."

"I have no idea what you're talking about."

"You do. I can help you. I have resources available to me that will keep you from getting caught. I can make your emails and your telephone calls anonymous, for certain. I want to help. I believe in what you are doing."

"I really don't know what you are--"

"Do not try to call the number from which I am calling. No one will answer. Do not try to trace the number. You will find no listing. I only use a phone number one time. Write down the following telephone number. When you are ready to accept my help, call it from a pay telephone. I shall be waiting for your call. The number is 410-555-1212. Again: 410-555-1212."

And he was gone. Quick. Paper. Pen. 410-555-1212. 410-555-1212. 410-555-1212. 410-555-1212. Got it: 410-555-1212.

"What was that all about?"

"Sit. Let me think for a minute."

"What?"

"Wait! I'll tell you. But, wait."

He knew. That was very obvious. He knew? How? Cops? No, they would be here. They would have broken down the door. Unless they're playing me. I don't think so. But, who is he? He said he wants to help. Why? He said he's a sympathizer. But why? Why does he want to help? Does he? Really?

I replay, as best I can, the details of the phone conversation to Rachel. She looks as baffled as I feel. I repeat to her all the questions I asked myself. For once, she is speechless.

"Zowee."

"Yeah. Zowee."

"So, what do we do?"

"For now, nothing. If it's the cops, we're screwed. If it's not the cops, nothing will happen. Let's just cool it for a few days."

"Zowee."

"Still in the mood?"

"Huh?"

"You said you had plans."

"Not now, Greg. Talk about a cold shower. This is definitely *not* 'the stuff that dreams are made of.' More like nightmares. I think I just want to go home and hide."

"Yeah. Okay. Call me."

CHAPTER 53
(Mirsab)

That was the most difficult telephone call I have ever made, but I had no choice. Hamad directed me to do it. I dare not disappoint him. I called from one of the few working pay telephones left in Torrance. In the few years that I have been in the United States, I have seen cellular telephones quickly make pay telephones essentially obsolete.

Hamad gave me the number to call. I knew what I must say. It was five p.m. here, and therefore, eight p.m. there. I said a prayer to Allah. I beseeched his guidance and strength, and I dialed the telephone number. A recorded voice asked me to enter my credit card number. I entered the number on the Master Card that Hamad mailed to me. The name on the card is unfamiliar to me. I assume that the card is stolen.

The telephone rang many times. I thought Gregory must not be at home. I would call again later. As I started to hang up, I heard the click of the telephone being answered. I remember the dialog perfectly.

"Hello?"

"Hello. My name is Justin. You do not know me, but I have something important to say to you."

He was irritated. I had disturbed him. He said something about begging, and he hung up before I could say anything more.

I dialed his telephone number again, and used the credit card again. He answered again. He was even more angry. He started to yell, but I interrupted before he could hang up again. "I know that you destroyed the cellular telephone towers."

He was silent for a moment. He asked who I was.

I talked calmly. I convinced him to listen. I explained that I had traced his email claiming credit for destroying the cell phone tower. I warned him that the government can do so as well.

He was silent again for a moment. He was considering my statements.

I continued with, "My name is Justin. I am calling from California. I am a sympathizer with your cause."

I asked him to listen. He did so, and I explained that I have resources available to me that will keep him from getting caught.

Gregory tried to deny that he knew what I was talking about, but I did not allow him to do so. I interrupted him, and told him the telephone number at which to call me. I repeated it one time slowly, and broke the connection. It was finished! Hamad will be pleased!

The number I gave him is that of one of the TracFones that Hamad has sent to me.

Gregory will return my call. Perhaps today, perhaps in a few days, but he will return my call. He knows that he needs my help.

Just as importantly, I need his help in preparing for the coming jihad!

CHAPTER 54

Sunday

(Peter)

My son, Mike, is ex-Army Rangers. He retired after twenty years to become a U.S. Marshall. But he also has a degree in computer science. I once asked him why the U.S. Army Rangers needed a computer science major. His answer was a rather vague statement that the Army uses computers as well as guns. "Hi, Mike."

"Hi, Dad. I'm surprised to hear from you so soon. Last I heard you and Nick decided to 'give it a few days to percolate.' What's up?"

"Well, it's still 'percolating,' but I have a question for you. An Internet question."

"I'm listening."

Mike is still a computer whiz. I suspect that if I asked him why the U.S. Marshall Service needs a computer science major, I'd get an answer similar to what I got when he was in the Army. Anyway, I get right to it. "You mentioned that Gregory has some postings on YouTube and Facebook. I'd like to look at them, but I know nothing about either of those sites. And I'd like to."

"That's an easy Internet question. Let's take them one at a time. Are you at your computer?"

"Yeah, I am."

"YouTube is easy. Just go to www.youtube.com on the Web. There is a search box on their home page. Enter the name you're looking for and you'll see a bunch of video postings. If you don't get the hit you want, try different spellings, different combinations, diff--"

"No need! I found him -- and his video -- immediately. You are right, YouTube *is* easy. I'll watch the video later. How about Facebook?"

"That's a little different. Facebook is a social networking site where you *make friends* with people you know or want to know. The bad thing is that you have to set up a Facebook account with your name and an email address. The problem I see is that you don't really want to identify yourself to this Zaremba character just to see what he is up to. Depending on how this thing develops, you may want to identify yourself to him later. But, I think, not now."

"Could I build a bogus email account with a bogus name on a free service like Yahoo, and use that to set up an account on Facebook?"

"Yes, you could. That will work, but make your bogus persona sound real because you'll have to ask Zaremba if you can be his friend."

"If I can 'be his friend?' Sounds like Mr. Rogers Neighborhood."

"It is, a little. To tell the truth, I've never really understood the fascination with Facebook. But you can dig around to your heart's content once you set up an account. You can see who his friends are, who their friends are, etc., etc., etc. You can look at people's profiles to find out their likes, dislikes, and so on."

"Okay. I'll build a bogus persona and play."

"Two things, Dad: One, tell Nick about your bogus persona, because I'm sure they are watching Zaremba. And two, you might tell Zaremba you found his video on YouTube and that you sympathize. See what happens."

"Two very good ideas, Mike. I won't take any more of your time. Tell Eric I said hello."

"You just want to go play on the Internet, Dad, but I understand. I'll tell Eric. Be careful, Dad."

"Bye, Mike."

And he was right. Two hours later, I'm still playing. The YouTube video is wild. Gregory definitely has some extreme ideas -- he probably *is* the perp, as Nick would say.

YouTube in general is fascinating. It's amazing what's on there.

Facebook was less satisfying. I am now Frank O'Brien, a twenty-something Ohio State student with an email address of knarfo@yahoo.com. That bogus persona was amazingly easy to build. No wonder the bad guys use the Internet. I found Gregory, and looked at his friends, but that's about all I could do. I asked him if I could "be his friend," but I haven't gotten a response yet.

The more I dig into Gregory Zaremba, the more I think Nick is right. He *is* the perp.

I ought to check Rachel on YouTube and Facebook. I wish I knew her last name. My gut says I've got to call Greg, and find out what I can about him -- and Rachel.

But I've been at this long enough. Kate's starting to make impatient noises. I'd better get downstairs and see what she wants to do this afternoon.

CHAPTER 55

(Gregory)

"Well, my dear, we've got two big decisions to make."

"Two?"

"Yeah, we have to decide if we're going to call this Justin back. And we have to decide if we want to try to recruit Pete."

"Zowee. You're right. Two biggies. 'Have you ever danced with the Devil in the pale moonlight?'"

"And I should interpret that how?"

"Well. Okay. Justin worries me. He just may be 'the Devil' -- the cops or the FBI or something. If he is, we're screwed. But assuming that he is not 'the Devil,' he is right. If he found us, so will the government. If he can keep us anonymous, we can use him. Another thing to our advantage is that you said he's in California, so we can keep him at a distance."

"That makes sense. Okay, I'll call him."

"No, let me call him. I want him to think we are part of a group."

"That makes sense, too. What about Pete?"

"He's old, but he's cute. I like him. I'm amazed that he is as sympathetic with our cause as he is. We just may be able to make him member number three of our little group. I think you should call him and see where you can go with him. He strikes me as somewhat suspicious, and also somewhat mysterious. That fascinates me. I'd call him too, but I think he'd be more comfortable if you called him again."

"I keep saying this, but it's true. That makes sense, too. When should I call Pete, do you think?"

"Now."

"Okay." I go over to the desk and sit down. I don't think I've called him on my landline, so he won't know the number. Do I have caller ID blocked? I don't remember. I'll have to check.

"Hello?"

"Hi, Captain. It's Greg Zaremba."

"It's Greg now? You've always used Gregory. Which do you prefer?"

"Rachel said Gregory sounded too 'stilted,' so I am now Greg."

"And how is Miss -- I don't know her last name. What is it, anyway? And how is she?"

"Her last name is Goldmann, with two *n*'s, and she is fine. She's here now, in fact. We're just watching TV. We've been talking cell towers during the commercials, and there are so many of them anymore: commercials, I mean. Cell phone towers, too. Anyway, I told her I wanted to talk to you again. Find out what's new. See where we ought to go from here. Hence the call."

"Greg, I'm still squirrely about discussing this over the phone. I know some of the things they can do with the Cray Supercomputers buried under Langley. They have to be looking for key words on phone calls."

"You mean like 'cell tower'"?

"Don't use that word again. Not while you're talking to me on the telephone. If you want to talk, let's meet."

"Okay. Okay. I don't believe the frickin' government is that good, but I'll play along. When do you want to meet? And where? Starbucks, again?"

"No, I've got another place in mind. Get off 480 at Tiedeman Road. It's a little farther west than where you got off to go to Starbucks, and go left instead of right. The second light is Brookpark Road. There is a bar on the corner called The Icehouse. Can you meet me there tomorrow about 5:15?"

"You sound like you've got this all planned out."

"No, not really. I just went by The Icehouse at lunchtime today. I've never been in there, but bars are good places to meet."

"You sound like you have experience setting up secret meetings."

"Maybe in a previous life."

"Right. I'm done with classes early tomorrow, so I can meet you there."

"And don't bring Rachel."

I look at Rachel hard. She has been listening to my end of the conversation. "'Don't bring Rachel'? Why not?"

"Because I want to talk about Rachel before we go much further. Okay?"

She gets up and starts walking toward me. I turn the phone so she can hear, too. "She won't like it."

"I don't care. If she is there, I'm not. And this ends."

"Well. Okay. If you insist."

"I do. I'll see you tomorrow night, Greg. Enjoy your evening with Rachel."

He hangs up. Rachel is standing in front of me looking at me. She turns her hands palms up, shrugs her shoulders, and gives me a "What?" look.

"He said he doesn't want me to bring you because he wants to talk about you before we go much further. I don't know what he meant by that exactly, but I suspect he wants to know where you fit into the scheme of things."

"So, go tell him where I fit into the scheme of things, 'My little chickadee.' And by the way, you promised me you'd quit saying frickin'. I'm going home."

Oh, the fucking frickin' thing again. Is she mad about that? "Are you mad? What about calling Justin?"

"No, I'm not mad. I just don't want to call Justin from here, or from home. I'd call him on my cell phone, but I don't want him to have that number. And if he is as good as he says he is, he just might be able to do a GPS fix on my cell phone. So, I'll stop halfway home and call him from a payphone. 'Chance is the fool's name for fate.'"

"Okay, Rachel. Call me after you've talked to him. And I'll call you after my meeting with Pete tomorrow night."

"Sounds good, 'My little chickadee.' And, Greg -- we've got to move ahead on the next tower. They're *still* not listening."

CHAPTER 56

(Mirsab)

The TracFone rings. Gregory is the only person to whom I have given the number. "Hello, this is Justin."

"Hello. I am a friend of Gregory's. I was there when you called him last week."

I do not know who this woman is. I must act like I know of her. "I know who you are. How may I help you?"

"How do you know who I am? We want to discuss what you can do for us. We want to know how you found us. And we want to know why you want to help us."

"One question at a time, please. Are you calling from your own telephone?"

"No, I'm calling from a pay phone so you can't trace me. Okay, how do you know who I am?"

I do not know, but I will, if Hamad can identify her. Perhaps Gregory's telephone records or emails will reveal her identity. If she used a credit card to make this telephone call, that will make identifying her even easier. "I would prefer not to say. What is your next question, please?"

"How did you find us?"

"The answer to that is quite technical."

"I'm quite technical, too. Try me."

"Any time one connects to the Internet, one's service provider keeps a record of the IP address from which the connection is made. No matter what email account is used, the connection can be cross-referenced to that IP address. The IP address in turn can often be cross-referenced to a geographical address. A geographical address can be cross-referenced to an individual. I have access to those records and databases. I made the necessary cross-references. I can go into more detail if you require."

"No. I get the picture. I'm something of a computer nerd myself. Given enough time, I could probably hack into those databases and do the same thing, maybe. Given enough time. Maybe. 'Pay no attention to that man behind the curtain!'"

"I beg your pardon?"

"Never mind. So, if you're out on the west coast, why do you want to help us in Ohio?"

"I shall be open with you. I represent a competing cellular telephone company. It is in their interest to eliminate competition from Vista Tel. I have been tasked with helping you."

"Zowee. That is scary! So, what can you actually do for us?"

"First, I must know if you have plans to destroy more towers."

"Well, yeah…"

"Then know that we will make all future contacts using disposable cellular telephones that I will provide. They are absolutely untraceable. You can tell me what you wish to say in your emails to Vista Tel and to the media. I will make it appear that those emails originate in the Middle East, or perhaps in Indonesia. Vista Tel will think that you have a connection to international terrorists. The police and the government will divert their resources to looking for those connections rather than to looking for you in Ohio -- in Euclid, Ohio."

"Zowee. I need to talk to Gregory about this, but I think we might want your help. Can I call you back at this number, Justin?"

I must be very careful. These two must understand the protocol from the outset. "This number will work one more time. Simply call me and say, 'Yes.' I will send a number of disposable cellular telephones to Gregory's address. I will include instructions on how to use them."

"'I'm here to fight for truth, justice, and the American way.'"

"I do not understand."

"Never mind. You don't watch many movies either, do you?"

She uses many strange phrases. "I still do not understand you."

"It's nothing. I'll call you. Maybe. Maybe not!"

"Goodbye."

The conversation was not as difficult as I expected. I believe that they will accept my offer of help. I also believe that I will be able to enlist them to help me prepare for the coming jihad without their being aware that they are being used. My only difficulty was in understanding the strange phrases that Rachel uses. I have lived in the United States for three years now. I still do not understand much American slang.

I must find out who this Rachel is. She must be part of Gregory's group. Hamad will help.

CHAPTER 57

Monday

(Peter)

Kate was only moderately okay with this meeting. She is genuinely concerned about my safety, I think. She realizes that these guys are not normal, law abiding citizens. And she knows that their kind do bad things. I assured her that I will bail out at the first sign of trouble.

I told Nick that, too. He said, "Let's just take it one step at a time." He wants a report each time I contact them. And he was glad to know about my digging around on YouTube and Facebook. He said he would notify the appropriate people. I always feel a little weird when he talks about "the appropriate people." It reminds me that this *is* for real, that Gregory and Rachel *are* radicals, that this *could be* dangerous.

It's been another exciting day in Cleveland with the three stooges. Sometimes that place functions just like the old Abbot & Costello "Who's on First?" skit. I think it continues to exist in spite of itself. Oh well.

The Icehouse. I don't go into bars very often. I quit drinking thirty years ago. If you don't drink, there is really no reason to go into a bar. The food is passable, at best. They smell. They are noisy. The patrons are, as a group, depressing. But as I learned in a previous life, for all those reasons, they are a good place to meet. For this kind of meeting, at least. A long time ago, an instructor of mine described meeting in a bar to do this kind of business as, "Hiding in a crowd."

I get a tonic water with a twist of lime. It's a good drink to disguise the fact that I don't drink. Unless you hear me order it, you'll assume it's vodka and something, or gin and something. Greg does not need to know I don't drink, that I wanted to meet here to "hide in a crowd." I sit at the bar near the front door.

* * *

Greg comes in. Alone. I offer to buy him a drink. He drinks draft beer. We move to a booth. People will probably think we're father and son having a drink together, but I don't really care since I'll probably never be here again. As long as nobody bothers us.

I decide to jump right in. "Greg, you said that you wanted to meet to find out what's new, to discuss where we go from here. Well, let's discuss."

"And you said you wanted to talk about Rachel. Why?"

Touché. I decide to go into intimidating mode. Kate says I'm good at intimidating people. "Because I need to know what part she plays in this. There is more going on here than you have told me. I need to know how you and her fit together."

"What do you mean by what part she plays in this? We're just curious about who is doing these cell phone towers. I don't know what you're talking about. You make it sound like some kind of conspiracy, or something."

Time to pounce. "Don't bullshit me, Greg. I saw your video on YouTube: your rant about the evils of cell tower proliferation. It was posted months ago. You did *not* just get curious about who is doing the cell phone towers."

Greg just looks at me. He is speechless. I continue. "I am the Frank O'Brien who you just accepted as a friend on Facebook. I know that you have friends who sympathize with your cause, Greg. I think you know a lot more than you have told me. I think that either, A, you know who is demolishing these towers, or B, you are the one doing the demolishing. Whichever it is, know that I agree with the destruction. I may not be as adamant about the issue as you are, but I find the proliferation of cell phone towers ugly and unacceptable. And from a technical point of view, completely unnecessary."

Still no words from Greg. He looks pale. A little sick. Like the kid who just got caught doing something bad. And I'm the person who caught him. I don't let up. "Greg, your face says it all. Which is it? Do you know who's doing this? Are you helping? Are you doing it? Is Rachel doing it? Are you in this together?"

"I--"

I don't let up. I have to know. Now. Time to switch from intimidating mode to fatherly mode. "Look, Greg, believe me. I'm on your side. I believe in your cause. I understand, and I want to help. I can and will keep your secrets. If you have a part in the destruction of these towers, I want to join you. If you know who is doing it, I want to join them. What do you say?"

Greg looks like the kid who got caught and now knows that his only option is confession. So, he confesses everything. He talks for ten minutes. He explains how destroying cell phone towers to drive Vista Tel out of business has been *his idea* -- his dream -- from the start. How he took down the first tower single-handedly. How he came to meet me at Shawn's Deals On Wheels. How he enlisted Rachel's help in investigating Shawn and me. How he and Rachel have become lovers. And how she has become his partner in his dream.

Greg tells me how he and Rachel took down the second tower. And about the third one they are planning.

He confides in me about his concerns about Rachel, about how she is becoming more radical than he is. About how she is pushing him to go faster than he wants, and to do more damaging things than he wants. He looks ready to cry. I think he is scared. In his idealism, he has created a monster. And he's losing control of it.

I reassure him. "Greg, it's okay. It *will* be okay. I think I can help. I've had some experience doing clandestine things in the past. I can help you control Rachel, and I can help keep this thing on track. One company at a time, we can force them to capitulate and combine. I'm pretty conservative politically, some call me far right. I'm a serious capitalist, but when it comes to public utilities, I'm very liberal, definitely far left. I border on socialist. There needs to be a government-controlled monopoly for each utility. There *must* be one electric company, one gas company, one phone company. And I truly believe that we can make that happen. At least we can force a start in that direction. When they understand what we are doing and why, others will join us. As Rachel would say, 'This could be the start of something big.'"

Slowly, I see Greg relax, then smile, then laugh a little. And he says, "Actually, I think the quote is 'Louis, this could be the beginning of a beautiful friendship.'"

We finish our drinks and walk out into the cool March evening. I've got to get to Nick. Fast. "I'll call you as soon as I digest all of this, Greg."

"Okay. I'll be waiting for your call."

CHAPTER 58

(Gregory)

Pete, the Captain, is sitting at the bar near the front door. He's drinking some kind of frickin' mixed drink, complete with a twist of lime. Rachel has been introducing me to wine, but I'm still basically a beer drinker.

I say hi to Pete, and he asks me what I'm drinking. I tell him a draft will do just fine. The bartender asks what kind, and I say, "Whatever." He draws me a draft, Pete pays, leaves a tip, gathers up the rest of his money and says, "Let's go sit and talk before we eat." Eat?

When we get situated, I ask, "What's this about eating?" He says that we're not eating. that the statement was just an excuse to come sit where we can talk without being overheard.

I say, "Oh," and he continues. "Greg, you said that you wanted to meet to find out what's new, to discuss where we go from here. Well, let's discuss."

I decide to go on the offensive. "You said you wanted to talk about Rachel. Why?"

And he answers. He says he thinks there is more going on than we have told him. He wants to know how Rachel fits in.

He's fishing. I play dumb.

He looks mad. He says, "Don't bullshit me, Greg," and he tells me he's been checking me out on YouTube and Facebook. He knows.

I just look at him. I'm speechless. He goes on. He says that either I know who is demolishing the towers, or I'm the one doing the demolishing!

Oh, shit. I feel sick. I'm busted. It's like when I was fourteen years old and I got caught shoplifting. I was screwed, and I knew it.

But then Pete's voice becomes softer. He says he's on my side. I believe him. I don't know why, but I do.

And it's like a dam breaks inside of me. I come completely unglued, and tell him everything. Just like when I was fourteen, when I confessed to shoplifting. It was at a hobby shop, and I not only confessed to the train car I put down my pants, I confessed to all the other things I had stolen from them. They called the police chief who called my father. Without a word, my father took me home and sent me to my room to worry. Then he made me return to the store and apologize to the owner. He knew both the police chief and the storeowner. Then he made me work to pay the store back for everything I had stolen. I never shoplifted again.

This is the same kind of confession. I start with my long-standing hatred of cell phone towers as a blight on the landscape. I explain how destroying the frickin' cell phone towers to drive Vista Tel out of business has been my dream from the start. I tell him about taking down tower number one, about going back the next evening and meeting him at Shawn's Deals On Wheels.

I can't stop blabbing. I need to tell somebody besides Rachel. I tell him how we took down the second tower, even about almost having sex there before it fell. And I tell him about the third one we're going to do, about how Rachel wants to hit the house and how I don't. I can't stop talking.

Finally, I run down. I'm drained. I just look at him. I want to cry.

He looks at me for a minute. Like my dad did. He leans forward, smiles, looks me in the eye. "Greg, it's okay. It *will* be okay. I think I can help."

I'm dumbfounded. I'm still speechless. But now for a different reason. I have help. Not just the excitement I get with/from Rachel. Real help. He knows. I'm safe. I'm not busted.

Slowly, I relax. I smile. I laugh a little. He comes up with a quote from Casablanca, but he's off by a little. I correct his quote. We both laugh about it, and we talk about what a pain Rachel is with her quotes.

We talk a little about sailing as we finish our drinks.

As we leave the Icehouse and head for our cars, I feel relieved, almost elated. I've got to tell Rachel.

CHAPTER 59

(Mirsab)

Just as I will provide Gregory and this Rachel with disposable cellular telephones, Hamad has provided them to me. The cellular telephones that he sent me have 857 area codes. That is a Boston, Massachusetts, area code, but I do not know where Hamad lives. It will be the same with my new friends from Ohio. They will not know where I live.

I will use one of Hamad's cellular telephones to report my progress to him. I am to use each telephone only once, and then destroy it. And he was very clear about that procedure: I am to destroy it, not just discard it. I questioned him on this, and he pointed out that a discarded cellular telephone might be recovered and reused. It might then be traced, perhaps. Destroying the cellular telephone prevents such problems. Hamad explained that if a cellular telephone is used only once, it is absolutely secure.

I have never met Hamad. He called me one day, and said that a mutual friend told him I spoke flawless English. His friend said that I would perhaps be willing to work with a group of Americans. Work with them, and deceive them into helping us prepare for the coming jihad. He would not identify our mutual friend.

He told me that he had been able to identify the American who is destroying cellular telephone towers in Ohio. He is a college student living near Cleveland, Ohio. It was Hamad's idea that I pose as an American mercenary. I was to explain to this Gregory in Cleveland, Ohio, that I had been hired by a competing cellular telephone company to help him. I was to tell him that I would aid him in eluding the police, and assist him by providing any resources he might need. Hamad explained that when we had a sufficient number of such individuals in place, we would be able to use them to disrupt communications all over the United States when the jihad starts here.

"Hello?"

"Hello, Hamad, this is Mirsab."

"It is not necessary to identify yourself. I know from your cell phone number who it is. It is better that you do not use names. Do you have something to report?"

"Yes. I have contacted the American who lives in Ohio. And I have discovered that he has an accomplice named Rachel. I do not know her last name."

"How did you find out about this accomplice named Rachel?"

"After I offered Gregory my help, she called me back to ask me more questions and to tell me that they may want my help."

"What sort of questions did she ask?"

"She asked how I found out about them, why I wanted to help, and what sort of help I could offer. I answered her questions as you instructed. She told me that she would discuss my offer with Gregory and call me back. I told her that she could call me one more time at the number I gave Gregory. I explained that I would send Gregory a number of disposable cellular telephones so that we could communicate safely."

"And she agreed to this?"

"Yes, but this Rachel uses many expressions that I find difficult to understand. I do not understand her meaning sometimes."

"You did well. Americans use many expressions that have unexpected meaning. Do you know the term 'idiom'? As you interact more with the Americans, you will learn the idioms they use."

"I know the term. I will learn."

"Speaking of idioms, Americans never say, 'cellular telephones,' they say simply, 'cell phones.'"

"I will remember that."

"I'm sure you will. When Rachel calls you back, encourage them, offer them whatever help they require: secure communications, anonymous emails, research, assistance, money, weapons, even explosives. Anything. You have done well. Keep me informed of your progress. Do you have any questions? Do you need any help from me?"

"Not at this time."

"What American alias have you chosen for your contacts with them?"

"The name I have used is Justin. Justin Brown. Is that good?"

"It is excellent. Your accent is flawless. That name is very neutral. It has no ethnic connotation, and that is good. I, myself, have such an alias. Contacts who do not know me as Syrian believe that my name is John Collins."

"I see, John."

"That is good. I will say goodbye for now. I repeat, Justin, you have done well."

"*Ma'a Salaama.*"

"Never speak Arabic to me! You never know who might overhear. Goodbye."

"Goodbye, then."

CHAPTER 60

(Peter)

"Hi, Cutie"

"Hi, honey, I'm glad you're home. I'm dying to know how your meeting with Gregory went. Did he bring Rachel?"

"No, he was alone. And it went well. Very well. Too well. He blabbed everything. Nick was right: he is -- they are -- the perpetrators!"

"Oh, wow."

"Gregory took down the first tower all by himself. Then he enlisted Rachel, and together they took down the second tower. They're already planning the third."

"So, now what?"

"Obviously I have to call Nick, tonight. Let's go to the Moosehead for dinner. I'll tell you the whole story on the way."

The Moosehead Grill is a great barbecue joint about a half hour away. I follow Kate around the house continuing my story as she gets ready. I continue during our drive, and by the time we pull into the Moosehead parking lot, I have pretty much told her everything that Greg told me. Including the fact that at Rachel's insistence, he now goes by Greg, not Gregory.

"All I have to do is convince him to call me Peter or Cap'n. He insists on calling me Pete. You know how I feel about being called Pete."

"Yes."

As we walk across the parking lot toward the Moosehead, I make a suggestion. "Let's talk about other things at dinner. We can continue talking about this stuff on the way home."

"Okay, that makes sense. Very good sense."

We discuss the rest of our day over pulled pork, baked beans, and coleslaw for me, and a half rack of barbecued ribs, a baked sweet potato and a salad for her.

* * *

When we get home, I call Nick. Kate's only advice is, "Cap'n, be careful. Please!"

Nick is his usual completely calm, unemotional self. He doesn't sound the least bit surprised about my revelation. He just says that he wants me to tell him everything that Greg said. Right now, while the details are fresh in my mind. He asks if he may record our conversation, and I tell him that he may and that I'm glad he at least asked. He laughs, and says he would have recorded it regardless. I tell him I figured he would, and he laughs again. He says I know the game. And I laugh.

Kate has changed into her pajamas as I've been talking to Nick. She's got on the cute snowflake patterned flannels I got her for Christmas at Victoria's Secret. Yes, Victoria's Secret has some really sexy lingerie and negligees, but they also have high quality and really cute PJs. Their flannels are Kate's PJs of choice. These are called "Boyfriend Pajamas." They are styled masculinely, but they look anything but masculine on her.

She comes over, kisses me on the cheek, and asks if she can get me anything. I ask her to bring me a Diet Pepsi. I spend the next hour being debriefed by Nick. He is good at what he does.

When he has sucked every detail out of me, I get up, stretch, and tell him that Homeland Security has to stop them. He says, "No!"

He explains that it is worth losing another tower to find out who else in involved. When I tell him again that Rachel wants to escalate the damage they do, he says that that's their concern, and that they will deal with it. He says my job is to get involved with Greg and Rachel, to join their group, to find out who else is involved.

I get a little angry. Sarcastically, I say, "What is it exactly that you want me to do? Help them destroy cell tower number three?"

Nick says, simply, "Yes."

CHAPTER 61

(Gregory)

On my way home from my meeting with Pete, I call Rachel. She wants to know all the details. I tell her, "Not on the phone," and ask her if she can come over. I think I'm learning paranoia from Pete. Rachel says she's doing laundry and asks me to come to her place instead. I tell her no problem; it's actually closer than my place. It takes over a half hour to drive to her place in Little Italy. I have to go straight through downtown Cleveland, but the drive gives me a chance to organize my thoughts, and to plan how to explain to Rachel that Pete now knows all about us.

* * *

Even at home doing laundry, Rachel looks good. She just has jeans, the usual hip huggers she wears, and a knit top on, but it's attractive. I have a definite urge to pull her knit top up and off over her head and...

But first. There's no easy way to do this. "Pete knows everything."

"What do you mean?"

"I mean, I told him about us. He knows that we are the ones destroying the cell phone towers."

"'Looks like I picked the wrong week to stop sniffing glue.'"

"He pretty much frickin' knew. He's been on YouTube and Facebook. He saw my stuff. He figured it out. And he sympathizes. He wants to help. It will be okay."

"No *frickin*! Are you sure? Do you trust him? Because if you are wrong, we are going to jail, 'My little chickadee.'"

"I know. And I do trust him. He will be the third member of our group."

"What about his son, the U.S. Marshal, and his sister, the Secretary of Defense, or whatever she is?"

"Coincidence. He won't involve them. He'd go to jail, too. He admitted to me that he has experience in doing what he called clandestine things. He said he can help us."

"Oh well. It's done. 'Life moves pretty fast. If you don't stop and look around once in a while, you could miss it.'"

Rachel leaves the room to go do something with her laundry. She has a washer and dryer. I don't. I hate laundromats, but that's my only option right now. Oh well.

* * *

"Come sit while I tell you my news. Then we'll go get something to eat."

"Sounds good, Rachel. I am trying to quit saying 'frickin.'"

"I know you are, Greg, and I appreciate it. I called Justin. He talks funny, somehow. Too precise, too correct. And he's completely clueless about movie quotes. It was like I was speaking a different language when I threw a couple into our conversation."

"So, he's probably a businessman with an MBA and no life. Or maybe he's a techie who is clueless about the real world. I wouldn't worry. What did he say? Can he help us?"

I listen as Rachel replays her conversation with Justin. I especially like the part about him taking over our public relations efforts. I was uncomfortable with us sending the emails. I think he's right. They will trace them. Maybe he can do the phone calls, too.

I ask Rachel if she figured out where he lives. "He said California, but the number he gave us is a Maryland area code. It's probably a cell phone. He could be anywhere."

Calls to the media from a third person in some other city will really throw them off track. That could be good.

But I have the same question that Rachel had about Pete. "Can we trust this Justin guy?"

"At least as much as we can trust Pete. Greed, for lack of a better word, is good. Assuming he is who he says he is, their company is motivated strictly by money, and that's probably safer than if they were motivated by idealism or something. There is one thing, though."

"What's that, Rachel?"

"After Vista Tel, Justin's company is next!"

"So much for 'greed is good.' Fair enough. They are next. Do we know the name of his company?"

"Not yet. But we will. Let's go get something to eat. How about a good hamburger?"

Rachel takes me to a place near where she lives. We have a pleasant dinner. It's an Italian joint, but they have great burgers. We just talk about stuff. Nothing important. Just stuff. Kind of getting to know each other better. We hold hands over coffee.

"Can you stay the night, Greg?"

I kind of stammer, "But I don't have anything with me, not even a toothbrush."

Rachel smiles. "We can stop and get whatever you need. Maybe you should start keeping a few things at my place."

As Rachel would say, Zowee!

CHAPTER 62

(Mirsab)

I am confident that Gregory or Rachel will call me again. They surely realize that I can assist them in ways that are important to them. After they call me, I will destroy the cellular telephone for which I gave them the telephone number. It was sent to me by Hamad, and I have only one more. I must request more cellular telephones -- no, more cell phones -- from him.

While I wait for their call, I will prepare the six TracFones that I purchased.

I will create labels with the numbers one through six, and attach them to the telephones. Label one will have the telephone number of the telephone with label two, and vice versa. The same will be true of labels three and four, and five and six. I will pack the cell phones with odd numbers in a box, and include instructions to use each phone in order, and then destroy it. I will keep the even numbered telephones for my own use. As Hamad did to me, I will stress that the telephones are to be destroyed, not simply discarded.

I shall invent a return address for the box and send it to Ohio via Priority Mail using the wondrous United States Postal Service.

These six phones will only serve to allow three telephone calls between me and my new friends in Ohio. I will have to purchase more shortly.

* * *

It concerns me that Hamad wishes to allow the Americans to continue to destroy cell phone towers at this time. It seems to me that further destruction should await the start of the jihad.

I asked Hamad about this. He told me that I must encourage them to continue as they are doing now, that I must work with them, and that I must help them. Their activities provide a source of distraction to the American Homeland Security forces. Personnel that are investigating the destruction of the cell phone towers are not available to investigate other, more important activities that we are performing.

Hamad also said that as I move forward, I must gain the control of my Cleveland group. At some point, I must prepare them to be ready to destroy several towers at once. That destruction will coincide with the start of the jihad!

CHAPTER 63

Tuesday

(Peter)

Well, this is as good a time as any. I'm pretty sure Greg will be home by now. I've been agonizing over this call since I talked to Nick last night. A couple of times today, I almost called him. I went to Big Creek Park at lunchtime, and just hung out. It was nice. Spring is definitely springing. The crocuses are starting to push through. Soon we'll see them and then daffodils in bloom.

I don't like talking on my cell phone while I'm driving. I view talking while driving, even with a hands-free headset, as a dangerous distraction.

But I'm on the Turnpike now, and through most of the traffic. I might as well get this over with. I'll keep it short.

"Hello?"

"Hi, Greg, it's Peter."

"Oh, hi. What's up?"

A little white lie will make this easier. "I want to keep this short. I'm on 480 and traffic is a little crazy. Bottom line, like I said yesterday, I'm in. I want to be a part of this."

"Great, Pete. I was hoping you wouldn't change your mind. I really need your help."

God, I hate that. "Please don't call me Pete. I prefer Peter or Captain. I don't want to talk right now, but I want to meet soon and talk about where we go from here. Are you free Thursday at lunch time?"

"Yeah, I can be. Where do you want to meet?"

Big Creek Park *is* nice this time of year. "Near where we met last time is a place called Big Creek Park. You can MapQuest it. I was there today at lunchtime."

"Actually, I'm sitting at my computer right now. I prefer Google Maps."

I've never used Google Maps. "You'll come west on 480 to Tiedeman Road, and south to the Icehouse, but then go left on Brookpark for just a quarter mile or so to the park entrance."

"Wait just a minute. Okay, I'm following you on the Google Maps. Then what?"

Cool. "About a quarter mile into the park is a picnic area on the right. I'll be in the parking lot about ten after twelve. Can you meet me?"

"I can see the parking lot in the Google Maps satellite view. No problem. Peter, I'm really glad you're on board."

Google Maps does sound cool. "I'll have to check that site out. It sounds cool. I'll see you in the parking lot on Thursday. I've got to go. Traffic is backing up."

"Bye, Captain."

"Bye."

That wasn't so bad. But I suspect that the meeting Thursday will be. Can I convince him that I want to do this? Do I even want to do this? To get involved? As Rachel would say, "Zowee."

CHAPTER 64

(Gregory)

"Hi, Rachel. Am I allowed to say I miss you already?"

"'You aren't too bright. I like that in a man.' Last night was nice. Let's leave it at that for now. Is that why you called? To tell me you missed me?"

"No. Well, yes, I do, but that's not all. I just got a call from Peter. He still wants in, and I think that rocks. He wants to meet with me on Thursday."

"Rats. I have to work Thursday."

"That's too bad, because I think Peter is okay with you now." Rachel sounds pleased to hear that, so I don't bother to tell her that Peter and I didn't talk about her at all yesterday. Actually, I'm sure he would have said something if he still had a problem with her.

"I really like him, Greg. I think he'll be a great asset. He's mature, and I get the impression that he knows what he's doing. I'd like to know more about him and about his background."

The way Rachel gushes about Peter irritates me a little. Am I jealous? Of an old man? Enough. "Rachel, there's something else."

"What, 'My little chickadee'?"

"You need to call Justin back and tell him that he is in, too."

"Why me?"

"You told him you would call him back. He's expecting you to call. Besides, I want you to be our primary contact with him, at least, for now."

"Okay, I'll call him as soon as we hang up. What do you want me to tell him?"

"Just tell him we want his help. See what he offers. Let him do most of the talking. Let's go real slow on this, okay?"

"Sounds good, 'My little chickadee.' Do you want me to call you back?"

"No, I don't think so. Not unless you've got some earth shattering news. I'm sure you'll handle it just fine."

"Do I detect a note of sarcasm, 'My little chickadee'?"

"No. Not at all. I meant what I said. You are one of the most competent girls I've ever met, Rachel."

"I'll take that as a compliment. But, I'm not sure if I'd rather be thought of as competent or cute."

"Cute, too, 'My little chickadee'."

"'Nite…"

* * *

We end our call, and I feel just a little unsettled. I'm not sure why. Can we trust Justin? Can we trust Peter? Can I even trust Rachel? Is my group growing too fast? It's what I thought I wanted. Do I? It was easier when I was alone. Not as much fun, perhaps, but easier.

CHAPTER 65

(Mirsab)

I receive the call for which I have been waiting. It is Rachel. "Hello. Justin? It's Rachel."

"Do not use names. I know who will call me on various telephones. We must be careful."

She speaks rapidly. "Okay. Is this a good time to call? I don't know where you are. I don't know the time difference. Where *do* you live?"

"We will not discuss our locations either. We must keep our conversations brief and vague. All you needed to do was call me and say, 'Yes,' as I directed."

"Okay, okay. *Yes!*"

"I am pleased that you and your friend have decided to accept my help. We can accomplish much together. I will cause a box containing several TracFones to be mailed to your friend in Euclid. The box will contain instructions on how to use the cell phones. He should receive it in about two days. Do not call this telephone number again. Wait for the cell phones to arrive."

"And that's all you have to say?"

"That is all. We will talk when you receive the phones. Goodbye."

"'*Hasta la vista*, baby.'"

* * *

I will deliver the box of cell phones to the Post Office today.

But first, I call Hamad. "Hello, I have news. I have been accepted by the Americans in Ohio."

"That is excellent. You I have done well, my friend!"

"However, I need more TracFones to send to the Americans."

"So, go buy them."

"I do not like to purchase them. When I bought the last cell phones at a Radio Shack here in Torrance, the clerk tried to sell me another variety with a Family Plan. The clerk was younger than I am, but he was typically American. He did not respect me. He argued with me about what I wanted, and tried to intimidate me. Such behavior by a shopkeeper is alien to me, difficult to cope with. Is there not another way?"

Hamad is angry. "Suck it up and do it."

I am stunned. "I do not understand the idiom."

He speaks more gently. "The idiom means to be strong and do a thing that you do not want to do. I will continue to use American idioms with you so that you may learn them."

Hamad then suggests that perhaps I can find a trusted friend to help me purchase the cell phones I need. "That is an excellent suggestion."

I do not tell Hamad, but I think I know who I can ask. I will purchase another group myself, and then I will enlist her help.

"Very good. Keep me informed of your dealings with your new friends in Ohio."

"I shall." We say our goodbyes -- in English.

CHAPTER 66

Thursday

(Peter)

God, what a beautiful day. It is spring! I love it. I don't really hate winter, but this is sure nicer.

I park in the sun, and put the top down. I recline the seat, close my eyes, and wait for Greg. I hope he's not late. Then again, I can do this for a while.

In about two minutes, I hear a car pull in beside me. I turn my head and open one eye, squinting because of the sun. It's Greg. Good timing.

He gets out of his car. He comes around to the driver's side of the Mustang, and says, "Hi."

He's dressed in his usual Joe College attire. I should clarify that. I don't mean Joe College as he dressed in the forties or fifties. I mean Joe College as he dresses in the twenty-first century -- as a complete slob! He's got on his usual jeans with holes. What's that about? A T-shirt advertising some band I never heard of. Where do they get these names? Of course, the required gray hooded sweatshirt, the *hoodie*. And, the crowning *pièce de résistance*, the knit hat! Why, oh, why?

"Hi Greg. Let's take a walk. I'm not a big walker, but it's a beautiful day." I pull the keys out of the ignition, and get out of the car. We walk down the path toward Big Creek.

When we're away from the other cars in the parking lot, I ask, "So what's the plan for the next tower?"

"Vista Tel is still not responding. We have sent them another message. If they don't respond by early next week, the tower comes down. As I said, there will be collateral damage. It will hit a building!"

I don't want to sound too curious. "Hit a building? Sounds like that should get their attention! What do you want me to do?"

"I'm not sure. I think maybe drive. Rachel almost got us caught last time by not following orders. This time the tower is near a busy exit and close to Lorain. The cops will get there quickly. If we screw this one up, we will get caught. I'm concerned that the location is too out in the open, but we want the media to get there quickly. We want lots of publicity. We need to coordinate the job carefully."

I assure Greg that I will make sure it gets done right. Again, I hint that I've done things like this before, that I'm much more experienced at this kind of stuff than Rachel is. I need to gain his trust. Completely. And soon.

As I'm considering this, Greg shocks me with a truly monumental revelation. They have added another member to the team! He won't go into detail. He says this person doesn't live around here. It seems that he works for another cell phone company. This other cell phone company supposedly wants to help us drive Vista Tel out of business. This person -- Greg won't even name him -- is willing to do the emails to Vista Tel and make them appear to come from offshore. He is willing to make the phone calls to the media for us from outside of Ohio. He will provide whatever help we need to drive Vista Tel out of business. Greg says he and Rachel want to use him because it will help keep us from getting caught.

This is more scary shit. I'm suspicious. This doesn't even sound right. Kids can be so naive.

I act as if I don't like this development at all. I ask Greg how he knows that this isn't a trap. I tell him that this guy could be an undercover cop. He could be setting us up, gathering evidence to bust us. I tell him I want to know more about this character.

Greg says, "No." He says that if this guy *is* a cop, we're already screwed. I tell him that *he* may be screwed, but I'm not. I act mad. Worried. I tell him that if he even hints to this character that someone other than he and Rachel are involved, I'm gone. Greg says to relax. Rachel is his single point of contact.

I say, "So, big deal. How does that keep me from joining you in jail when he busts you and Rachel?" Greg says he will tell Rachel my feelings; tell her not to mention me. He promises to keep me out of any discussions with this guy.

I act as if I'm somewhat placated for now. I tell him that I think I trust Rachel to protect my identity, but I also tell him that I want to talk to Rachel myself. I want her phone number when we get back to the car. He somewhat reluctantly says okay.

I've got to find out more about this guy. And tell Nick. Quickly.

CHAPTER 67

(Gregory)

Pete, Peter, the Captain, whatever. He's already here. He looks like he's snoozing. Nope. He squints at me as I pull in to his left.

I get out, go around the front of my car and up to his door as he sits up. I open with, "Hi."

He says, "Hi" back, gets out of his car, and starts down the path toward the creek.

Pete said he came from work. I don't know what kind of work he does, but it sure doesn't look like he's been working. He looks like he's going out to dinner or something. He's got on nice khaki pants, and one of those light blue dress shirts with a button down collar. At least he doesn't have on a necktie. His shoes are nicely polished, and very expensive looking. Penny loafers, I think they call them. No pennies, though. His hair is a little longer than most men his age wear, and he has a full beard. The beard looks like he trims it every day. He always looks this way!

As we get near the creek, he asks about the next tower.

I tell him if Vista Tel doesn't respond by early next week, the next tower comes down!

He asks what he can do. I've been thinking about this, and I know exactly what I want him to do, but I act like it's a question I'm just considering. "I'm not sure. I think maybe drive." I explain that Rachel almost got us caught last time by not following orders, and I don't trust her to follow orders this time.

I decide to drop the bomb. I tell him about Justin. I keep my explanation vague. I don't name him. I don't go into a lot of detail. I explain in very general terms who Justin is, who he works for, and what he can do for us. I try to stress how he can help us keep from getting caught.

Peter gets really squirrely about Justin. He thinks the guy is a cop! I do my best to reassure him. I tell him if he was, we'd already be busted. Peter looks and sounds ready to bolt. Basically, he says he doesn't want us to mention him to this new guy at all. I'm really surprised at his reaction. This guy is frickin' paranoid!

I assure him that Rachel is Justin's only point of contact, and I promise to tell her not to mention Peter to him. He says he wants to talk to Rachel about this. I reluctantly agree to give him Rachel's number.

Peter looks at his watch and says he has to get back to work. We turn around and head back toward our cars.

CHAPTER 68

(Mirsab)

` I do not expect another call on this telephone. "Hello?"

"*Ciao*, Justin. It's Rachel again. I just wanted to tell you that we have enlisted another mem--"

Stupid woman! "*Ghabi!* Stop!"

"But I didn't think--"

"Idiot woman! I told you never to call this number again. Now you have compromised its usefulness! I must now destroy this telephone!"

"But--"

"Do you not understand that the authorities are listening? When you use the same telephone more than once, connections are made. The supercomputers see patterns. Telephone calls are no more anonymous than emails. They can be traced. They *will* be traced. You will cause us to be arrested! Wait for the telephones that I sent! Use them as directed!"

And I hang up without allowing her to respond.

The woman does not understand how dangerous her actions are. She has no idea of the power of her own government. I think that most Americans do not.

I must call Hamad. I must tell him that I can not work with this woman. She is endangering the whole operation. Hamad will know how I should deal with this situation. He seems very knowledgeable about the Americans and about working with them. After three years here, I am not!

CHAPTER 69

(Peter)

I tried to call Nick right after I left Greg, but I got his voicemail. I told him I'd call him back on my way home. I desperately wanted to alert him to these latest developments, but I didn't dare do it from work. This whole subject is simply too sensitive to risk someone at work overhearing and asking questions.

Finally, it's quitting time. As soon as I get through the local stop and go stuff and get on to 480, I try Nick's number again. He answers, "Nick Patridis."

"Hi, Nick. Boy, have I been anxious to talk to you. I met with Greg at lunchtime today. Two big things we've got to talk about."

Nick is amazing. He looks like a fireplug. And most of the time, he talks with as much emotion as one. He simply says, "I want to meet as soon as we can and get all the details, but give me the bullet points."

I'm excited. This is heavy shit. "Okay. Bullet point one: They have picked out tower number three. It goes down next week if Vista Tel doesn't start responding. It will hit some sort of building. I think I'm driving the getaway car."

And Nick is calm. "And bullet point two?"

I tell him the biggie. "They have enlisted another member! Greg says he's not local, that he works for a competing cell phone company. He's going to do the emails and the phone calls. Maybe provide financial support. Whatever we need."

Nick's not emotional. But he's obviously interested. He responds with, "We have to talk. You teach a class tomorrow night, don't you?"

I knew this would get his attention. "Yeah."

"How about we meet at the McDonalds by the school?"

"You mean the one right near the Interstate 90 exit?"

"That's it. What's a good time for you?"

"How about after class, about 8:30?"

"That works. This is important. I'll be waiting. Peter, what's your immediate gut reaction on this new person?"

"Sounds weird. Suspicious."

"See you tomorrow night, Cap'n."

CHAPTER 70

(Gregory)

I tried to reach Rachel at her place this afternoon but got her answering machine. She must be either working or in class. I really need to get her schedule and give her mine.

I didn't want to leave a message, and I didn't want to call her at work. So, I had to wait 'till this evening. "Hi, Rachel."

"*Ciao*, Greg. What's up?"

"Not a lot. I just wanted to update you on a couple of things. I met with Peter at lunchtime today. He is definitely in. I told him our plans for tower number three. He wants to drive."

She sounds pissed. "And what, may I ask, is wrong with *my* driving?"

"Nothing, Rachel, but he wants to be a part of this, and we have to let him. We need to get him involved and committed."

"Well. Okay. He drives... Both of us."

Now what? "What do you mean?"

"He drives. I go with you to the tower!"

Oh, shit. "But…"

"'But me no buts.' Remember?"

"But…"

"Gregory, I am part of this. Get used to it, okay?"

I'm screwed. "I know you are."

"Okay. That's settled. Greg, there's something else. I called Justin today."

She sounds hesitant. "Yeah, I asked you to. But you said that funny."

"Well. He went bullshit. He screamed about me calling him again on his landline. At least I think it's his landline. He called me an 'idiot woman,' and something I didn't understand. He told me I was going to get us caught. Told me to wait for the cell phones and hung up!"

Trouble with my troops? "Well, maybe he was just being very careful. Maybe he's a little paranoid, too. I know Peter is."

"Greg, I don't know for sure."

Now what? "You don't know what for sure?"

"When he was screaming and yelling."

"What?"

"I swear he lapsed into some kind of foreign accent."

CHAPTER 71

(Mirsab)

I can not work with this woman, Rachel. I must call Hamad.

I use one of the TracFones that he has provided. I wonder where Hamad lives. I never know if it is a good time to call, but he always answers, and always sounds ready to talk. I must remember to always respond to Rachel and Gregory in the same way. Of course, unlike Rachel, I follow the protocols.

I explain to Hamad what Rachel has done. I explain how she continues to not follow instructions. I tell him that, in my opinion, she is endangering our cause. As I get more angry, I lapse into Arabic.

"Stop! English only! Always!" And Hamad adds, "Deal with it!" Another idiom.

This time, he explains the idiom. Then he continues, "I know that you find it frustrating, but you must learn to work with Rachel."

"But she is difficult. Her manner is so alien to me."

"You should know by now that in the United States, women have more power than in our country. Women have, in my opinion, too much power, but it is the Americans' way. You must learn to cope with this fact, this abnormality, at least until the jihad."

"She does not understand how dangerous her actions are. She has no idea of the power of her own government."

"I agree. Let me tell you a story about a character in American children's literature from many years ago. Her name was Pollyanna. She was a blindly optimistic young girl who always believed the best about everything and everyone. Americans are Pollyannaish about their own government. That they have no idea how evil it is."

"I think I understand, Hamad."

I use his name without thinking, and I expect a reprimand. Instead, Hamad makes me a promise. "Learn to deal with Rachel and lead this group, this cell -- your cell -- toward our goal for the coming jihad. Your actions will prove to me and to our leaders that you are worthy of more responsibility. If you do that, I promise to use you for even more important tasks in the future."

I am awed. I am honored. I am afraid.

CHAPTER 72
Friday
(Peter)

Class seemed long tonight. I'm antsy. My students sensed it, I know. I think I just need to talk this through with Nick. I *really* don't want to become an urban terrorist. I don't want to drive the getaway car. Even if it *is* for the greater good. Even if it will help them catch these creeps.

Greg is one genuinely screwed up kid. He needs a serious reality check. Some time in jail will open his eyes.

I like Rachel, but she is so misguided. Sometimes, I just want to shake her and say, "Use your potential! Quit listening to this loser. Be your own woman. You have so much more going for you than he does!"

I can't think of any place I'd be less likely to go on my own than McDonald's. Oh well, it was Nick's choice, not mine.

At least this one is full of college kids, not kid-kids. Last time I was in a McDonald's, a herd of six year olds were having a birthday party. That experience made me swear off McDonald's for a very long time!

Now that I think about it, I'm not sure that McDonalds was a good choice. I know too many people on and around campus. Perhaps a better way to put that is too many people know me. I've touched the lives of hundreds of kids over the years that I have been an Adjunct Professor here, and it's likely that someone who knows me will see me sitting here talking to Nick.

And Nick walks up to me. I didn't see him pull in. "Hi, Nick."

"Hi, Cap'n. Let's go get some coffee."

I tell Nick what I was thinking. "Are you sure this is a good place? I'm well known around here."

"Sometimes the best place to hide is in a crowd."

Sounds familiar. McDonald's. My choices in coffee consist of -- coffee. I remember being in Paris last fall with Kate and the Garrets and Susan. We spent a few days there on our way back from our vacation in Russia. The McDonald's on the *Champs-Élysées* was awesome. It was huge. It had a counter like this one that sold the usual Mickey Dee stuff, and then a second counter that was a coffee bar and *pasteria*. Their *Café Americana* was great!

We've *got* to go back to Paris. I was there thirty years ago when I worked as a contractor to the DIA. I forgot how much I loved it. The atmosphere, the ambiance, the Parisians make it very special. And contrary to popular American opinion, the French *do* like us.

We get our coffees and find a reasonably quiet spot. In plain view of the world, but away from the larger groups of students hanging out and/or studying. I do like college kids. "What do you want to know, Nick?"

"You know the drill. Start at the beginning and describe the conversation as nearly verbatim as you can." He discretely sets a small digital recorder on the table between us and hits a button. A red LED comes on.

I tell Nick about our walk in the park -- Big Creek Park -- yesterday. I tell him again about the fact that Greg and Rachel have already picked out the next tower. I remind him that they've said it will hit a house or a building. And I tell somewhat agitatedly that they intend to destroy it next week if Vista Tel doesn't start responding.

Nick is calm. I'm getting more agitated. "Nick, Greg wants me to drive. I don't think I want to do that."

"You've got to."

"No, I don't think I've 'got to.' How about you *want me to*?"

"No, I think 'got to' is the right phrase. You've been in this business before. I don't have to remind you why we do it. You know that we need to identify this new player. You know that that will only happen if you immerse yourself in this role completely. Gregory and Rachel must believe that you are one of them. You must have their complete trust. You've 'got to' do this."

I shouldn't be, but I'm a little incredulous. "You're just going to let this happen?"

"Yes."

"But what about their collateral damage? What if there are people in this house or building or whatever it is?"

"We'll deal with that. You need to identify the location of the tower so that we can be proactive."

"Actually, that won't be hard. We know it's Vista Tel. We know it's near Lorain. And we know it's near a busy exit on Route 2."

And Nick almost nonchalantly switches topics. "So, tell me about the new guy." God, but he is smooth. It's almost irritating. He reminds me of me when I was in the business.

I tell him that Greg wouldn't name him. All he'd say is that this new guy works for another cell phone company. He said that this other cell phone company supposedly wants to help us drive Vista Tel out of business.

I explain to Nick that I acted as though I didn't like this whole deal. I tell him that I told Greg I thought that this guy could be an undercover cop. That he could be setting us up, gathering evidence to bust us.

I tell him how I tried to use my anger as a lever to find out more, but how Greg didn't bite. He simply would not divulge any more about the guy.

"Anything else? Anything?"

"Yeah, actually there was. Greg said that this new guy was communicating with Rachel and Rachel only. He said that they would be communicating with TracFones."

"That makes sense, Cap'n. Things have changed a little since you were in the business. Cell phones have changed the world. The bad guys like to use disposable or stolen cell phones. They use them once and destroy them. They're virtually untraceable. And virtually impossible to monitor."

"That makes sense. What do you want me to do? Try to find out where they're getting these phones?"

"The more information we have, the better. We have to identify this new player. He can lead us even further into this maze."

Much as I hate to say it, I'm excited. Spy vs. Spy, from *Mad Magazine*. I loved it when I was a kid. Do they still even publish that? I guess I still love the idea of Spy vs. Spy. "I'll do two things over the weekend: find out more about the phones, and find out more about the site."

And Nick, as nonchalant as ever, says, "Please note that I said 'virtually' before. You *do* know the meaning of virtually?"

"Yes, I do."

"You'd be amazed at what we can do with just a little information."

"No. I wouldn't."

CHAPTER 73

(Gregory)

"Let's go check out our next tower, 'My little chickadee.'"

In the movie *White Christmas*, Bing Crosby said to Danny Kaye, "Pushy, pushy..." I'd love to say it to Rachel right now, but instead I say, "We can't go now. There's too much activity around there."

"'Wait a minute, wait a minute. You ain't heard nothin' yet!' We'll drive out that way, drive by the site, and then go get something to eat. After dark, we'll go back and check things out. Sounds like a great way to spend a Friday night."

Like Bing said, "Pushy, pushy..." Oh well. Pushy but hard to argue with. "How about we leave the 'check out the site' part optional? We'll do it *if* it's quiet around there."

"I really want to say, 'Frankly, my dear, I don't give a damn.' But, you're right, Greg. We'll leave checking out the site optional. Do you know any place good to eat around there? I'm buying."

Damn her incessant movie quotes. I do know a place: Red Clay on the River in Vermilion. "As a matter of fact, I do. Do you like fish?"

We take Rachel's Jeep. I drive. We get off of Route 2 at the Broadway exit, and I drive as slowly as I dare past the house and the insurance office. The tower sits a little way back between the two of them. Rachel looks absolutely in awe.

"Zowee."

I drive a little way past the site, make a u-turn in a Doctor's office parking lot and go back toward the exit. I pull into the gas station across the road from the insurance office, house and tower. "I have to go pee. Not really, but it'll give you a chance to stretch your legs and look around."

"'Sometimes there's so much beauty in the world I feel like I can't take it, like my heart's going to cave in.'"

When I get back, Rachel is sitting in the Jeep looking at the tower. She has a smile on her face that's hard to describe. Kind of like a kid who just opened a Christmas present and found a toy she's dreamed of but never expected. Cute. Rachel *is* cute.

I get in and we head north through Lorain and then along the lake toward Vermilion. We miss most of the *barrio* this way, but Rachel is surprised at the number of storefronts that have Spanish signs. I tell her the story about the steel mill importing Puerto Ricans to work the mill during World War II. She finds my little history lesson interesting.

And she finds the difference between Lorain and Vermilion even more interesting. In fifteen miles we go from typical rust belt mill town to very upscale tourist area. She's never been to Vermilion before. We take a quick driving tour of the downtown area and then go back across the bridge to the Red Clay. It's touristy, but they have good fish, and the springtime view of the Vermilion River is pretty neat. We take a quick walk along the public dock, McGarvey's Landing. There are no boats in the water yet, but Rachel is impressed. It's getting cool though, as evening approaches. We head into the Red Clay.

* * *

The perch at the Red Clay is good. Very good.

But we're both antsy. Rachel is anxious to get back to tower number three. I'm anxious to avoid going there again tonight.

We don't talk much during dinner. Before long, it's getting dark and we're on our way to the tower.

* * *

"There are entirely too many people around, Rachel."

"I still want to say, 'Frankly, my dear, I don't give a damn.' But you are still right, Greg. Can we come back tomorrow night? Late?"

"That works, 'My little chickadee.'" And she kisses me. Very soundly.

"Zowee."

CHAPTER 74
(Mirsab)

I do not like it, but I must call Gregory and Rachel. I must explain my outburst at Rachel. I must reassure them that I am their ally and not their enemy.

I use the first of my newly purchased TracFones to call one of the units that I sent to Gregory. Rachel answers. "Hello?"

"Hello, Rachel. It is Justin. I am glad that you answered. I must apologize to you for my behavior the last time we talked."

"'Well, nobody's perfect.' I do think that you went a little crazy just because I called you on your landline, though."

"It was not a landline. Rachel, you have no idea of the power of the government. They monitor telephone conversations for key words, for repeated themes. They will find us and arrest us, if we are not very careful. That is why I sent you the TracFones on which we are now talking. If we use them one time and destroy them, it will make it very difficult for the government operatives. I overreacted, though. I am sorry."

And her answer indicates that I have placated her. At least, I think so. More idioms! "'Et cetera, et cetera, et cetera.' Let's just move on, okay?"

"Okay."

"So, what's up? Why did you call? I thought the TracFones were not to be used lightly."

I really do not understand her at times. "I called to apologize for my behavior. I think it is important that we be allies."

"That's all?"

This may make her more at ease with me. "I would like to ask your address. The three TracFones I sent to Gregory will not last long. I have more that I would like to send, but I want to send them to you rather than to Gregory so that the postal authorities will not become suspicious."

"I can't imagine the kind of mail carriers we have around here thinking about the packages we get or much of anything else. But if it'll make you happy."

"It will. I am ready to write down your address." She gives me what I assume is her home address. Not only will I send the new group of TracFones that I have purchased to this address, but I will give it to Hamad. He may be able to use it to find out more information about her.

"Justin, the reason I called the other day..."

I should have asked her why she called that day. It was foolish of me not to do so. She must have considered it important to break protocol. "Yes, Rachel?"

"Two things, actually. First of all, we have enlisted a new recruit."

"That is marvelous. May I know his name?"

"'Lions and tigers and bears, oh, my!' Greg says I shouldn't, but I'm tired of all this secrecy. He's a sixtyish guy from Lorain by the name of Peter Bradovich. He believes in our cause and wants to help."

This is more very useful information for Hamad. I quickly write down the name. "It is good to know that you are now three. But you said there were two things?"

"'Yeah, baby!' We have selected the next Vista Tel tower. We will destroy it next week if they do not respond to our demands!"

My cell is moving more quickly than I expected. I hope Hamad approves. "What can I do to help?"

"Well, I'm glad you asked. This tower will hit a building when it is brought down, and it is located near a major highway interchange. We want to alert the media as soon as it goes down. That way, we'll get the media coverage we need. They will jam the intersection with all of their mobile units during rush hour. Vista Tel will *not* be able to continue to ignore us!"

Rachel is very excited. "When will this happen? What day and what time?"

"I don't know the day yet. Probably mid-week. I'm thinking just before dawn. Maybe five a.m."

"Please call me as soon as you have decided on a day and time. I will make the necessary advance plans here. When the day comes to destroy the tower, I will await your call telling me that the mission has been accomplished. I will have several media outlets in Cleveland called immediately. We will force Vista Tel to acknowledge us."

"That sounds great, Justin. I knew you would be an asset to our cause."

"What else may I do?"

"That's it for now. I'll call you when we have picked the day and time. And send more phones. We'll need them."

"I shall do that."

"'*Hasta la vista*, baby.'"

CHAPTER 75

Saturday

(Peter)

I'm relatively certain that I have found tower three! I found a website that shows cell phone towers on a Google-like map. You can click on a tower and it tells you who owns it. Amazing.

The amount of information available on the Internet is absolutely mind-boggling. How did we ever get along before the Internet? I'm really glad that Al Gore invented it.

The location that I've found on the website fits Greg's description, and I think I remember it from passing it on the way home from work. Only one way to find out. A little Saturday morning expedition.

* * *

This has got to be it. It sits about a hundred yards north of Route 2 and fifty yards east of Broadway. It's on the edge of an abandoned cornfield, sort of between a rather ramshackle farmhouse and a slightly shabby independent insurance office. If you planned it right, you could hit either the house or the office with the tower.

Greg and Rachel are getting scary. This is going beyond just property damage. Now it's endangering people. I really hope Nick knows what he's doing. I know that he does, of course. This is what they do. But still, I need reassured. I need to talk to Mike about this. I need to talk to Kate about this.

I wonder if Greg and Rachel have thought about how hard it will be to drop the tower where they want. It's not like felling a tree: you can't notch it the direction you want it to fall like a woodsman would do to a tree.

How would I do it? Force applied to the tower when you remove the base bolts. Hmm. One idea: a come-along from as high up on the tower as you can get to the base of one of the fence posts. Maybe. Or steel wedges between the tower flange and the base. Or both. It's a good engineering problem. I'll have to think about it.

* * *

Before I call Nick, I need to confirm this with Greg.

"Hello?"

It's ten o'clock, but I think I just woke him up. "Hi, Greg. It's Peter. Did I wake you?"

"Yeah. I was up pretty late last night. What's up?"

Now's a good time to ask, while he's still half asleep. "I need to know something. I think I just drove by the cell phone tower you were talking about. Our next victim. Is it at the intersection of Route 2 and Broadway, south of Lorain?"

"Uh, why do you need to know?"

"If I'm going to drive, I need to do a little reconnoitering."

"Yeah, that's it. How did you find it?"

"It was pretty easy really. I knew it was Vista Tel, you told me that it was near a busy exit on Route 2, and that it was near

Lorain. I found a website that locates cell phone towers on a map and identifies their owners. I didn't have to be Sherlock Holmes to find it."

"Oh. So, what do you think?"

"Lots of people around. And it'll take some engineering to drop it where you want."

"Yeah, I've been thinking about that. But we'll do it."

"What about this new guy? Can he help? What's his name, anyway?"

"I only know him by his first name, and he has asked me not to tell even that to anyone."

"Sounds kind of paranoid to me."

"Well, that's what he wants."

I decide not to push it. "Okay. I just wanted to verify the site. I'll let you go back to sleep, Greg."

* * *

After I get off the phone with Greg, I call Mike. I cry on his shoulder for a while. I bring him up to date on what's going on. I tell him that his dear old Dad has become an urban terrorist. I tell him about the plan for me to drive the getaway car. And I tell him I'm not sure I want to do this.

He's not a lot more sympathetic than Nick. He says he thinks that for all my complaining, I sound excited. He reminds me that I can still walk away from this.

"No, Mike, I don't think I can."

"Dad, you can, but you won't. Just be careful. Okay?"

"Okay, Mike. I will. I'll stay in touch."

* * *

Maybe I can get some sympathy from Kate. She's sitting by the fire checking her email on her laptop, her pink Sony Vaio. I ask her if I can interrupt. I tell her that I need to talk.

She sets her laptop aside, and I go though the same spiel that I did with Mike. And have about the same result. She worries, too. And she tells me so. But she's starting to find this as exciting as I am. We're both getting sucked into this. We're both becoming urban terrorists!

CHAPTER 76

(Gregory)

It's eight o'clock when the door bell rings. "Hi, Rachel."

"*Ciao*, Greg. Can I come in for a minute before we leave? I have to pee."

"Sure. You know where it is. I even spent some time today doing a little house cleaning."

"I'll just be a minute and we can head out. Do we need to take anything?"

"I already have gloves, flashlights, and bolt cutters in my car. I want to take my car -- it's less noticeable than your Jeep."

* * *

When we get to the site of tower number three, it's after ten p.m., and it's quiet. There is no sign of life at the insurance office or at the house next to it. There are no cars at either place. The only activity is at the gas station across the road, and even that is deserted except for the attendant. He's inside, and really can't see anything going on across the road.

We pull into the insurance company parking lot. It's behind the office, on the opposite side of the building from the road. The only way anyone will see us is if they come behind the building and into the lot. We're a little more exposed here than I would like, but we don't dare walk along the road and back to the tower. This is as good as it'll get.

"Let's go check this out. We'll move low and quick to the side of the fence by the cornfield and hit the ground. Ready?"

We've both worn dark clothes and gloves. Rachel even has a black watch cap on. Her hair's tucked up inside. I have to smile. We look like caricatures of spies sneaking up on their objective, and we do just that. Nobody sees us. When we get to the fence, we hit the ground like a couple of amateur commandos. "I know this is serious stuff, but we really must look like a couple of characters out of a bad spy movie."

She kind of snorts and then starts giggling. I have to try very hard not to join her. "Let's make a door."

The moon is bright enough that we can see what we're doing without flashlights. I use the bolt cutters to cut two two-foot long vertical cuts in the fence a little less than three feet apart. I fold up the flap of fence and we're in.

We crawl up toward the base of the tower. I tell her to keep her butt down and she starts giggling again.

When we finally get there, we move to the side of the tower opposite the parking lot. We're completely invisible -- from the road, the house, the office, the parking lot. We can work here.

I turn on my flashlight and look at the tower base. It's the same design as the others. The tower base is a square steel plate bolted to a concrete pad. But there are five bolts on each side and they are bigger than the other towers. Each lock nut is tack-welded to the bolt. Breaking the welds won't be a major problem, but we'll need a bigger socket.

"Shit. These nuts are bigger than the other towers. We'll have to buy another socket. I didn't bring a tape measure. I think they're about three and a half inches, but I'm not sure. We'll have to come back with a tape measure or a ruler. Shit!"

"No, we won't. 'E.T. phone home.' If he can phone home with junk he collects from a toy box, we can measure these bolts."

Without saying a word, she crawls back to the fence. What is she doing? I want to holler at her, but I don't dare. I watch her scurry back to the car, open the door, disappear for a minute, close the door, and scurry back. In less than a minute, she's back at my side with a sheet of paper from the yellow legal tablet that was in the back seat.

"What?"

"Shush. 'With my brains and your looks, we could go places.' Just watch. Learn."

She folds the sheet of paper into fourths, and carefully tears a corner off. When she unfolds it, there is a hole in the middle big enough to go over the end of the bolt. She lays the paper on the nut with the bolt protruding through the hole, and carefully bends the paper down along each of the six sides of the nut, one at a time. When she's done, she holds the paper up -- a perfect outline of the nut.

"*Viola*! Anything else, 'My little chickadee?'" She looks very smug. And she should.

"That's it! The only thing left to do is to figure out how to make it fall where we want to. Let's get out of here."

"'Listen to them. Children of the night. What music they make.'"

CHAPTER 77

(Mirsab)

Nura's parents are from Qatar. Though they are Wahhabi Sunni Muslims like me, I believe that they follow the Hanbali Madhhab. They came to America perhaps fifteen years ago, but still follow the old ways. Nura's mother comes to the door dressed in a long *Jilbab*. I'm certain that she wears the *Hijab* -- the modest head covering when she goes out in public.

The Qatari speak a dialect that is significantly different from my Syrian dialect. I decide to greet her mother in English. "Good evening. May I speak with Nura, please." I make eye contact only when speaking, and then look down as is the old custom.

I have met her mother before, but she does not remember my name. "I shall see if she is available. May I ask your name?"

"I am Mirsab Bin Saleh al-Fulani. I know Nura from college."

"Ah, yes. Now I remember. Come in, please." She offers her hand. I shake it, bow slightly, and enter their home. It is a beautiful home, decorated with a pleasing mix of Arab and American furnishings.

I don't remember what Nura's father does, but he obviously does it well. Palos Verdes is a very expensive neighborhood, Paseo

233

del Mar is one of its most desirable streets, and their house is one of the nicer ones on the street. I can't even guess at its value.

* * *

I haven't seen Nura in several months. She is as attractive as I remembered. "Hello, Nura. I tried to call your cell phone, but I got someone else."

Her mother is the image of a typically conservative Arab woman, but Nura is the image of the modern American young woman. She has lived in America since she was a child, and looks and talks like it. Her skin and hair and eye color identify her as Arab, but her makeup and clothes identify her as American. She looks exactly like what she is, an MBA candidate from a wealthy family on her way toward a successful career.

Nura has a touch of an accent, but it is very pleasing. "Mirsab, it's good to see you. I'm so sorry you couldn't reach me. I got a new cell phone -- an iPhone. I should have had my old number transferred, but I didn't. They must have reassigned the number. I am sorry. Come back by the pool, please. Can I get you something to drink?"

"Iced tea, if you have it, thank you." We move through their impressive entrance hall, through the huge great room, and out onto the back patio that adjoins a stunningly blue swimming pool overlooking the ocean. I believe it is called an Infinity Pool. She seats me in a white wicker loveseat, and goes into the house to get my tea.

Nura and I shared some classes as undergraduates. We went out a few times, but I was more interested in American women then, and I think she was more interested in American men. My thinking has changed, though. Perhaps hers has as well.

After we got our undergraduate degrees, I went on to graduate school at UCLA and she enrolled at USC. We drifted away from each other. Perhaps it is time to drift back together.

Nura comes back with a tray containing two glasses, a pitcher full of tea and ice and a sugar bowl. "I'll let you pour your own. That way you can add sugar as you like, Mirsab."

"Nura, you look well. How have you been?"

"Busy. As I'm sure you've discovered, grad school is very intense. Being a woman, an Arab woman, in business school puts me at a disadvantage. It really is quite a *boys club*. I have to work extra hard, but I am enjoying it immensely. And you?"

"I don't have the boys club disadvantage that you do, but engineering is, well, engineering. 'Intense' is a good word."

I have had trouble dealing with the American woman, Rachel. My immediate reaction to Nura is very different. She is smart and capable, and very westernized. But somehow, with her, it is acceptable. She seems a fascinating mix of Arab and American, of old and new. The difference in my feelings bears examination.

"Is this a social visit, Mirsab? Or do you have something on your mind?"

"It is both, Nura. To be very bold, as soon as I saw you just now, I thought to myself, 'Why did I allow us to drift apart?' Perhaps we can fix that."

"That takes care of the social visit part. And yes, I would like very much for us to renew our acquaintanceship. And the other reason for your visit?"

Nura is smart. I must be forthright with her. She will either say yes or no. "I need your help. I can not explain why, but I need you to go to a store like the one where you bought your iPhone. I need you to buy four pre-paid TracFones for me."

She looks at me, steadily. She is looking for clues about my motives. If I show nervousness or uncertainty, she will see it in my eyes. I look back at her and say nothing. It was socially unacceptable to look Nura's mother in the eyes, but it is not so with Nura. I wait.

She has made a decision. "Mirsab. I have not seen you in a few months, but I think I know you a little. I trust that you would not ask me to do anything that would endanger me or my family. I will do this for you."

"Thank you, Nura. This was a difficult thing for me to ask. I do not want to jeopardize our relationship, whatever it is, or whatever it may become. However, I simply could not think of anyone other than you to ask."

"I think I should ask why you cannot buy these TracFones yourself, but I think you must have your reasons. I think I will not ask. When do you need them?"

I am relieved. I am very relieved. "This is Saturday. Can you have them by Monday evening? Perhaps we can go out to dinner Monday."

"I can have these TracFones phones by then, and I'd love to go out to dinner. Do you still live in Redondo Beach?"

"I do."

"I'll bring the phones to your house. About seven? Then we can go to dinner from there. You pick the place. But I should warn you that my B-school friends have turned me into a carnivore. I love a good steak!"

CHAPTER 78

Monday

(Peter)

"Peter Bradovich."

"Hi, Captain. Is this a good time to talk?"

It's Greg. And no, it's not a good time. I'm a little paranoid about doing non-business stuff during business hours. And I'm more than a little paranoid about talking to Greg with any other people around. What we are doing must not get out. "It's never a good time when I'm at work, but what's up?"

"I just thought you'd like to know. Vista Tel is still ignoring us. We made a decision to take down the next tower Wednesday night. I want you to drive."

I need to know more. "Greg, can I call you back during my lunch hour?"

"Yeah. That'll be okay."

"Is this a good number? It's your cell phone, I think."

"Yeah, it is. I'll keep it with me until you call."

"Okay. Great. Talk to you in a couple of hours."

I'm not surprised that they -- we -- are doing it Wednesday night. But it's still a little upsetting to actually be a part of doing this. Talk about knots in your stomach.

What do I have to do when I call him back? Find out what part Rachel is going to play. I know she'll be involved. Find out if the new guy knows yet. I need to know what part he is playing. And tell Nick, as soon as possible.

* * *

At lunchtime, I head for Big Creek Park. It's overcast today, but still pleasant. It's still a good day to go to the park. The guys at work know I like to do this, so it works out well.

I call Greg as soon as I get there. "Hi, it's Peter. Let's talk about the next project."

"I thought talking about this stuff on the phone made you squirrelly."

He's got a good point. I wouldn't be at all surprised if HS was monitoring my phones, and I don't have a problem with that. Gregory would, though! "I guess I'm getting more comfortable with the subject. Let's avoid using key words though."

"Okay. I can do that. Anyway, here's the plan. I want you to drive. Rachel insists on coming with me. Her frickin' bossiness is really getting on my nerves, but I don't know how to disinvite her."

No surprise there. He tells me his plan for how the job will come down. He finishes by bitching again about Rachel's pushiness. "That's your problem, I guess. Actually, it may be a good idea to have her with you. I think this will be a two-man job."

"Why do you say that, Cap'n?"

"Getting the tower to go where you want is going to be a challenge. Have you given it any thought?"

"No, not really. Maybe a rope?"

"Well, where do you *want* it to go? You said it's near a house and an office building."

"I want to drop the tower between the farmhouse and the insurance office, but Rachel wants to hit something! I talked her out of hitting the house because I think somebody might still live there. She says she'll settle for the office. Rachel will be pissed, but I'm still going to try for the empty space between the house and the office."

"So, how are you going to do that?"

"I'm not sure. Maybe a rope?"

I tell him my ideas. "I've been thinking about it, and I've got a couple of ideas, Greg. You can put tension on the tower with a come-along and pound wedges in between the steel plate and the concrete base as you loosen the bolts on the side away from where you want the tower to go."

"That sounds like a plan. Do you have any of the stuff you're suggesting, or do we have to go buy it?"

"Yeah. Actually, I've got it all. I have a come-along from some project I did at some time in the past, and I have some steel wedges that I used to use for splitting wood."

"That's frickin' great!"

"My concern is that that's a lot of stuff to carry. And a lot of stuff to deal with at one time. That's why I think it's a two-man job."

"I guess maybe Rachel *will* come in handy."

"Question. What's the new guy doing?"

"Justin lives in California. His role will be to call the Cleveland media as soon as the tower comes down. If we time it right, they will be on their way to the site as we are making our getaway!"

I can't believe he just said that! Justin. California. Nick needs to know this! "Greg, I've got to get back to work. Think about some of the things we just talked about. We'll talk again before we do the deed."

I say goodbye and leave Greg to ponder my ideas.

* * *

My next call is to Nick.

He answers on the first ring. He must have had his phone in his hand.

"Nick Patridis."

"Hi, Nick. Peter Bradovich."

"That's what my caller ID says. I was just getting ready to call you. I figured it would be your lunchtime, and I hoped you'd be out and about."

"I just finished talking to Greg. I've got some important stuff to pass on." He listens carefully as I recount my conversation with Greg. He asks a lot of questions about Justin. Both about what I know from talking with Greg, and about what I think. About my impressions.

"I can't add much more detail. Greg just wouldn't say a lot. I do question why California. That seems a long way away for a competing cell phone company."

He agrees, and he gives me a new mission. He wants me to try to get a number from one of the TracFones.

"I'll see what I can do, Nick. I have another concern, though. Greg says he is going to aim for the space between the farmhouse and the insurance office, but I'm not sure he can pull it off. I'm worried that there might be people living in the farmhouse."

"There are. Husband, wife and three young kids."

"Nick, we've got to *stop* this!"

"No, we don't." And he explains that it is their plan to evacuate the family before the tower comes down. He says that we have to let this happen. We have to know who Justin is. We have to find out who else is involved.

I ask him how in God's name he is going to evacuate the family without word leaking out that Homeland Security knew the tower was going to come down. He has a simple answer: "We lie. And we convince the family to lie."

CHAPTER 79

(Gregory)

I called the Captain on my way to school. He basically blew me off. He said he'll call me back at lunch time. I do manage to get in the fact that tower three comes down Wednesday night. That should motivate him to call me back quickly.

* * *

My controls class was over at noon, and as I was walking back to my car, my phone rang.

It was Peter. He wanted to know all about the plans for Wednesday night.

I told him that I want him to drive. I explained that the plan is for him to drop Rachel and me off behind the insurance office, and then for him to hang out somewhere nearby until we call him on the walkie-talkies. He's more than a little surprised that Rachel's going to help me bring the tower down. I explain that I really don't have a lot of choice in the matter, that she insists.

Peter has a couple of good ideas about how we can make the tower fall in the direction I want. He'll even supply the stuff we need. I knew he was going to be a valuable addition to our group.

He wanted to know what part Justin is going to play, and I told him about the plan to call Justin as soon as the tower goes down. I explained how he'll be standing by to call the media from California while we're boogying.

Unfortunately, I not only said "California," I said "Justin" as well. I just got a little excited. Big frickin' deal. Justin will just have to get over it!

Peter didn't seem to react to the name Justin or to California.

As we said goodbye, I was wondering how Rachel and I are going to carry all this shit from the parking lot to the tower and back again.

* * *

Rachel is waiting for me when I get home. She says we've got to call Justin and tell him the plan so he'll be ready to alert the media. I agree.

We go in the house, and I get us each a beer while she goes into my office to get one of the TracFones.

She comes back, sits down on the couch with the phone and the beer, and dials the number on the label. Justin has a label on each phone that tells the order to use them in, and the number to call. He's efficient, if nothing else.

Rachel gets a baffled look on her face and says, "Oh, I must have the wrong number. I was calling Justin."

Pause. An even more baffled look, and, "Is this 424-555-6773?"

Another pause, and, "Uh. Okay. Sorry. Bye."

I have to ask, "What?"

"That was so weird. Some girl answered the phone. She said she didn't know anyone named Justin. So I hung up. I dialed the right number. *Now* what? How do we get in touch with Justin?"

I tell her I don't know. We check the labels on the phones. There is a definite pattern. Each phone has a label that shows the very next phone number. Our phone ending with the number 6772 is to call 6773. Our phone ending with the number 6774 is to call 6775, and so on. All the numbers make sense. The girl who answered the phone doesn't.

We sit here, drinking our beers and trying to figure out what to do next. I finish mine, and ask Rachel if she wants another one. "Might as well. 'Can't dance.'"

And the TracFone rings!

Rachel answers it. She listens hard for several minutes. Then she says, "Okay, Justin. That all makes sense. We were really worried when she answered the phone and said she didn't know you."

Another pause. I'm really getting curious. What is going on here?

Then, "The reason I called in the first place was to tell you that tower three will come down Wednesday night -- or actually Thursday morning -- about five a.m. our time. What time is that for you?"

Another frickin' pause. Shit. This is really frustrating. "The tower is at the interchange of Ohio Route 2 and Broadway Avenue in Lorain. I don't know the exit number."

Crap. I should have told her I want to listen. Next time we'll figure out a way to do that. "Okay, so you'll be up and ready for our call?"

Come on! "Okay. Be expecting our call Thursday morning, and be ready to call every media outlet you can think of. '*Hasta la vista*, baby.'"

"Hearing half a conversation is driving me nuts! What's going on?"

Rachel explains. "The girl who answered the phone is Justin's part-time cleaning lady, Nura. Her English is not as good as it sounds, and she knows Justin only as Mr. Brown."

"That's weird."

"He said she usually does not answer the phone, but she was dusting his desk when one of the several phones laying there started to ring. She knew he was in the shower, and she panicked about him missing a call. She got confused when I asked for Justin."

"Nura? Did she sound like a foreigner? In California I would have expected a Hispanic cleaning lady, but Nura doesn't sound Spanish."

"I thought I heard a slight accent, but she didn't sound Hispanic. Whatever. Justin said that he has reprimanded her and told her to never answer the phone again, or he would fire her. There will be no reoccurrences. I think he was kind of harsh."

"Like you said, whatever. What else did he have to say?"

"We're supposed to destroy the phone I just used. Justin said to not just throw it away, but to destroy it so it can't be reused or reprogrammed. He's sending more phones to my place. We should have them tomorrow or the next day."

"More phones. I'd really like to know which company is paying him."

"By the way, we were right, Justin is in California, or at least on the west coast. When I said that the tower would come down at about five a.m. our time, he said that would make it about two a.m. his time."

"So why does a west coast company want to help us?"

"I don't know, 'My little chickadee.' The good news is that he will be waiting for our call. He will call all of the Cleveland TV and radio stations, and he'll call the newspapers just for good measure. He told me that he has ways of doing this virtually simultaneously."

"This guy's got to have some high tech shit."

"I agree. Enough terrorism for one night. Let's kick back and watch some TV. Come sit by me."

CHAPTER 80

(Mirsab)

Nura had brought me the telephones I asked her to purchase. I expressed my gratitude, and I asked her to wait while I went into the bathroom to change clothes before we went to dinner.

* * *

When I came out of the bathroom, Nura told me that she answered one of my many TracFones. I was furious! Women! "What do you mean, you answered the telephone? You must never do that again! Which telephone did you answer? What did the caller say?"

She looked shocked. "It was a girl -- an American girl. She wanted to talk to someone named Justin. I told her that there was no Justin here. She was certain that she was calling the right number. She said to tell Justin that Rachel called."

"Leave me. Wait in the living room. I must call her back immediately! Which telephone did you answer?"

She went over to my desk and picked one up. "This one. What is going on, Mirsab? What is this about?"

"I will explain later. I must undo the damage you have done first. Leave me, please."

I close the door on Nura. My apartment is an open arrangement. Nura is in the large space overlooking the ocean that contains the living, cooking, and dining areas. The door separates that area from the bedroom and office area in the rear. I sit at my desk and take a moment to meditate and calm myself. I call the number that shows on the caller ID of the telephone that Nura answered. Rachel answers with a very tentative, "Hello?"

I identify myself, and I quickly explain that Nura is my housekeeper. I do my best to repair the damage that Nura has done. After a few moments of explanation, Rachel indicates that she understands, and I can hear in her voice that she is somewhat placated.

We briefly discuss the location of the next tower and the timetable for destroying it.

I can find the location using Google maps, and then use a Google add-on that I know of to find the latitude and longitude. I will need this information to notify the media in Cleveland. I must also give this information to Hamad as soon as possible.

I assure Rachel that I will be waiting for her telephone call when the tower is destroyed. I explain that I will immediately notify all of the major media outlets in the Cleveland area. I imply that I have the technology to notify them all simultaneously. I do not have such technology. I will simply call each television station with the same short message. I will tell them the street address, and the latitude and longitude of the tower. I will tell them that it has just been destroyed and that they must dispatch their news crews immediately.

The damage repaired, I say goodbye.

Now I must calm myself to face Nura.

* * *

I open the bedroom door and find Nura staring out the window at the ocean. She looks troubled.

"Nura, I am sorry."

"Mirsab, your behavior just now bordered on inexcusable. I am not some shepherd girl from the hills of Syria. I am an American. I was raised here, I was educated here. I am your equal, and I demand to be treated with respect. If you cannot do that, we can never be anything beyond two individuals who share a common heritage."

"I am truly sorry, Nura. I know you are my equal. I accept that. I like that. I have not lived here as long as you have, but I have lived here long enough that I can never go back. I could never be happy with a 'shepherd girl.' I find you fascinating, challenging, beautiful. Please forgive me."

"You must explain that telephone call to me. Who is Justin? Why were you so upset?"

"When we talked at your house, you said that you knew I would not ask you to do anything that would endanger you or your family. Answering that telephone could have done just that."

She looks at me expectantly. "Go on…"

I must convince her. "Nura, I am involved with a group of Americans in Cleveland, Ohio. I am serving as the conduit between them and the Arabs in America who are planning the jihad to come."

I am very careful to mask my feelings about the coming jihad from Nura. I am not certain that she is sympathetic to our cause. She is too Americanized to really understand our goal. "I really have no choice in what I am doing. My family in Syria might be harmed if I do not perform this task."

I think she believes me. She looks pained that I am in this position. She looks like she might hug me. Or kiss me. She does neither, though. She says, "Mirsab, I need time to process this. When you asked me to buy the TracFones, I knew that you were involved in something I might not approve of -- or even understand. I need to think about this before we do anything more."

"I understand, Nura. Take what time you need. I pray that you will understand my situation. Be that as it may, I must ask if you would still like to go out to dinner? I have made reservations at a restaurant called the Charthouse. I am told that they have excellent steaks."

"I know the Charthouse. You're right, they do have great steaks, but it's expensive. I thought you were just a poor grad student. Can you afford it?"

"No. I can not afford it. I *am* a poor grad student. But I would like very much to take you there."

"Well, a girl's got to eat, Mirsab. Let's go."

CHAPTER 81

Wednesday

(Peter)

I live fairly near tower number three, but Greg and Rachel live a substantial distance away, so we decided to meet at a truck stop west of Cleveland. They will leave their car there and I'll drive the Denali to the tower. It's got plenty of room for people and tools. Their car parked at a truck stop late at night will attract no attention whatsoever.

It's just at two a.m. when I see Greg's beat up Honda pull in to the truck stop. I flash my lights so he knows where I am. He drives back to the side of the truck stop, pulls in beside me, and shuts off his lights and engine. As Rachel gets out of the passenger side, I roll down the window and tell her that the back of the Denali is unlocked. They can dump their tools in there. Rachel walks back and opens the Denali's tailgate. Greg opens the Honda's trunk. As they transfer the tools, I watch them in the rear view mirror. They are both dressed completely in black: pants, sweatshirts, watch caps, even gloves. Everything but camouflage face paint. I can't decide if they look menacing or silly.

Everything is moved: pipes, bolt cutters, come-along, rope, a dark canvas gym bag kind of thing that I assume contains the wedges, hand sledge, flashlights and other little stuff. They close the

Honda's trunk and the Denali's tailgate. They both head for my passenger door. Rachel passes Greg, gets there first, opens the door, and slides in. Greg gets in the back seat, looks a little peeved that Rachel is riding shotgun, but wisely doesn't say anything.

The truck stop has an all night diner attached. "Anybody want coffee or anything before we leave?"

Rachel says, "I'd love some coffee."

Looking a little surly, Greg says, "I don't think we should go inside dressed like this."

I'm dressed normally, on purpose. I've told Greg and Rachel that while I'm driving around waiting for them to do the tower; I don't want to attract attention by looking like a commando. "I can go in. What do you want?"

I go into the diner to get three coffees: me and Rachel black, Greg a cream and two sugars. Sitting at the counter is -- Nick!

We make eye contact. He shakes his head "no" almost imperceptibly, and looks away. As I wait for my coffees, he looks at his bill, leaves three dollars on the counter, gets up and walks out the door. Through the window, I see him go around the corner toward where we are parked. I know he's going to check out Rachel and Greg.

* * *

I open my door, and hand the coffees in to Rachel. "Did some guy walk past here?"

Rachel answers, "Yes, but I don't think he saw us. We had the lights off. He kept walking and went back toward those eighteen-wheelers. I didn't see which one he got in."

He didn't get in any of them, I'm sure. And he did see them, I'm equally sure.

We pull out and head west toward our target. Knowing that Nick is around, I feel better. I'm sure he's not alone. I'm not alone.

* * *

Rachel pulls a cell phone out of the front pocket of her black hoodie, and puts it in the cup holder on the center console. "I want to leave this with you, Cap'n. It's the phone we're supposed to use to call Justin when the tower has come down. I don't want to take a chance on losing it or damaging it while I'm crawling around at the tower."

"Is there any reason I can't call him as soon as you call me on the walkie-talkie? I can call him while I'm on my way to pick you up. That way, he'll be calling the media a couple of minutes sooner."

Greg says, "Good idea. Do it."

Well, this will sure make getting a cell phone number for Nick easier.

* * *

It's about 2:45 as I pull into the driveway at the insurance office and drive around back. The parking lot is completely deserted. I also notice that there are no cars at the farmhouse next door, but I don't say anything. Greg points to a spot about in the middle of the fence and says, "Stop so the back door is even with there."

"Back door or tailgate?"

Somewhat sharply, he says, "Okay. Tailgate." He's nervous.

I stop as directed, and shut off the engine. The lights stay on -- built in delay -- I quickly override it. And I hit the switch to disable the dome light while I'm at it. It's virtually pitch black here, and I want to keep it that way.

Without either saying a word, Rachel and Greg get out. She opens the tailgate while he goes to the fence. She starts carrying tools as he kneels down and bends up a flap of chain link fence.

They have obviously rehearsed this. In less than two minutes they are inside and around on the far side of the tower. Even I can't see them. A flashlight flashes for just a second. That's the signal for me to leave. I start the engine and slowly pull out. When I get near the street, I turn on my lights. There are no cars around. Nobody sees me leave.

Well, that may not be so. I have a feeling that some of Nick's buddies see me leave.

* * *

I drive north on Broadway. I can't go too far. We have tested the walkie-talkies. They're only good for about a mile. I don't dare get out of range. I change my mind. I pull into an automobile body shop parking lot, turn around, and go back to the gas station across from the insurance office. It's open. I decide to hit the restroom and get some junk food to keep me occupied while I'm waiting.

I've been to many out of the way, open late at night gas stations. I don't believe I've ever walked into one and found an NFL linebacker tending the till. If this guy is not Homeland Security, I'm not a sailor. He only says, "What do you need?" I tell him I need to pick up some junk food to nibble on to stay awake, and I need to use the men's room. He says, "No problem," and hands me a key on a two-foot long piece of plastic. He says, "We only have one restroom. It's outside and around to the right."

I thank him and head for the restroom. The short walk gives me a chance to look across the street at the tower. I can see nothing. Rachel and Greg are well hidden there.

After I get rid of the coffee I drank, I go back inside. The linebacker eyes me. I'm sure he has a description of me. I look back at him pointedly, turn and go pick out my goodies: some Combos, a package of cheese and peanut butter crackers, a Snicker's bar, and a Diet Pepsi. I pay the linebacker. He hands me my change and thanks me.

252

I get back in the car with my goodies, pull out, and head north again. There is a Chiropractor's office just north of here. It's where I will wait for the next hour or so.

CHAPTER 82

(Gregory)

Rachel and I settle into our workplace. I set up the small LED work light and point it at the base of the tower. We're getting good at this. Experience matters, I guess. This one is similar to the two previous ones. It has bigger bolts, with one more nut per side, but otherwise, it's identical. The lock nuts are tack welded, but the pipe extension on the breaker bar works just fine to break the welds.

After I take off all twenty locknuts, I sit back and survey the tower. In a low voice, I tell Rachel, "I don't think the come-along will work. I brought rope to loop around the column, but it'll just slip down. I was hoping there would be rivets or bolts or something to hold it in place, but there is nothing that we can reach."

Without saying a word, Rachel gets up and walks over to where the ice bridge meets the equipment building. She jumps up, grabs the cables, and before I fully realize what she is doing, she's sitting on top of the ice bridge with one leg dangling over either side, like she's sitting on a horse. She holds her arms straight out at her sides, and in a loud stage whisper says, "I'm king of the world!"

She scoots along the ice bridge to the tower, and says, "I put two Crescent wrenches in the ditty bag. Toss them up to me. I'm going to unbolt the ice bridge so it won't interfere with the tower going over. The ice bridge brackets are welded to the tower. They'll hold your rope in place. Go secure the come-along to the fence and extend it while I unbolt the ice bridge."

I'm so surprised at her resourcefulness that I do what she says. The come-along needs to be fastened to a fence post west of the tower. The fence posts here are easily seen from the insurance office parking lot. I don't like it, but I carry the come-along and one piece of half-inch rope to the fence. I tie the rope to the base of the fence post with a bowline, and tie another bowline in the free end of the rope to make a loop for the come-along. I hook the come-along in the loop, release its clutch, and start pulling it out as I crawl back towards the tower. Suddenly, there are headlights!

A car pulls into the parking lot, moving slowly. Shit! It's a cop! If he aims his headlights toward the tower, he'll light me up like a deer caught in his headlights. I hit the ground. My heart is racing.

He hits his high beams and slowly starts to make a u-turn. His lights sweep over my back, but he doesn't stop. He continues to turn and his lights sweep across the equipment building, the ice bridge, and then the tower, but he doesn't stop. He keeps turning, and slowly moves away from us. In a minute he's back out on the road and gone. I can breathe again.

I crawl back to the tower. Rachel is still riding the ice bridge like a horse. "It's good to be the king!" She pauses. And chuckles. "To use what *used* to be your favorite word, I was so frickin' scared I almost peed my pants. I just sat here! Was that a cop?"

"Yeah. I saw the light bar on his car. He could have seen either of us if he looked. I think he was probably just making a quick sweep to look for kids parking or whatever. No cars meant all was well. It never occurred to him to look on the ground or up there. We were lucky. Extremely lucky. Let's just get this done."

I toss her the other piece of half-inch rope. While she loops it around the tower, and ties it to itself with a sheet bend, I get the come-along and hand her the free hook. When it's secure, I engage the clutch and work the handle to pull it tight. It looks pretty puny compared to the tower. I don't know if it'll help much, but it can't hurt.

"Let's start unbolting the base." I get the steel wedges out of the bag and jam them between the base plate and the concrete on the side opposite the house and office. I cover their exposed ends with several layers of rags, and whack them as hard as I can with the hand sledge. I don't like the noise, but they jam in place.

We want the tower to go west. I should say I want the tower to go west. Rachel wants it to go a little south or north of west. My way will put it right between the house and the office building, while Rachel's way will hit one or the other. I'm driving -- it'll go west. The square base plate is aligned the way I want it, the sides of the square face the cardinal points of the compass. I remove the ten bolts on the north and south sides, and stop to take a breather. "Boy, I wish I'd have brought some water!"

Rachel has climbed down from the ice bridge while I've been unbolting. She reaches into the canvas bag and comes out with a bottle of water! "'Here's looking at you kid.'" She tosses it to me.

"You're amazing."

With a smile, she says, "'The stuff that dreams are made of.'"

After I take a long drink of water, I tell her, "This is it!" I loosen the four bolts on the west side about two turns each.

Then I do the same to the four bolts on the east side -- and I hit the two wedges as hard as I can. I still don't like the noise. "Crank the come-along."

She does. "Is anything happening?"

"I don't know yet." Another two turns on the nuts on the east side, and a couple more whacks on the wedges. Another crank on the come-along.

Another two turns, a couple more whacks, and another crank.

"Well?"

"The wedges are going in. I can't see it, but the tower must be starting to lean. I'm going to take the east nuts all the way off.

When I give you the okay, crank the come-along, and I'll drive the wedges in!"

"'This isn't a dream! This is really happening!'"

I do it. She does it. I do it. The tower starts to go!

The cables pull out of the equipment building. They are accompanied by flashes and crackles and smoke, the lovely sights and sounds of electronics being destroyed.

The tower topples slowly and majestically. Toward the house! Oh, crap! It's going to hit the house! Rachel wins! God, I hope the house is empty. I don't want to hurt anybody. That's not the plan.

After what seems like hours rather than seconds, the tower hits the house. The last two towers made a loud whump when they hit the ground. This one makes a horrible crashing sound as it destroys the north wall of the house. And it creates a new bunch of fireworks -- more flashes and crackles and smoke. I didn't notice before, but the electricity to the house comes into the northwest corner, and one of the antennas caught the power line!

The flashes and crackles and smoke don't stop. Flames get added to the mix. The house is old, the wood is dry. It's catching fire!

Rachel is standing there completely transfixed. Her mouth is open, and she's panting a little. "Rachel! Call Peter. Start gathering up our tools. We've got to get out of here!"

She doesn't move. I yell, "Rachel! Now! Give me the walkie-talkie! Let's go!"

I push the call button on the walkie-talkie. Peter answers immediately, "Yeah?"

"It's done. The towers down. We hit the edge of the house. It's on fire. Come get us. Quick."

"Oh, shit. I'm on my way -- two minutes."

We start ferrying our stuff through the hole in the fence to the edge of the parking lot. I don't think the gas station attendant can see the fire yet, but he had to have heard the crash.

Oh, my God! The cops! I don't know if it's the same one. I can't tell. It doesn't matter. He stops on the road with his lights flashing. He opens his door, and he is illuminated by his dome light. He has his microphone to his mouth. He's calling for backup.

"Rachel. Cops. We're screwed. Leave everything. Head for the cornfield. Now!"

CHAPTER 83

(Mirsab)

Dinner with Nura Monday night was marvelous. The food was stupendous. As the evening progressed, Nura recovered from her displeasure with me, and we truly enjoyed being with each other. She is a wonderful young woman.

There are some aspects of life in America that far surpass what is available in Syria, or virtually anywhere else in the Arab world. The very good restaurants here are truly a wonder. Unless one is a sheik in Abu Dubai perhaps, there is nothing like the Charthouse in my world. We can learn from the Americans in this area.

The meal we had was quite expensive even by American standards. The average American does not eat at a place like the Charthouse. I can afford to do this only rarely. Monday night was a financial sacrifice worth making.

Dinner lasted nearly two hours. After dinner, we walked along The Strand at Hermosa Beach. We held hands. It was a most memorable evening. After dark, I took her back to my home to pick up her car. We said good night on the street next to her car, and she kissed me. I was in awe.

* * *

This evening, I am still in awe. Nura has affected me in a way that I have never felt before. I am confused. Do I want to be Syrian? Do I want to be American? Do I want jihad? Do I want America to become like Syria? Do I want Syria to become like America? I only know that I want to be with Nura.

I am to meet Nura at a Starbucks coffee house near where she works as a part time intern. We are going to go to buy more cell phones. She has made it clear that she does not want to see jihad come to America. But she has agreed to help me. Because I lied. Because she thinks my family is in danger.

We are going to go to Radio Shack first where we will each buy four TracFones. Then we will go to Wal-Mart and do the same thing. That will be a total of sixteen cell phones, eight for the Americans, and eight for me. That will be enough for eight more conversations, sufficient for some time, I think.

I park nearby and walk into the Starbucks. Nura is already sitting down and drinking some sort of creamy coffee drink. I approach her table and hold out my hand. She reaches up, puts her hand behind my neck, pulls me forward, and kisses me on the cheek. I blush a little. She is very Americanized. I like it very much.

I go to the counter, order a double espresso, pay, and wait until it is prepared. I stop at the condiment table and pick up a stirrer, some raw sugar, and several napkins. I join Nura. She smiles. Her smile is lovely. I am smitten.

"What are you drinking?" I have to make conversation to keep from sitting here and staring at her.

"It's called a caramel macchiato. Horribly rich, and horribly fattening, but I love them."

"May I taste?"

"Sure." She holds it up for me to sip. It is rich -- and very good. I like my espresso better, though.

"You've got foam." She wipes my moustache with her napkin. And smiles.

"Mirsab, after we do our shopping, can we go out for a hamburger? My treat. I so enjoyed Monday night. I want to get to know you better."

"I would like that very much."

* * *

We take Nura's red BMW Z4 Roadster. She knows this area better than I. She drives. She drives fast. The automobile is capable, and so is she. In ten minutes, we are in the parking lot in front of Radio Shack.

I tell Nura about my previous experience at a Radio Shack. I explain that the clerk wanted to sell me everything except what I wanted. She looks at me and smiles. "You've been doing too much engineering and too little living. You're not Americanized enough yet. Do you mind if I do the talking?"

"No, not at all."

We walk in, and she goes directly to the counter. I follow. The somewhat disinterested looking clerk looks up at Nura. She smiles and says, "Do you have eight TracFones in stock?"

"Uh, I don't know. I think so."

"Well, go find out. If you have them, go get them. I want to buy them. Now. Actually, I want to buy four, and my friend wants to buy four. Now. For cash."

The clerk looks stunned. He starts to say something about their other phones and all of the various plans they have. Nura holds a finger to her lips and say "Shhh."

"But…"

"I think I made myself quite clear. If you have eight TracFones, we are going to buy them. If you do not, we are going to go elsewhere. If you can't deal with that rather simple transaction, go get your supervisor, please." She smiles sweetly at him.

He walks into the back room. In about two minutes, another somewhat older clerk emerges from the back room with his arms full of TracFone boxes. "I understand that you want to buy these, ma'am."

"I'm not a 'ma'am,' and yes I do. Ring them up as two separate transactions, please. Four for me, and four for my friend. We will pay cash."

The clerk's badge says Ronald, Store Manager. Ronald does as he is told. We pay him, and collect our change and our phones. And we leave. In less than ten minutes, we're back in the BMW.

"You are amazing!"

"Not really. It's kind of like dealing with a dog or a cat. If you make it clear who is the boss, they will obey you. And not even mind doing it."

"I still think you're amazing."

"Oh well. You impress easily. Let's skip the Wal-Mart and do another Radio Shack. They're easier to get into and out of. I know of one on the way to Marina del Rey. We're having supper at a Fatburger there."

"I still think you're amazing." And I laugh. So does Nura.

It takes us a half hour to drive to the next Radio Shack. We do an almost exact repeat of the first transaction at the second Radio shack. In another ten minutes, we have our sixteen TracFones, and we are on our way to Fatburger. It will be a new experience for me. But a great one, I suspect!

CHAPTER 84

(Peter)

I've been sitting here for almost two hours. I'm starting to get really antsy. What's taking so long? I can't see the tower or much of anything else from here. Should I drive down past the site? Should I call on the walkie-talkie?

And the walkie-talkie buzzes! "Yeah?"

It's Greg. "It's done. The tower's down. We hit the edge of the house. It's on fire. Come get us. Quick."

He's elated -- and scared. "Oh, shit. I'm on my way -- two minutes."

I pull out of the Chiropractor's lot and start to head north on Broadway. I stop almost immediately. Even from fifty yards away, I can see the flashing red and blue lights. The cops are already there! How could that happen? He didn't go past me. He must have been near there when the tower went down -- he saw it happen -- coincidence?

Did he see Greg and Rachel? Did he catch Greg and Rachel? Does he know about what's going on? No. The local police must not have been warned by Homeland Security. Why not? I know why not. Too many players mean too many leaks. HS would have kept this close to their chests.

Shit! He can screw everything up if he busts them. Now what do I do? I don't dare try to go after Greg and Rachel. The local cop will nail me. They are either caught or not caught. They're on their own.

I see the cop get out of his car and head for the house. He hasn't seen Greg and Rachel, or he would be after them. I make a quick u-turn and go back to the Chiropractor's lot. I've got to call Justin, and then decide what to do about Greg and Rachel.

* * *

The walkie-talkie buzzes again. I quickly pick it up, and respond with "I see the cop car. What do you want me to do?" Greg is in a panic, but a controlled panic. "Don't come here. We left everything, and went into the frickin' cornfield. I don't think the cop saw us."

"He didn't. I saw him heading for the house, not for you. He's probably trying to alert the occupants. You're in the cornfield?"

Greg is panting with stress and exertion. He says, "Yeah, the cornfield. I'm not sure, but I think it goes pretty far north. Maybe all the way to that east-west road that intersects Broadway up by where you were waiting."

"I'm back where I was waiting before. When I saw the cop car, I got out of there. Take about six deep breaths and calm down. Let's figure this out. Is Rachel with you?"

He's not panting so bad now. "Yeah, she's here. Scared shitless, too."

"Okay. It's quiet here. We're not caught yet. But I'm sure backup is on the way. Here's the plan."

"I saw the cop using his radio as soon as he stopped. We've got to hurry."

"Yes, we do. But not in panic mode, that'll get us caught. I've got my Denali's GPS System on. I'm looking at the map. The road you're talking about is North Ridge Road, and there are no houses 'till you get there. You guys head north and a little east. The road is less than a half a mile from where you entered the cornfield. I'll drive up there and call you on the walkie-talkie as soon as I check the area out. Now get going."

I don't know how far away the cops and firefighters are. I assume he called for both. I don't hear any sirens yet, but they'll be here quickly, and we've got to be out of here before they show up. Getting caught by the locals will completely screw up Nick's plans.

I pull out of the lot, head north about a quarter mile, and make a right on North Ridge. There are houses here, but they're old, and widely spaced. The houses on the north side of the road are newer and closer together. The south side of the road looks like old farmsteads. I think I can see fields behind the houses. The same cornfield? I'm not sure, but it's possible. I buzz Greg.

Rachel answers with a ragged "Hello?"

"Rachel, are you okay?"

"I think so. Where are you?"

"To quote a dear friend, 'We're not in Kansas anymore.' I'm on the road north of you. And I'm waiting for you."

"How will we find you, Cap'n?"

"I'll find you. Listen carefully. You'll come out of the cornfield into some backyards. I can't tell if there are fences, but I doubt it. All of the houses are dark and there is nobody around. Just walk through one of the yards and out to the road. I'll see you and come pick you up. It'll be easy."

"Easy for you to say..."

I move up to about the third house. There is no ditch, so I pull off the road onto the lawn, shut off the engine, and kill the lights. To anybody driving by, I'll look like a car parked here for the night. I scrunch down and wait. Half a mile -- running -- that should take them about ten minutes. They should be here any minute. I drop the window on the passenger side and listen.

A dog starts to bark. Then two dogs. Then a whole neighborhood full of dogs. Shit. Why do people keep dogs outside? House dogs, I can understand, if you're a dog lover. Outside dogs make no sense. What's the point? But the pointless dogs must hear Greg and Rachel. Lights are coming on. This could get bad.

CHAPTER 85

(Gregory)

After I talk to Peter, we start north. The cornrows run east and west, so going north is hard. I bust through row after row of dry cornstalks. They're left over from last fall, so they're all jumbled up. They're noisy. They're scratchy. It's cool tonight, but I'm getting hot.

I stop and hand the walkie-talkie to Rachel. I take my watch cap off and cram it in my pocket. "You carry the walkie-talkie, so I can use both hands to break through this shit." I take off again.

We go about six rows and Rachel smacks me on the shoulder. "Stop. The Captain's calling. I can't hear." We're both panting hard as she listens intently.

She holds the walkie-talkie up to her mouth. "I think so. Where are you?" She listens again.

"How will we find you, Cap'n?" She puts one hand on her knee and leans forward as she holds the walkie-talkie to her ear with the other hand.

She straightens up and says, "Easy for you to say." She pulls her watch cap off and shakes out her hair. It's damp with perspiration.

"He says we should keep going 'till we hit some backyards up ahead. We're supposed to walk through somebody's yard like we own the joint, and go to the road. He'll pick us up when we get there. I don't like it, but..."

"But I don't think we have a lot of choice. Let's move out."

We take off again, moving as fast as we can. It's getting light in the east, and we can see where we're going, but the ground is uneven, and we're both sort of stumbling along. Me breaking the way, Rachel following with the walkie-talkie. It seems like we've been doing this for hours, but I know it's only been minutes. I stop for a breather. I'm panting hard. Rachel rasps, "What?" I wave my hand in front of my face and keep panting. In a minute, we're both breathing a little easier. I whisper hoarsely, "Let's slow down. Make less noise. We've got to be getting close." We start out again, but more slowly now.

* * *

I think I see lights ahead. Suddenly, we're out of the cornfield and on a rough lawn. I stop.

It's quiet. The houses are about fifty yards ahead. There are a few outbuildings in some of the back yards, and a couple of them have big country-style yard lights. It's open and fairly well lit -- too well lit. But we have no choice. We start forward slowly and quietly.

Behind the house to our left, a dog woofs once. A big dog. In the light cast by the yard light, I see him come out of his doghouse, dragging his chain, so he can't go far. That's good. He looks at us. That's bad. He's thinking, "What are you doing here?" I look at him. I'm thinking, "Go back in your dog house." It doesn't work. He let out another woof. Louder, this time. On our right, another dog noisily drags his chain out of his dog house and answers with a woof. I think loosely translated, his woof mean's "What's up, Spot?" Then he sees us. And starts barking seriously. Spot joins in and we have dogs to the left of us, dogs to the right of us. Was that a song? Jimmy Buffet? No, that was sharks. This is just as bad.

We both break into a run. I see a light come on in the house to our right. Oh, shit. We run faster. I see the road. More lights! More barking! This is not good.

We hit the road and stop. Now what? I look at Rachel. She looks at me. Spot and his buddies are telling the whole neighborhood there are intruders about. I don't know what to do.

I hear sirens in the distance off to our right! Headlights come on about twenty yards to our left! The car's engine starts, and the car comes toward us -- fast! Cops? Are we busted?

The car screeches to a halt next to us. Peter!

We snap out of our deer-in-the-headlights immobility. We each jerk open a door and dive in, me in the back, Rachel in front. Before we can get the doors closed, Peter tromps on the gas, and we're moving. I didn't know a car this big could peel out, but it does, and we're fast leaving Spot and his buddies behind. I watch out the back window for people or front porch lights. I see none. The farmers probably went out their back doors to check with Spot and the gang.

I turn around and see red blinking lights approaching. Peter pulls over -- and a fire truck roars by. Then another. We start moving again.

I sit back and relax just a little. I'm so wound, my teeth are almost chattering. "Do you know where this road goes, Captain?"

"No. And I don't really care. As long as it's away from here. That was entirely too close."

Rachel asks, "Did you call Justin?"

Peter takes a deep breath and lets it out slowly. Then answers, "I did. The media should know what we did by now. Let's put some miles between us and the tower. I've set the GPS to take us back to your car."

CHAPTER 86

(Mirsab)

It is almost three o'clock in the morning when the TracFone rings. I am dozing, and it startles me. "What was the delay?"

A voice I have never heard before says, "Is this Justin?"

I am shocked. I demand, "Who is this?"

I hear car noises in the background. The person almost shouts. "It's Peter. Is this Justin?"

I recover quickly. "Yes. Why are you calling?"

"Greg and Rachel just took down the tower. I'm going to pick them up in about two minutes."

I hear the stress and excitement in his voice. "Was it a success?"

"Yes, they destroyed the tower. It hit a house when it fell, and it has started a fire. The media will love it. But there are cops there already. We're okay so far, but it could get bad. I have to go. I've got to get us out of here before we get caught."

"I will immediately arrange to have all of the Cleveland media outlets notified. That will happen within minutes after I hang up. I will also have an email sent to Vista Tel from a Middle Eastern country. It will reiterate our demands. I will see to it that the media receive copies of this email. You will hear about it from the media, I am sure."

"Excellent. I've got to go get Rachel and Greg, Justin. Wish us luck."

This Peter sounds very much in control, certainly more so than either Rachel or Gregory. "Goodbye, Peter."

This is marvelous. Another tower has been destroyed. The police are already on the scene. The incident will cause much concern among the authorities. The media will demand an investigation. It will divert the attention of many forces. Hamad will be pleased.

* * *

I go to my refrigerator and get a bottle of water. I take a long drink of water, and meditate for a minute to calm my nerves. Then I make my telephone calls. I have a list of the telephone numbers of the four major television stations, the four news-talk radio stations and the three area newspapers. I use the same TracFone to make all of the calls. It is the one that Peter just called. I will destroy it tomorrow.

In each case, the message is identical. I say, "We have just destroyed another Vista Tel cell phone tower. The address is the corner of Broadway Avenue and Ohio Route 2 in Lorain. The coordinates are 41 degrees, 24 minutes, 43.8 seconds, north latitude, and 82 degrees, 9 minutes, 51.5 seconds, west longitude. You must dispatch your news crews immediately! You will soon receive a copy of the email we have sent to Vista Tel."

Some of the numbers I called were answered by a person, some by a recorded message. Some of the people tried to engage me in further conversation, but I did not allow that. I repeated the message one time, and then hung up.

The telephone calls took less than fifteen minutes, but I am exhausted. The stress was extreme. I take another drink of water and rest for a few minutes.

* * *

Now that I have called all of the media outlets, I must call Hamad. He must know that the tower has been destroyed. I must also ask him to have the email sent to Vista Tel.

I have just received another group of disposable cell phones from Hamad. It is a brand of which I have never heard. I use the first one to call Hamad at the number listed on the label of the cell phone. The area code is 843, one with which I am not familiar. Hamad answers immediately but sleepily.

I apologize for awakening him, but when I tell him the news about the tower and ensuing fire, he assures me that it is good that I called. I explain about Peter calling instead of Rachel. Hamad tells me that he has researched Peter Bradovich to some extent, and that he feels it is odd that a man this old and with his background would be involved.

I ask him to explain. He says not now, we have other more important things to deal with, but he warns me to be very careful in talking to Peter. I assure him that I will do so.

Hamad tells me that he will arrange to have the email reiterating our demands sent to Vista Tel. He tells me that all of the major news media, both Cleveland and national, will be copied. I ask him from where the email will originate, and he says that the exact location is not my concern, but that it will come from outside of the United States.

Hamad congratulates me on running my cell as the leaders of the coming jihad would have me do. He assures me that there will be greater things to come if I continue to do so well.

He surprises me by saying "*Tisbah ala Kheer*," and hanging up. Hamad never speaks to me in Arabic. He has reprimanded me for doing so to him. I am pleased that he has chosen to say goodnight in our native tongue. His accent is odd, though. I can't place it.

272

CHAPTER 87

Thursday

(Peter)

I can't believe I've agreed to do this. A "Victory Celebration." Pizza and beer at Rachel's place in Little Italy.

Actually, it may be a good opportunity to do a little informal debriefing. Perhaps I can add to our knowledge base about Rachel, Gregory, and Justin. It may be a chance to find out if anyone else is involved.

I told them I don't drink, but I'd like to come anyway.

God, but I'm tired. I didn't get much sleep last night. It was pushing four by the time I dropped Rachel and Greg off at the truck stop. A little way down the road, I stopped at a gas station and made some phone calls of my own.

First to Kate, to tell her I was okay. She was still up. And relieved, to say the least.

Then to Nick. The last I saw of him, he was at the truck stop where I met Rachel and Greg. He said that I may not have seen him at the cell tower, but he saw us. He watched the whole thing. He didn't go into much detail about where he was or how he watched us. I assume he was sitting somewhere nearby with Night Vision Goggles.

He confirmed that the linebacker at the gas station was one of their people. I was the only person of interest in the gas station all night. All the other visitors to the station have been vetted and found to be innocuous.

Nick also told me that the family who lived in the farmhouse just "happened" to be visiting relatives for the night. They heard about the tower -- and the fire -- on the morning news. It seems that they have much better homeowners insurance than they thought. Though little damage has been done, their home will be declared a total loss, and they will get a very nice insurance settlement. Enough to buy a nice home in a new development going in not very far from their farm. I told Nick I thought that was a very nice touch. He said, "We *do* repay people for helping us."

Nick verified that the local cop showing up behind the insurance office, and being nearby when the tower went down was strictly coincidence. As I suspected, the locals had not been notified. HS knew that there was the possibility of coincidental interference such as what happened, but they like to keep these kinds of activities as quiet as possible. He said they observed everything, and got no other surprises. He said that by keeping everything within HS, they can easily watch for other players, and they saw none.

As usual, Nick wanted debriefed. He said that he witnessed everything up until Greg and Rachel disappeared into the cornfield. He wanted me to start there and tell him everything up until we arrived back at the truck stop. He didn't say so, but I'm sure they had somebody watching Greg's car all the while it was parked there.

I filled him in on all the details: my call to Justin, Rachel's and Greg's cross-country dash through the cornfield, the dogs, the flying pickup, and the drive back. There was little useful information in my debriefing, but people like Nick always want the full story, from beginning to end. I did my best to accommodate him.

* * *

After I dropped Greg and Rachel at their car last night, and I made my calls, I scanned radio stations all the way home. There was no news of the tower anywhere. Of course, there is virtually no live radio late at night, so I wasn't too surprised. I was sure that it'd be the subject on all the morning drive-time shows.

Kate was still up when I finally got home. I chewed her out -- gently -- for not going to bed. But I was glad she was still up. I knew she would be.

And as I knew she would, Kate demanded another debriefing. It took an hour to tell her the whole story. She had made chocolate chip cookies while she was waiting for me to get home, so we did the debriefing to Diet Pepsis and cookies.

It was getting gray out by the time we crashed.

* * *

This evening over dinner, Kate reminded me that Sam and Janie are coming up for the weekend. They are friends of ours from Youngstown. Canfield, actually. We've know them forever. No big plans. Dinner together tomorrow night -- probably at the Moosehead -- and then just a goof off weekend together. It'll be nice, but I'll have to be careful. Sam's ex-Navy. Vets can sense things. It never goes away.

* * *

I park on the street near Rachel's place. I've never been to her place. She gave me her address and my GPS brought me here.

I like Little Italy. It's a compact neighborhood on a hillside not far from the Cleveland Clinic. In recent years, it has become yuppified. Old houses, apartments and businesses remodeled and sold or rented for lots more than they're worth. But it has quaint shops, good restaurants and safe streets. It's a nice place to live if you like the city life. I'm surprised Rachel can afford it. I'll have to do a little fishing there.

I ring the bell next to her mailbox at the outside door. I hear music and Rachel on the intercom. "Who is it?"

"Peter."

The door buzzes, I pull it open, and enter. She has the second floor of a three story building. I look around as I climb the stairs. Nicely done, and well maintained -- not cheap, I suspect -- I wonder if HS has looked into her finances.

I knock on the door, Rachel opens it, hugs me, and kisses me on the cheek. She is euphoric. "'Hello, gorgeous.' Come in Cap'n. I like that name, it fits you. Cap'n. 'Made it, Ma! Top of the world!' I love it."

It's going to be a long night.

CHAPTER 88

(Gregory)

We're both still tired from last night. It's good to just sit here, drink a beer, and listen to Rachel's very nice sound system. I like her taste in music. We're listening to Fleet Foxes at the moment.

I hope Peter gets here pretty soon. I'm hungry. This is supposed to be a little private victory celebration, but it'll probably wind up being an analysis session for last night's job: what we did right, what we did wrong, what we need to change, and most important, what's next.

Rachel gets up, turns down the stereo, and goes to the intercom by the door. I didn't hear it buzz, but I'm sitting on the floor right between the speakers. She pushes a button on the intercom and asks, "Who is it?"

The somewhat distorted answer is, "Peter."

She pushes another button to let him in. In about three minutes, he knocks and Rachel opens the door. Of course it's Peter, and of course she makes a big deal of it. She hugs him and kisses him on the cheek.

Peter smiles, hugs her back, and kisses her back. On the cheek, at least. Rachel asks what she can get him, and Peter says, "A Diet Coke or Pepsi if you have it. Something brown with caffeine."

Rachel says, "Comin' right up, sailor. I'm so glad you came."

Peter turns to me -- finally -- and says, "Hi Greg. Catch up on your missed sleep yet?"

"No, but I intend to do so tonight. What do you like on your pizza?"

"I'm essentially a carnivore. I like pepperoni, Italian sausage, that kind of stuff. I'm not big on veggies."

"Sounds good to me. I'll order a large pizza from the place down the street. It should be ready in less than a half hour."

As I'm finishing my call, Rachel comes back with Peter's drink. "Here you go, Cap'n. You really don't drink at all, huh?"

He smiles. "I used to. Too much. I didn't like what it was doing to me, and to my life. I quit almost thirty years ago. Used to smoke, too. Quit that about twenty years ago."

"Greg and I both smoke. Me a little, him a lot. Does it bother you if we smoke?"

I don't smoke *that* much. I start to say something, but they're both ignoring me. Peter responds before I can bitch. "Not at all. I just won't join you. Same with drinking."

Then Peter changes the subject. "This looks like a very nice place, Rachel. Do I get the fifty cent tour?"

Rachel gets up and says, "Sure. Come on."

Off they go. It *is* a nice place. It's not a big place, though, so they won't take long. I take a drink of beer, light a cigarette, and stretch out on the floor.

* * *

They get back from their little tour, and Rachel asks me when the pizza will be ready.

"It's time to go pick it up right now. Who's going?"

Peter says he wouldn't mind exploring Little Italy. "I'll drive if someone goes with me to show me the way."

Rachel says, "Why don't both of you go? It'll give you a chance to bond."

Both Peter and I look at her as if to say, "And what makes you think we want to bond?" I shrug, get up, grab my jacket, and say, "Okay. Let's go."

* * *

When we get back, Rachel has gotten out plastic plates, napkins, two more beers, and one more Diet Pepsi. She has even put a red, checkered tablecloth on her round glass table. How Italian.

We spend the next hour eating pizza, and dissecting last night. We all agree that we were damned lucky to not get caught -- that the site was just too open. But, we all also agree that it was a great site!

The news coverage has been amazing. Justin really did his job. All the local TV stations were there. Our handiwork has been the lead story on all the news broadcasts all day. Pictures of the wreckage of the tower. Pictures of the ensuing fire. Commentaries about the threat to the family that lives in the farmhouse. Question from the talking heads like, "What if those poor children had been home instead of visiting relatives last night?" Dramatic laments like, "These people have to be stopped before someone is injured or killed." It's great!

The coverage has also been pretty much nonstop on the local radio talk shows. We almost got caught, but we really got their attention. Vista Tel is going to have a hard time ignoring us now. And it's about frickin' time.

At one point Peter says, "So tell me about Justin. He obviously did his job. How did you make contact with him, anyway?"

"Actually Justin contacted us. He said that he traced the emails we were sending to Vista Tel back to us. I don't know much about computer network technology. I'm an engineer, but hardware is my forte, not software. Rachel is the software whiz -- a genuine computer nerd."

Rachel chimes in with, "My discussions with Justin point to the facts that one, he is very computer savvy, and two, he has lots of computer horsepower available to him."

I continue, "We don't really know much about him. He says he represents a competing cell phone company, but he won't name it. He says it's better if we don't know. He said if he can find us, the government can too. That made sense to Rachel and me, and we figure he's one more layer of insulation between us and the cops, feds, whatever."

Rachel interrupts again. "I'm going to call Justin right now and thank him for his part in the operation. Tell him he did good. Tell him the media coverage has been non-stop. Want to listen in?"

Peter says, "I'd like that. What's your plan?"

Rachel says, "The cell phones Justin provided are really cheap looking Motorola TracFones, but they have speakerphone capabilities. We'll just put him on speaker."

"When?"

"Right now. 'It's showtime!'"

CHAPTER 89

(Mirsab)

I have just gotten home from mailing the latest group of cell phones to Rachel, when one of the phones I have assigned to her cell rings. It is about six p.m. That means that it is nine p.m. in Cleveland. I answer with, "Hello?"

"'Louis, I think this is the beginning of a beautiful friendship.'"

She is speaking in idioms again! "Rachel? I am sorry, but I don't understand you. Who is Louis?"

"It's from a movie, Justin. *Casablanca*? Humphrey Bogart? Classic?"

And now she quotes movies, as well? "I have not seen it."

"Oh, never mind. I just called to tell you that you did an excellent job of notifying the media. You --"

I hear music and voices in the background. "Do you have me on the speaker?"

"Yeah, cutie. The gang's all here. Me, Greg, Peter. We want to thank you. We haven't heard from Vista Tel yet, but they can't ignore us now. The TV news coverage has been non-stop since this morning. The local radio talk shows are talking about nothing else. The networks have picked it up."

This is better. This I can talk about. "That is excellent. Congratulations to all of you. You did very well. There has been some coverage here today on CNN and MSNBC. I have not seen Fox News, but I am sure they are covering your work as well. I heard something about the local police almost apprehending you. Tell me, please, what happened."

"It was not as close a call as the local cops would like to let on. A cop on patrol swung by the tower while we were actually loosening the base nuts, but he never saw us. Another cop -- or maybe the same one -- we don't know -- drove by the tower within a minute of when it hit the house. Pure coincidence! We saw him. He didn't see us. We disappeared into a cornfield, cut cross-country and Peter picked us up. We were gone before they even started looking for us!"

"I am glad, then. I was concerned. The media made it sound much worse. Now that we have attracted national attention, we must increase our vigilance. We must be very careful when communicating. We must be on guard at all times. The local, state, and national police will be watching for any suspicious activity. They will be monitoring all communications channels."

"National police?"

Did I misspeak? "I simply meant the various federal police organizations: the FBI, NSA and so on."

"'Lions and tigers and bears, oh my!' We'll be okay, Justin. We'll be careful. Besides, we've got the Captain to keep us in line. He knows all about this spy shit. He used to work for the DIA, or something."

Is there a fourth person about whom I have not heard? I have heard of the DIA, but I do not know what it is, or what it does. Is this new person an ex-government agent? "Who is this Captain? Is he somebody new? I must know."

"Oh, cool it, Justin. You're so uptight! Cap'n is Peter's nickname. He is a sailor. He has a boat. And a Captain's License."

I am relieved. "Oh, I see. I thought you had enlisted a fourth person. Now would be a very bad time to do such a thing. The police will try to infiltrate your group if they identify any of you. Be wary."

"Okay. Okay. We just all wanted to say thanks. We'll be looking for tower number four. We'll have to do something even more spectacular!"

"Again I congratulate you. All of you. You Gregory. And you Peter, or should I say 'Captain'?"

"Cap'n works for me, Justin. You did well, too."

I need to end this conversation and report some of these details to Hamad. "Rachel, I mailed another group of TracFones to you today. As soon as we are finished, please destroy the one you are using now. Thank you for calling to apprise me of the situation. Good bye, for now, to all of you."

* * *

As soon as I hang up, I move to my other group of cell phones, the ones that I use to communicate with Hamad. As always, he answers almost immediately. Does he never leave the phones? Does he never sleep?

"Good evening. I have talked to the members of my cell in Cleveland. Have you heard anything of the destruction they have caused?"

"Of course. I know of the damage that has been done. We are very pleased with the attention you are getting. You have done well, Mirsab. Your efforts have not gone unnoticed by those in control of the coming jihad."

I am very pleased. I tell Hamad of my involvement of Nura. I explain that she is much more westernized than I am, and that she is more at ease dealing with shopkeepers than I am.

He is immediately concerned. "This is not good. What is her name?"

I am hesitant, but I must comply. "Her name is Nura Bint Taimurs al Thani. She was born in Qatar, but came here with her parents when she was very young. I can give you her address if you like."

"That will not be necessary. We will look into her background. Into her family's."

Her family's background? I am fearful of what I have done. Hamad continues. "You must be careful of involving others in the jihad. Especially women!"

"But you told me to enlist someone to help me. I--"

"I did not expect you to recruit a woman. But enough of Nura."

Hamad sounds calmer as he continues. "It is good that you have encouraged and helped the Cleveland cell. They must start planning their next target."

"Rachel said they have already begun planning, and that the next tower must be even more spectacular."

"I agree with Rachel. Stay in contact with them. As soon as you know more details of what they are planning, notify me."

"I will do so. There is another thing. Peter has a past connection to an organization called the DIA."

There is a pause. When he speaks, I can hear Hamad's concern. "Tell me what you know."

"I know very little, except that Peter once worked for this DIA. What is the DIA? Who are they? What do they do? Why are you concerned?"

"The DIA is the Defense Intelligence Agency, the military arm of the American intelligence network. They are tasked with gathering intelligence information on foreign militaries. The DIA should not be a threat to us, but anyone who has ever been involved with the American intelligence network can never be fully trusted. You must be very careful with Peter. You must never divulge your connection to me."

CHAPTER 90

Monday

(Peter)

We had a great weekend with Sam and Janie. Talked a lot. Ate a lot. Played Dominos, a game that Susan and her boyfriend Ted recently introduced us to.

Over Dominos, out of the blue, Sam asked me about my past. He said that we've known each other for twenty years, but the four of us have never really had a chance to talk. He said we always seem to be together with a whole group of friends, and that's nice, but it really makes it hard to get to know each other.

Sam said that he knew that I spent some time in Europe. He knew I was a contractor assigned to NATO. He said, "Do I remember you saying that you worked for the DIA?"

I don't think he was fishing. I don't think he picked up on my new career as an urban terrorist. I think he really did just want to know about how I got where I am. I told him, "Yeah, I was DIA. But that was a long time ago, and I don't talk much about those days."

Janie piped up with, "What's DIA, Peter?"

"Well, DIA is the Defense Intelligence Agency. It's sort of like the CIA, but it has to do with the military."

"You were a spy?"

"No, nothing that exciting. I was an electronics technician advising other NATO military forces on equipment that my employer, Raytheon, built."

"Oh, I thought maybe you were like a James Bond."

"I wish. He drove great cars and always got the girls. Let's play Dominos."

Sam looked at me, but didn't say anything. He was thinking. Processing is the word that Kate uses.

Saturday was a beautiful sunny spring day. Kate, Janie and Sam wanted to take a walk on the beach. Well, at least Kate and Janie did. I think Sam would have been quite content to just sit and look out the window. But he's a good sport, so he said he'd go along, and mind Daisy, our Maltese, while the girls looked for sea glass. I told them I had to make a quick call to Damien at work. Just some things I needed to tell him before Monday morning. I told them I'd catch up, and I went upstairs to my office in the loft while they went to the beach.

I called Nick to tell him about the victory party. As usual, he said little, but wanted to know all the details.

"I have two major bullet points that are worth passing on."

"Okay. What's bullet point one?"

"Rachel is already thinking about the next tower. She wants to do something even more spectacular."

He wasn't surprised. "Do you get the impression that she is kind of taking over?"

"Yeah, I think so. Rachel is the much stronger personality. Greg is in love -- or at least in heat -- and he is allowing Rachel to lead."

"I thought so from what you've said in the past. What's your second bullet point?"

I told him about our speaker phone call to Justin. "Justin got very agitated when he thought we had recruited a fourth person with a past connection to DIA."

He asked an odd question. "Did you detect any accent at all when you were listening to Justin?"

That caught me off guard. "No. None at all. If I had to place him, I'd say somewhere in the Midwest. If anything, his English was too good. Why do you ask?"

"In a minute. What do you mean by 'too good,' Cap'n?"

"I'm not exactly sure. Yes, I am. He speaks English learned as a second language. No accent, no slang, no idioms, not even any contractions. Again, why do you ask?"

"Could he be an Arab?"

"He could be anything. What's going on Nick?"

"The cell phone you used to call Justin was purchased from a Radio Shack in California. Homeland Security has a standing request out to cell phone sellers that they be notified anytime someone purchases more than three disposable cell phones at one time. Several such purchases have been made this week at Radio Shacks in the Torrance, California, area. Two persons, one male and one female, have purchased four TracFones each at two different stores for cash. Unfortunately we have not been able to get good likenesses from the surveillance cameras: one was down and the other poorly aimed. The description we have from the store personnel in each case is, 'Well dressed, well spoken, Arabs.'"

"Oh, shit."

CHAPTER 91

(Gregory)

Today was a real frickin' pain-in-the-ass day at school. Some of my classes are so irrelevant. I don't like going to school. I'm glad to be home.

Supper time. I don't like cooking either, but I'm pretty broke. Going out is not an option. Maybe there's something in the freezer.

Knock -- knock, knock, knock, knock -- knock, knock. Only Rachel knocks a tune. "Hi, Rach. I was just thinking I'd better call you and find out if you were still alive."

"'It's alive! It's alive!' I've been busy. Exploring. And please don't call me Rach. That's not what my mother named me. Rach is in the same class with frickin'."

"Well then, come in, Rachel. I was just trying to figure out if I had anything to eat in the house. I'm hungry. And broke."

"'As God is my witness, I'll never be hungry again.' That's why I work for a living *and* go to school."

"Is that a crack?"

"No, Greg, it's really not. I wish I had parents who would support me while I'm going to school. I'd much rather just concentrate on school. I don't like working full time and going to school full time. I'm tired, all the time."

"Your parents won't help at all? You never talk about them."

"My father deserted us when I was two. My mother is a drunk. She can't even support herself. 'I have always depended on the kindness of strangers.'"

"Oh. I didn't know. You must have worked very hard to get where you are. You should be proud of what you've accomplished. I was just thinking about how much better you are doing than I am. Your apartment, your--"

"Shush. Don't say anything else. Just give me a hug and a kiss. Then let's go find some food. I have things to share with you."

* * *

Rachel has a new place in mind. La Bodega in Tremont is known for its huge deli sandwiches. Tremont is only about eight miles away, but it's on the other side of Cleveland. Tremont is kind of a neat area. It's on the bluff west of the Cuyahoga River, and overlooks the old industrial area. Like Little Italy, it's getting yuppified. I guess Rachel likes these kinds of areas.

Driving there gives us a chance to talk. Rachel says she has spent the weekend looking for tower number four, and she found it! This one is off of Interstate 90. She says it's *spectacular*!

I ask her what makes it so spectacular. She says, "It's like real estate -- location, location, location."

"What do you mean?

"I can't believe that they actually built it where they did. Do you know those high voltage lines that run along Interstate 90 and Route 2?"

"Yeah. If you're talking about the really big ones, that's the 345,000 volt line that runs all along the great lakes. It's the one that went down in 2003 and caused a blackout all over the Midwest and New England."

"You got it, 'My little chickadee.' That's the one I'm talking about. Vista Tel built a cell tower so close to it that when we take down the tower, it will hit the lines. We'll take out Vista Tel and the power to millions of people!"

"Rachel, that's crazy. We can't do that."

"Oh, yes we can, 'My little chickadee.' We most assuredly can…"

CHAPTER 92

(Mirsab)

I must call Hamad again. I do not understand the reasoning behind destroying cell phone towers now. I can understand why we will want to do this once the jihad has started. We will want to disrupt all forms of communication, but I need a better explanation of why we must do this now.

I also must tell Hamad of my continuing concern about Rachel not following the protocols I have developed. I think I did not tell him that she had me on a speakerphone, and that now Gregory and Peter know my voice.

For the first time, when I call Hamad, he does not answer. I leave a message asking that he return my call.

* * *

When I return from my afternoon class at UCLA, I note that the message light is flashing on the cell phone I used to call Hamad. I listen to the message. It is brief. "Call me."

I pour myself a glass of wine. This is a newly acquired habit, a glass of wine in the evening before dining. I feel somewhat guilty. I am behaving like a rich decadent American. But I enjoy the wine.

Hamad answers immediately. "Your call surprises me. Has your cell selected their next target?"

"I have not heard from them yet. I assure you that if I do not hear from them soon, I will call them."

"That is wise. You must maintain close contact with them."

I tell him of my concern about Rachel. I tell him of the speakerphone incident.

"That was not wise of her, but there is no harm done."

"But I am fearful of being identified."

He tells me not to be concerned. "Your English is as near to perfect as I have ever heard. Even if they recorded you, it would be extremely difficult to identify your voice. Voice identification is a much less certain fact than fiction writers would like one to believe."

"I see."

Hamad is somewhat impatient. "Others are taking chances much more serious than being overheard by virtual strangers two thousand miles away. You must quit worrying about such things, and do your job."

I use his speech as a segue into my other reason for calling. "Hamad, I must ask you to explain again why we are destroying cell phone towers now, before the jihad has begun."

He tries to sound patient, but I know that he is not. I sense his irritation, his anger even. I sense that he does not like being asked for explanations. It is the way of our leaders. They expect unquestioning loyalty, unquestioning obedience.

He explains. "There are several reasons. First, it occupies the time and resources of the authorities in investigating these very obvious, public actions instead of investigating other less obvious actions that are occurring in preparation for the coming jihad. Second, by carefully escalating the level of violence, we can measure their ability to respond, we can calculate how much time we will have before our operatives are in danger of being caught."

"I see. That is why information about the police arriving so soon is important to you."

"We think that was coincidence. There is a third purpose. By your immediate and unquestioning obedience to our orders, you are proving yourself worthy of a larger role in the future. Do not waste this opportunity."

"I will not. I want to play a bigger role in the future."

Hamad says, "Goodbye then," and hangs up. As I sip my wine, as I think of Nura, I ask myself, "Do I really want to play a bigger role in the future?"

CHAPTER 93

Tuesday

(Peter)

It's lunchtime. I'm out of the office for an hour, as usual. I'm on my way to a hobby shop in Parma when I drive by a Radio Shack. Oh, shit!

I pull into the lot and stop. I'm shaking.

Oh, shit! Why didn't I think of it yesterday when I was talking to Nick? I was in Torrance three weeks ago. I was at a Radio Shack. I watched an Arab buy TracFones!

I call Nick. No answer. "Nick, it's Peter. Call me immediately. I have vital information."

The hobby shop doesn't seem quite so important now, but I might as well go. Maybe Nick will call back before I return to work.

As I pull into the lot of the Parma Hobby Shop, my cell phone rings. It's Nick.

"Nick. I don't know why I didn't think of this yesterday. I was in Torrance three weeks ago. I was at a Radio Shack. I watched an Arab buy TracFones!"

"You're kidding!"

"No, I'm not. I was buying an RS-232 cable for the job I was on, and I noticed him because of the fuss he was making." I explain the whole experience to Nick. How the Arab wanted TracFones, and how the clerk tried to sell him something else. How the Arab got agitated and threatened to leave. How, because I was curious, I watched the whole transaction while I was pretending to look at cables.

Nick asked if the male was alone. I said he was, but he fit the description. Then he asked if I saw him get in a car, and I said no, I didn't pay attention.

Nick explained that the tapes HS got from the security cameras at one of the Los Angeles area Radio Shacks showed a fair shot of the female, but only a partial shot of the male. Mostly what they got of him was the back of his head and a little bit of a profile. He said he will send me the wmv files. He wants to know if I saw Justin.

So do I.

* * *

I'm on my way back to work and the phone rings again. As I flip it open, I notice that the display says UNKNOWN. Not Nick. Probably not a customer. Not with an unlisted number. "Hello?"

"Hello, this is John Collins. I'm calling from Sprint headquarters in Alexandria, Virginia. I'm sorry to bother you, but we are having some issues that you may be able to help with. Is this Peter Bradovich?"

"Yes, it is. But if you're Sprint, why is your number showing up as UNKNOWN?"

"I'm with the Sprint Fraud Unit, sir, and for obvious reasons we do not encourage callbacks. I can give you our unit's extension. You can call 611, and verify that I am, in fact John Collins of Sprint."

"No, that's not necessary. What can I do for you?"

"For identification purposes, can you please give me the name and address of your employer, Mr. Bradovich?"

"Why do you want to know that?"

"As you know, the phone you are talking on is a company phone. I need to verify that."

"Oh. Okay. That's true."

I give him the info he wants, and he continues. "Some of your employer's phones were stolen and reprogrammed for private use. We are just verifying which ones are still legitimate. That's all I need for now."

"That was easy."

"Yes, it was. Thank you. Have a great day. Goodbye."

* * *

When I finally get back to the office, I tell Cindy, Stan's Administrative Assistant, about my call from John Collins at Sprint. She looks at me blankly. Says she doesn't know what I'm talking about. Says she knows nothing of stolen phones. That's weird. Cindy knows everything that's going on.

CHAPTER 94
(Gregory)

I just don't know what to do with -- or about -- Rachel. She's nuts. She's lost sight of our goal. We can't take down the electrical grid. That's insane.

One, I don't want to cause that kind of damage. As I recall, dozens of people died because of the last blackout. That's not my goal.

Two, it'll detract from the message we're trying to deliver to Vista Tel. People will be concentrating on looking for us. Vista Tel will get a pass.

I've got to slow her down, if I can.

I know she's getting off on taking these towers down. I'll never forget how turned on she was after she helped me take her first one down. I didn't know a girl could become that open about wanting sex. I didn't know they could be that demanding. It was like something out of some porn story.

And the tower last week had the same effect on her. We didn't zoom back to her place, or my place, and get it on. But she was hot. I still get a little excited thinking about how hot she was after Peter dropped us off at my car. If we could have had sex in the parking lot without being afraid of getting caught, we'd have done it. And we came pretty frickin' close.

By the time we got back to her place, we were both emotionally exhausted, though. I just kissed her good night, and went home -- alone.

* * *

Crap. Her answering machine. "Rachel, we've got to talk. I don't like what you want to do next. I don't want to leave any details on your answering machine. Call me when you can."

That'll get her attention. I just hope it doesn't end what we've got going for us.

* * *

I'm still sitting here contemplating my call to Rachel when my cell phone rings again. As I flip it open, I notice that the display says UNKNOWN. I think that means someone with an unlisted number. "Hello?"

"Hello, this is John Collins. I'm calling from Verizon headquarters in Alexandria, Virginia. I'm sorry to bother you, but we are having some issues that you may be able to help with. Is this Gregory Zaremba?"

"Yes, it is. But I don't really want to add any services. Besides, it's late, and this is not a good time to be calling about my account. And if you're from Verizon, why is your number showing up as UNKNOWN?"

"This is not a sales call, sir. I'm with the Verizon Fraud Unit, and for obvious reasons we do not encourage callbacks. You can call Verizon at 611, ask for the Fraud Unit, and verify that I am, in fact, John Collins, of Verizon."

"No, no, I don't need to do that. Look, it's late. What do you want?"

"For identification purposes, can you please give me your home address and your land line phone number, Mr. Zaremba?"

I give him my address and phone number, and he continues, "Some of our customers with numbers similar to yours are being called and offered upgrades for what seems like very good prices. These calls are fraudulent, and the perpetrators are using this ruse to obtain customer's credit card numbers. Have you received any such calls?"

"No, I haven't."

"Very good. If you do receive any such calls, just hang up and call us at 611."

"That's it?"

"Yes, it is. Thank you. I'm sorry for calling so late. Have a great evening. Goodbye."

* * *

"Hello, I have a complaint about a call I received from you guys late last night." I explain the call from their Fraud Unit and tell the girl I don't appreciate being called late at night. I tell her they need to do business during business hours, not at almost midnight. She asks me to wait one moment, and I get the usual boring music. I think they used to call it Muzak. I wonder if Muzak still exists. She comes back on the line.

"Sir, we have no record of anyone from Verizon calling you last night. Moreover, our Fraud Unit is not calling customers about any sort of scam in operation. Are you sure the caller was from Verizon?"

"That's what he said. His number showed up as UNKNOWN, though."

The girl said that their calls will *always* show up on caller id as VERIZON. She went on to say that they would investigate the call. I thanked her, and hung up.

Weird...

CHAPTER 95

(Mirsab)

I regret very much that I have involved Nura in my activities with my Cleveland cell. Hamad's reaction to my disclosure of Nura's limited role concerns me. It is what I would expect from a Syrian living in Syria. His comments verify the extreme chauvinism that is common among my countrymen, especially the older men.

But Hamad sounds so American. In all else, except this, he sounds and acts as I would expect any well educated, upper class American to sound and act. Perhaps he is not as western as I surmised. His reaction to Nura certainly seems to indicate that.

I think I must tell Nura of my concerns. I must warn her that I had to give my superior her identity. I must allow, even encourage her, to disassociate herself from my cause. I gave her my word that I would not involve her in anything that would endanger her or her family.

I find myself caring for Nura more than I have cared for any woman. I think our relationship might develop further. I must not jeopardize that relationship.

* * *

I call Nura on her cell phone. She does not answer.

I do not understand why people do not answer their cell phones. More and more, I see my American friends and associates look at their cell phones when they ring, but not answer them. They wait to see what message is left, and then call back, if it suits them. It is their way of screening their incoming calls. I consider being screened in this way an insult. It indicates that the recipient of the call feels that the caller is not important enough to warrant their immediate response. I hope Nura has not adopted this habit.

I receive a text message from Nura almost immediately after I hang up. I find text messages even less understandable than screening one's incoming calls. Entering a text message takes much longer than talking and accomplishes nothing that talking would not accomplish.

In this case, however, I must admit that texting does make sense. At least I think it does. Her text message reads "CT. IN CLASS. CMB@4. <3." The first part is clear, I think, "Can't talk. In class." The next part I am fairly certain is an abbreviation for, "Call me back at four." I have no idea of the meaning of, "<3." Less than three? What is less than three?

I will text her back. I have never done this before. After much aggravation, and many false tries, I think I have sent her the message, "Can we meet tonight, Nura?" It has taken me approximately five minutes, but I have sent my first text message!

Almost immediately, I get the message, "GR8 CU <3.'" Again, the less than three? I understand the rest of the message, though. "Great. See you."

I text her back, "I'll call you at 4:00 p.m." I may be slow, but at least my messages are grammatically correct.

I must learn the meaning of her *less than three* abbreviation.

* * *

I am preparing to call Nura when one of the cell phones Hamad sent me rings. This is unexpected.

"Hello?"

"Hello, Mirsab. I have some assurances to pass on to you."

I am a little confused. "What do you mean by 'assurances', Hamad? Also, I thought you disapproved of using names."

"There are times when the friendly salutation seems appropriate. This is one." Hamad explains that he has personally talked to Peter, Gregory and Rachel. I am shocked. He says he posed as a representative of their respective cell phone companies. I ask how he was able to determine their companies, and he says with obvious mirth in his voice, "It's my business." I don't understand his meaning, but I am glad that he finds it humorous, and I don't pursue the question.

He says that the reason for his calls was simply to listen to their voices. "I am very good at sensing lies and deception in people." He says that his continued survival depends on that ability.

"I have found that when people are hiding their identity, when they are living in deception, when they are playing a role, they almost always divulge it by the tension in their voices, especially when talking with strangers. I detected no such tension in any of them."

Hamad assures me that these people, the members of my cell, are exactly what they seem to be, clueless American's who have no idea they are being used.

I thank Hamad for his call, for his assurances. I am afraid to ask if he can give me the same assurances about Nura.

I call Nura as soon as I have finished my call with Hamad. She answers immediately, and says she is in her car on the way home. She asks, "What's up?"

"I would like to see you tonight if possible."

"I'd love it. Do you mind if I pick the place? It won't be fancy. I'd like to broaden your dining horizons."

I can hear the smile in her voice. "That will be fine, Nura. I just wish to spend time with you."

I ask about the *less than three* abbreviation. She laughs. "It's not less than three, silly."

"Then, what?"

"Turn you head sideways and look at it again. It's a heart! 'Bye." She hangs up.

It is just as well that she hung up. I am speechless...

CHAPTER 96
Wednesday
(Peter)

It's right before lunch when my phone rings. "Hello?"

It's Greg. He's agitated. Very Agitated. "Can you meet me? We gotta talk."

"Where are you?"

He's close to panic. "I'm at Big Creek Park. At the spot where we met last time. We really *have* to talk."

"I can be there in less than ten minutes. Sit tight."

I put on my jacket, get two cans of Diet Pepsi out of the vending machine, stuff them in my jacket pockets, and leave.

* * *

When I pull into the park, I see Greg sitting on a picnic table about fifty feet into the trees. I park, get out, and start to walk towards him. He sees me coming and jumps up. Boy, is he wired. When I get close, I say, "As Barry Manilow would say, 'Sit, sit, sit.' I didn't know if you preferred diet or regular."

I hand him a Diet Pepsi. "What's up?"

He pops the tab and takes a long drink. "I don't know what to do about Rachel."

"What do you mean?"

"Rachel found the next tower she wants to take down."

"Yeah?"

"You know the high voltage line that runs along Interstate 90 and Route 2?"

"Yeah?"

"That's the 345,000 volt power line that caused the huge blackout in 2003. When it went down, it took out power all the way from Detroit to New York City."

"Where is this heading, Greg?"

"Rachel found a cell tower that Vista Tel built so close to the power line that when we take the tower down, it'll hit the power line!"

"You're kidding!"

"No, I'm not. I wish I was. She's getting frickin' nuts."

Greg says that Rachel told him about finding the tower on Monday. He tried to talk her out of it last night, but she dug her heels in. She will not be deterred.

I don't believe what I'm hearing. "Who the hell is in charge here, Greg?"

He says, "Right now, Rachel, I guess."

And it all comes pouring out. He says Rachel has lost sight of our mission, that she's gone off the deep end. He says he thinks he's in love with her. He tells me he doesn't know how to stop her without losing her.

Greg goes on. "I did some Internet research. Wikipedia has a big write up on the blackout of 2003. A dozen people died. Dumb shit like one guy who died of carbon monoxide poisoning while running a generator indoors, and another guy who died by falling off a roof while trying to break into a store. But people died. I don't want to be responsible for that."

Neither do I. Harassing Vista Tel is one thing, but this is terrorism pure and simple. I agree with Greg. We've got to stop Rachel. We can't allow this.

I do my best to calm Greg down. "Where is the tower located? I want to check it out myself."

"I'm not sure, exactly, but I know it's along Interstate 90. From Rachel's description, it may be Vista Tel's next tower to the east of the one we just took down."

"I'll find the location on the Internet and check it out. Then I'll talk to Rachel."

Greg starts to unwind a little. I tell him what he needs to hear. "Listen to me, Greg. We will get Rachel under control. You won't lose her. She's just gone off the deep end a little. She's gotten caught up in the excitement of it all. She's getting a rush from it right now, but she'll cool down. This whole campaign was your idea. You're the one who has to guide it and control it. I'll convince Rachel to find another tower that'll put us back on track. I'll explain to her why her tower is a very bad idea. I can be very convincing. We'll work it out. It'll be okay."

He looks visibly relieved. And almost ready to cry. Like he did the day he first told me about this whole mess. I smile at him. I almost want to hug him. Almost. "We'll work it out. It *will* be okay, Greg."

But I'm not so sure.

* * *

When I get home, I tell Kate the whole story. She is incredulous. She says these kids are nuts. I have to agree. She asks what I'm going to do. I tell her step one is to check out the site to make sure the tower will really hit the power lines. "I can't believe they would build a tower that close to the power lines. That would be phenomenally stupid!"

"Was it Forrest Gump who's mother said 'Stupid is as stupid does'?"

Not Kate, too. "Then I'll call Rachel and talk her out of it. And then call Nick to warn him about what Rachel was planning. Or maybe call Nick, then Rachel. I don't know who I'll call first. Do you have any thoughts on it?"

"We'll figure it out tomorrow after we've checked out the site."

"We?"

"Yes, we." Kate says she has a plan. Kate always has a plan. She approaches most problems in life like a project that needs managed. But then that makes sense. She *is* a Project Manager after all.

She tells me to get on the Internet tonight and figure out exactly where this tower is. She says that when I get home from work tomorrow night, we'll take Daisy for a walk.

"Huh?"

"We'll pack up the dog, go for a ride and check this tower out. We can stop and get a pizza on the way home."

And Daisy starts bouncing around the room. There are three things Daisy loves: rides, walks and pizza! I know dogs don't understand the meanings of words. I don't know how they think. But they do think. And I do know that they connect the sounds of words with emotions. "Bad" = I screwed up -- look repentant. "Jill" = Painful time getting washed and combed and poked -- go hide. "Ride" or "Walk" = Fun time and lots of new smells -- let's go, let's go. "Pizza" = Oh boy, oh boy, oh boy -- gourmet people food!

CHAPTER 97

(Gregory)

When I get home from talking to Peter, Rachel is sitting on my porch. I sit down next to her. "Hi, Rachel. I'm surprised to see you here. Not working this afternoon?"

"'One, two, Freddy's coming for you...' That's what we're going to tell Vista Tel! 'I'm as mad as hell, and I'm not going to take this anymore!' They *will* take us seriously. Or we'll have half the population of the United States down on them!"

God, I hate the movie quotes. "Have you been drinking or something? You're not making sense."

"I'm making perfect sense, 'My little chickadee.' We've got their attention now. It's time to go in for the kill. No more screwing around. If they don't listen, we black out the whole northeast. That's probably close to half the population of the United States. Well, maybe a fourth of the population. Or ten percent. Whatever. It's a bunch of people. And they will be really pissed off when they find out Vista Tel could have prevented the blackout."

"Rachel, what are you talking about?"

"I talked to Mirsab this afternoon. I told him we are doing tower number four a week from Friday night. I told him we are going to cause a massive power blackout. Here's the plan-- "

"But I just talked to Peter. He thinks causing a blackout is a big mistake. He wants to talk to you about it-- "

"No -- more -- talk -- ing! '*Carpe diem*. Seize the day, boys. Make your lives extraordinary.' We are done talking. We are now doing. Here's the plan: Sunday, Mirsab sends emails to Vista Tel and the media telling them that they have forty-eight hours to capitulate or we do the next tower and it'll make the last one look like a minor inconvenience. If we don't hear from them by Wednesday, he sends another batch of emails telling them that the clock is ticking, that every day they wait will make the damage worse. Thursday he sends another batch of emails telling them the damage will be in the millions of dollars. Friday he sends yet another batch that tells them people will die. And we do it Friday night!"

"Rachel, what are you saying? You can't mean this."

"Yes, I can, Greg. Come on. Don't be such a wimp. Look, my little speech there was a bit overly dramatic perhaps. But Mirsab will send the emails. The damage won't be in the millions. People won't really die. But we have to scare them. We have to make them listen to us and do what we want them to do, or we have to simply give up on the whole thing. We have to admit that Vista Tel has defeated us simply by ignoring us. Is that what you want, Greg? Is that how you see your dream ending?"

I don't know what to say. I don't know whether she is nuts -- or right. I don't want my dream to end in defeat. I believe that my dream is worthwhile. I believe that we can win. That we should win. Maybe Rachel is right. Maybe we have to keep escalating the stakes until they give up and capitulate.

"Rachel, I just don't know. I don't want anybody to get hurt, but we've got to win. My dream *is* valid. My dream is necessary. We have to keep fighting. It's just getting scary. Very scary."

"Come here, 'My little chickadee.' You need hugged. Or maybe laid. Let's go inside."

CHAPTER 98

(Mirsab)

Rachel is a very trying person. I have had a great deal of trouble understanding what I thought was her use of idioms. When I explain that to her, she laughs. "They aren't idioms, they are movie quotes." She explains that it is just a habit of hers.

"I was raised in a religious denomination that forbade attending movies. Now that I am an adult, and living on my own, I am trying to catch up on many things that I missed while growing up."

She laughs again, but it is a sympathetic laugh. "I promise to cool it on the quotes, or at least educate you about where they come from."

She even promises to put together a must see list of movies for me. "You have heard of a cable channel called TCM -- Turner Classic Movies?"

"Yes, I have."

"My list will be Goldmann Classic Movies."
"Goldmann?"

"It's my name. Rachel Goldmann. With two *n*'s. A good Jewish name, if there ever was one!"

Rachel? A Jew?

When I recover, I asked her why she has called, and she tells me that they have located tower number four. She goes on to explain that it is located next to the 345,000-volt transmission line that circumscribes the Great Lakes. She explains that when they destroy the tower, it will hit the transmission line causing a huge power blackout. I ask her what she means by huge and she says, "I assume you have a computer. Google 'Northeast Blackout of 2003.' That big. Millions will be affected!"

"Is that wise? Such a blackout will remove the focus from Vista Tel."

"Justin, you sound like Greg, now. We're doing it! Here's what I want you to do."

She explains the series of emails she wants me to send. Starting next Sunday, I am to send a series of increasingly threatening emails warning of escalating violence if Vista Tel does not capitulate. The plan will culminate in destroying the tower next Friday night. Actually, the plan sounds well conceived. However, I must discuss this with Hamad.

I tell Rachel that I will prepare the emails. I ask her to call me again in a few days to verify the expected date and time of the demolition. I explain that I must make plans to notify the media again as soon as the tower is destroyed.

She says, "Good enough, Justin. In the meantime, I'll be working on the Goldmann Classic Movie List. We've got to catch you up on everything you missed!"

* * *

As soon as I end my call with Rachel, I start Internet Explorer on my computer, go to Google.com, and type 'Northeast Blackout of 2003' into the search box. The first hit is a Wikipedia article. I open it and read.

The article is several pages long, and it is accompanied by many photographs. I think it will be a great mistake to allow my cell to destroy a Vista Tel tower that will cause a repeat of this incident. All of the interest and media coverage will be on the blackout, and not on Vista Tel.

I have two groups of cell phones. The group to the left of my computer is the group I use to call my cell, and the group to the right of my computer is the group I use to call Hamad. I mark the phone I just used in my conversation with Rachel for destruction and choose the next phone from the group on the right. I dial the number marked on the phone. Hamad answers immediately.

I explain the conversation I just had with Rachel. "They plan to destroy a tower that is adjacent to a 345,000-volt transmission line along Lake Erie. It will cause a massive blackout. I have a great concern about allowing my cell to do this."

He does not agree with me. He agrees with Rachel. He says, "They have chosen an excellent target!"

I am surprised. "I have read the Wikipedia article on the blackout of 2003. Is doing this much damage wise? My thought is that the focus will be on the blackout, and not on Vista Tel."

"You are being short sighted. People will focus on the blackout, yes. But, my friend, they will blame Vista Tel, and that is what we want. They will not be thinking of who did it, they will be thinking of who allowed it to happen!"

I see his point. I had not thought of it that way. "I value your insight in these matters."

"Thank you. It comes from many years of fighting these battles, Mirsab. You will learn."

Hamad has an odd request. He wants me to call Rachel back and find out the exact location of the tower. I ask why. "My people will want to know. They will want to investigate this site before my cell destroys the tower. They will want to look for security measures that may be in place and for vulnerabilities that may be repeated in other locations."

"I see." But I'm not sure I do.

"Just get me the location. Call me back tomorrow. I have people to contact now. You have done well, Mirsab. Goodbye."

* * *

I find myself thinking about Nura. Last night, she took me to a Chinese restaurant. I have eaten Chinese food before, but have always found it rather bland. This was nothing of the sort. It was a type of food called Hunan Chinese. It was very good, and very spicy. We washed our dinner down with a drink called *huangjiu*. It was very good and very powerful.

I told Nura more about the group of Americans in Cleveland. More, perhaps, than Hamad would like. I told her about what they are doing, about the cell phone towers they are destroying in the guise of radical environmentalism. I made it sound like I had a very small part in their actions though. I did not tell her that I am controlling this group. She seemed fascinated, however.

Both Nura and I were a little drunk by the time we finished dinner. She was not too drunk to drive me home after dinner, though.

And she was not too drunk to kiss me goodnight. To kiss me very soundly. I was surprised and elated. I still think of Nura as Arab. She is Arab -- and American, at the same time. It is a marvelous combination.

CHAPTER 99

Thursday

(Peter)

I'm on my way home to pick up Kate and Daisy and go check out the site when my cell phone rings. I figure it's Kate. "I'm on my way home right now. Be there in fifteen minutes, cutie,"

"Well, dad, I don't think you've ever called me 'cutie' before."

"Oh. Gabe. I thought you were Kate. Hang on one. I've got a traffic situation."

Gabe is my younger son by my first marriage. He's a mutual fund manager and lives in Charlottesville, Virginia. I don't see him much. And we don't talk very often. No real problem with our relationship. It's just that neither of us is a good communicator.

"I'm back. This is a surprise. What's up?"

"Dad, I've been talking to Mike. He told me about your little spy game. I thought you outgrew that kind of stuff."

"Well, it just sort of jumped out in front of me. Did Mike go into much detail?"

"Actually, yes. We discussed you and your escapades for the better part of an hour."

"Then you know pretty much everything that I can tell you. And it's not really spying. More like gathering information."

"Mike said you drove the getaway car last time. That's not 'gathering information'."

"Well. Yeah. My guess is it's going to end soon."

"I hope so too, Dad. I worry about you."

I tell him I'll be careful, and that the yahoos I'm involved with are pretty non-violent, at least when it comes to people. I reassure him somewhat by telling him that Kate knows exactly what's going on. He knows Kate. He knows she'll keep me in line.

"Gabe, I'm pulling into my drive now. Kate's waiting for me to get home so I can change clothes and leave again. We've got a pretty tight schedule tonight." He says he understands, that he's got a wife, too. I tell him to say hi to Karen and the girls for me. He tells me he will, and tells me to say hi to Kate, too. We hang up.

I thought it better not to tell him exactly why we had a "tight schedule" tonight.

* * *

Kate, Daisy and I park just off the edge of the road on a grassy spot near the Interstate 90 underpass. We're right under the high-tension power lines and about fifty feet north of the service road leading back to the cell tower. We can hear the hum from the overhead high-tension power lines. We can almost feel the energy. It's a little scary. Daisy doesn't like it here.

We walk along the asphalt two-lane country road back to the service road. Actually, the service road is more like a path. It's just two dirt tracks with grass growing up between them. There is a culvert over the ditch and no gate or barrier to block access to the track. Now that I see how dry it is, I realize I could have parked here and been less conspicuous.

It's about a half a mile east back the dirt track to the tower. The trees and brush have been cleared on either side of the track for about fifty feet. The cleared track runs parallel to the cleared space under the power lines, so we have an unobstructed view of the Interstate, and they have an unobstructed view of us. The total distance from the track to the road is probably close to a hundred yards, so at least we're not real obvious to passersby.

Now that we're a little bit away from the power lines and on the track, Daisy is happy. So many new smells! Bugs! Birds! Rabbits!

We get to the cell tower. It's very similar to the other Vista Tel towers. Galvanized tubular tower connected by an ice bridge to an equipment building. Chain link fence around the whole thing. The area enclosed by the chain link fence is bigger at this one. And the tower itself is bigger. Bigger in diameter, and taller. Definitely tall enough to hit the power lines if it goes down to the north.

I can't believe they built the tower this close to the power lines. That is absolutely insane! Did they all forget about the power outage of 2003? That was caused by a tree limb hitting these lines. What do they think a gigantic steel tube will do? What was Vista Tel thinking? Who has to approve these things? What were they thinking? I have to tell Nick about this as quickly as possible.

The fenced in area has a good-sized clearing around it. For some reason, they bulldozed the trees for about thirty yards all around the installation.

Looking north, it's open under the power lines and to the Interstate. The only thing blocking the view at all is a string of scraggly bushes along the wire mesh fence at the edge of the road's right-of-way. There are scruffy second-growth woods south and east of the clearing, but they don't provide any useful cover. This site is entirely too exposed.

I ask Kate to take Daisy so I can get a closer look at the installation. They walk toward the woods and I go up to the fence, looking to my left at the cars passing on the Interstate. A hundred cars must have gone by since we got here. Anyone could have noticed us. And reported us.

There is a man gate and a bigger truck gate on the east side of the fence. The lock on the main gate is open! No sign of forced entry, somebody just forgot to lock up. I'd love to go in and get a closer look. It's just too exposed, though.

I've seen enough, really. We need to get out of here. I holler for Kate. I yell, "Pizza time!" Daisy starts yapping happily. And they start running toward me, seven-pound Daisy almost dragging 120-pound Kate. I head back for the main road and they catch up quickly. "I've seen enough. Let's get out of here and go get a pizza."

"Sounds good to me! And Daisy!"

"Will you drive while I call Nick? I've got to tell him this can't happen. If they aim right, they will take down the power lines. It'll be a tragedy. It just can't be allowed to happen."

CHAPTER 100
(Gregory)

The sun is setting as I get to the tower Rachel wants to take down. It took me a while to figure out how to get here. I drove by the tower on the Interstate almost an hour ago, but I couldn't figure out how to get here from there. I should have pinpointed the tower on that website that shows all the cell phone towers and then done a Google map. Oh well, I'm here.

I park at the entrance to the access road. It's really not much of a road. More like an off-road. Perfect for a Jeep, but not for a Honda. I'd love to just drive back to the tower. It's got to be a half a mile, anyway. With my luck, I'd get stuck. That would be a little hard to explain.

Somebody has been back this way today. A couple of people, actually. The tall grass between the two tracks is trampled. Kids? Hikers? I don't think there is anything back there except the tower.

It's starting to get dark when I finally get to the site. It's a big site. Bigger clearing. Bigger fenced in area. Bigger equipment building. Bigger tower. Much bigger tower. Probably bigger bolts and nuts.

From here, it is obvious that Rachel is absolutely right. The tower will hit the lines when we take it down. If we can get it to go due north. This site is crazy. They never should have been allowed to build this tower here. I can't believe our government. They want to control everything -- except the important stuff!

I've got to talk Rachel out of this. We can't do this. Vandalizing cell phone towers is one thing. Yeah, it's a felony, but it's not really hurting anyone or anything. It's *radical environmentalism*. Knocking out power to millions of people is a whole different thing. It's major bad. They will come looking for us. Big time. And nobody will be worrying about Vista Tel.

I move up to the chain link fence to try to get a better look at the tower base.

Thank you, Vista Tel! There is a gate where the trail meets the fence, and they left the frickin' lock unlocked. It's pretty dark now. They probably can't see me from the Interstate, even though it's open all the way there. I go in. I wish I had brought a flashlight.

I can't see much. It feels like the nuts have more welding on them than the last towers. And they are definitely bigger. I'll need a bigger socket. We lost ours at the last tower anyway. No way could we drag that stuff with us on our mad dash through the cornstalks. I've got to come back. During the day. Or at night -- with a flashlight. I'll bring my bolt cutters just in case they decide to lock the gate.

* * *

It's about forty-five minutes from tower number four to home. I decide to call Rachel. I know Peter said he is going to talk to her, but maybe I can convince her. I *don't* want to do this tower.

"Hi, Rachel. I'm glad you're home."

"I just called your house to see if you want to go get a beer or something. Where are you, 'My little chickadee'?"

"I'm forty-five minutes from home, maybe a half hour from your place. I just left the tower you want to take down."

"I thought we weren't supposed to talk about this stuff on the phone. Justin will give you hell."

"Screw Justin. And screw Peter. They're both paranoid. The cops and the government aren't listening in on all the phone conversations going on in the world. That's bullshit."

"'Lions and tigers and bears, oh my!' Somebody is wound up."

"I'm tired of all this spy shit. I just want to get back to my dream of making Vista Tel go away."

"Don't you just love my little discovery? Isn't it just 'the stuff that dreams are made of'? Can you believe they built a tower that close to those high voltage lines? You gotta love it."

"No, I don't gotta love it. I think it's a huge mistake. We have to talk. Yeah, I'd like to go get a beer. I need one. Or two. Or three."

"Don't get your shorts all twisted, Greg. We'll sort this out. Do you remember Peronne's Bakery just across the street from my place?"

"Yeah, I think. But a bakery? I thought you said we were having a beer. Or beers."

"I did. They serve beer. You'll like the place."

"Okay. I'll meet you there. But we need to get this tower choice resolved. We'll--"

"'Listen to me, mister. You're my knight in shining armor. Don't you forget it.' I mean that, Greg. I really do. You have given me a dream that I never could have conceived of by myself. Your dream. And we *can* make Vista Tel go away. You'll see. We just have to convince them. And we will. I'll be waiting at Peronne's."

* * *

Shit. Rachel scares me. I really do think she's a wacko. I've never met a girl like her. I don't understand her. I don't want to listen to her. But then -- she talks to me and I fold. I'm so captivated by her. What the hell ever happened to 'Just say no'? I can't. I know it. And I think she does, too.

* * *

Little Italy is absolutely crazy crowded on weekends but it's quiet on weeknights. I find a parking space with no problem. I walk into Peronne's. I've never been here before. It looks like a plain old bakery from the street. Now that I'm inside, I see it's a lot more. Along the back wall are bakery cases and a counter with a cash register that looks like an antique. And a cashier that looks as old as the cash register. *Senore* Peronne?

The bakery cases are full of goodies even at this time of night. A few tables are near the front windows. Kids my age hanging out. Better dressed, though. Yuppies. A couple of girls my age waiting on the tables. Cute girls. And well built girls. *Senore* Peronne has good taste.

I don't see Rachel. I walk further into the bakery and notice that there is an archway next to the counter. At first I thought it was a hallway to the restrooms or kitchen or something, but there are people going in and out. I head that way. It leads to a back room that is bigger than the front room. There is a bar with about ten stools, all taken, along one wall. There is a small dance floor, and some tables opposite the bar. And along the back wall there are some old wooden booths. I walk into the room. It's amazingly busy for this late on a weeknight.

I hear, "'Shane. Shane. Come back!'" from a booth in back. I have to smile. She is something. Oh, crap. Is she something, or what? Rachel looks absolutely stunning. Cute. Sexy. Wow.

"Wow."

Rachel is sitting on her legs in the booth. "'Oh, fiddle-dee-dee.' I'll bet you say that to all the girls." She beckons me to lean down. I do. She kisses me on the cheek.

I sit down opposite her in the booth. The table is bare. "All the girls don't look like you."

"You sounded like you needed cheering up when we talked. I decided to get cleaned up a little."

"I thought you were going to have a beer waiting for me."

"I do, 'My little chickadee.' At my place. It's too noisy in here tonight to talk, and too public for serious cheering up. Let's go."

She smiles impishly, slides out of the booth, grabs my hand, pulls me out of the booth, and heads for the archway. Before I really have a chance to think about what she means, we're through the front room and waiting to cross the street. "I called Justin while I was waiting for you to get here."

"Why?"

"I told him we were doing tower four next Friday night."

CHAPTER 101

(Mirsab)

"*Ciao*, Justin. Is this a good time to call?"

It is Rachel. "It is always a good time to call if you have information to provide to me."

"No, I mean is this a good time of day? I don't really know where you are. California, I think."

Why does she wish to know? "Yes, I live in California. I live in the Los Angeles area. Why do you want to know?"

"No big deal. I just don't want to call you in the middle of the night."

Now I understand. "It is not a problem. You may call me at any time, but why are you calling now?"

"I just want to tell you that we are definitely taking the tower down next Friday. I want to go over the plan with you. I don't want to waste this opportunity. This is going to be big. Stupendous!"

Rachel's excitement is contagious, but I am still uncertain.

She reiterates her proposed plan for the emails I am to send. I explain to her that each day's emails will come from a different location, and be sent from a different and untraceable email account.

I ask Rachel if she would like to have telephone calls made as well as emails sent. She is ecstatic! "That would be fantastic, Justin. Can you do that without endangering yourself?"

"Yes, I believe I can. The calls will appear to be made from somewhere in the eastern United States. Our power and apparent wide range of locations will intimidate Vista Tel, the media, and the government. They will believe that we are a large and international organization. That is exactly what we desire."

There is one last piece of information I need. I ask Rachel, "I must know the precise location of this tower, Rachel. Can you give me that information?"

"Can I email it to you?"

"No, that would not be wise."

"I need ten minutes to get on my computer and find the latitude and longitude of the site."

"Please call me back using the cell phones on which we are now talking when you have the information."

"Roger that, Justin."

She hangs up. Roger?

* * *

In about eight minutes, the TracFone rings. It is Rachel. She gives me the latitude and longitude of the tower.

"May I ask you how you obtained this information so quickly?"

"Peter found a website that locates and identifies cell phone towers on a Google-like map. There is another website that gives the latitude and longitude of any point on a similar map."

I write down both URLs. I must explore these websites.

I tell Rachel that I must now begin to make my preparations. "We will talk again in a few days."

I do not tell her that I wish to discuss this tower and this plan with Hamad before I proceed. I think I also want to verify the details of this tower and this plan with either Gregory or Peter before I proceed.

* * *

"Hello, Peter. It is your friend from California."

"This is a surprise."

"Do you have caller ID?"

"Yes…"

"Write down the number from which I am calling. Go to a payphone, and call me back at this number as soon as possible. I shall be waiting."

"But..."

"Goodbye."

* * *

I wait impatiently for Peter to return my call. It takes him nearly fifteen minutes.

He explains the delay. "I have not used a payphone in years. It took me a while to remember where the nearest one was."

"It is not an issue. It was necessary as you have no TracFones."

I apologize for disturbing him at home, and tell him that we need to discuss tower number four. "I need to verify that it will hit the power transmission lines. Have you seen the tower? Do you know for certain that it will hit the lines?"

"I visited the site today. The tower will definitely destroy the power lines."

He goes on. "I think this is a mistake. A major power outage will detract from our message, and jeopardize our mission."

I tell Peter that I agree, and that I must discuss this with my superiors before allowing it to happen. Peter seems considerably easier to deal with than Rachel. I ask him if I may send him some TracFones so that we, too, can discuss issues such as this more safely. He agrees and I write down his address. I will ship the phones tomorrow.

* * *

"*Aasalaamu Aleikum*, Hamad. *Ismee* Mirsab. *Kayf Halak?*"

"I told you I know who will call on this telephone. You need not identify yourself. And I told you no Arabic!"

"But, the last time we talked, you --"

"I made a mistake. It won't happen again. What is it?"

I tell Hamad of my conversation with Rachel. "Rachel is a Jew."

He seems not the least bit concerned. "We will use the American infidels, be they Christian or Jew!"

"Hamad, I am still concerned about this site. If I allow my cell to destroy this tower, it will destroy a high voltage transmission line and cause a blackout that will affect millions. I believe this to be a mistake."

Hamad violently disagrees. He is very angry that I am questioning his judgment. I tell him that I spoke directly to Peter and he becomes even angrier.

"Fool! I told you not to trust Peter. He may not be who you think he is. You are jeopardizing the entire enterprise!"

Hamad goes on to explain that he has already told his superiors of our plan. "They agree that this diversion is an excellent idea. It must happen as planned. Contact your cell, and tell them that in all probability, Vista Tel will not capitulate. Tell them that they must move forward with their plans to destroy the tower and the power transmission lines next Friday."

"I will do as you wish."

"Your future depends on it."

Before I can respond, he hangs up.

CHAPTER 102
Friday
(Peter)

It was about ten o'clock last night when I got the surprise call of my life. "Hello, Peter. It is your friend from California."

I was absolutely dumbfounded by the fact that Justin called me directly. If his name is Justin.

He told me to call him back as soon as possible from a payphone.

About two miles down the road is an off-brand gas station and a shaky looking bar called The Galleon. There is a payphone in a parking lot between them. Sitting at the payphone in my Mustang at ten o'clock, I probably looked like someone trying to score some drugs. I half expected to be arrested -- or mugged -- while I was talking on the phone.

If the location was a little weird, so was the discussion. Justin apologized for calling me at home, but said he had to talk to me about tower number four. He said he had talked to Rachel and wanted to verify some of the facts with me.

I verified for him that the tower will definitely hit the high tension lines. I told him that in all probability it will destroy them and cause a massive blackout. This obviously upset him.

I can't decide if he is legitimate or not. Well, I guess legitimate is not really the appropriate word for a mercenary who is arranging the destruction of one cell phone company's towers at the behest of another cell phone company. I guess I should be thinking mercenary performing illegal acts versus jihadist performing terrorist acts. That's really weird, now that I think about it.

Justin said he has to clear this with his superiors before he can allow it to happen. Allow it? I don't think he can stop Rachel and Gregory. I doubt that I can either.

And just to add to the weirdness, he wants to send me some TracFones so he can call me. Nick will love that! I told him okay. He asked for my address.

As soon as I got off the payphone with Justin, I got out of there. I tried to call Nick from my cell phone as I was driving back home. I got his answering machine. I told him I had important information. I said if I don't hear from him before then, I'd call him in the morning on my way to work.

$* * *$

Nick answers on the first ring. "Where were you last night?"

"I do have a life you know. Other than chasing bad guys. I was out with a girlfriend."

"With your girlfriend?"

"With *a* girlfriend, not *my* girlfriend. You should know that lasting relationships are difficult when you're in this business. You were there."

"Yeah, I was. And you're right. It didn't work for me either."

"So, why was it so urgent that you talk to me last night? You said you had information. What's up?"

"I had a call from Justin."

"Oh, really?"

And I explain the details of our conversation to him. I tell him I can't figure out if Justin is a mercenary or a terrorist, but that it's obvious that he has serious reservations about knocking out the power line. And I tell Nick that Justin said he must clear this with his superiors before allowing us to do it. I tell him it was almost like Justin thought he was running the show instead of assisting us.

Nick says he may think just that!

"Homeland Security's theory on this whole thing is that Justin is either an extremist Muslim jihadist or under the control of the jihadists. They think that the jihadists are using you to distract attention and resources from them while they are preparing even bigger things."

"Justin is a jihadist? An Arab?"

"So it would appear. HS thinks that Justin is playing you. Pretending to help so that he can guide what you do and when you do it."

"That's absurd. I've talked to him. He's not an Arab."

"Are you sure? Really sure? You were in the middle east…"

"That was a long time ago. But no, I'm not sure. Not really."

"Neither are we. Yet."

"So, what do we do, Nick? We can't let this tower happen!"

"We won't let it actually happen. We can't allow you to cause a large scale blackout. But we must allow it to continue for now."

"That's crazy!"

"No, it's not. Two points. Point one, the power grid is a lot more failsafe now than it was in 2003. The power companies don't talk about it for obvious reasons, but they have spent millions of dollars making the grid less susceptible to disruptions such as happened then."

"And the second point?"

"I can't go into much detail, but I do have permission to tell you that HS is monitoring selected cell phone conversations in California. The information you have provided has gone a long way toward helping HS unearth the next level in the jihadist hierarchy."

"Okay…"

"We must let this play out for another week. A week could make the difference between nailing just Gregory and Rachel, and nailing them *and* Justin *and* his superior or superiors. Justin and his superiors are the ones Homeland Security really wants."

I can't argue with the logic. Another week can't hurt. Much. I hope.

* * *

I don't think there is much that Mike can do. I'll just feel better if I share some of this with him. "Hi, Mike. It's your dear old Dad. If you can, give me a call between twelve and one my time. We need to talk."

* * *

I'm at my usual spot in Big Creek Park. It's kind of drizzly today, but it's reasonably warm. And it's better than the office. All three stooges are in today.

My phone rings. It's Mike. "Hi, number one son. I was hoping you were somewhere where you could call me."

"I just got back last night from a week in Paris. It's still one of my favorite cities. Even if it's full of the French."

"Business?"

"Business. So, what's up?"

I don't think I've talked to him since before tower number three. So I tell him all the details of that one, and my part as an urban terrorist/getaway car driver.

And I tell him about tower number four. Nick didn't say I couldn't tell Mike about Homeland Security's theory on this thing, so I tell him about my call from Justin and about just who HS thinks he is.

"Oh, Jeez, Dad. I had no idea this thing was going to get this messy. I don't like this at all."

"I know. I'm about ready to bail."

"It's too late for that. HS will see this through to its conclusion. They will go after Gregory, Rachel, Justin, and if they can get to him, Justin's handler. I've got to call Nick. We've got to get you out of this safely and anonymously. What needs to happen is that when the bust comes, you need to appear to escape without being arrested or implicated. If you get arrested and released, the bad guys will know that you're one of the good guys. And they'll come after you."

"That is scary, Mike. Very Scary. They know who I am. They know where I live."

"This is not a new situation, Dad. I have had some experience with this sort of thing. Actually, it's similar to what I was doing in Paris. Nick just needs to do the bust right. I'll work with him to make sure that he and his guys do it the way it needs done, Dad. Don't worry. It's a little complex, but it is doable."

CHAPTER 103

(Gregory)

It's the first Friday night I've spent without Rachel in a while. I don't think I like it. I was quite happy as student/bachelor until she came along. Well, if I'm honest, I have to admit that I led a pretty boring and lonely life. I also have to admit that she didn't just come along. I actively recruited her to join in my cause. Whatever.

Dinner alone consists of a beef and cheese toasted sub from Marco Polo's, Lay's bacon and cheddar potato chips, a Diet Coke and TV. Boring.

The phone rings. Rachel, maybe? "Hello?"

"It is your friend from California."

"This is a surprise. Why are you --"

"Do you have caller ID?"

"Yes, but --"

"Write down the number from which I am calling. Go to a payphone, and call me collect at this number as soon as possible. I shall be waiting."

"But --"

"Goodbye."

Shit, I didn't even get a chance to tell him I'm eating. Well, all of a sudden the evening is no longer boring. Why is he calling? On my land line? Rachel has all of the TracFones. He could have called her and -- and I don't know what.

I might as well do as he wants. There's an outside pay phone at the gas station at the end of the block. You'd think that in this age of cell phones, pay phones would be dying out. Not so. At least not in this neighborhood. There always seems to be someone on that phone. Curious.

* * *

How do you make a collect call from a payphone? The instructions, if there ever were any, are long gone. Of course, there is no phone book. I make a guess and hit the "0-Oper" button. A bored operator answers. I tell her I want to make a collect call. She tells me that I have to dial zero, and then the number. She hangs up and goes back into hibernation.

So I dial zero and then the number. Another equally bored operator answers and says, "How may I help you?" I tell her I want to make a collect call. She asks my name. I ask her if "Gregory" is sufficient. She says, "One moment, please" and I hear clicking and eventually ringing.

Justin answers. I say hello. There is no response. Then the Operator asks Justin if we will accept the charges for a call from Gregory. He says yes. She says thank you, there is a click, and she, too, goes back into hibernation.

Justin apologizes for the inconvenience, but says that it was necessary because Rachel has all of the TracFones, but he wanted to talk to me.

This is odd, to say the least. "Why do you want to talk to me?"

"I just want to verify that the next cell phone tower will be destroyed a week from tonight, and that it will destroy the high voltage transmission lines."

Oh, come on. "It will be destroyed *if* Vista Tel doesn't capitulate. Didn't Rachel tell you that?"

"Yes, but because of the -- to use Rachel's word -- stupendous nature of this endeavor, I just want to verify it with you. As I told Rachel, I will make the necessary arrangements to have the emails sent and the telephone calls made. I have little confidence that Vista Tel will capitulate, so you must prepare to destroy the tower as planned."

Wait a minute. Now he's trying to take over, too? Rachel was bad enough. This fool gets put in his place right now. "Look, Justin, this is my project. I plan it. I run it. I decide what we do and when. You just do your part. Okay?"

"I am sorry. I did not mean to offend you. Of course it is your project, as you say. I just want to verify the plan so that I may do my part."

I wish Rachel was so easy to dominate. "Okay. That's better. Is there anything else you need?"

"No. Goodbye, Gregory. And thank you."

This guy is just plain weird. "See you."

CHAPTER 104

(Mirsab)

I suspect that I may have upset Gregory somewhat. I meant no harm by suggesting that they should prepare to destroy the next tower. I wonder why that upset him. It was really a quite innocuous comment.

In the end he seemed placated, so I shall not be overly concerned. The important thing is that I suggested to him that Vista Tel will, in all probability, not capitulate.

I wonder what Hamad would order if Vista Tel did, in fact, capitulate. My cell would feel that they have accomplished their purpose. What then?

* * *

As always seems to be the case, Hamad answers almost immediately.

"Hamad, it seems that it does not matter at what time I call you. You always answer the telephone almost immediately. May I ask how it is that you are able to do that? I would like to be as timely with my telephone communications."

"It is really quite simple. Whenever I am away from my desk, I carry three cell phones: the next one on which my superior might call, the next one on which you might call, and one other."

"You are right. It is quite simple. I shall start carrying the next one that you might use and the next one that my cell might use with me at all times. Thank you."

"And you called now because?"

"My cell will destroy the next cell phone tower one week from tonight. I have advised them that, in all probability, Vista Tel will not capitulate, and that they should proceed as planned."

"You have done well. Your performance will not go unnoticed."

"Thank you. I would like to ask you to help me with the notifications to be made when the next tower is destroyed."

I explain to Hamad the series of emails Rachel has asked me to send. He agrees that her plan is an excellent one. Again he approves of the carefully considered escalating threats. I tell him that I will send these emails from public locations using fictitious email accounts I shall create. I have several public libraries in mind.

"Excellent. Include in each email some fact about the previous destructions that is not publicly known. Contact your cell for details that have not been made public."

"I shall do that. Perhaps you can make the phone calls to the media when the tower actually goes down."

There is silence for a minute. "Why do you want me to do that?"

"The phone calls announcing the last tower's destruction came from California. Perhaps this time, the telephone calls should originate elsewhere."

Hamad agrees. "Call me as soon as you receive word that the tower has been destroyed. I will cause the telephone notifications to be made immediately."

I remind him that the tower will be destroyed before dawn in Ohio. "The time is not important. The media will be notified virtually immediately."

I am very pleased that Hamad is willing to do this.

I have been thinking of something else. Perhaps this is a good time to discuss it with Hamad. "I am considering something else next Friday night."

"And what is that?"

"I am considering traveling to Ohio to witness this act of destruction and its aftermath in person. I might even be able to catch sight of the members of my cell. Perhaps near their homes the day before or the day after. I --"

"Are you insane? You are an Arab! Do you not realize that any Arab traveling to Cleveland will be suspect? We are very fortunate that the authorities believe that these acts of urban terrorism are the work of far left-wing American environmental activists. But they will be watching for *any* suspicious persons!"

"But surely they won't be monitoring all passengers flying into Cleveland. They believe that this is the work of locals. They--"

"*No!*"

Hamad will brook no discussion. He has made his position quite clear. "I apologize for my foolish idea. I will call within the week to verify that all is proceeding according to plan."

We say our goodbyes. They are strained.

It was not a good time after all to discuss my plan to travel to Cleveland. I expected Hamad to object, but I did not expect him to object so violently. It is good that I did not tell him that I was going to ask Nura to accompany me.

* * *

The more I consider it, the more I believe that Hamad is wrong. It is impossible for the police to be monitoring all travel activity. Moreover, I am certain that they believe the perpetrators of these acts are local and American. They actually are just that, after all. We have led the authorities to believe that. We have misled the authorities into believing that they have international connections, but the message has been that they are local far left radical environmentalists.

Hamad is wrong. Nura and I will fly into Cleveland early Friday morning. We will attempt to catch glimpses of Gregory and Rachel and Peter. I know their home addresses. It will not be difficult. We will witness the destruction of the tower and the high voltage transmission lines from somewhere safe but nearby. We will return to California Saturday evening.

CHAPTER 105

(John)

I don't know who is more stupid, the Arab, or the Americans! In the Bible, Jesus Christ compared people to sheep because sheep are dumb -- and easily led. These people are sheep!

* * *

The Arab believes that he is aiding his countrymen in preparing for some great jihad here in the United States. Jihad? Give me a break! There are tons of Arabs here, true, but they will never be well enough organized to wage a holy war. Isolated -- even horrendous -- damage like nine-eleven, yes, but war, no!

If the Arab population had any self-reliance at all, they'd be busy making money and making a good life for themselves instead of blindly following a bunch of extremist holy men. Talk about sheep.

Just as I told him to, Mirsab pretends to be working for some mysterious competing cell phone company, contacts Gregory and his little band of fools, and convinces them to accept his help.

The fool has no idea how he is being used. He may be well educated, but he's remarkably gullible.

He has involved his Arab girlfriend, and now he wants to go to Cleveland? Fool. Luckily, he is a sheep. I play the mean Arab jihadist, and he caves. He does what he's told.

* * *

And then there are the Americans. More sheep! These fools really believe that they can force Vista Tel to start using another provider's towers! And they think the Arab is some kind of industrial espionage agent who is willing to help them!

I almost understand Gregory and Rachel. They're young, idealistic, foolish -- sheep. They can be easily led. I don't understand Peter, though. He's old enough to know better. Then again, most Americans are old enough to know better -- but they don't. Look who they elected president for God's sake! Still, Peter surprises me. He just doesn't seem the type to get involved in this crap. I'm glad he did though -- he makes leading the rest of the sheep easier.

* * *

The great irony here is that the Americans think Mirsab is Justin, the industrial espionage agent -- and Mirsab thinks I'm Hamad, the Arab jihadist! If the Americans found out that Justin is really an Arab jihadist, they'd poop their pants! And if Mirsab found out that *I'm* the American industrial espionage agent, he'd poop his pants, too!

* * *

I love this country. It truly is the land of opportunity. I have managed to parlay a couple of tours as a Ranger Officer in the Middle East into a very nice career. I speak enough Arabic, and understand the Arab mind enough that I've built a reputation as a person who can use them to do what others want done. My clients get their little jobs done, and the Arabs get the blame.

Actually, I'm not at all convinced that this group in Cleveland will do any real damage to Vista Tel, but my employers think they will. The important thing is that they are paying me very good money to make this all happen. What a country! I love it!

The chain is simple. My very anonymous employers pay me a lot of money to make life difficult for Vista Tel. I pretend that I'm an Arab jihadist and convince Mirsab to follow my orders. Mirsab pretends to be an American industrial espionage agent, and directs and helps the Americans in Cleveland. The Americans destroy Vista Tel towers. This disrupts Vista Tel's service and generally makes their lives difficult. They give up and go out of business, or sell out, or something.

The nice thing is that there are lots of layers between my employers and the towers. They're safe, they're happy. They pay me. I'm safe, I'm happy. The sheep do what they're told, Vista Tel is unhappy.

And the truly great thing is that if anybody gets caught, if anybody goes to jail, it'll be the American sheep!

* * *

They may be dumb sheep, but their plan is sound. This will be, to use Rachel's words, a truly stupendous event.

The mayhem it will cause will be unprecedented. When the media break the news that Vista Tel could have prevented this very major blackout, the shit will hit the fan. Their stock will nosedive. Their customers will be so pissed that a significant number will bail. Who knows, it just may drive Vista Tel out of business. In any event, it will be a great event to witness.

* * *

I was in Afghanistan in 2003. I missed that great blackout. Maybe I don't have to miss this one.

Mirsab can't go to Cleveland -- Homeland Security will be watching for any even slightly suspicious activity.

A slightly disabled Veteran returning home for a visit with old friends and relatives will not be the least bit suspicious, though. There is no reason that I can't go to Cleveland. I can do my part of the job from there via the modern miracles of cell phones and Wi-Fi.

CHAPTER 106

Sunday

(Peter)

I had to tell Kate about my talk with Mike. I had to tell her that the Arabs know who we are.

She is a little scared. Maybe more than a little. I hate it when I have to tell her something that makes her frown. That's not what I want for her. I want to tell her things that make her smile. That, as I see it, is my job.

Kate said she would never have encouraged me to get involved if she had known the danger it would bring to us. I agreed.

But I tried to reassure her by explaining that Mike is getting involved. She questioned how he could do that. She said she thought he was a U.S. Marshall. I reminded her that Mike won't talk much about what he actually does. I suggested that an ex-Army Ranger with a Computer Science degree has to be doing more than escorting bad guys around the country. She asked if he could be doing international spy stuff like I used to do -- if that's why he went to places like Paris.

"Kate, I didn't do 'spy stuff.' I was a field engineer working on electronic systems for NATO."

"Yeah, right. I think they call them *contractors* now. Mike has got to be involved with that kind of stuff. If he can watch our backs, I'll be forever grateful."

"So will I, cutie, so will I. It'll be over soon."

I tell Kate that I have to go to meet Greg and Rachel tonight, that we're doing our final planning. She asks if I'll be late. She says she doesn't really want to be alone. I reassure her that I will not be late. "I promise."

"Call me when you're heading home."

"I will. I love you. Bye." And we kiss like we haven't kissed for a very long time.

* * *

The meeting at Rachel's is a complete waste of time. They start talking about what to wear. I kind of take charge. "What's wrong with the shit you wore last time? You looked like Ninjas or something, but the same outfits will work again. And we'll use the same MO. It worked the last time, and it'll work again."

Greg looks skeptical. Rachel looks worried. "Just like last time, we'll meet at a truck stop, pile you and your tools into the Denali, and I'll drive you to the site. Just like last time, I'll hang out somewhere nearby 'till you're ready for me to pick you up."

Rachel is a little white. "But we almost got caught!"

"That was because the site was too open. This is a much better site this time. It's secluded. There will be nobody around late at night. You really did pick a stupendous site, Rachel. The results will be epic!"

She smiles. "'You want the moon? Just say the word, and I'll throw a lasso around it and pull it down.'"

That's the Rachel I know and love. "From *It's a Wonderful Life*. And you got us the moon, Rachel!"

Greg looks disgusted. And miserable. I want to smack him. To just say, "Oh, lighten up, punk." But instead, I try to involve him.

"Greg, what about tools? We lost everything last time. How long will it take to re-equip ourselves? What can I do?"

He starts to look less pained and more interested. "Nothing, I guess. Rachel and I have been rebuilding our tool kit."

I ask him where they have been getting the stuff like the pipe and the big sockets. He names some names -- the places are widely scattered. I tell him he did well, and it's his turn to smile. He blabs on about inconsequential stuff. I say the supplier names to myself over and over -- Nick will want to know them.

Now that I've got them both feeling a little smug, it's time to bail. "I've got to visit a plant in the morning, so I have to go. Is there is anything I can do?"

They look at each other and shake their heads "No."

I think they're thinking about each other more than the tower right now. That's good. I'm out of here.

* * *

As soon as I'm on my way home, I call Kate and tell her I'm on my way. She's relieved. She asks if I want to play some Dominos when I get home. "Yeah, it'll help us both relax."

And my cell phone beeps -- an incoming call. "I've got another call, cutie."

"Call me back."

I flip over to the incoming call. It's Nick. "Hi, Nick. What's up?"

"I've got some information I can pass on to you."

"Yeah?"

"Justin Brown is Mirsab bin Saleh al-Fulani."

"Oh, shit…"

346

"It's not as bad as it sounds."

"What do you mean?"

"Mirsab is an amateur. He's an engineering grad student at UCLA. He's the son of a fairly wealthy Syrian merchant family and he's been in the United States about three years. He has no known connections to any terrorist group here, in Syria or anywhere else. We think he is being used by others that we have yet to identify, but we're getting close to his connection."

"So, now what?"

"We proceed as planned. We've also identified his female accomplice. She is Nura bint Taimurs al-Thani -- she could be his girlfriend. Another amateur, or more likely, an unwitting accomplice. Mirsab probably conned her into helping him buy the phones, but she doesn't seem to have any other involvement."

"Yeah, but--"

"Nura has lived in the United States virtually all her adult life. She's the only daughter of an independently wealthy Qatari. We think her father has a connection to the Royal family, some distant relative. No hint of any terrorist connections there, either."

"You said you think this Mirsab is being used?"

"Yes. We're still working on his handler. We have warrants to monitor Mirsab's Internet activity and phone calls. In addition to the TracFones he uses to call you guys, he has another set that he uses to contact his handler, a character in Alexandria, Virginia, named Hamad. We're close to nailing down a more precise location for him. We need just a few more phone calls."

"I'd like to say I'm amazed at how you've been able to put this all together, but I'm not. I know what we were capable of thirty years ago when I was in the business. I suspect that's primitive by today's standards."

"That's a pretty good assessment, Cap'n."

CHAPTER 107

(Gregory)

I really get tired of this cutesy stuff between Peter and Rachel. It's almost flirting on his part, and Rachel just sucks it up. If he weren't so old and so married, I'd think he was trying to get in her pants. Maybe he is.

Peter finally realizes I'm here, too. He asks me, "Greg, what about tools? We lost everything last time. How long will it take to re-equip ourselves? What can I do?"

Maybe he does know that I exist. I tell him that Rachel and I are taking care of it.

I start telling him about some of the new places I'm going to start using when Rachel catches my eye. She smiles her flirty little smile. The one that says, "I want to get you alone." I kind of lose interest in talking about tools.

Peter says he's got to get up early tomorrow to go on some job, and starts to look like he wants to leave. I look at Rachel. We don't argue.

Peter leaves. Rachel walks him to the door, and says goodbye. She turns. I'm still sitting on the couch. She takes four quick steps across the room -- and pounces on me! "'Hello, gorgeous.' I need laid. But I'm hungry, too. Let's go to Peronne's and get something to eat. Then come back and solve my horniness problem."

"To paraphrase the Godfather, that's an offer I can't refuse!"

* * *

While we wait for our food, we go over the things we need to buy before Friday night. There's not much we still need, but we go over our mental list carefully. We don't want to write anything down, so we quietly discuss the assault on the tower step by step, verbally checking off the equipment we'll need for each step.

Preparing: Peter is right. The dark clothes we wore last time will work fine. And his Denali proved to be a great getaway car.

Entering: gloves, flashlights, bolt cutters. I'm really sorry to have lost the bolt cutters on the last job. They were my dad's, probably older than me. Oh well.

Unbolting: breaker bar, pipe, socket, WD-40. I tell Rachel I'll make a quick trip to the site this week to check the socket size. She wants to come along -- I'll make that not happen -- I want to go alone.

Toppling: two pieces of rope, come along, steel wedges, sledgehammer. This time I get a real sledge, not a hand sledge. And four wedges instead of two. The tower is bigger. It'll need more help to go where we want it to go.

Escaping: walkie-talkies. The one thing we didn't lose. We should think about getting some with a better range, though.

Just as we finish going over our list, our food arrives. We ask the waitress for two more drafts, and dig in. I'm hungry, too, so we get quiet as we eat. As we start to satisfy our hunger, we start talking again. Now it's more about what's next. We have to be careful about who might overhear, so it's difficult. Neither of us would ever admit it, but I think we're both getting tired of our campaign. I know I am. I really hope it won't take too many more of these to break Vista Tel's will. I think I'd rather just be getting on with my life. Maybe with Rachel.

As we finish our supper, Rachel leans over and says, "I still need laid, 'My little chickadee.'"

* * *

An hour later, I'm heading home. I have a class tomorrow morning. No doubt about it. Being an urban terrorist is starting to lose its appeal.

But I told Rachel I'd make sure we have the right socket. The wrong size socket would be a complete showstopper.

I don't have a class on Tuesday 'till afternoon. I can go to the site tomorrow night and sleep in Tuesday morning.

Rachel is getting the rope and the come along from Lowe's. I'll stop at Home Depot tomorrow after class and pick up the wedges and the sledge hammer. That'll complete our shopping. We'll be ready to go on Friday night.

CHAPTER 108
(Mirsab)

It is truly amazing how easy it is to set up a completely fraudulent email account. All that is required is a fictitious name and address. In ten minutes, I have set up four fraudulent accounts: Gmail for today, AIM for Wednesday, GMAX for Thursday, and Yahoo! for Friday. By using each only once, there will be no record to be traced.

I go to the Long Beach Public Library instead of right around the corner to the Torrance Library. Torrance is just too close to home. Long Beach is an easy trip over Sepulveda to the 710 and south to Ocean Boulevard.

I sit down at a public access computer, make sure nobody is behind me, and log on to Gmail and my email account. I send the first of my emails to Vista Tel. It is brief, but succinct. As Hamad directed, though, to verify that we are, in fact, the perpetrators and not some *copycat* pranksters, I include a fact that has not been made public.

Because the police arrived at such an inopportune time during our last demolition, we were forced to leave our tools. Among them was a very old pair of bolt cutters with H K P cast into the handles. They are a family heirloom. We will miss them.

You have forty-eight hours to indicate your intent to capitulate, or we will destroy another tower. The damage caused by the next tower will be orders of magnitude greater than the damage caused by the last tower.

I look around and verify that nobody is interested in what I am doing. I open the manila folder I have brought with me and take out the paper with the list of email addresses. I quickly but carefully copy them into the TO: box on the email editor. I hit send, log off of Gmail, and quickly type in www.msnbc.com into the browser address bar. Then I go to the Outlook Internet Options Window and delete the history of websites visited. There is no point in leaving the link to Gmail in the computer.

I gather up my folder, return the guest pass to the library desk, and walk out into the warm evening air.

If they do not publicly indicate their willingness to cease building towers and to remove their existing towers by Wednesday, I will find another library and send them the next email. I will do it again on Thursday if necessary.

And Friday, I will send the last email from Cleveland!

* * *

I am so glad that Nura has agreed to go with me to Cleveland. When I told her the purpose of the trip, she hesitated not at all. She said simply, "Mirsab, I got involved in this of my own free will. I want to see it through to the end. I want to do this with you."

I was a little awed by her determination. She is a strong woman.

When I told her I would rent us a car and two hotel rooms for Friday night, she smiled somewhat impishly and said, "Make it one room for two nights. Pick a nice hotel in downtown Cleveland. I'll rent the car -- I have an Emerald Club Card. We'll play tourist for the weekend. I want to see the Rock and Roll Hall of Fame."

After her comment, I was more than a little awed.

* * *

When I get home, I log on to Travelocity. Tickets are expensive this close to departure, and a lot of flights are sold out, but I find seats on Continental for a non-stop flight from LAX to Cleveland leaving late Thursday night and arriving in Cleveland Friday morning. I find a return flight leaving Sunday evening.

I will starve for several weeks, but I select the best hotel I can find, the Marriott Renaissance Cleveland. It is in downtown Cleveland and within walking distance to the Rock and Roll Hall of Fame.

I have heard of this place, the Rock and Roll Hall of Fame, but I know little about it. If it is important to Nura, it is important to me.

Rachel used the word "stupendous" to describe the tower they will destroy. For many reasons, I expect this weekend to be -- stupendous.

CHAPTER 109
(John)

Mirsab called and said he sent his email to Vista Tel. I would like to have seen it. I wonder.

I know I can set up a bogus email account on a site like Yahoo. I also know that IP Addresses can be tracked to pretty specific locations.

I think the way to go is to find a place with a public Wi-Fi connection -- like a Starbucks -- and build a bogus email account. I can then tell Mirsab to send his emails to that account as well. I don't want him to copy me on the ones he sends to Vista Tel and the others. I don't want even a bogus email address available to them. He needs to do a cut and paste of the text to a separate email. That will isolate me.

I can then log on to my bogus account from wherever there is a Wi-Fi hot spot and monitor what he's doing.

As I crush the cell phone Mirsab called me on, I realize that we only have two sets left. I need to call my supplier and have them send some more out to me and to Mirsab. One nice thing about having a phone company as a customer: the supply of cell phones is endless -- and free.

I definitely need to go to Cleveland. This will be, as Rachel said, a stupendous event. I can watch my sheep in action. From a distance of course.

I'll fly in Friday morning and make a long weekend of it. Stay in a nice hotel, eat some good food, watch the fireworks. Maybe even do some sightseeing. I've always wanted to see the Rock and Roll Hall of Fame.

If the phone calls I have to make come from Cleveland, it'll seem perfectly plausible to Homeland Security. It'll be another pointer to a local group.

When I get home, I log on to Expedia. Continental has non-stops from Washington National to Cleveland Friday morning with return flights Sunday evening. That'll work.

I tack on a room at the Marriott in downtown Cleveland and I'm all set.

Almost. There is public transportation, the RTA train, from the Cleveland Airport to downtown, but I'll need a car to get around. I'll definitely want to check out this site before Friday night.

Mirsab did have one good idea. I'll do a drive by of the homes of my little flock of sheep. Maybe I can see what my sheep actually look like. I've got a mental image of each of them, but the reality will be worth seeing.

I log back on to Expedia and add a car. National is not cheap, but their Emerald Club makes it easy. Is it too cold in Cleveland for a convertible? It probably is, but one thing I do want is a GPS.

* * *

There's nothing on TV tonight -- big surprise there -- so I decide to do a little homework before the trip.

Even though I'll have a GPS in the car, I still like paper maps. I get on Google and print road maps of the area around the tower, and around Peter's house, Gregory's house, and Rachel's apartment.

I also switch from the map to the satellite view and explore the area around the tower. I never cease to be amazed at the detail available to the public. The aerial view allows me to see the tower itself -- the maximum resolution on Google Maps is about fifty feet of terrain to each inch on my computer screen.

Even more amazing is the little gold man at the top of the zoom gadget. When I drag him over to Route 2, the view changes so that I can see what the tower looks like from there. Absolutely amazing. I rotate his viewpoint and zoom in to see the tower through the scrub along the road! How many photos must Google have stored to make this sort of thing possible?

And that sort of amazement with technology always leads me to ask myself the question, "What can the government do that they are *not* allowing us to see?"

CHAPTER 110

Monday

(Peter)

Last night after Nick told me about the definite Arab connection, I told him about my meeting with Greg and Rachel. He didn't seem very surprised by anything I said, and kept stressing that we had to let this play out.

Another sleepless night. I am definitely getting too old for this shit!

And another lunchtime call to Mike. I tell him I really don't like the way this is coming down. I tell him I'm worried about our safety. I tell him I don't want Kate and me to wind up in some witness protection program kind of thing because Arab terrorists are looking for me.

Mike is less than totally reassuring. He says he's confident that if HS does it right, the Arabs will not know of my dual role. I tell him that someone once said, "Military operations never go as planned." And I tell him I think that probably applies to Homeland Security, too.

"Dad, I've got to go back to Paris next week, but I'm free until them. I'm going to call Nick and tell him I want to be involved in this."

"You can -- will -- do that?"

"Yeah. I don't think he can refuse me."

"You have no idea how much more safe that will make me feel. And Kate, too. She is really, really regretting that she encouraged me to get involved. She's scared, Mike."

"Tell Kate we'll come out of this okay. I won't let anything happen to you guys. I love you both."

I do feel better. Kate will, too. "Well, kid, I've got to get back to the loony bin before the stooges miss me. Kate will be very reassured that you're getting involved. Me, too."

* * *

I'm on my way home. Thinking about my lunchtime call to Mike. I want so bad to tell Kate that he's getting more involved. But I want to do it in person. Twenty minutes. And the phone rings.

"Hello, Peter, it's Nick."

"That's not what my phone says. It says you are Mr. PRIVATE. Isn't caller ID wonderful?"

"Do I detect a note of sarcasm?"

"I'm just getting tired of this whole thing. If I'd have known it was going to go on this long, to get this messy, I would not have gotten involved."

"I suspect you would have. I've gotten to know you, Cap'n. I respect you and what you're doing. So does my organization. You will be thanked when this is all over, and it will be over this week."

"We'll see. Why'd you call?"

"More information. Mirsab and Nura are coming to visit you!"

"What?"

"We intercepted some conversations between Mirsab and his handler, Hamad. Mirsab told Hamad he wanted to come to

Cleveland to witness this tower's destruction. Hamad went bullshit and forbade it."

"But you said they were coming."

"They are. Mirsab is disobeying Hamad. He made plane reservations for him and Nura -- under their own names!"

"You're shittin' me."

"I told you they were amateurs. Nura even rented a car using her National Emerald Club card. He made a reservation at the Marriott Cleveland Key Center. One room, so we can assume that she *is* his girlfriend. They're coming in on the red eye on Friday morning. We will be with them every step of the way."

"So, you'll nail four of them: Gregory, Rachel, Mirsab and Nura. What about Hamad?"

"We're still working on him. He's slippery. We need about two more phone calls and he's ours!"

CHAPTER 111

(Gregory)

This crap really is getting old. Tromping around in the dark. What's worse, it's foggy and cold and damp tonight. I'll be soaked by the time I get out of here.

The good news is that this site is completely isolated. There is absolutely nobody around here. This spot is like the second tower we did. The little county road crosses under Interstate 90, the power line is just south of the Interstate, and the access road is just south of that. There are no houses within a mile of here. There is nothing but old, no-longer-used farmland and some second growth woods scattered around.

A mile and a half east is an interchange with a gas station and a little truck stop sort of place, but nothing here. Crap! Except mud puddles! Now I'll have wet feet to match my wet pant legs.

At least the fog will keep me from being seen from the Interstate. I get to the fence around the cell tower. The gate is still unlocked. Idiots. They can't be taking us very seriously if their security is this crappy. They will after Friday night, though.

I go to the base of the tower and move to the side away from the Interstate just in case the fog is not as thick as it seems. I get the socket I brought out of my pocket and turn on my flashlight.

Oh, shit. Now what?

These nuts are not just tack welded like the others have been. These are frickin' welded all the way around. They will never come off!

* * *

I'm back in the car. And wet from the knees down. And cold. I've got to think. That truck stop is a mile and a half away. I need a cup of coffee.

* * *

The coffee is crappy. It matches the night and my mood.

No way are those nuts going to come off. This is not going to work. Now what? Another site? Can we find one in time? Do I even want to?

That must be why the gate was unlocked. Vista Tel probably has crews going around welding all the lock nuts in place to make it impossible for us to just unscrew them. Are all the towers going to be the way this one was?

I've got to figure this out. It's my show, even if I am getting tired of it. Shit. Shit. Shit!

* * *

It's midnight. I'm still almost an hour from home. If I'm up and miserable, there's no point in being the only one.

"Hello?"

"Hi, Rachel. Did I wake you? We've got to talk."

"No, you didn't wake me. I was in bed reading. What's up? Do you want to come over?"

"I don't want to come over. I'm cold and wet. I just left your tower a little while ago. We have a problem. A serious one."

"What?"

"The lock nuts on the tower base are welded in place -- not just tacked like the others -- welded. We'll never get them off!"

"There must be a way."

"Not without a cutting torch and tanks of oxygen and acetylene or a power hacksaw and a very long extension cord or a bomb!"

"Greg. There is always a way. You're an engineer. You know that. Why don't you come over. I'll do two things while you're en route. I'll call Justin and tell him our dilemma. Maybe he'll have an idea. I'll dig around on the Internet -- it's amazing what you can find."

"I really don't think I want to come over, Rachel. I am cold and wet and grumpy and still an hour from home. But call me if you come up with anything. Okay?"

"I will, Greg. Give yourself a hug. Sounds like you need it. 'After all, tomorrow is another day!'"

Oh, stop! "Yeah. Right."

* * *

In forty-five minutes, Rachel calls me back. "Justin thinks he can help."

"How?"

"He's pretty sure he can get us something called a cutting charge."

"A what?"

"A cutting charge. I looked it up on the Internet. Have you ever seen a video of a building being demolished, where it just kind of collapses in on itself?"

"Yeah…"

"Well, they do that with cutting charges. They are specially shaped explosive charges that literally cut though the I-beams. Like a hack saw but quick. We can use them to cut the tower off at its base!"

"And Justin can get these?"

"He thinks so. He'll call me tomorrow."

"'Toto, I've got a feeling we're not in Kansas anymore!'"

CHAPTER 112

Tuesday

(Mirsab)

I slept little last night. My thoughts kept returning to what I told Rachel. I do not know if Hamad will approve of what I told her. I do not know if it was wise to assure her that we can help. I do not know if Hamad can provide what they need.

I was caught off guard by her call and by my cell's dilemma. It was necessary to make a fast decision. I had to act as though I am in charge.

I do know, however, that my plan will work. I have no experience with explosives or with Thermite. Certainly no experience with cutting charges. However, I have read of them extensively on the Internet.

A few foolish American conspiracy theorists still believe that some of the World Trade Center buildings were brought down with Thermite linear cutting charges. They are wrong. The Trade Center was destroyed on nine-eleven by Arab heroes using the Americans' own aircraft as weapons. It is not what the American politicians mean when they use the phrase, "Weapons of mass destruction," but I believe it is an appropriate phrase.

Because of their conspiracy theories, however, there is a huge amount of information on the Internet about Thermite and about its use in metal cutting.

My hope is that Hamad can provide what my cells needs. My fear, though, is that he can not do so quickly enough to allow them to maintain their schedule.

Since dawn, I have been waiting until it is a reasonable time in Virginia. I call. "Hello?"

"Hamad, my cell has a problem. I hope you can help."

"What is the problem?"

I explain that Rachel called me late last night and informed me that Gregory has discovered that the lock nuts on the bolts at the tower base are securely welded in place. They will not be able to remove them and bring down the tower. Gregory told her that their alternatives were to either cut the bolts with an oxy-acetylene torch, to cut them with a power hack saw, or to use explosives.

"And what did you tell Rachel?"

"I hope I have not overstepped my authority. I told her I might be able to supply Thermite linear cutting charges."

"Thermite? Cutting charges? What do you know of this technology?"

I tell Hamad that I know only what I have read on the Internet. However, I explain that I have studied the technology extensively, and I think it can be used to cut the bolts, or even the tower itself. I remind him that though I'm an electrical engineer, I have studied chemistry and physics.

Hamad is not upset. He agrees that Thermite is a possible solution. "Thermite is not illegal in the United States. It is a simple mixture of powdered iron oxide and powdered aluminum, usually ignited by magnesium. However, there may be better solutions. Let me talk to my superiors and have them query our scientists and engineers. We have experts available in these areas. We have experts here in the United States as well as in the homeland."

"Then what I told Rachel meets with your approval?"

"Yes. You did well. The tower must be destroyed on schedule. The only decision that must be made is how to best accomplish this. The difficulty that must be overcome is getting the necessary materials to Cleveland in time. Though Thermite is legal, we must be very careful about how we transport it. We must not attract unnecessary attention to ourselves."

"I see."

"I will call you soon. Be certain that you have the next of our cell phones with you at all times."

"I shall. May I call Rachel and tell her that we will provide what they need?"

"Yes. Goodbye."

* * *

"Hello?"

"Hello. Rachel. It is Justin."

"Hi, Justin. I've been waiting for your call. What did you find out? Are we dead in the water?"

"I do not yet know exactly what we will supply. I do not yet know how we will get the material to you. I do know, however, that our organization will supply what you need to destroy the tower on schedule."

"'All-righty then!'"

CHAPTER 113

(John)

It's exactly eight a.m. when Mirsab calls. He is agitated. He must have been waiting impatiently until he thought it was a reasonable time to call.

I ask him what the problem is, and he tells me about the base plate bolts being welded in place. It's about time that Vista Tel started to take some action to try to stop my Cleveland sheep!

Mirsab tells me that Rachel said their choices are limited. "And what did you tell Rachel?"

"I hope I have not overstepped my authority. I told her I might be able to supply Thermite linear cutting charges."

He is right on, but I need to act surprised. "Thermite? Cutting charges? What do you know of this technology?"

He basically says he doesn't know shit. He's an Internet expert!

I give him a thirty second lesson on Thermite, and tell him I've got to talk to our experts. Hah! I'm the expert! I was doing demolition work while my sheep were still peeing in diapers!

Mirsab is looking for a pat on the head, so I give it to him."Yes. You did well. Thermite is legal, but we must be careful about how we have it transported to Cleveland so that we do not attract attention."

I tell him I'll call him back soon and hang up.

I've got to think a little. Thermite will work. The sheep can form plasticized Thermite into a band around the tower near the base, and ignite it with a strip of magnesium. It'll cut the tower like a chainsaw through a tree. The trick will be to get it to fall in the right direction.

Another alternative is a shaped explosive charge. A shaped charge is noisy but fast. And they can place it on the side of the tower opposite the direction they want it to fall. The explosion will give the tower the nudge it needs. Really, out there in the boonies in the middle of the night, who cares about the noise. That's the way to go.

This is Tuesday. Plenty of time. I can contact my supplier today, and he'll have the material ready for me tomorrow. I can double seal it in high density plastic bags, box it, and ship it UPS Red Label. It will be there Thursday morning.

I just have to make sure one of my sheep is home to receive it.

* * *

"Hi, George, it's John Collins. I have a short shopping list."

He tells me to bring him my list. "I'm in Alexandria. It would take me three hours to get to Norfolk."

"Oh. Do you remember my other phone number?"

I tell him I do. "Call me in ten minutes."

His other phone number is a payphone he uses sometimes for extra security. The idea is to call him there from a random payphone. That makes everything virtually untraceable.

Payphones are getting hard to find in Alexandria, but I've got ten minutes and a couple of ideas.

* * *

"George?"

"Yeah. You said your list is short. What do you need?"

"One item: a shaped explosive cutting charge. I need to cut through a tubular steel tower about three feet in diameter. I want to control the direction of the fall."

"Sounds interesting. Will I hear about it in the news?"

"I guarantee it."

"You do such interesting work, John. Did I ever tell you that John Collins sounds like an alias?"

"I assure you that it really is my name. Scout's Honor. You'd be amazed at what my alias is."

"I'm sure I would be. When do you need this?"

"Can I pick it up tomorrow afternoon?"

"We can do that. Do you care to know the cost?"

"Nope. I'll bring adequate cash. See you tomorrow, George"

"Always a pleasure, John."

* * *

"I need you to call your people in Cleveland. The package containing the material they need will be shipped via UPS Overnight Air Freight. It will be delivered in Cleveland before eleven a.m. on Thursday."

"I can do that--"

"Silence. It is imperative that somebody be there to receive the package. Call them, find out who can be at home on Thursday morning, and call me before the end of the day. Make sure to get the proper street address."

"I will call Cleveland immediately, but it may take a while to determine who can receive the package."

"Do it quickly. I shall be waiting for your call. Goodbye."

CHAPTER 114

Wednesday

(Peter)

Kate is still squirrely. So am I. We decide that a good steak will help us settle down, so we head for Crocker Park. There's a steakhouse there that's every bit as good as a Morton's.

Crocker Park is about a half hour from home. East on Interstate 90. It's an upscale shopping/eating/living development that we enjoy frequenting. It's only a couple of years old, but it's designed to look and feel like Main Street, USA. About twelve city blocks of genuine fake nostalgia. But we really do like it.

By the time we get there, we've changed our plans twice. From Hyde Park Prime Steakhouse, to Brio Tuscan Grill, to The Cheesecake Factory. A step down, but you've got to love their humongous variety of humongous servings of cheesecake. It'll be dinner there, and cheesecake to go home.

* * *

At seven p.m., on a Wednesday night there is no wait, but we request a booth overlooking the boulevard and that takes a few minutes. We occupy our time by studying the cheesecake display. They have something like thirty different varieties of cheesecake.

Our booth is ready. We no sooner get seated than my cell phone rings. I hate to see people talking on cell phones when they are with other people, but I flip it open to see who it is. It's Mike. "Kate, it's Mike. I'd better take it."

"Yes. Do. By all means. See what he wants."

"Hi, Mike. What's up?"

I tell him that we just sat down to dinner at The Cheesecake Factory. I warn him that it's very public here but ask him why he called.

"Just wanted to give you a heads up that I'm coming into Cleveland this weekend, Dad. Thought we might get together."

"Mike, that's great news." I look very pointedly at Kate, she gets the idea and leans forward. The waitress comes to our table just then. I ask her to come back in a few minutes. I explain that it's my son calling long distance. She nods, smiles and leaves.

"When are you coming in?" I say loud enough for Kate to hear over the general restaurant noise. Her face lights up.

"I'll be there sometime Friday. I'm not sure just when, but I'll call you."

Again loud enough for Kate to hear, "Friday. Great. How long can you stay, Mike?"

"At least until Monday. Actually it's a working trip, Dad, so at this point it depends on how the work goes."

"Until Monday? Great!" Kate pantomimes clapping.

"I've got a flight to catch right now, Dad, so I've got to go. But I need you to understand that this is a working trip. I may be tied up for part of the weekend. Did I ever mention a coworker named Nick from our Cleveland office?"

"I think so."

"I'll be working with him. Got to go. Love and kisses to Kate. Bye."

The waitress comes back as I flip my phone shut. She smiles as if to say, "Is everything okay?"

"My son lives in Denver and just called to tell us he's coming to Cleveland on business this weekend but will have time to visit."

She says that's great. We order. She leaves.

Kate says, "Well?"

I tell her I don't know many details, but that Mike stressed that he's working this weekend. And that he's working with a coworker from Cleveland named Nick.

I can see the relief in Kate eyes. She smiles. "Thank God, Cap'n. You have no idea how much comfort that gives me."

"Yes, I do."

CHAPTER 115

Thursday

(Gregory)

I cut classes today so I can be here to receive the package. I can't believe I'm waiting for a shipment of explosives.

Explosives? What was I thinking when I agreed to this? What was Rachel thinking? What was Justin thinking? This is crazy. I know I'm going to get busted.

The UPS guy is going to ring the bell. I'm going to go to the door. I'll have to sign some touch screen UPS gizmo. When I hand the gizmo back to the UPS guy, about a hundred cops are going to jump out of the bushes! There'll be city cops and state cops and FBI guys and Homeland Security guys and four different kinds of military troops!

Okay, I don't have enough bushes to hide a hundred guys. They'll jump out of cars, rappel off the roof, spring up out of manholes. I've seen it on TV a hundred times. I'll be busted. You can't ship explosives via UPS! This is crazy.

I'm going to get an ulcer waiting. UPS said my package will be delivered before ten. It's now nine. I've been up since seven. Shit, shit, shit! I really have had enough of this urban terrorist shit. Whatever made me think I wanted to do this?

* * *

I've got to start another pot of coffee. Like I'm not wired enough. Shit, shit, shit! I should have made Rachel do this. It was her idea. Poor dear just had to work. Just couldn't take off.

Oh, crap! Door bell!

I carefully pull aside the drapes enough to check the street. Brown truck. Nothing else. I look out the peephole. Brown uniform. Nothing else.

I open the door. Nobody in sight but the man in brown. "I have a priority package for Gregory Zaremba." He glances down near his feet. He's standing behind a box about two feet square with red stickers all over it. He looks bored, and in a hurry at the same time. He doesn't look stressed.

"That's me."

"Sign here, please." He hands me a thing like a giant cell phone with a touch sensitive yellow screen. I take it. He hands me a pen. I take it.

I look around. He sees me looking over his shoulder and he looks confused. "Is there a problem, sir?"

"No." I sign. And wait for the assault by the one hundred cops. Nothing. Maybe they're waiting for the UPS guy to leave.

He takes back his gizmo and pen, says thanks, turns and starts walking quickly back to his truck. I wait. Nothing.

He gets in his truck, and slides the door shut. He looks at a clipboard. Still nothing.

He drives away. Still nothing.

I look up and down the street. Two cars moving this way, but not anything that looks like a threat. I walk down the fifteen foot walk to the curb. The UPS truck turns the corner and disappears. The two cars pass. Kids. Teenagers. Skipping school? What's new?

But no cops. I look at the manhole cover in the street right in front of me. It stays closed. I turn and look at my roof. No rappelers. Nobody jumps out of my scraggly shrubs. I guess I'm not busted. Yet.

I go back up the sidewalk, up the three steps to the porch, and pick up my box. It's heavy, maybe twenty pounds. I carry it inside, and close and lock the door. All three locks.

I pull aside the curtain and check the street one last time. Still nothing.

* * *

I look at the box for at least ten minutes. Now what? I look at the shipping label. My name and address are in the "TO:" spot. And "Acme Importing, 123 Fourth Street, Norfolk, VA 25000" is in the "FROM:" spot. Sounds like an address from a Roadrunner cartoon.

Justin didn't say not to open it. He didn't say open it either. He just said, "You will receive the required shipment on Thursday morning before eleven a.m. It is imperative that you be there to receive it." Sometimes he talks weird. I don't know if he's trying to impress us with his vocabulary or what.

Well, shit. I get out my utility knife, carefully cut the tape, and open the flaps. It's full of those little plastic airbags. In the middle is a heavy clear plastic bag. I carefully remove it. Inside I can see a brown plastic bag and several eight and a half by eleven sheets of paper that are folded in half. I cut the clear plastic bag and remove the papers. I unfold them. It's a how-to manual about six pages long. It looks like it was printed on a computer, but there are hand done drawings interspersed throughout the text. The top line reads "DO NOT OPEN THE BROWN BAG UNTIL YOU ARE READY TO USE THE PRODUCT!"

I set the manual aside and take out the amazingly heavy brown plastic bag. I can see the shape of a coil of hose or wire or something inside of the bag. I feel it gently. The coil is about twenty inches in diameter and eight inches thick. The hose itself is about an inch in diameter.

I set it down very carefully, and go back to the manual. I think I'm about to get my first lesson in the care and use of explosives.

CHAPTER 116

Friday Morning

(Mirsab)

Now I know why they call it the "red eye" flight. My eyes are very red. They are full of grit. I feel like I have been caught in a sandstorm. Nura says that she feels the same.

Our non-stop flight left late last night and got in shortly after seven a.m., Cleveland time. The time in the air was four and a half hours, and it was very nice to have Nura sleeping next to me. She snuggled up against me and slept peacefully for most of the trip. I slept very little.

As we walk through the terminal to the baggage claim area, our bodies are still on California time. They think it is now three a.m. We are tired, and our biological clocks are confused, but we are excited.

After we get our luggage, we decide to have a light breakfast here at the airport before we obtain our rental car. We find a table at the Cinnabon, I guard the luggage, and Nura goes to get our breakfast. While I wait, I open my laptop computer and turn it on to see if the airport has Wi-Fi service. It does have this service, but apparently, there is a charge because the site to which I am connected asks for a credit card. I turn off my laptop. We will find a

Starbucks on our way to central Cleveland. Nura told me that they have free Wi-Fi. I must send my last email to Vista Tel!

* * *

At the National Car Rental counter, Nura asks the girl if she knows of a Starbucks on the way to downtown Cleveland. She says she needs a Starbucks fix. They both smile.

The rental agent says she does, it is only slightly out of our way, and she goes there frequently herself. She marks the route on the map she provides. We are to go east on Interstate 480 to Ridge Road. The Starbucks is only a fraction of a mile north of the intersection. When Nura has had her coffee fix, we can get back onto Interstate 480, continue east to Interstate 71, and take it north into the city.

We thank her and drag our luggage to our Chevrolet Trailblazer. Nura has also rented a GPS so we will have no trouble finding our way around.

* * *

Once we settle in at the Starbucks on Ridge Road, I get us drinks while Nura starts my laptop. When I return, she has connected to the Internet and is looking at Google maps. I ask her what she is doing. "Nothing, Mirsab, just familiarizing myself with the area."

"I noticed a pay telephone in the parking lot, Nura. I am going to use it to call Gregory. I shall be back in a few minutes."

* * *

"Hello?" He is sleepy. It is still early.

"Gregory, this is Justin. It will not be necessary to destroy the cell phone on which you are talking. I am calling from a pay telephone. This call will be untraceable."

"Yeah. Okay. It's early. I just got up. What's up?"

"I simply want to verify that our plans for tonight have not changed. I am about to send an email to the company with which we are dealing."

"Oh. Yeah. We're still on for tonight." I must have awakened him.

"You have received the shipment?"

"Yeah, I did. It came complete with instructions. We should be okay." That question awakened him.

"Very good. Then I will be waiting for your call tonight. If you need to talk with me, use the number on the label on your cell phone. Goodbye." I hang up before he can respond.

* * *

When I go back inside, I tell Nura that I have successfully contacted Gregory, and that our plans for tonight have not changed. "May I use the computer? I must send an email." She slides the laptop to me. I log on to Yahoo, and connect to my fraudulent email account. I have saved the text I wish to send in a text file. I open the file, and cut and paste its contents into an outgoing email. I enter the email addresses of the recipients and -- I click SEND.

It is done. I do not expect Vista Tel to publicly announce by tonight that they will meet our demands. Tonight, we will do something that has not happened since 2003! We will cut power to millions of people! Vista Tel will self-destruct!

* * *

When we have finished our coffees, Nura suggests that we drive in to Cleveland and see if we can check into our hotel early. She suggests that we take a nap this morning, and then take a drive to check out the tower this afternoon.

For many reasons, this sounds like a very good idea!

CHAPTER 117

(John)

God! Arabs everywhere. Even in Cleveland. At the airport. At eight a.m.!

For a Friday morning, the line at the National counter is not long. Three agents are working. All three have customers, though. All the customers look like foreigners. Figures. The good news is I'm next in line. Probably as soon as the Arab couple in front of me is done. It looks like they're wrapping their rental up. The clerk is trying to show them directions on the little National map. Tourists.

The Arab girl is cute though. Extremely cute. For an Arab. Arab, but very American looking.

Ah, they're done. The agent waves at me as the Arabs gather up their luggage and move off.

The agent smiles as I take their place. I suspect she's thinking something like "Thank God, an American." But she just says, "Good morning. How may I help you, sir?"

I want to say something snide about Arabs. I decide to be nice. "I have a reservation. John Collins." And I hand her my driver's license and Amex card.

She pulls my reservation, looks at it and says, "Oh. You're in the same situation as the last couple. I'm sorry to say that we are out of the intermediate sized car you requested. Computer screw-up. I can offer you a compact, a full sized car, or an SUV at our compact car rate, sir."

"What kind of SUV?"

"A Chevrolet Trailblazer. It's a nice vehicle, Mr. Collins. And you can get it cheaper than the G6 you requested."

I check her name tag ."Sounds good, Meg."

She starts hitting keys on her keyboard. God, it was an early morning. I wonder if I can check into the hotel early? Maybe take a nap. It's going to be a long day. And an even longer night.

* * *

Very nice room. Great view of the city. I love classic old hotels like the Renaissance.

I'm too wired to sleep, though. I wonder if they have a coffee shop in the lobby. If not, I'm sure there's one close by.

* * *

The Arabs again! The ones I saw at the National counter. They are just getting into another elevator as I get off mine. If they're just checking in, they must have gotten lost on the way from the airport. Good!

I ask the concierge if they have a coffee shop, and she asks my room number. "Room 817. Why?"

She smiles as she looks at her computer screen. "I suspected as much, sir, and it's why I asked. Your room number identifies you as a Club Level guest and we have a private lounge on the top floor for people such as yourself." She has been discretely hitting a few keys on her keyboard as she talked.

"May I call the lounge and ask them to have something waiting for you, Mr. Collins?"

"Just coffee, Ashley. Thank you."

Those Arabs bother me. I wonder. Nah.

* * *

It really is just like they said. There is absolutely no doubt that the tower will take out the 345,000 volt line when it falls. Assuming that they make it drop to the north.

I can't believe that Vista Tel was allowed to build the tower there. Did anyone -- the engineers, the power company, the contractors, Vista Tel -- think about putting the thing where it could hit the power line? Who issued the permits? Don't they remember 2003? The location is just amazing.

It is perfect for our purposes. Clearly visible from Interstate 90. It'll be a media circus. Yet the approach to the tower is completely out in the boonies. I drove by the tower twice on 90, but it took me the better part of an hour to get to the tower access road. There is nobody and nothing around, just old and deserted looking farmland. It looks like it's not been farmed in years. There are some crappy looking woods around here and there but no houses or anything. Of course, why would anyone want to live around here, anyway? The place has nothing to recommend it.

I'm really tempted to park and go back to the cell tower site itself, but the last thing in the world I want to do right now is attract attention to the site or to myself. It will get lots of attention tonight. I don't want to be a part of that attention.

The interchange where I got off of 90 is only about a mile and a half east of the tower. It's about ten miles of country roads from there to the tower though. There's not much at the interchange except a small truck stop. It may be a good place to hang out tonight and watch the fun. I've got to check it out.

CHAPTER 118
Friday Night
(Mike)

As soon as I got into Cleveland, I contacted our field office. They had been briefed by HS but they're not involved. I convinced the station chief to loan me a fellow Marshall for the duration of this little operation. Tom is about my age and has a similar Ranger background, so we understand each other just fine.

We catch up with Nick about dark. He's not happy to see two of us. I tell him, "Look, you're the SAIC on this job, the Special Agent in Charge. I'm already cleared for this op. Tell your boss I brought some backup. I got my dad into this and I need to be a part of getting him out. The bad guys must not know that he's our asset!"

Nick grudgingly says okay. I promise to stay out of the way. Yeah. Right.

* * *

Nick has found a job that will very effectively keep Tom and me out of the way. Or at least keep us away from the tower site.

We are to follow Mirsab and Nura tonight. Our job is to keep Nick informed of their whereabouts, and to arrest them when the bust at the tower actually happens. Nick's people have put a tracking device in Nura's rental car. Actually, they put two in her car. One that will be fairly easy to find, and one that will be much more difficult to find. If they look, they will find the easy one, and figure they are safe. Cute idea.

* * *

Nick will deploy his people at the tower. He will have teams in the woods just south and east of the tower, in the scrub along the fence line to the north, and a couple people actually in the equipment building. Gregory and Rachel are screwed. There is no possible way they will escape Nick's people.

The plan is that when they don't call Dad, when they are caught and the sirens and red and blue lights start to go off, Dad will "panic" and boogie. Mirsab and anybody else he's working with will assume Dad did what any getaway car driver would do under the circumstances: "Get outta Dodge!" Should work. Dad will *not* be implicated.

* * *

Our efforts are being coordinated by a group in a mobile unit parked at a rest stop west of here. They're *Control*. Not very original, but it works. All of us are wearing throat mikes and ear buds. They are digital and encrypted. HS has some nice stuff. Straight out of *24*.

It's shortly after two a.m. We have been following Mirsab and Nura since they left the hotel at midnight. "This is Mike. Our *Easterners* have taken up residence at a truck stop approximately one point five miles east of the site. Looks like they plan to stay a while."

"Nick here, Mike. Stay with them. All is quiet on the western front. *Control*, where are the *Natives*?"

"*Control* here. *Dad* is en route from Lorain, traveling east on Route 2. The *Kids* are moving west on Interstate 90, about a half hour from the site."

It looks like this is going to happen, and happen soon.

* * *

"Mike, this is *Control*. What's your precise twenty?"

"Back in the truck lot behind the diner. Tom is in the diner drinking coffee and monitoring the *Easterners*."

"*Dad* just pulled into the lot in front of the diner. He's sitting still."

"I see him. Gray Denali. Lights out, engine off. Sitting."

Dad said they were going to meet at a truck stop near the tower. I should have realized that it would probably be this one. Is it a coincidence that Mirsab and Nura are here, too? "This is Mike. Just an FYI. I'm going into the diner."

"Mike, this is Nick. Stay put!"

I ignore him and walk through the small group of trucks to the diner. As I pass in front of Dad's Denali, I stop and tie my shoe. I want him to see me. To know that we're here.

I go inside. There's a counter with two males sitting at opposite ends. One, obviously a trucker, looks like he's finishing up. The other, a tired looking, semi-bald headed businessman type looks like he's just getting started. Mirsab and Nura are sitting at a booth with coffee and maps in front of them. They're trying to look like traveling tourists. It's not working. There is one other couple at another booth. They look old and tired and grumpy. They look like they're getting ready to leave, too.

I nod to the lone waitress and head for the men's room. "*Control*, this is Mike. There are a couple of citizen's in here that I'm going to get rid of."

Nick is a little pissed. "I told you to stay put!"

I ignore him. "Tom, it looks to me like the only citizen who may be here for a while is the guy at the counter near the register. I need you to go flash your badge at him and tell him he needs to go talk to another U.S. Marshall here in the men's room. I'll have a talk with him. If the old couple doesn't pack it in soon, we'll do the same with them."

"Will do, Mike."

I'm standing by the door with my ID in my hand and my jacket open so he can see my gun. He stops dead when he sees me. He looks close to panic, like he's about to turn and run. "What's this all about?"

"Sir, we have this facility under surveillance for national security reasons. I need to ask that you leave the premises. If you like, I can get you directions to the next open diner."

He looks more than a little relieved. And interested. "Is this about those Arabs in the booth? Are they the ones under surveillance?"

"Sir, I really can't say. I just need to ask you to leave as soon as possible."

He starts acting very animated. Very interested. "Is this about the cell phone towers that those terrorists are destroying? Is there an Arab connection?"

This guy is a pain I don't need. "Sir, I'm sorry. You need to leave the diner."

"Look. I work for a cell phone company. I'm curious. This could affect us next."

I need to put a stop to this. Now. I open my jacket pointedly. "Sir, I need to see some ID."

"But…"

"Now."

He looks a little sick. He pulls his wallet out of his back pocket, and takes out a driver's license and a business card. I look at the license. John Collins, Alexandria, Virginia. And the business card. John Collins, Security Advisor, Sprint.

"Well, John Collins, Sprint Security Adviser from Alexandria, Virginia, if you're in security, you know I'm not going to answer your questions."

"Not that kind of security, sir. Internet security. I just got excited. We really are worried about this stuff that's going on in Cleveland."

"What are you doing at an Ohio truck stop at two a.m.? Kind of a long way from home, aren't you?

"I'm on my way to see family in Detroit. Look, I'm sorry. Why don't I just leave?"

"Sounds like a very good idea, John Collins, Sprint Security Adviser from Alexandria, Virginia. You have a good night now." And he backs out the door. Very quickly.

"Tom, this gentleman will be leaving soon. What about the old couple?"

"They're paying their bill now. We're clear."

* * *

"This is *Control*. The *Kids* just pulled into the truck stop. They are going around back. *Dad* is moving, going around back as well."

"Tom, this is Mike. Go back to our vehicle and see what you can see with our Night Vision Goggles. Get back to me if anything significant happens. I'll stay in the diner."

* * *

"Heads up everybody. This is Tom. *Dad* and the *Kids* have all piled into the Denali. They're moving out."

"Nick, are you there?"

"I'm here, Mike.

"Nick, when I talked to him earlier this week, my dad said it'd take him a half hour to get to the site and drop them off. Then he's supposed to hang out 'till the tower goes down. They will call him on the radio, and he's supposed to come get them."

"We know all that, Mike. It won't happen. The *Kids* will be walking right into the midst of twenty of the best agents that HS has. And they're all listening right now. Gentlemen, we have a half hour until this happens. We illuminate them when they breach the fence. Mike, your dad knows to just go home after he drops off the *Kids*. They won't be calling him."

"Nick, this is my father. He shouldn't be doing this."

"Mike, your dad volunteered to do this. We'll get him out of it safely. When you hear us apprehend the *Kids*, your team is to apprehend the *Easterners*. Are you clear on that?"

"Yeah, Tom and I will do our job. Did you ever get anything on Mirsab's superior, Hamad?"

"We're working on it. All we know at this point is that his alias is John Collins."

"Oh -- my -- God!"

"What?"

"He was here! I met him. He's not an Arab. He's an Anglo. And he walked out of here ten minutes ago!"

"What? Which way did he go? What was he driving?"

"I don't know. He's gone. I think he might have been watching Mirsab and Nura. He knew what was happening. We won't find him. Damn. Damn. Damn!"

* * *

"This is Nick! Heads up everybody. Here come the *Kids*. Steady. Steady. Now! Light 'em up!"

"Halt! This is Homeland Security! Put your hands on your heads! Drop to your knees! You are surrounded! You are under arrest!"

* * *

"Tom, let's do this!"

In about two minutes, Tom comes in the front door. He nods and stops there with his arms crossed. The waitress takes one look at him, realizes that something serious is happening, and looks at me as if to say "What's going on?" I smile and lay my badge on the counter. She scurries toward the kitchen.

I get up from the counter and slip into the booth beside Mirsab. I lay my badge on the table. Mirsab looks like he is going to be sick. Nura does a good imitation of a rabbit caught in the headlights of a car. Nobody says anything.

Tom moves down the counter and stops opposite the booth. He opens his jacket so that they can see his flak jacket and his gun.

I smile at Mirsab. "We just arrested Gregory and Rachel. We know everything, Mirsab. You and Nura are under arrest."

THE END

EPILOG
Fourth of July Weekend
(Captain)

The weather has finally gotten nice. It's eighty degrees and sunny. Life is finally getting back to normal. Kate and I are sitting in the cockpit of our boat watching the tourists go by.

Leamington is a great place for people watching and for just relaxing. The Canadians *do* know how to relax. This is one of our favorite cruising destinations. It's about six hours straight across the lake, almost due north from Vermilion. When the wind is right, we can set up the sails, tie them off, turn on the autopilot, and just relax. We take turns watching out for other boats, and just enjoy the ride.

And we deserve it this summer. After the spring we had. Our urban terrorist days, our secret agent days, are over.

*   *   *

Gregory and Rachel are in jail. They are both being held on several million dollars bail, and waiting indictment on all kinds of federal charges. Stuff I never even heard of. Stuff that will keep them in jail for a long time to come.

Their story has been the subject of everything from local newspaper stories to Nancy Grace and Geraldo Rivera. I think HS *wants* it that way. Their being in jail -- and staying there for a long time -- is an excellent deterrent.

I have mixed feelings about them. Gregory certainly deserves to be right where he is. It was his rather bizarre plan from the start. Rachel, I'm not so sure about. Greg kind of sucked her into the plot. But then again, she convinced him to make a bizarre concept even worse.

*   *   *

Mirsab and Nura are gone. They went back to their home countries. Nick was right. Nura's father is related to the Qatari royal family. They put pressure on the State Department to let both Nura and Mirsab just quietly go home.

There was very little on the news about their involvement. Some stuff about Mirsab being duped by an unidentified American mercenary, and Nura, in turn being duped by Mirsab. That's all. They're home free. Literally. Oil rules.

I've heard from Mike that they are trying to immigrate to Canada, but so far, the Canadian government is fighting it. That's a surprise. Canada is pretty liberal. But a nice surprise.

*   *   *

And then there's John Collins -- Hamad Sharif. Those are in all probability, both aliases.

He's gone. Evaporated. Mike met him at the diner that Saturday night. Talked to him. Watched him walk away.

Homeland Security suspects that he was at the diner watching Mirsab and Nura. Before they left the country, Mirsab and

Nura were questioned. They both professed to not have noticed him in the diner that night. They say they never met him, only talked to him on the phone.

I talked to him, as did Gregory and Rachel. He called each of us one night and professed to be from our cell phone companies' fraud units. Nobody knows why.

It's really bothering Mike that he let him walk. There are no photos of him, only Mike's recollection of what he looks like. He has made it his mission to check every John Collins and every Hamad Sharif for whom he can find a photo. I suspect that will be futile.

Mike has another idea that I think has a better chance of success. He's spending his spare time looking at photos of every Army Ranger Officer who ever served in the Middle East. He's convinced that John/Hamad learned his skills as a Ranger, and his Farsi while deployed there.

Who knows? Maybe.

*   *   *

And Kate and I are sailing. And enjoying the summer. I'm still working as a consultant, but I'm down to three days a week and working from home again.

One day shortly after the destruction of tower four was thwarted, Stan, the owner of our company called me into his office. He said that my nemesis, Howard, was leaving and that I could go back to working from home again if I wished. He also told me I could work part time if I wished, as many days a week as I wanted.

He offered no real explanation, just said that's the way it was. The Three Stooges were no more.

I've often wondered if Stan got a call from Homeland Security. I don't think I want to ask.

*   *   *

Life is good again. It really *is* good. But I have this one little doubt: I think about it every once in a while late at night when I look out at the dark lake.

Gregory and Rachel and Mirsab and John/Hamad know who I am. But they don't know I was a good guy. They don't know that I was the one who got them caught. But if it *ever* leaks out...

ACKNOWLEDGEMENTS

I would like to thank two people who have been very instrumental in bringing *Cell Tower* to you, my readers.

First, to my wife and constant fan, Debbie. For encouraging me. For listening to my ideas. For reading and rereading, and rereading… And then reading aloud so that I could listen to the dialog. I thank you, cutie.

Second, to my proofreader and editor, Karen Rumple. For all your work and suggestions. For combing through the manuscript with the detailed eye of a court recorder. And for your faith in this project from day one. Thank you.

Breinigsville, PA USA
21 February 2011
256033BV00003B/14/P